NO LOVELIER DEATH

NO LOVELIER DEATH

Graham Hurley

The right of Graham Hurley to be identified as the author of this
work has been asserted by him in accordance with the
Copyright, Designs and Patents Act 1988.

First published in Great Britain in 2009 by Orion
An imprint of the Orion Publishing Group
Orion House, 5 Upper St Martin's Lane,
London WC2H 9EA

An Hachette UK Company

A CIP catalogue record for this book
is available from the British Library

ISBN 978 0 75286 885 1 (Cased)
ISBN 978 0 75289 906 0 (Export Trade Paperback)

1 3 5 7 9 10 8 6 4 2

Typeset by Deltatype Ltd, Birkenhead, Merseyside

Printed in Great Britain by Clays Ltd, St Ives plc

The Orion Publishing Group's policy is to use papers
that are natural, renewable and recyclable products and
made from wood grown in sustainable forests. The logging
and manufacturing processes are expected to conform
to the environmental regulations of the country of origin.

www.orionbooks.co.uk

That England, that was wont to conquer others,
Hath made a shameful conquest of itself

Richard II, William Shakespeare

Acknowledgements

My thanks to the following for their time and patience: Rory Beard, Klone Boams, Dorothy Bone, Theo Chadna, Martin Chudleigh, Dr Debbie Cook, Nigel Crockford, Shirley Dinnell, Robert Doolan, John Hamer, Mark Harper, Martin Harrison, Jack Heasman, Barry Hill, Jack Hurley, Cheryl Jewitt, Neil Keeping, William Lambert, Terry Lowe, Tina Lowe, Jane Moody, Simon Parker, Lara Pechard, Jennifer Pollitt, Kevin Prior, Dave Sackman, Katie Sage, Christine Searle, Danielle Stoakes, Tony Tipping, Scott Whiffing, Nathalie West, Jessica Wretlind and Charles Wylie.

Bruce Marr and Paul O'Brien from the Portsmouth Preventing Youth Offending Project gave me valuable insights into Pompey youth culture while James Priory, Headmaster of Portsmouth Grammar School, was extremely generous with the temporary loan of a handful of his sixth-formers.

Viv Firman shared her poolside coaching secrets and introduced me to the awesome world of high-performance swimming. Dedication, at this level, is too small a word.

For D/I John Ashworth, a special mention. Along with Roly Dumont and Steve Watts, he's been with Faraday from the beginning. If the series has won a reputation for authenticity, then much of the credit should go to their collective experience, wisdom and trust.

The usual bouquets to my editor, Simon Spanton, who has piloted the series into extremely challenging fictional waters, and to my wife, Lin, who is – as ever – in charge of the survival gear.

To Jack and Hannah
with love

Chapter one

Craneswater is the best address that money can buy in Portsmouth. Tucked away at the bottom of the island, with a Southsea postcode and regular calls from the Waitrose home delivery service, it offers privacy, neighbourliness and a certain peace of mind. Handsome Edwardian villas behind high brick walls. Ample space for the Volvo Estate and the wife's Porsche. Invitations to tennis tournaments, with the promise of a poolside barbecue afterwards. Craneswater, Faraday had always believed, was the one corner of Pompey that somehow belonged to another city. Respectable. Civilised. Safe.

Faraday pulled his rusting Mondeo to a halt. It was half past two in the morning. Beyond the *No Entry* tape at the end of Sandown Road, he could see a line of white minibuses. On the other side of the road, two uniformed patrol cars and three white Ford Transit vans. Two of the vans, with their heavy metal grilles, belonged to the city's Police Support Unit. The third, an incomer, was badged with the logo of the FSU.

The presence of the Force Support Unit was the clearest possible evidence that Detective Chief Inspector Gail Parsons hadn't been joking. On the phone, summoning him from a hard-won sleep, Faraday's immediate boss on the Major Crime Team had sounded shaken, even alarmed. Something substantial had clearly kicked off.

There were coppers everywhere: FSU guys in the full ninja gear, little knots of officers staring up at a big house on the left, an obviously harassed uniformed Inspector muttering into a mobile. Further down the road, a guy with a boisterous Alsatian was locked in conversation with a couple of blokes in forensic suits from Scenes of Crime.

Faraday produced his warrant card for one of the uniforms behind the tape. As he lowered the window, the music engulfed him, hammer blows of drum and bass, loud enough to make his bones ache. The uniform bent to the window. Parking was already tight. There might be spaces round the corner. Faraday nodded, still gazing at the scene

I

in Sandown Road. The big house on the left, he thought. Party time.

The car parked, he found DCI Parsons round the corner in a huddle with Jerry Proctor. Proctor was a Crime Scene Coordinator. He rarely attended for anything less than homicide. The music, this close to the big house, was deafening, the shuddering bass line overscored with the drunken yells and whoops of partying adolescents.

'What's going on?' Faraday mouthed. Windows in the house were all curtained, occasional chinks of light framing a glimpse of faces peering out.

Proctor spared Faraday a nod of welcome, then bent again to catch something Parsons was trying to say. She was a small squat woman with a huge chest and a definite sense of presence. Faraday had yet to draw his own conclusions but she'd arrived in the Major Crime Department with a reputation for ruthless self-advancement. Thirty five was young to have made Detective Chief Inspector.

He stepped back into the road. An investigator from the Scenes of Crime team hurried past with a couple of lamps on lighting stands. Faraday watched him as he disappeared into a driveway further down the street. This property, equally grand, was next door to the party house and something familiar about the heavy metal gates snagged in Faraday's memory. He stared at them a moment, blaming the lateness of the hour and a lingering befuddlement that went with the best part of a bottle of Côtes-du-Rhône. Then he had it.

'Bazza. Our old mate. Wouldn't believe it, would you?'

Faraday, recognising the gruffness of the voice, turned to find a familiar looming presence beside him. Jerry Proctor was a big man, slightly intimidating in his sheer bulk, a veteran of countless crime scenes. Faraday rated him highly, trusted his judgement. DCI Parsons had disappeared.

'So what's the score?' Faraday shouted. 'What's going on?'

'Bunch of kids. Hundreds of the little scrotes. The party kicked off early and it's got worse ever since. If it was my house, and you came back to that, I'd be suicidal.'

'Who owns it?'

'Some judge. He's away on holiday, poor bastard.'

'And that's it?' Faraday was looking at the line of police vehicles, the suited SOC guys, the heads bent to mobiles. Even a riot didn't merit a response like this.

Proctor shot him a look. 'No one's told you? About Baz?'

'No.'

Proctor studied Faraday a moment, then gestured down the road towards the still-open gates. Somewhere quieter. Somewhere they could have a proper conversation.

2

Faraday fell into step beside him, picking his way between the mill of officers. Bazza Mackenzie was a career criminal who'd turned his monopoly on cocaine supply into a major business empire. On one famous occasion Major Crime had tried to bring him down. Operation *Tumbril*, largely covert, had been blown to pieces by Mackenzie himself and Faraday was one of the CID officers who'd been hurt in the subsequent post-mortem.

Since then, years down the line, Bazza had gone from strength to strength. Twenty million quid's worth of washed narco-loot had given him a portfolio of businesses from tanning salons and seafront hotels to property developments in Dubai and Spain. Faraday had never believed in the inevitable triumph of virtue and justice but Bazza Mackenzie, in his new incarnation, was the conclusive evidence that crime paid.

They were standing across the road from number 13, denied access by more tape. The Crime Scene Investigator must have set up his stands in the garden because the back of the house was washed with a hard bluish light. Faraday looked up at the rooftop balcony with its apron of smoked glass. The beach and the Solent were barely half a mile away. From his Craneswater chateau, Faraday thought, Mackenzie was King of the City.

'He's still living there?'

'Yeah. Though just now he's down at the Bridewell.'

'We've arrested him?'

'Too right, we have.'

'What for?'

'Sus homicide. Two bodies. Both beside his pool.'

Winter was asleep when his mobile began to trill. He groped on the floor beside the bed and struggled up on one elbow to check caller ID. Sweet Marie. Bazza's missus.

'Paul? Are you there? Speak to me.'

'It's two in the morning.' Winter rubbed his eyes. 'What's the matter?'

'It's Baz, Paul. He's been arrested. In fact we both have.'

'Where are you?'

'The Bridewell. I haven't seen him yet, not to talk to, but he's definitely here.'

'The *Bridewell*?'

Winter had a sudden vision of the custody suite at the city's central police station. On a Saturday night, about now, the evening's mayhem would be coming to the boil: drunks from the clubs, infant drug dealers nicked on supply charges, predatory psychos who'd handed out a

3

beating to some passer-by. Most weekends the queue for the Custody Sergeant stretched round the block. Where did his new employer fit into all this?

'It's complicated, Paul. Baz has phoned Nelly. She's coming down from Petersfield. We need you here too.' Nelly Tien was Bazza's solicitor, a ferocious Hong Kong Chinese.

The tremor in her voice told Winter she meant it. The best part of a year working for her husband had, to Winter's surprise, cemented a real friendship. Marie was a strong woman. Coping with Bazza Mackenzie, you'd be nothing less. Whatever had taken the pair of them to the Bridewell deserved Winter's full attention.

'I'll be there in ten.' He tried to raise a smile. 'Put the kettle on.'

Old times, Winter thought. He parked his new Lexus in front of the Magistrates Court and sauntered the fifty metres to the adjacent police station. A white minibus had just arrived and a couple of uniforms were shepherding a line of preppy-looking adolescents across the tarmac and into the station itself. One glance told Winter that most of them were pissed. He watched until the last of them, a gangly youth in surf shorts and flip-flops, disappeared inside, wondering what might have brought middle-class kids like these to the attention of Pompey's finest. They didn't look violent. They'd didn't look sullen. Since when did an evening on cheap lager get you nicked?

Winter gave the kids a minute or two to clear the front desk before making his way inside. He hadn't been inside a police station for over a year, not since the night they arrested him on the drink-drive charge, but the moment the door closed he felt his former life close around him. The same smell of unwashed bodies and over-brewed coffee, the same queue for the fingerprint machine, the same lippy drunks shouting their innocence from the cells along the corridor, the same waste-paper bins, overflowing with copies of the *News* and grease-stained all-day breakfast boxes. An informant of his, an old lag with loads of previous, had once told him that the custody suite on a Saturday night was your first real taste of life inside, and one look at the sweating turnkey beyond the desk told Winter he'd been spot on.

The Custody Sergeant was a forty-something veteran called Frank Summers. The last time Winter had seen him was up in the bar when one of the Major Crime D/Is had scored a big result and was shouting everyone a drink.

'Well, well.' It might have been a smile but Winter wasn't sure. 'Can't keep you away, can we?'

Summers stepped across to the PC on the desk and it was a second or two before Winter realised he was about to be booked in.

'Not me, Frank.'

'No? Shame. What can we do for you, then?'

Winter explained about Marie Mackenzie. He understood she'd been nicked. He was here to lend a hand.

'In what respect?'

'Legal representation.'

'But you're not a brief. Not last time I checked.'

'Friend, then. Appropriate adult. Any fucking thing, Frank. Just give me a break, let me see her. Couple of minutes and I'll be out of your hair.'

'Can't do it, Mr W. As you well know.'

Winter held his eyes for a moment, knowing it was true. The last thing these guys would do for him was any kind of favour.

'That's a no, then?' He said at last.

'Afraid so.'

'Has their brief turned up? Nelly Tien? Chinese lady?'

'On her way down, as I understand it.'

'So what's the story? Why the drama?'

Frank Summers shook his head, dismissing Winter with a wave of his hand. Behind him, emerging from an office used by the duty solicitors, Winter recognised another face.

'Jimmy ...' he called.

D/C Jimmy Suttle paused. In his late twenties, he was tall with a mop of ginger hair and a dusting of freckles. He was carrying a couple of files and looked preoccupied. Spotting Winter, he stepped across to the front desk. Like the Custody Sergeant, he assumed the worst.

'Not another DUI?' Driving Under the Influence.

'Very funny.' Winter nodded towards the street. 'You got a moment?'

Suttle frowned and glanced at his watch. Then, aware of the Custody Sergeant's eyes on his back, he accompanied Winter towards the door.

'Good lad.' They were out on the pavement, walking towards Winter's car.

'That yours? The Lexus?'

'Yeah.'

'Legal, are you?'

'No problem. We took the disqual to appeal, got it reduced to a year.'

'Luck?'

'Money. Shit-hot lawyer. Chinese woman. Work for Baz and you get the best.'

'So I see.' Suttle was looking at the Lexus. 'What's this about then?'

Winter took his time. As a working detective he'd taught Suttle everything he knew, and when the scan came through on the brain tumour, three long years ago, the boy had repaid him in spades. Working with Jimmy Suttle had been the closest Winter could imagine to having a child of his own and one of his few regrets about joining Mackenzie was the loss of a relationship he regarded as precious.

'You doing OK, son?' He put his hand on Suttle's shoulder. 'Life been good to you?'

'I'm doing fine.' He looked, if anything, impatient. 'How can I help?'

'Baz and Marie are in there.' He nodded towards the Bridewell. 'They got nicked tonight and I need to know why. Is that a problem for you?'

Suttle studied him a moment, reluctant to answer, and Winter realised what was different about him. He'd aged, and with age had come a wariness he'd never associated with the impulsive, gifted, tireless D/C he'd happily introduced to the darker arts of crime detection.

'I got my sergeant's exams a couple of months ago,' he said at last. 'I'm acting D/S on Major Crime.'

'Nice one.'

'Thanks. That's pretty much what I think.'

'Waiting for a job to come up?'

'Yeah. They're gold dust at the moment. That's why I could use a result. It's been quiet lately.'

The silence between them was broken by the howl of a police car braking for the roundabout. Seconds later, an ambulance. They were both heading east, a route that could conceivably take them to Craneswater. Suttle turned back to Winter. Winter returned his look.

'Well, son?' he queried.

'I know fuck all, except we've got a riot next to Bazza's place and a couple of bodies by that new pool of his.'

'Bodies? You're serious?'

'Yeah.'

' And Bazza's down for them?'

'Dunno, boss, but if I were you I'd toddle off home.' For the first time the old grin. 'Who knows? The next address on our little list might be yours.'

Faraday finally cornered DCI Gale Parsons as she ducked into her Audi. A lengthy kerbside conference with the duty Inspector and a

6

middle-aged officer in a black jumpsuit had just come to an end and she had some calls to make. She gestured at the passenger seat.

'Keep the windows up,' she said. 'You can't hear yourself think out there.'

The calls were over in minutes. The first of them went to Detective Chief Superintendent Willard, the Head of CID. Parsons rarely wasted time on small talk and tonight was no exception. Faraday gathered that the guy in the black jumpsuit was the Tactical Adviser for Public Order, which went some way to explaining the Transit vans. His advice, it seemed, boiled down to containment.

By now, kids upstairs were yelling from the open windows, winding up the melee of figures below, wanker gestures supplemented with a volley of empty wine bottles. The pavement outside number 11 was littered with broken glass.

'So how does containment work?' Faraday couldn't resist the question.

'We're buying time, Joe. The kids downstairs aren't a problem. We started controlled release half an hour ago, got the first batch off to the Bridewell. Favourite is to clear the ground floor first, one minibus at a time. Then the FSU boys will sort it. You know the way it goes.'

'On this scale?' He shook his head. 'Never.'

'Me neither. Sign of the times.'

The Force Support Unit, she said, were on standby, awaiting the call to intervene. She was looking across at the party house. The property was surrounded by uniforms. Controlled release meant exactly what it said on the tin.

Curtains on one of the upstairs windows had been ripped down. Faraday watched a couple of kids mooning the street below.

'Jerry Proctor says the house belongs to a judge.'

'He's right. It's Ault's place. Just now he and his wife are off sailing in the South Pacific. They're in for a nasty shock, poor things.' She took off her glasses and rubbed her eyes. 'You know Ault?'

Faraday nodded. Peter Ault was a Crown Court judge. His hard-line summings-up in a number of recent cases, widely publicised, had won him a devoted following amongst right-wing correspondents to the letters page of the city's daily paper, the *News*. He was popular in CID offices too, largely because he had little time for social workers.

Faraday glanced at his watch. 02.37.

'So what's the state of the place?'

'I gather it's pretty much wrecked. Not just that. One of the bodies we recovered turns out to be the Aults' daughter.'

'Shit.'

'Exactly. Total nightmare.'

7

Faraday looked away, trying to imagine the welcome home awaiting this luckless pair. One moment, the bluest of oceans; the next, the
worst news in the world.

'These bodies were by the pool next door?'

'Yeah. We think the other one's a lad called Gareth Hughes. If
we're right, he's the boyfriend.'

'Injuries?'

'According to one of the CSIs, we're looking at bruising and abra-
sions on both of them, plus blood beside the pool, plus multiple stab
injuries on the girl. Early days, though. Jenny's still en route.'

Faraday nodded. Jenny Cutler was the on-call forensic pathologist.
She lived in a farmhouse in the wilds of Somerset. Hence her late
arrival.

Faraday was looking at the house again. Through the open front
door he could see a couple of uniforms talking to a gaggle of kids.

'What's the plan here? Are we arresting them? Or do we treat them
as witnesses? Either way, Jerry seems to think the resource implications are horrendous.'

'Jerry's right. We're estimating one hundred-plus kids. Apparently
the invite went out on Facebook and half the world turned up. The
girl was planning for a cosy soirée. Instead she ended up with a riot.'

'Girl?'

'Rachel.' Parsons glanced across at Faraday. 'The one by the
pool.'

Faraday nodded. As the story unfolded, it wasn't difficult to track
the implications. Two bodies triggered a major homicide inquiry.
Next door, more than a hundred partying kids were either suspects
or witnesses. Either way, they'd need to be taken to a custody suite,
medically examined, and housed overnight before being interviewed
in the morning.

'So are we arresting them?'

'Not in the first place, no. We're asking for their cooperation and
their mobiles. If there's any difficulty, we'll go for arrest.'

'Grounds?'

'Hasn't been necessary yet. A few kicked up when we seized their
mobiles but you'd expect that. If push comes to shove Mr Willard's
suggesting breach of the peace or criminal damage. We're not fussy.
Either will do.'

'What about transport? Jerry said he was pushing for full forensic
cleaning.'

'Jerry would. That's his job. But given the situation, I'm afraid he's
got no chance. I talked to the cleaning contractors a couple of hours
ago. We'd be here all weekend if we went down that road so we're

settling for low-mileage minibuses. That way they might be at least half-clean. I'm afraid it's the best we can do.'

Faraday nodded in agreement. With every passenger a potential suspect, the evidential textbooks called for each vehicle to be forensically pre-cleaned to prevent cross-contamination. That would leave the Crown Prosecution Service flameproof against later defence challenges in court but Parsons was right: sorting out a fleet of minibuses to Jerry Proctor's satisfaction would bring the entire operation to a halt.

The DCI's mobile began to ring again. While she was busy with the call, Faraday tried to tally the rest of the night's implications. The booking-in process at the custody centres, especially at weekends, could itself take nearly half an hour per person. Every witness or suspect would need access to a lawyer. If they were sixteen or under, they'd require the presence of an appropriate adult. If they were foreign, they'd be calling for interpreters. They'd need to be swabbed, fingerprinted, and medically examined by a police surgeon. Their clothing would be seized, bagged, tagged and put aside for possible dispatch to the Forensic Science Service.

Every step in this journey carried a price tag or resource implications. Would there be enough cell space county-wide? Would there be sufficient replacement clothing? And who would pick up the tab for the lab tests? Only last week Faraday had countersigned an invoice from the Forensic Science Service. For DNA analysis on just five items of clothing, the bill had come to £3460. Multiply that one hundred times and they'd be looking at over a third of a million quid. Parsons was right. Total nightmare.

She was off the mobile. Willard, she said, had been talking to the Assistant Chief Constable responsible for CID. On a busy Saturday night the force operations room had so far identified a mere thirty-seven available custody cells county-wide and a call had gone out to abandon further arrests unless absolutely necessary. Given the shortfall in custody space, the ACC had no choice but to invoke the standing mutual aid arrangements and control room staff were now in touch with neighbouring forces. Kids who'd started their Saturday night by necking a litre of Diamond White on Southsea Common might well end their evening in a cell in Reading. Or Dorchester. Or Worthing. Such was the thinness of the thin blue line.

Parsons was gazing at the house across the road. Another dozen partygoers were being escorted towards a waiting minibus. One of them stumbled and fell. Heavily gelled, he was wearing Adidas track bottoms and a Henri Lloyd top. Face down, he lay sprawled on the pavement. Seconds later he began to throw up. None of the other kids, stepping carefully round the spreading pool of vomit, stopped to help him.

Faraday glanced back at Parsons. She looked exhausted.

'What's the story on the party?'

'Too early to tell. Word obviously got round. This city can be rough. Nice Craneswater kids? Loads of booze on the premises? Easy pickings? Who knows ...'

Faraday, watching the kids again, knew she was right. In a city as claustrophobic and tightly packed as Portsmouth, the script would write itself. The invite would have spread from estate to estate. Nowhere was more than a couple of miles from anywhere else. Who fancies a trip down to leafy Craneswater? All those posh kids? Be a laugh, wouldn't it?

'Spot of social revenge, then? Is that what we're thinking? Booze? Drugs? Chance of a decent ruck?'

Parsons didn't answer. Instead, she spelled out the way she wanted to handle the coming days. Over the weekend the duty Detective Superintendent would babysit the operation, with Parsons acting as his deputy until Martin Barrie, in charge of the Major Crime Team, returned from leave. Jerry Proctor, as Crime Scene Coordinator, would be steering the forensic operation. D/S Glen Thatcher would supervise Outside Enquiries, with acting D/S Jimmy Suttle in charge of the Intelligence Cell. Jenny Cutler would doubtless be pushing for a Sunday morning slot at Winchester for the post-mortems and forensic teams would be starting on the multiple crime scenes after daybreak. The investigation already had a codename. Operation *Mandolin*.

'What about the kids upstairs?' Faraday was looking at the house again.

'The FSU lads have scoped a rear entry. As soon as we've shipped the rest out, they don't anticipate a problem.'

Faraday nodded. At close quarters, a confrontation with the Force Support Unit could be a terrifying experience. They worked in shield pairs, moving from room to room, cornering the stroppiest customers, lots of noise, lots of verbal, lots of aggression, a slap or two if needed before the cuffs went on. On special occasions, like tonight, they might even put a dog or two in. They called them 'land sharks'.

Parsons was scribbling herself a note. Faraday watched two uniforms handcuff the youth on the pavement then manhandle him into the minibus. White faces stared out as the boy tried to wipe his mouth on the sleeve of his shirt. The door slammed shut and the minibus growled away towards the seafront.

'And what do you want me to do, boss?'

'Sort out the interviews, Joe. We're talking God knows how many custody centres. Thames Valley. West Sussex. Dorset. You name it. We need a strategy. We need command and control. We need a grip on the witness statements as they become available. We need to jigsaw all this stuff together, put it alongside the forensic and the intelligence and whatever else, recreate the party, establish a timeline, sort out what exactly happened. We might get lucky. We might even get a cough by lunchtime. But we'd be crazy to plan for that. This thing's a monster already.' She looked up from her notepad. 'So we need to get on top of it, Joe. And that's not going to be easy. I gather the duty Det-Supt will probably be handing over to me, by the way, if this thing goes into next week. If that happens, you'll be Deputy SIO. Did I mention that?'

Faraday studied her a moment. Then, unaccountably, he was back in bed, the warmth of Gabrielle beside him, wondering who'd be phoning at half one in the morning.

'Thanks …' he said drily. 'Piece of piss.'

Chapter two

Winter resisted the temptation to go back to bed. Instead, he headed for the seafront, curious to know what remained of the evening's festivities. A riot and two bodies sounded extremely promising. There'd be a call for the full chorus line: Scenes of Crime, uniforms, plus a small army of detectives. A year ago, and he'd already have been totting up the overtime.

In the cold half-light of dawn the seafront was deserted. A highish tide nibbled at the bank of shingle that passed for a beach and when he slowed on the approach to the pier he could just make out the figure of a lone fisherman at the seaward end, silhouetted against the blush of pink away to the east.

Craneswater lay inland beyond the Rose Garden and the tennis courts. Winter brought the Lexus to a halt, glad of the chance to stretch his legs. A couple of swans were on patrol amongst the pedalos on Canoe Lake and he paused for a moment or two, poking at a waste-paper bin in a search of bread. His eye was caught by a sandwich container and he extracted the remains of a BLT. Were swans allergic to curls of cold bacon and a smear or two of mayo? He hadn't a clue.

The water in the lake was slime green, the colour of a heavy cold, and Winter gazed at it for a moment, waiting for the swans to show some interest. In one sense the news that Bazza had been arrested was no surprise. Winter himself knew that the girl next door was planning to throw some kind of party. Marie had mentioned it only the other day, confiding to Winter that she thought it was a bad idea. Bazza and the judge – a relative newcomer to Sandown Road – had become the best of mates, and Baz had promised to keep an eye on things while Peter and Belle were away. Quite how he'd square this assurance with a riot and a sus double murder was anyone's guess but Winter knew that Baz would have got stuck in if the situation called for it, especially if he thought the girl was under any kind of threat.

Was that the way it had been? Had Bazza done his neighbourly best to defend his new mate's daughter, his new mate's house? And maybe gone too far in the process?

Somehow Winter doubted it. A year of working for Bazza Mackenzie had taught him how much the man had calmed down. He'd always been bright, clever even, but now that cleverness was tempered with something close to maturity. His days of seizing life by the throat had gone. He seldom did anything without good cause and a bit of a think.

Not that Bazza was any stranger to violence. On the contrary, his years of front-line service with the 6.57, Pompey's marauding army of football hooligans, had given him a city-wide reputation as a top face. On one occasion, totally fearless, he'd taken on half a dozen Millwall fans practically single-handed. The ruck had kicked off in south London, the 6.57 trapped in a clever ambush, but Bazza had hospitalised three of them before being knocked unconscious himself. In certain Pompey pubs the following weekend he'd drunk his body weight in free Stella, and even coppers on the force had given him a passing nod. Not bad for a bloke your size, they'd said.

Done with the swans, Winter zipped up his new leather jacket against the early chill and stepped out of the park. Sandown Road was within sight and already he could see the uniform in his hi-vis jacket, standing guard at the end of the avenue. Anticipating another rebuff, he decided against a conversation. He'd walk past, give the bloke a nod, see what was on offer, draw his own conclusions.

In the event, the P/C looked barely young enough to be up so late. No way would he have a clue who ex-D/C Winter was.

'What's all this, then? Mind if I ask?'

'Not at all, sir. Bit of an incident.'

Winter nodded. In twenty years he'd rarely seen so many vehicles at a single scene. Traffic cars. CID Skodas. Ninja vans. Minibuses. An ambulance. The fancy bespoke Transit used by the imaging people from Scenes of Crime. Peugeot vans full of more forensic gear.

'What happened, then?'

'Afraid I can't say, sir.'

'Kids, was it? Party? Things got a bit out of hand?'

'Something like that.'

'Lot of fuss, though. Can't be just that alcopop shit they drink.'

'No, sir.'

Winter, bored with getting nowhere, was about to ask about rumoured deaths when the early-morning quiet was shattered by a roar of voices and the distant thunder of stamping feet. Winter guessed it was coming from the judge's house beyond Bazza's place. He was right. Seconds later, a tight knot of blokes in full riot gear emerged from the rear of the property, dragging two youths. Handcuffed, they disappeared into the back of one of the waiting Transits. Then came the noise again, louder if anything, and three more youths – one of them covered in blood – made an equally brief appearance. The biggest, still full of fight, swung a leg at a nearby WPC. Winter heard the crack of an ASP, then a yelp of pain and a string of oaths before he too was bundled into the Transit.

'I thought this was a nice area? Quiet? Peaceful?' Winter was frowning. 'And on a Sunday too?'

'Yes, sir. On your way now. I'm sorry I can't be more helpful.'

Dismissed by an infant, Winter thought. He gave the P/C a nod, lingered for a final look down the road, then strolled on. Some distance ahead, on the pavement across the road beside the pitch and putt, he spotted a pedestrian walking his dog. Quickening his pace, Winter crossed the road, recognising another of Bazza's neighbours, an old guy in polished brogues with an equally ancient Scottie. In these situations a handshake always helped.

'And you are ...?' The man was looking confused.

'The name's Paul Winter. I'm a friend of the Mackenzies. You'll have seen me around.'

'Really?'

'Yeah ...' Winter gestured back towards Sandown Road. 'So what's been going on?'

The old man looked briefly troubled. He didn't know quite what to make of this stranger. Then he asked exactly what connection Winter had with the Mackenzies.

'I'm a business partner, really. Ex-copper, if that helps.'

'Policeman?'

'Detective. CID. Twenty-plus years, man and boy.'

'Ah ...' The man smiled, plainly relieved, then said he'd been up most of the night with his wife, up in the top bedroom, watching events unfold. His wife wasn't too well. They'd moved to Craneswater from Gunwharf for a quieter life. He'd tucked her up in bed an hour ago and decided to take the dog for an early stroll.

'I'm in Gunwharf,' Winter volunteered. 'And I couldn't agree more. Let the riff-raff in, and you have to put up with all kinds of aggravation.'

'You find that?'

'Definitely. It's the tenant situation. Half the apartments are lettings, and say what you like but people don't know how to behave any more. And the younger they are the worse it gets.'

'You really think that's true?'

'I do, I do.' Winter nodded. One of the lessons he'd learned over the past year was just how many people had come to the same conclusion. In the Job he'd always been aware of what the management called 'low-level disorder' but out on his own he'd quickly sussed what a pain inner-city life could be. It was like a kind of collective toothache, he'd decided. Now matter how hard you tried to ignore them, no matter how thick your front door, the scrotes were always in your face.

'So how's it been?' He nodded again towards Sandown Road.

'Dreadful. The noise. The music. Just unbearable.'

The trouble, he said, had started around ten. Everyone in the road knew that the Aults were away, and no blame attached to young Rachel for taking advantage, but no one in their right mind would have invited so many people to a party.

'How many are we talking?'

'It seemed like hundreds. We weren't counting, of course, but they just came and came.'

'What sort of kids?'

'All sorts, and some of them young too, really young, thirteen, fourteen years old, swarms of them.'

'On foot?'

'Yes. And lots of them ...' he offered Winter a weary smile '... obviously the worse for wear.'

The music, he said, had started soon afterwards. Quite decent stuff to begin with, melodic, bit of a tune, but then coarser, much uglier, much *louder*.

'I think it must be the frequency they play this stuff in. It's totally unreasonable. It gets to you. It shakes you up. So in the end we decided to phone the police.'

He frowned, jerking the lead to extract the Scottie from a scatter of broken glass. Winter caught sight of the label on the neck of the bottle. Cheap vodka. Co-op's own brand.

'And what did the police say?'

'They said they'd call by. They asked us if it was more than just the noise. We said no.'

It was an hour before a patrol car arrived. Two officers, he said, knocked on the Aults' front door. One of them was a woman. There was a short conversation, then they drove away.

'And the music?'

'It made no difference. For a minute or two, to be fair, it was a bit quieter. But then they just turned it up again, louder if anything.'

A neighbour, braver than most, had lost his rag and crossed the road. When he finally got someone to open the Aults' front door, the place was evidently on the way to being wrecked. The youths on the doorstep told him to fuck off back to bed. Just like that. Fuck off back to bed. They were rough, he said. Really rough. Another call to the police.

'What happened this time?'

'They said they'd come back.'

'Your neighbour mentioned the damage?'

'Yes.'

'And what happened?'

'Nothing. Not for half an hour or so. Then the Mackenzies turned up. My wife recognised the Range Rover. I must say we were relieved. Mackenzie might have a reputation but at least he speaks these people's language. Unlike us poor souls.'

The Range Rover, he said, stopped outside Mackenzie's house. The pair of them got out and stood in the road for a minute or so. Then Mackenzie went and rapped on the door. In the end someone opened it and Mackenzie disappeared inside. For a while his wife waited for him on the pavement. Then he reappeared.

'He had blood all over his shirt. It was on his face too.'

'You could *see* that?'

'We have binoculars. For the sea view.'

'So what happened?'

'His wife sent him back home. Then she got on her mobile. God knows what she said but there was a police car here within minutes. And another one shortly afterwards.'

'Maybe she mentioned Peter Ault.'

'Maybe she did. If so, God bless her. But that's when it started getting complicated.'

The police, he said, kept looking up at the house but stayed in the road. No attempt to intervene. No knocks on the Aults' front door. Pretty soon afterwards a white van arrived, full of more policemen.

'At that point Mrs Mackenzie went home. I saw her walking down the road. I assume she wanted to check on her husband. She went in through those big front gates of theirs but she was out again within a minute or so. And this time she was running.'

'Where to?'

'To the policemen. There were lots of them by now, more than a dozen. A couple of them went back with her to the Mackenzies' place. Then one of them reappeared. He was talking on his mobile. Within half an hour or so you couldn't see the road for police vehicles. They were everywhere. At that point we realised something serious had happened, something really serious.'

'And do you know what that something was?'

'No. And we still don't. Except the men in those strange suits turned up. They're the ones with the small white vans. My wife said it looked like an episode of *Silent Witness*.'

'Scenes of Crime investigators?'

'I imagine so.'

The old man looked down again and spotted a smear of blood on the pavement. The dog had cut his paw on the glass. 'Damn,' he said softly, producing a handkerchief.

Winter asked him if he had any idea of the time when the Mackenzies returned.

'Yes, as a matter of fact I do.' Still bending to the dog, he looked up.

'And?'

'Twenty-three minutes to one. I expect they'd been to a party themselves.'

'You're sure about that? Twenty-three minutes to one?'

'Absolutely certain. I was keeping a log by this time. It's a habit, I'm afraid. I used to be in the merchant navy – bridge officer. I somehow felt that this thing had got completely out of control and that if there were ever to be ... ah ... repercussions, then it might help to have an accurate chronology'

'But you've no idea of what might have happened? At the Mackenzies'?'

'I'm afraid not.'

Winter brought the conversation to an end and wished him a very good morning. Walking on, he took the first road on the left, then left again at the bottom, wondering what else he might pick up from the other end of Sandown Road.

It was full daylight by now, the rich yellow spill of sunrise throwing long shadows across the road. With Sandown Road in sight, he suddenly came to a halt. The greying bearded figure walking towards him was unmistakable. Faraday.

Winter ducked into a front garden, watching the D/I fumbling in his jacket for his car keys. Same old clapped-out Mondeo, he thought. Same RSPB sticker on the top corner of the windscreen. With the door open, Faraday took off his jacket and then had a stretch, his face to the sun, his chin tilted up. Watching him Winter realised how much he seemed to have aged. There were lines in Faraday's face that he'd never seen before, and when his head came down, his whole body seemed to slump.

Over the last years of his service Winter had developed a soft spot for Faraday. They'd never been mates, and never would be, but he recognised a loner when he saw one, and he knew too that in a job that was rapidly becoming impossible, Faraday would never make it easy for himself.

Younger D/Is with an eye on promotion were cluey enough to buy the right drinks for the right bosses. Older detectives might succumb to the odd short cut. But Faraday did neither, maintaining a prickly independence that won him more respect than friendships. With his passion for birdlife and his deaf-mute son, he'd won himself a reputation as something of an oddball. Before Winter left the force, Faraday had also added a new girlfriend to this strange life of his. Not some retread divorcee from over the hill, standard MO for detectives of his age, but a youngish anthropologist. And French, to boot.

Winter watched Faraday check the road behind him, then execute a messy U-turn before accelerating away. He's knackered, Winter thought. And it's starting to show.

Faraday was at his desk in the Major Crime suite by quarter past five. The tiny kitchenette was at the end of the corridor. He filled the kettle, scoured the empty fridge for milk, scraped a spoonful of instant off the bottom of the catering tin of Nescafé and then ducked into the lavatory next door. The mirror over the handbasin told him everything he needed to know about a night's work after an evening's drinking. His eyes were bloodshot. His face was pouched with exhaustion. A splash or two of cold water certainly helped but he knew he needed Ibuprofen. Month by month he was aware that the tablets were becoming a habit. He drank too much and too often, every night if he was to be honest, but still preferred self-medication to the nauseous thump of an early-morning headache.

Back in his office with the milkless coffee, he popped a couple of tablets and then settled down with a pad and a pencil. The key to the next twenty-four hours, as Parsons had already pointed out, was some kind of matrix to impose the beginnings of order on the chaos of Sandown Road. For a start he needed to prioritise the interviews, take a first stab at a list of possible suspects, then match that list to his best teams of interviewers.

Already, he had a scribbled tally from the duty Inspector who'd been supervising the controlled release of partygoers from number 11. In all, he'd taken ninety-four names and addresses and anyone with visible traces of blood on their clothing had been heavily underlined. These youths, nineteen of them, would have joined the rest of the partygoers in custody suites scattered across four counties.

By now the booking-in process should be complete – including fingerprinting and checks on the Police National Computer – and with luck Faraday would soon be looking at printouts indicating whether or not they had previous form. This of course indicated nothing beyond an early taste for mischief, but a great deal of experience had taught him how helpful a PNC profile, supported by intelligence from Hantspol's own database, could be. Everyone belonged to some kind of network. Mates. Fellow criminals. Ex-girlfriends. And in a city as tightly knit as Pompey, this kind of information could open all kinds of doors.

The list began to take shape, name after name transcribed from the duty Inspector's notes. Curtis. Jason. Damian. Carl. Some, he knew, would be Grammar or High School kids, friends of Rachel Ault, offspring of Pompey's moneyed middle class. Others, often badged by their Christian names, came from the other side of the tracks. Quite how all these paths had come together and knotted at 11 Sandown Road would be the subject of countless interviews but on the face of it the social mix would have been all too combustible. Put a bunch of rugby-playing toffs alongside youths from the inner-city estates, and literally anything could happen.

Faraday sat back and tried to imagine how it might have kicked off. Part of Pompey's charm to him had always been the sheer numbers of people heaped together on this marshy little scrap of land off the Hampshire coast. He could think of no other city where areas of serious deprivation – Portsea, Buckland, Landport, Somerstown – lapped so closely around enclaves of relative wealth. Buy yourself a four-bedroomed villa in Southsea or a half-million-pound apartment in the new Gunwharf development, and you were – often literally – a stone's throw from the sixties tower blocks that housed some of the city's most damaged and challenging families.

The fault lines between these areas were often hard to detect but it was always the kids who were more aware of the consequences of social and territorial difference than anyone else. In inquiry after inquiry, over the years, he'd dealt with twelve-year-olds who'd rarely leave their own tight web of streets, let alone the city. Straying into Somerstown, if you were a Buckland boy, was a journey fraught with danger. Making it down to Craneswater, with all its rumoured poshness, was a glimpse of another planet.

He gazed down at his list, unsurprised that so many kids seemed to have arrived mob-handed, then realised that he'd yet to make room at the top of the page for Bazza Mackenzie.

Mackenzie was the city's best example of what the politicians were now calling social mobility. He'd come from the backstreets of Copnor, a journey that had taken him into the property business. Unlike his mates, he'd avoided getting his hands dirty on a building site, preferring to chance his arm working for an estate agency. On a rising market he'd watched other faces in the city make serious money by buying old terraced properties for a song, toshing them up and selling on. It was silly money, there for the taking, and Bazza had seen no reason not to help himself.

Drug-dealing gave him the working capital – first Ecstasy, then cocaine. Within a couple of years he'd banked, spent or reinvested more cash than his dad had ever seen in his entire life. The wheel went round and round – drug money, property, more drug money, more bricks and mortar – until his accountant grew more ambitious and drew up a blueprint for a wholly legitimate commercial empire. Not just property but a raft of other businesses: café-bars, hotels, shares in a taxi company, tanning salons, nail bars, developments abroad, and most recently a security consultancy offering a variety of services. The latter was the richest of ironies but Mackenzie himself didn't care a stuff. It was a chance to make silly money ... again. Because these days people were really scared of the bad guys.

Word had already come in from the custody suite at the Bridewell that Mackenzie had completed the booking-in process with barely a word of protest. This in itself was a bit of a surprise, as the Custody Sergeant had pointed out, but when Faraday had pressed him for more details it seemed that Mackenzie's only real concern had been Marie, his wife. After an hour or so at the Bridewell, she'd been transferred to Fareham, a ten-mile drive away, and Bazza wanted her treated with a bit of respect. Beyond that, he'd been as good as gold. His solicitor had booked into the Holiday Inn down in Old Portsmouth. She'd be back at the Bridewell first thing Sunday morning for disclosure ahead of the interview. Bazza seemed confident he'd be home in time for lunch.

On the face of it, Faraday could understand why. Bazza had plainly waded into the party and tried to restore a little order but in the end sheer numbers had overwhelmed him. Hence all the blood, his own and others'. That of course gave him an obvious motivation to settle a debt or two but Faraday doubted whether he'd do it there and then. Everything he'd learned about Bazza Mackenzie in his new incarnation – business tycoon, pillar of the community – told him that the man would bide his time and administer a cuffing, probably through a lieutenant, and preferably at a time of his own choosing. Not tonight, surrounded by a small army of pissed adolescents.

So where else might this list take *Mandolin*? Faraday was still transcribing the last of the priority names when he heard footsteps down the corridor. Alerted by the light beneath his office door, the footsteps paused. Then the door opened, revealing Jerry Proctor's unmistakable bulk. If anything, he looked even more knackered than Faraday.

'How's it going?' Faraday nodded at the empty chair.

Proctor was eyeing Faraday's abandoned coffee cup. When Faraday told him the catering tin down the corridor was empty, he sank into the proffered chair.

'Great,' he muttered.

Proctor, as Faraday knew only too well, had an appetite for challenging jobs. Years ago he'd spent six months on a secondment to Kosovo, disinterring hastily buried bodies in a bid to gather evidence for the War Crimes Tribunal at the Hague. More recently he'd had a spell in Basra, teaching the elements of forensic crime procedures to the Iraqi Police Force. But nothing, just now, compared to events in Sandown Road.

'I've been counting the crime scenes,' he said. 'Do you want to hear something seriously funny?'

'Go on.'

'OK.' Proctor leaned forward on the chair, counting the scenes one by one. 'First off there's the victims. Young Rachel. The boy Gareth. Second, the poolside at Bazza's. Third, the inside of Bazza's house. Fourth, that Range Rover of his. Fifth, the bit of pavement that leads next door. Sixth, the judge's place, what's left of it. Then, last of all, ninety-four dickhead twats who should have been tucked up in bed with their iPods. I make that exactly one hundred and one crime scenes. Try working out the manpower implications. The time. The bodies. The bills. I just hope someone's got deep pockets.'

Faraday could only chuckle. It was, as Proctor was the first to point out, surreal. If a single party in leafy Craneswater could fill custody suites in Dorchester and Reading, and bring the Scenes of Crime machine close to breaking point, what would happen if two weekend parties kicked off? Or three? Or four?

'We've made a cross for ourselves,' Proctor concluded. 'We're too bloody careful.'

Faraday sensed he meant it. These days, crime investigation was driven by fear of defence counsel months down the line – if an inquiry ever made it into court. A single tiny detail overlooked in the heat of the moment could blow an entire case. Hence the meticulous evidence-gathering at over a hundred crime scenes. Hence the endless cycle of management meetings over the coming days. Hence the prospect of DCI Parsons bent over the investigation's Policy Book, committing every decision to paper in case of a later legal torpedo that might sink *Mandolin*'s fragile boat. Every year, it seemed to Faraday, the business of matching crime to punishment became more fraught and more complex. You maximised your chances in court by minimising risk on the job itself. But that, as he knew only too well, could reduce an investigation to walking speed.

'We've no choice, Jerry. Unless you're braver than me.'

Proctor smothered a yawn, knowing it was true. Then the silence was broken by the sound of the door opening at the end of the corridor. The footsteps this time were rapid. DCI Parsons. Had to be.

Seconds later she was standing at Faraday's office door. She must have had a change of clothing in her office because she was wearing a black two-piece, nicely cut, that gave the impression of a waist. Proctor was too tired to hide his smile.

'Looks great, boss. Going anywhere nice?'

She ignored the dig. She was looking at Faraday.

'How are you doing, Joe?'

'Fine.'

'Names for the interview teams?'

'Next on my list.'

'Good. Run them past me when you're ready. In the meantime wish me luck.'

Parsons had produced a slip of paper. It had come from the party house. Faraday glimpsed a line of digits.

'We recovered this from a corkboard in the kitchen.'

'What is it?'

'A number for the Aults. God knows where they are but it seems they've got a satphone on board.'

Chapter three

Faraday was asleep when Detective Chief Superintendent Willard appeared at his office door. He awoke to find the bulky figure of the Head of CID conducting a shouted conversation with someone down the corridor. Faraday rubbed his eyes and reached across the desk to open the window. An hour's kip had made him feel, if anything, worse.

'Sir?'

Willard had stepped inside now. He had Jerry Proctor's bulk. The office felt suddenly cramped. He wanted to know where DCI Parsons had gone.

Faraday did his best to remember. The last time he'd seen Parsons, she was emerging from her office having put the call through to the Aults.

'She went over to Netley, sir. Then she's going on to Winchester for the PM.'

The force training HQ at Netley housed all the forensic departments. The post-mortem was scheduled for ten o'clock at the Royal Hants. With luck, Parsons would return with preliminary findings by lunchtime.

'She knows about the TV people?'

'I've no idea.'

'Did she mention it at all?'

'Not to my knowledge.'

Willard grunted, peering down at the hastily pencilled lists on Faraday's desk. He was wearing a sober three-piece suit with a Royal Yachting Association tie. A waistcoat in mid-August was a sure sign of an impending media interview.

'Tell her it's taken care of, OK? Sky and the Beeb are set up at the end of Sandown Road. I'm off down there now. What should I be telling them?'

It was a good question. Faraday listed the known facts. The party that had got out of control. Umpteen kids in custody centres across

23

the region. Two bodies beside the neighbour's pool. Two prime suspects under arrest.

'Mackenzie?'

'Yes, sir. And his missus.'

'What's the strength?'

'Highly doubtful. Even if he was pissed he wouldn't be that silly.'

'My thoughts entirely. Be nice to have a nose round his property, though. You've got the warrant sorted?'

'Suttle's onto it now. Jerry'll put his blokes in after they've finished round the pool.'

'I hear we've found a guy across the road, kept tabs on the incident throughout the evening, even made a log. Is that right?'

The news startled Faraday. He said he didn't know. It had been a long night. Twenty-four hours without much sleep wasn't the best preparation for a job like this.

Willard wasn't listening. He'd found the list of interviewing D/Cs Faraday had scribbled before his head had settled softly on the desk.

'What's the plan here? You've been in touch with this lot?'

'First thing, sir, a couple of hours ago. They're all due a briefing at half eight. I'm putting Yates and Ellis into the Bridewell. The rest of them I'm spreading around.'

'What about Thames Valley? West Sussex? Dorset?'

'I've booked conference calls for nine o'clock onwards. In every case they're bringing in D/Is as coordinators. So far they've been bloody helpful: kit seizures, police surgeons, PNC checks, the lot. It's arm's length, I'm afraid, but it's the best we can do. We're looking to sieve out the bystanders and get some kind of handle on a timeline. The probables and possibles we'll ship back down here. Unless of course we get a result first off.'

'No chance.'

Something in Willard's voice put the ghost of a smile on Faraday's face. He wants this to run and run, he thought. He's guaranteed headlines already and he wants some kind of return for all the holes in his budget.

Willard was checking his watch. He'd call by later in the day. Faraday was to bell him if he needed more leverage with the neighbouring forces.

He stepped out into the corridor, colliding with one of the civilian indexers from the MIR. The Major Incident Room had been firing up for an hour now, staff hauled in on overtime. Faraday got to his feet. Most of the indexer's coffee was dripping down the opposite wall. She must have found a new tin, Faraday thought vaguely. Thank Christ for that.

Willard turned back to him. One more question before he went.

'The judge ...' he said. 'They're bound to ask.'

'It's Peter Ault.'

'I know. Where is he?'

'In the middle of the South Pacific. DCI Parsons raised him a couple of hours ago.'

'And?'

'He and his wife are on a friend's yacht. They're turning back to their last port of call. He's estimating Heathrow on Thursday morning.'

'Sure, Joe. But how does he feel about it all?'

'*Feel*, sir?' Faraday was watching the indexer mopping up the coffee. 'I imagine he's quite upset.'

It was the TV news that called Winter back in from the sunshine. With some reluctance he hauled himself out of the new recliner on his balcony and stepped back into the shadowed cool of the big living room. Beyond the picture windows a jet ski from the Harbour Patrol was scrolling lazy circles on a flooding tide and he lingered for a moment, thinking of Bazza's dead brother, before settling himself on the sofa in front of his new widescreen TV. Plans to commemorate Mark Mackenzie with a jet ski Grand Prix had come to nothing, but he knew he owed this new life of his to Mark's accident. Every cloud, he thought, reaching for the remote.

BBC News 24 was promising a live update on overnight events in Southsea and within seconds Winter found himself looking at a pretty Asian reporter framed against the well-heeled villas of Sandown Road.

Scenes of Crime teams, she said, had moved into two of the properties behind her. In one of them, the party house, investigators were already talking of substantial damage and looting. Entire rooms had been wrecked, furniture overturned, pictures and ornaments smashed, carpets ruined. No one was counting as yet but the bill could easily run to five figures.

Worse was the tragic news that two young people had been killed, not in the house itself but in the garden of the property next door. Police had yet to release names but were believed to be working on the theory that the party and the double murder were linked. In a huge overnight operation Hampshire police had called on neighbouring forces to help house and interview nearly a hundred partygoers, many of them far from sober. This morning, she said, was a time for sore heads and a deep, deep sense of loss. But where next for this mammoth investigation?

The shot widened to discover Willard by her side. His tinted lenses had darkened in the bright sunshine, emphasising the pallor of his skin. Ignoring the reporter's question, he took issue at once with her use of the word 'looting'. Looting, he said, was associated with natural disasters, with earthquakes, with floods. This was something totally different, something man-made. Many of the young people at last night's party appeared not to have been invited. That raised issues of trespass, of housebreaking, of criminal damage, possibly of theft. Add the tragic deaths she'd already mentioned, and the implications were profoundly disturbing. Not just for the friends and family of the victims. But for all of us.

Scenting a headline, the reporter asked him to explain. Given an invitation like this, Willard couldn't help himself. He was on live television. On a Sunday morning half of suburban Britain would probably be tuned in. Fighting the temptation to turn directly to the camera, he tallied the real damage these young people had done. Two needless deaths were bad enough but what people might live to remember was the spectacle of an entire city left virtually unpoliced while officers did their best to deal with a bunch of partying thugs.

These people, in his view, were the tip of a very dangerous iceberg. What we'd seen last night was near-anarchy. Only patient police work – and a huge amount of money – had restored some semblance of law and order. As it was, force resources had been stretched to breaking point. Any more parties like that, and good people, decent people, might find themselves living under a state of siege.

The frankness of his admission surprised even Winter. He looked round the apartment. Was it time to change the locks on the front door? Buy himself a Rottweiler? Borrow some of Bazza's more inventive heavies? He turned back to the TV but Willard had said his piece and the smile on the reporter's face told Winter she'd got her scoop. Top Cop Warns Of Anarchy. Kids Rule, OK?

The picture cut to a pre-edited piece shot an hour or so earlier. A couple of suited CSIs were carrying forensic gear in through Bazza's front door. Winter recognised the steel-grey case that housed a Quasar. This was a wonderful bit of kit that used a special light frequency to bring out latent marks – blood, fluids, fingerprints – invisible to the naked eye, and it meant that Bazza might be in deeper shit than he'd previously thought. What if he'd dragged a couple of scrotes in from next door and given them a slapping? What if a lesson like that had got out of hand? What if Marie had got her Marigolds out, swabbed away the blood but left a tiny trace or two for the man with the Quasar?

He thought about the possibility for a moment or two, watching pictures of a P/C sweeping broken glass from the pavement of the house next door, then dismissed it. He'd no idea who'd be SIO on the developing investigation but in his or her place he'd jump at the chance of getting a Section 8 warrant on Bazza's pad. The sense of grievance after the collapse of Operation *Tumbril* would still be there, lingering like a bad smell in certain CID offices. The chance to settle a debt or two would be irresistible. Paperwork that might offer a way into Bazza's ever-expanding empire. Bank statements that might contain evidence of fraud or corruption. Even a line or two of recreational Class A drugs. None of these would have any conceivable link to last night's events but that, as Winter knew only too well, didn't matter. Anything to give Bazza's perch a poke. Anything to make the cocky bastard wobble.

The reporter at last signed off and Winter wandered through to his kitchen, knowing already that any kind of fishing expedition at 13 Sandown Road was doomed. The best part of a year on Bazza's payroll had taught him how disciplined the man had become, and how careful. The days of hands-on involvement in the drugs biz were well and truly over, and while Bazza still enjoyed keeping a benevolent eye on some of the younger players on the scene he was far too busy making legitimate money to take the slightest risk with his growing reputation.

In the early days of Winter's contract, back in the late autumn, he'd been dispatched to a residential development on the Costa Dorada south of Barcelona. The project had always been more Marie's baby than Bazza's. She'd bought it for a song after the collapse of a Spanish property company, and finished it with an eye to attracting modestly well-off retired couples. As well as sunshine and cheap booze she was selling peace of mind, and it had been Winter's job to sort out security on the place.

He'd stayed a couple of months, occupying a freezing makeshift office beside the unfilled pool, but after successfully bonding with an ex-inspector from the Policia Municipal who'd been more than happy to supply some local muscle, he'd quickly tired of whinging sixty-five-year-olds who'd run out of HP sauce and drunken ex-squaddies who desperately wanted a new best friend. By Christmas, he'd become a kind of welfare officer, a job description that in no way matched the excitements of the life he'd left behind. On the phone, minutes after receipt of his plaintive email, Marie had tried to make a joke of it and then offered her apologies. Bazza, she said, was cooking up another little idea. Less than a week later, Winter was on the plane home, director-designate of Mackenzie Confidential.

Just the title had won Winter's heart. It was billed as 'the ultimate screening service', and the glossy brochure offered in-depth pre-contract recruitment checks, full-spectrum competitor analysis, a range of supplier information and bespoke customer profiles. On signature of a two-year contract, local entrepreneurs – big or small – could take the risk out of free enterprise. Whenever a hotelier had a moment's doubt about a new chef, or a block booking, or the bona fides of the Pompey builder who'd put in a bid for the planned rear extension, then all he had to do was lift the phone and talk to Mackenzie Confidential.

The service didn't come cheap, as Mackenzie was the first to admit, but from the off Winter had loved the challenge of the job. He'd spent most of his working life being paid to be nosy and this, in essence, was no different. Except the paperwork never got out of hand, there was no one down the corridor to make life difficult for him, and when push came to shove he could always call on one or other of Mackenzie's lifelong buddies to apply a little extra pressure.

He grinned, reaching for the kettle. He'd known already that personal data was as available as apples in an orchard. Find the right guy, pay him the right money, and there was nothing you couldn't nail down about an individual. He'd started trading in February and word about Mackenzie Confidential had quickly spread around the city. Paul Winter. Ex-cop. Brilliant connections. Sharp as you like. And a laugh too.

To Bazza's delight, the contracts had come rolling in and by early summer Mackenzie Confidential had spawned Mackenzie Sunrise ('buying your new life abroad'), Mackenzie Poolside ('taking the risk out of foreign relocation') and Mackenzie Courier ('distance no object'). The latter was the love child of Bazza's drug smuggling operations back in the nineties – importing vast quantities of cocaine from middlemen in the Dutch Antilles – and Winter found himself employing faces he'd last seen in court. This time, though, they were dealing with totally legitimate high-value items, hand-carried to any corner of the globe, and although some of the veterans complained of boredom on the longer flights, the profit margins – like the pay – made up for everything.

Sunrise and Poolside had naturally involved a lot of foreign travel on Winter's part, and lately he'd begin to tire of the drive to Gatwick, but he'd discovered that his natural ruthlessness coupled with a seeming affability was the perfect combination if you fancied your prospects as a tyro businessman, and it pleased him a great deal when even Bazza himself had been surprised at his success. The Lexus had been one way of saying thank you. Rumours of an invite to Misty Gallagher's, over on Hayling Island, might well turn out to be another. Either way, Winter was warmed by the prospect of the coming months.

Spooning sugar into his tea, he kept an eye on the TV through the open kitchen door. Already, Willard's comments had sparked a modest studio debate on BBC News 24. A woman from a London-based charity for delinquent kids was talking about problem families. We reap what we sow, she was saying. We worship money, and power, and easy pickings. We live in a help-yourself society and we measure happiness by the thickness of our wallets. Too right, thought Winter, beaming at the set.

Faraday was late getting to the Bridewell for the first of the interviews. The conference calls had taken longer than he'd anticipated and the opening session with Bazza Mackenzie was well under way when he slipped into the monitoring room alongside the interview suite.

The Tactical Interview Adviser was sitting at the table, scribbling himself a note. Mackenzie's battered image hung on the monitor set cabled to a camera next door. Beside him sat his lawyer, Nelly Tien.

Mackenzie had put on a little weight since Faraday had last seen him and he must have been somewhere hot because his face was heavily tanned under a night's stubble. A crêpe bandage around the top of his head hid the worst of the damage but a bruise had virtually closed his left eye and there was more bruising on the side of his neck. He was on the small side, five seven, five eight, and Faraday wondered whether the overlarge tracksuit that hung from his shoulders was a deliberate act of malice by the Custody Sergeant. The clothes he'd been wearing at arrest, liberally splashed with blood, had already been bagged and tagged, awaiting dispatch for analysis by the Forensic Science Service.

'How's it going?' Faraday took a seat beside the TIA.

'It's going nowhere, boss. He couldn't be more helpful. Names, times, the whole nine yards.'

'Names?'

'Kids in the house next door. Turns out he knows half of them.'

'And what's he saying?'

'He's saying they were out of their heads. And he's saying they were ...' he glanced down at his notes '"... a fucking disgrace".'

Mackenzie, according to his own account, had arrived back at Sandown Road a bit past midnight. He'd been to a dinner party with his missus. He'd had a few to drink and she was driving. As soon as he got out of the Range Rover, he'd realised what had kicked off. He'd never fancied young Rachel's party idea and now it had all turned to ratshit. Marie had told him to leave it but there was no way that was going to happen. He'd given his mate his word. The kids needed sorting.

'His mate?'

'Ault. Apparently they're top buddies. Before Ault went on holiday, Baz promised he'd keep an eye on things. Like you do.'

Mackenzie had therefore waded in.

'In his own words, the place was already a khazi. Apparently they'd liberated Ault's cellar. He kept some really tasty reds. Half of them were over the carpets. The rest they'd had away or they were necking. Baz couldn't believe it.'

'So what happened?'

'He set about finding some faces he knew. Like I said, he didn't have to look far. The kids who did the real damage were out of Somerstown. One of them called him a silly old cunt. Apparently that did it.'

Bazza, in his own words, had totally lost it. He'd been a scrapper most of his life but he'd lost his edge recently and an evening's drinking didn't help. He'd whacked a couple of them before he took a bottle of single malt, full force, on the top of his head.

'What happened?'

'The bottle smashed. It was full. He was lucky the cuts weren't deeper and I guess the alcohol was a pretty effective antiseptic but you should read the Custody Sergeant's notes. Even this morning he still stank.'

'And that was it? Inside the house?'

'Pretty much. He was on the carpet after they bottled him so he took a bit of a kicking but another lad lent him a hand.'

'We've got a name?'

'Yeah, boss.' He flicked back through his pad. 'Matt Berriman.'

'Where is this kid?'

'Newbury. Apparently Mackenzie knows him from way back. Which might explain the intervention.'

'And that's when Mackenzie left the party?'

'Yeah. He says his missus had treble-nined us by then. I checked with Charlie One. They logged her call at 12.39.' Charlie One was the force control room at Netley.

'What did she say?'

'Basically she told us to get our arses down to Sandown Road. The house belonged to a Crown Court judge. She said we were looking at serious grief.'

'She's right. Probably righter than she knows.'

Faraday broke off to watch Mackenzie. One of the interviewing D/Cs was quizzing him about exactly what happened after Marie had sent him home.

'I went to bed, didn't I? Like you would ...'

'You didn't clean up at all? Have a bit of a wash?'

'Yeah, I must have done, but to tell you the truth I felt shit, totally knackered, plus I had a headache like you wouldn't believe. Four Ibuprofens, couple of mouthfuls of Scotch, out like a light.'

Faraday was staring at the screen. There were implications here. And one of them was suddenly all too obvious. He turned to the TIA.

'We arrested him in bed, am I right?'

'Spot on, boss.'

'And his wife we arrested outside?'

'Yeah. In the street.'

'So they never talked, never met, not after he got back from next door?'

'Absolutely right.'

'So he doesn't know that one of the bodies was Rachel? Is that what we're saying?'

'No, boss. Not yet. He was arrested for sus homicide. No names. No details.'

'What about his brief?' Faraday nodded at the screen. 'The Chinese lady?'

'She knows. We had to disclose it.'

'And she hasn't told him?'

'As far as I can gather, no. I think she's playing it long. We're going to get to Rachel in the end, probably soon, and she wants Baz to react for real. He's not going to be pleased. And that says there's no way a killing like that is down to him. Good move on his brief's part. Fucking smart.'

Faraday nodded. The TIA was right. Fucking smart.

Next door there seemed to be a problem with the audio cassettes. One of the D/Cs brought the interview to a formal pause while the other one tried to sort it out. Mackenzie went into a huddle with his lawyer. Seconds later, the door opened. D/C Dawn Ellis was holding an audio cassette. She asked the TIA to call for a techie.

Faraday looked up at her. He'd worked with her for more years than he cared to remember, trusted her judgement completely.

'Mackenzie? What do you think?'

'No chance, boss. The way he's calling it is the way it happened. I'd put my life on it.'

'You're going to tell him about Rachel?'

'It's next on our list.' She nodded at the screen. 'Stay tuned.'

The TIA returned with a technician. Within minutes the interview had restarted. The other interviewer was D/C Bev Yates. Another veteran.

'Mr Mackenzie, we're dealing with two bodies beside your swimming pool. Do you know how they got there?'

'No.'

'No idea at all?'

'None.'

'You didn't see them when your wife sent you home?'

'I couldn't have done. I went in through the front door. The pool's at the back of the house.'

'Really?' There was quickening in Yates's voice. 'So why didn't your wife use the front door too? When she came back to check on you?'

'Because I'd locked it. Probably chained it too. Tell you the truth, I wasn't thinking straight. A night like that, you wouldn't blame me.' He leaned forward. 'Check it out, son. Have a look for yourself.'

'We will.' Yates scribbled himself a note then sat back.

'These bodies, Mr Mackenzie.' It was Ellis.

'Yeah?'

'Would you have any idea who they might be?'

'How could I?'

'That's not an answer. I'm asking you whether you might have any suspicions, any ...' she frowned '... clues.'

Nelly Tien broke in to protest but Mackenzie shut her up with a look. There was something in his face that told Faraday he'd scented bad news. He wanted the names. Now.

There was a silence broken, in the end, by Yates.

'One of them was a lad called Gareth.'

'Gareth Hughes? I know him, met him round at the Aults'.' Mackenzie's head was cocked at an angle, his undamaged eye bright. 'And the other?'

'Rachel.'

'Rachel Ault?'

'Yes.'

He stared at Yates for a long moment, then shook his head. 'Shit. Shit. *Shit.*' He turned to Nelly Tien. 'You knew this?'

'Yes.'

'Then why the fuck didn't you tell me?'

'Why do you think?'

'I don't know, love. I'm not paid to think. *You're* paid to think. And you're also fucking paid to keep me in the fucking loop. That girl's my responsibility. She's my neighbour's daughter, for fuck's sake, his *only* daughter, his only fucking *child*. She's precious, she's what it's all about, and pretty soon he's going to be back in Sandown fucking Road wondering just what's happened to this wonderful life of his. Not just his house. Not just his fucking cellar full of posh wine, but his *daughter*, for fuck's sake. Out there by *my* pool. What do you say to a man who's just lost everything? What do you say when you were the one who promised to keep things cushty?' He stood up, shaking his head, distraught. 'I'm out of here.' He turned on Yates, scarlet with rage. 'Just fucking sort it, son, yeah?'

Next door, in the monitoring room, the TIA glanced sideways at Faraday. Then he reached forward and closed his notepad.

Chapter four

Summoned to his video entryphone, Winter found himself looking at three tiny faces peering up at the camera guarding Blake House. Guy, Lucy and Kate, Bazza's grandchildren, his pride and joy.

'Ezzie? You there?'

The kids shuffled sideways and Esme appeared. Esme was Bazza's daughter, a qualified lawyer who lived with her husband and three kids on a seven-acre spread in leafy Hampshire. She was wearing a halter top Winter recognised from her last expedition to the Maldives. The scowl on her face told him she'd been tuned in to BBC News 24.

He buzzed the door open. The kids loved banana smoothies. He kept a regular supply for just these occasions.

They were up in the lift seconds later. Winter could hear them laughing as they ran along the corridor towards his apartment. At three, four and six, he thought, they still lived in a world of their own. Winter was their favourite uncle. They'd told him so. Uncle Paulie. With the well-stocked fridge.

The moment they romped into the flat, Guy headed for the kitchen. Winter heard a *clunk* as he pulled the fridge open for the smoothies, and then the usual squabble over who was to clamber on the kitchen stool to grab the yellow plastic Lion King mugs.

He was right about Esme. She needed to talk about her dad. Badly.

'What's he done this time?'

Winter laughed. Things had been tricky between him and Esme to begin with. She hadn't bothered to hide her misgivings about letting an ex-cop so close to the family business but they'd slowly fumbled their way towards some kind of truce. Esme was a girl who always spoke her mind, and Winter liked that.

'From where I'm standing, I doubt he's done anything.'

'So why all the hassle?' She nodded towards the TV. 'Nelly phoned me first thing. Dad *and* Mum?'

'It's routine, Ez. We're not talking subtle here. Show cops a crime scene and they grab what looks obvious. Baz? These days he might be pushing to join the Rotary Club but that's not the first thing they're going to remember.'

'Nelly said he'd got into some kind of fight.'

'More than likely.'

'And ended up with two bodies beside his pool.'

'Spot on.'

'So how come that happened?'

'Christ knows. You want coffee?'

They talked in the kitchen while the kids played in the lounge next door. In Winter's view, unless he'd misread the situation, Ezzie had nothing to worry about. Bazza and Marie would doubtless remain in custody until Scenes of Crime had taken a good look at the house itself but that shouldn't take long and he'd be surprised if they spent another night in the cells. As for the bodies beside the pool, Winter was as clueless as everyone else.

'We're dealing with kids on the piss,' he said. 'It could be they necked so much vodka it all just got silly.'

'In Dad's garden, you mean?'

'Yeah. They'd have known from Rachel there was a pool next door. So they hop over the fence and stagger around and maybe one of them falls in and the other one gets him out, and then ...' He shrugged. 'Fuck knows.'

'So why all the drama?'

'A body's a body. Blokes in the Job take death seriously. It's what they do.'

'So maybe we're not talking murder at all? Is that what you're saying?'

'Yeah, maybe we're not. Just a bunch of kids trashing someone else's house. What did Nelly say?'

'She didn't know. Not when I talked to her first thing.'

'Fine. Just relax, then. It's cushty. No way would Baz have done anything silly. He'll be sitting it out until they can't think of anything else to ask him. Then he'll be home again.'

She nodded, unconvinced, then turned to find her youngest daughter standing in the kitchen doorway. Her tiny face was covered in the tangerine Post-its that Winter kept by the telephone. Each carried the logo of the Burj al-Arab hotel, one of the many trophies Winter had brought back from a thank-you trip to Dubai.

'Guy did this, Mummy,' she piped. 'He's always horrible to me.'

DCI Gail Parsons was back in Portsmouth by half past two. She'd rung ahead, asking Faraday to convene the first of the *Mandolin* management meetings for 14.45. She'd borrowed the Detective Superintendent's office and wanted all the principals to attend. That, she emphasised, included the hard-pressed civvy ex-journo who headed Media Relations.

Faraday had done her bidding. It was strange seeing the DCI behind Martin Barrie's desk. Parsons seemed to occupy it with an instinctive air of entitlement, as if she'd been storing her handbag beside the battered old chair for months. The forbidden tang of Barrie's roll-ups still hung in the stale air, and Parsons had both windows open before the *Mandolin* team began to gather around the conference table at the other end of the office.

As brisk as ever, she kick-started the meeting with news from the post-mortem. Marie Mackenzie, she said, had found two bodies lying full-length beside her pool. One was Rachel Ault, the other Gareth Hughes. Rachel had stab wounds and was plainly dead. Marie had tried to revive Gareth, thinking he might be unconscious, but quickly realised he too was beyond help.

Hours later the attending pathologist examining Hughes had noted a number of facial injuries including a patterned stamp mark on his left cheek. There was blood on the paving stones beneath his head, with more blood beside Rachel's body, and the pathologist had found evidence of an impact injury on the rear right-hand side of his scalp. In Jenny's view, this might be consistent with a backwards fall.

'Stamp mark?' Jimmy Suttle wanted to know more.

Parsons was leafing through her notes. She produced a digital print taken last night at the poolside. Hughes had milky white skin and reddish gelled hair. He lay cheek down on the paving stones beside the swimming pool. His mouth hung open, revealing a line of crooked teeth, and blood was caked around an injury to his left eye. More blood pinked the whiteness of his T-shirt.

Faraday lingered for a moment over the image before passing it down the table. The stamp mark on the lad's cheek was clearly visible, a windfall lead, but what caught Faraday's attention was the hint of vulnerability, even surprise, in the still-open eyes. Whatever Gareth Hughes had been expecting from last night's party, it certainly hadn't included this.

Suttle briefly studied the stamp mark. The sole pattern suggested a trainer of some sort. In due course the imaging department at Netley would be supplying full albums of photographs but this one was high priority.

'Nice one.' He made himself a note. 'I'll action it.'

Parsons ran through the findings on Hughes at post-mortem. Periorbital haematoma around the left eye with areas of laceration to the inner eyebrow. Superficial scratches on his forehead. Bruising inside his mouth plus a single-line fracture running from the rear of his skull. That was pretty much it.

'Any self-defence injuries?' It was Proctor.

'None that Jenny could find.'

'That makes him unlucky, doesn't it? Either it was over in seconds or he didn't put up much of a fight.'

Parsons nodded in agreement. In the pathologist's view a backward fall onto the paving stones could have been fatal.

'So we're looking at some kind of confrontation?' Jimmy Suttle again.

'I think that's a safe assumption.'

Heads nodded around the table. Proctor asked about Rachel Ault. Eyes turned towards Parsons.

'She was beside the pool as well, four metres from Hughes. She had injuries to her face and neck, and more bruising to her lower ribcage. Jenny found multiple stab wounds to her chest and abdomen. She had a major internal injury to the aorta. There was certainly enough blood loss to kill her. The size and depth of the entry wounds would suggest a ten-centimetre blade. We might be talking about a kitchen knife, a hunting knife, a switchblade, whatever.'

'Nothing recovered?' Faraday this time.

'Not yet.'

Faraday turned to the other photo. The brightness of the flash on the camera had done her no favours, but Rachel Ault had been striking. Her face was bloodied but it spoke of a strength and purpose that had survived sudden death. She had a full mouth, her lips drawn back in what – to Faraday – looked like a gasp, and it was all too easy to imagine the scene by the swimming pool, the unimaginable strangeness of a knife driving into her flesh, the sudden flooding warmth as her belly filled with blood. He gazed at the photo a moment longer. Her eyes were open, a startling green.

'Some of the blood by the pool is presumably hers?' he asked.

'Could be. We're talking two locations by the poolside. The samples went off this morning. We'll know for sure within a week or so.'

Faraday nodded, returning to the photo. Even now, after years on the Major Crime Team, he was always fascinated by the way that a lab analyst a hundred miles away could begin to coax a narrative from a few drops of blood.

Parsons hadn't finished.

'Jenny took body swabs at the poolside, and a fresh set before the

PM began. She found semen in the girl's vagina. More in her throat. She also mentioned a strong smell of alcohol.'

'And the lad? He'd been drinking as well?'

'The tox results won't be back for weeks, and Jenny's not prepared to chance her arm on an exact time of death, but the party had probably been going on a while by the time they died so it's a reasonable assumption that he'd had a few. Probably more than a few.'

Faraday finally passed Rachel's photo down the table. In his morning briefing he'd alerted interview teams to the importance of sightings of Rachel and Gareth. When had they last been clocked at the party? Who had they been with? What had they been up to?

Parsons had finished with the PM. The pathologist's full report should be available within three weeks, she said, but now she wanted to concentrate on the interviews and statement-taking. She'd couldn't remember a homicide with so many potential witnesses. In some ways it reminded her of the aftermath of a train crash or a terrorist incident: multiple points of view knotting into a single complex story.

'Joe?'

Faraday glanced up, nodding. He'd had a brief phone conversation with one of the Crime Scene Investigators starting work on Ault's house. In many ways the DCI's image of a bomb attack was all too telling: blood and wreckage everywhere, almost beyond belief, and an aftermath that might stretch – for some – deep into the future. The picture of last night's events, just now, was still chaotic. Facts first, he thought.

'We're dealing with ninety-four individuals,' he began. 'Most of them agreed to attend as witnesses. We've filled all fourteen custody centres within the force, plus eight more under the mutual aid arrangements. Interviews out-of-county are being handled by their own personnel. We're obviously processing the rest.'

'How are you prioritising?' There was an edge of impatience in Parsons's voice. Busy lady. Lots to do.

'I drew up a matrix first thing. We need to winnow out the chaff. Anyone with obvious signs of injury or blood on their shoes or clothing goes to the top of the list. Likewise anyone with previous. Ideally, I'd have preferred to put the bad eggs in one basket but last night that was impossible. We batched them in the order they came out. That means the possibles and probables are pretty much dispersed. By now, most of the kids will have been released. Potential suspects we'll bring back to the Bridewell.'

'How many are we talking?'

Faraday glanced down at his notes. He'd been anticipating exactly this question.

'Nineteen,' he said carefully. 'I'm assuming whoever had a hand in the killings probably legged it. But they would have had mates. And they're the ones we'll be talking to.'

'Anyone top of the list?'

'Not so far, not to my knowledge, but Jimmy and I won't be looking at statements until this afternoon.'

Suttle nodded. It would be his job to comb every statement and begin to match one account against another. Parsons caught his eye.

'You've got something to add?'

'Only that I took a phone call from Thames Valley just before we kicked off. They've got a girl up in Reading. Samantha Muirhead. It turns out she was Rachel Ault's best friend. She's slightly older too. Lives out in the country. Agreed to be a DD.'

'DD?'

'Designated driver. Which means she was sober.'

'And?'

'She's upset, obviously, but if we're looking for a decent account the D/I up there thinks she'd be a good place to start.'

'You want to re-interview her?' Parsons was looking at Faraday.

'Definitely.'

'Is she happy to do that, Jimmy?'

'According to the D/I, yes. Her parents are up there with her. They're driving her down from Reading. I told him we'd have someone at the Bridewell.' He glanced at his watch. 'About now.'

He'd alerted the Custody Sergeant to expect them. Faraday shot him a look, said they'd talk to the girl together. The Thames Valley D/I had been right. At this stage in the game *Mandolin* needed an overview.

Parsons agreed. Already briefed by Faraday, she'd virtually dismissed Mackenzie as a prime suspect. Regretfully, there was every indication that he'd simply been playing the good neighbour. She gave Faraday a nod, asking him for more detail.

Scenes of Crime, he said, had found blood in Mackenzie's kitchen. There'd been smears on the lip of a glass beside the sink, and there'd been more blood on a flannel and a towel in the upstairs bathroom, and on one of the pillows in the Mackenzies' bedroom.

Challenged to explain these stains, Mackenzie had claimed the blood as his own. To be honest, he couldn't remember going to the kitchen but he must have fancied a glass of water. Upstairs in the bathroom, still bleeding, he remembered mopping his face with a flannel. Marie kept Ibuprofen in the cabinet over the sink. He'd popped four of them before calling it a night.

Monitoring the interview from the adjoining suite, Faraday had phoned through to the scene and minutes later the CSI had re-confirmed Mackenzie's story in every detail. Blood had tracked Mackenzie's path to bed. Then, still leaking onto the pillow, he'd crashed out.

Mackenzie's solicitor, said Faraday, was pushing hard for early release. Swabs from the bloodstains would be dispatched for analysis but full DNA results wouldn't be back until the end of the week. Under these circumstances there was no point in holding him with a view to any kind of custody extension. His wife, Faraday added, had corroborated every element in her husband's account.

Turning to Suttle, Parsons asked about mobiles. He said that sixty-seven had been seized last night, and another fourteen recovered from the house or the garden. Numbers had been tallied for billing purposes, and the lot had gone to the Comms Intelligence Unit at Netley for analysis. He was anticipating a wealth of images, including video, and in the shape of three seized digital cameras *Mandolin* was looking at another windfall.

Faraday, collecting his notes, briefly pondered this development. Suttle was right. Kids these days were obsessed by images and material retrieved from phones might well wrap up the investigation. Live by the mobe, he thought grimly, die by the mobe.

He glanced up to find Parsons on her feet. She wanted another conference late afternoon for a Scenes of Crime update ahead of the full squad meet. In the meantime she'd be briefing the duty Detective Superintendent. Was there anything else that couldn't wait until five?

There was a brief silence, broken by D/S Glen Thatcher. His Outside Enquiry teams were already doing house-to-house calls the length of Sandown Road and beyond, hunting for any shred of evidence that might help with the bigger picture. He was looking at Parsons.

'We're getting a load of grief from the residents.' He said, 'Putting it bluntly, they think we were piss poor. Some of these people are well connected. Maybe you should pass the word, boss.'

The civvy in charge of Media Relations sat at the end of the table. She'd once been a reporter on BBC South. Parsons favoured her with a smile.

'Yours, I think, Debbie. Maybe we should have some kind of strategy in place. Glad you could find time to attend.'

Nelly Tien's call found Winter looking for his trousers. After Esme and the kids had departed he'd gone back to bed for a kip. Nelly sounded harassed.

'Mr Mackenzie is about to be released from custody. He wants to know where you are.'

'Gunwharf, love. The flat.'

'Fine. I'll drive him round.'

'And Marie?'

'She's sitting beside me. She got out an hour ago.'

Nelly ended the call without saying goodbye, even more clipped than usual. Trouble, Winter thought, wondering whether he ought to sort out a fresh shirt.

Bazza and Marie arrived twenty minutes later. Unusually, Bazza had a protective arm around his wife. Under the summer tan she looked nervous and distracted. When Winter asked her whether the Fareham custody suite still had a poster up for last Christmas's CID bash, she didn't bother to raise a smile. A night in a custody cell had clearly concentrated her mind. She wanted to get home, she said. She wanted a long hot shower, a decent cup of coffee and a chance to work out what to say to the Aults. But until SOC released their house, even that wasn't an option.

'Where will you go?'

'The hotel, mush.' It was Mackenzie. 'Where do you think?'

The Royal Trafalgar was on the seafront. Drug money had restored the place to its pre-war glory. To date, it was Mackenzie's biggest stake in the city.

Ignoring the offer of coffee and a doughnut, he told Winter to sit down. The swelling on his face had begun to subside and he'd abandoned the swath of crêpe bandage around his head. Blood had crusted around the wound on his scalp and there was more damage to the knuckles of his left hand. Southpaw, Winter remembered.

'Listen, Paul. We have a problem, all of us. What happened last night was totally out of order. The more I think about it, the worse it fucking gets. You don't pay good money for an address like that to have a bunch of arsehole kids come and wreck it. And I'm certainly not having some numpty or other dumping bodies beside my pool. Neither should my missus have to put up with a night in the fucking cells. Respect is where this begins and ends. Peter Ault's a good bloke. I gave the guy my word of honour. I told him I'd look after things and I've completely fucking blown it. He'll be back any day, poor bastard. By then, my old mate, I want a name. *Comprende?*'

'Name, Baz?' This was a new Mackenzie. Accepting responsibility. Administering justice.

'Yeah, name, mush. Or maybe names. I've no fucking idea but just sort it, OK? You told me once you were the best fucking cop this town had ever seen. You told me you'd taken more scalps than any other Filth that ever lived. So now's your chance to prove it. You might start with Matt Berriman, the kid who hauled those animals off me. I used to know his mum. She had a Somerstown address unless she's moved.'

Winter was missing something here, and he knew it. He eyed the TV for a moment. Maybe going back to bed hadn't been such a great idea.

Marie stirred. She was standing by the window now, gazing out at the harbour.

'One of the bodies by the pool was Rachel,' she said quietly. 'We somehow assumed you knew.'

Chapter five

Sam Muirhead and her parents were late getting to the Bridewell. Faraday and Suttle had been waiting fifteen minutes by the time they arrived. The Custody Sergeant brought them into the office he'd made available, and Suttle fetched more chairs while Sam's mother offered her apologies

'We stopped on the way for a bite to eat. It's been a bit of a trial, I'm afraid.'

The father was a thickset man with a firm handshake and a weathered, outdoors complexion. He wanted to know why his daughter had to go through the whole thing again. She'd been as helpful as she could. The detectives in Reading had been pleased with her statement. Surely she could be spared another interview?

Faraday asked them all to take a seat.

'Your daughter knows about Rachel?'

'Yes. It was on the news coming down. Sam's pretty upset, to be frank.'

There was a silence, broken in the end by Sam. She was a tall girl with a long pale face, and she had her mother's auburn hair. Faraday sensed she'd been crying.

'I'll do whatever you want,' she said quietly.

Faraday explained that the interview would take place in one of the special suites across the corridor. Sam said no to the offer of legal representation and shook her head when Suttle suggested her mum or her dad sit in.

'Let's just do it. Then we can get home.'

In the interview suite Suttle cued the audio and video tapes. Faraday, after a snatched conversation with the D/I in Reading, knew exactly where to start.

'I understand you knew Rachel pretty well.'

'We were best friends.'

'For a long time?'

43

'Yes. Years and years.' She sniffed and tipped her head back. 'We were like sisters really. That's what other people said and in a way it was true.'

'So what sort of girl was she?'

'She was brilliant. Brilliant as a friend. Brilliantly clever. Brilliantly kind. Brilliant in all kinds of ways.'

Faraday consulted his notes then looked up. 'You mentioned the swimming club this morning. Care to tell me about that?'

'It was something she started young, really young. We were at primary school together. She was swimming even then, you know, proper swimming, not just messing around. She got spotted. A coach from Northsea came along. I think she signed her up, I'm not sure.'

The Northsea Club was Pompey's pride and joy. Based at the Victoria Baths, it won honours at every level and had produced a string of contenders for the UK national squad. Rachel, said Sam, had found herself training six days a week, two sessions a day. Her commitment had been awesome. Just like Matt's.

'Matt who?'

'Matt Berriman.'

'The Matt Berriman who was at the party? The lad who helped the neighbour next door?'

'Yes.' She seemed surprised. 'He and Rach have been together for years. Ever since they both started at the swimming club. I'm sorry ... I thought you knew that.'

'No.' Faraday shook his head. 'Tell us more.'

'Well ...' She was trying to remember. 'He was a bit older than Rach when they first met. I think he was already at secondary school. St Mark's.'

St Mark's was a troubled comprehensive that straddled the fault line between Portsmouth and Southsea. Socially, Matt and Rachel would have been on different planets.

Faraday studied her a moment. PNC checks on Berriman at Newbury custody suite had revealed a recent conviction for a motoring offence: 132 mph on the M27 in a borrowed BMW.

'You know Matt?'

'Of course. We all do.'

'What's he like?'

'Big. Tall. Ripped.'

Faraday glanced at Suttle.

'It means fit, boss.'

'Thank you.' He looked back at Sam. 'So they were training together? Twice a day? Saw lots of each other?'

'Absolutely. And as they got older they began to go away together.

44

There's a place up in the north somewhere, Sheffield maybe. They do special training weekends if you're really good. Rach and Matt were both in the national team. They went to London too. She lived for those weekends. She said they were brilliant.'

'They had a relationship?'

'Definitely. Full on.'

'How old was she by then?'

'Fifteen. Rach swam the longer distances, I don't know exactly which race. Matt was a sprinter. That suited him, believe me. He did everything flat out. He was just immense. One time we were all on the beach, pitch black, and someone dared him to swim round the pier, and he just did it – just stripped off to nothing and did it.'

Faraday frowned. Round Southsea Pier couldn't be more than a couple of hundred metres. Nothing surely to a swimmer like Matt?

'It was December. Christmas Eve.'

'Ah ...'

Sam, for the first time, smiled. The smile widened into a grin. Memories of the young Matt Berriman had brought her to life.

'So how long did this relationship last?'

'Until six weeks ago.'

'Really?' Faraday leaned forward. There'd been no mention of this from the Thames Valley D/I. 'So what happened?'

'She met Gareth.'

'Gareth Hughes?'

'Yes. I've known Gareth for a while. We're in the sixth form to-gether at PGS.' She hesitated. 'Or we were ...'

Faraday scribbled himself a note. Portsmouth Grammar School, like the Girls' High, was fee-paying.

'Tell me about Gareth.'

'He was different to Matt, nowhere near as sporty. He wasn't spastic, nothing like that, and he wasn't a boff either, but he was much more ...' she frowned, hunting for the word '... *sensible* than Matt. There'd been some problems between her and Matt. Rach was trying to nail down all the stuff she had to do for the Oxford entrance exam and Matt definitely wasn't helping.'

'Like how?'

'Like he'd buy tickets for a big festival, the whole weekend, expensive tickets, tickets he could no way afford, and when Rach said she couldn't spare the time he'd get really ... you know ... difficult. He really knew how to make her feel guilty too, and in the end she'd always give in and then regret it.'

'Why?'

'Because he was just getting wilder and wilder. He was into all

45

kinds of stuff. He just had to try everything, which obviously made things hard for Rach.'

'And the swimming? The training?'

'That was the other thing. Matt had pretty much given up. Rach was the same, though for different reasons.'

'And did she get into Oxford?'

'Yeah. In fact she got a scholarship. That's why her dad gave her a car.' She began to sniff and then fumbled for a Kleenex. 'Shit, this is really hard.'

Faraday gave her a moment or two to blow her nose. Then he wanted to know about the party. Whose idea had it been?

'Rach's. She just wanted a bunch of friends around, people who maybe didn't know Gareth that well.'

'So how did she sort out the invites?' It was Suttle this time.

'She's got a page on Facebook. You can have a best mates list. You can tell everyone whether you're in a relationship or not. You can do all kinds of stuff. She just sent word round all her mates.'

'Including Matt?'

'Must have. Matt had been on her Facebook page, obviously. Rach was incredibly bright, like I've said, but I think she just forgot to take him off the list. Either that, or she couldn't bear to. She could be really silly sometimes about that kind of stuff, really soft in the head.'

'So that was how he got to find out about the party? Is that what you're saying?'

'Yes. Must have been.'

'And how was the invite worded? Do you know?'

'I can't remember. You could check it out. It was something about Rach's new squeeze. She made a joke of it really. It was just supposed to be really casual, a chance for people to come and crash for the night, you know. Big old house, loads of space, DVDs, music, stuff to drink. It was no big deal, honestly ...' She tailed off.

'Do you think Matt might have spread the word? Because of Gareth?'

'Out of jealousy, you mean? I've no idea. He could have done, I suppose, but it would surprise me because he's not that organised really. With Matt it was always last-minute stuff ... impulse ... you know what I mean?'

'But did he miss her? To your knowledge.'

For the first time there was hesitation in her face.

'Yes,' she said finally. 'He did.'

'He wanted to get back with her?'

'Yes, definitely.'

'She told you that?'

'I knew.'

'How?' Faraday this time.

The wariness again. A longer silence.

'Because he told me.'

A week ago, she said, she'd bumped into Matt at Gunwharf. He was with a couple of mates. He'd sent them packing and insisted on buying her a coffee. He'd just been done for some stupid driving offence and the woman he'd borrowed the car from had gone bonkers.

'Why?'

'He'd taken the car without asking. And he wasn't insured.'

Faraday made a note. The pull on the M27, he thought.

He looked up. 'You were having coffee ...'

'Yes. That's when Matt told me he wanted him and Rach to get it on again. He was really wound up about it. He said she was the best thing that had ever happened to him and next time he wouldn't ... you know ... mess it up.'

'He thought there'd be a next time?'

'Definitely. But that's Matt. He makes things happen.'

Makes things happen. Faraday leaned back in his chair, gazed up at the ceiling.

'Let's go back to the party. Rachel got the place sorted before everyone arrived?'

'We both did. Gareth helped. We locked the bedrooms upstairs, put little notices on the doors, hid stuff we didn't want to leave lying around.'

'What kind of stuff?'

'Family bits and pieces, games consoles. Rach's dad's a bit of a wine expert. He had crates and crates of really expensive stuff downstairs in the cellar. Gareth went and bought a padlock and put it on the door at the top of the cellar stairs.'

'Who were you worried about?'

'No one in particular. No one we really knew. But any party you sometimes get walk-ins off the street. It's best to be careful, especially in a house like that.'

'But you'd no idea so many people ...?'

'Absolutely not.'

The party, she said, had kicked off around nine. Friends had wandered in from Southsea Common. Most of them had been drinking since six or seven. It was a warm night.

'You're telling me they were drunk?'

'Happy. Gareth had made a kind of punch thing with lots of fruit and stuff in it and we had a couple of crates of WKD. Some lads from the rugby team turned up. Three of them had cases of Stella. It was cool. No trouble. Good vibe.'

'So what happened?'

'Like I said, it was fine to begin with. One of the rugby guys had brought some laughing gas and a bunch of balloons. We were just fooling around. Then Matt turned up.'

'What time was this?'

'It's hard to say. Maybe around ten. Maybe a bit earlier.'

'He was by himself?'

'No. He had some other guys with him – friends, I guess. None of us had a clue who they were.'

'What kind of guys?'

'Chavs. Definitely. Maybe St Mark's boys. I've no idea.'

'Not your sort, then? Or Rachel's?'

'No ... but there was no hassle, no trouble, not at that point. One of them had even brought some cans of Carling. He couldn't have been more than fourteen. I remember he wished Gareth a happy birthday.'

'It was his birthday?'

'Not at all. The kid was pissed. Not stroppy. Just ... you know ... stupid. Pretty much like everyone else was. A situation like that, you just hope it stays cool.'

'And did it?'

'No. More kids turned up. Then more and more. I knew it was getting out of hand but there didn't seem much I could do about it. I tried to lock and bolt the front door at one point, just to stop more people coming in, but as soon as I did that someone else came along from inside and unlocked it again. To be honest, it was quite scary. We'd completely lost control.'

'What about the rugby lads?'

'A couple of them tried to sort it out. They asked the older ones to leave and take the younger kids with them. That was pretty hopeless because they just got a mouthful back. Some of these people were vile. At one point it was pretty obvious there was going to be a fight but I managed to calm things down.'

'*You* did?'

'Yes.'

'What about Rachel?'

'She was out of her head. She must have been drinking most of the day. When she saw what was happening she just seemed to lose it. Vodka, mainly. With lemonade.'

The first sign of real trouble, she said, was a bunch of guys she didn't know doing lines of coke on the upstairs landing.

'It turned out there was a dealer with them. They called him Danny. I don't know whether it was his real name or not but apparently he was practically giving the stuff away. They couldn't get enough of it. I tried to tell Gareth but he was pretty pissed too. When he finally cottoned on he made me promise I wouldn't call the police. He was really worried about Rach's dad finding out. He was sure Rach would get the blame.'

By now, she said, the house was full of strangers. That's when it really kicked off.

'I heard this terrible yelling. Then a stamping noise and the sound of breaking glass. Rach heard it too. Her dad's study's up on the first floor. I was sure we'd locked it but someone had kicked the door in. Her dad's got a big leather-covered desk and some of these kids were dancing on it. They'd piled all the family photos they could find on the desk, nice shots in frames, and they were just trashing them. There was a girl on the desk too. She was the one who told the kids to … you know …' She gestured at her lap.

'What?'

'Piss. Piss all over them.'

'And they did?'

'Yes. Right in front of us. Rachel just freaked. You can imagine. I don't think she really grasped what was happening. She did her best to stop them but they just laughed at her. Told her to fuck off. That's when Matt appeared.'

Matt, she said, had taken charge. The kids seemed to know him. When it got difficult he just started hauling them off, one by one. A couple of them tried to have a go at him but he just threw them into the hall. Then he took Rach off.

'Where to?'

Once again Faraday sensed reluctance. He repeated the question. Finally, she shrugged. 'The bathroom.'

'And?'

'I think he tried to get some sense into her. When I next saw her, there was water on her T-shirt and she seemed to have sobered up a bit.'

Faraday glanced across at Suttle.

'Were they in there a long time?' Suttle asked.

'Quite a long time.'

'And was the door locked?'

'How would I know?'

'Because I expect you tried it.'

Sam stared at Suttle for a long moment.

Then she nodded. 'I did.'

'And was it locked?'

'Yes.'

'Why do you think that was?'

She wouldn't answer. Suttle was looking at Faraday.

'What happened after that?' Faraday asked. 'Did you talk to her at all?'

'Yes. Just to ask if she was OK. She said she was. She said that Matt had been ... you know ... brilliant.'

'And her boyfriend? Gareth? Where was he?'

'I've no idea. It was just chaos by now. Kids everywhere. One of them had a paint aerosol. Black. He was tagging with it. It was everywhere, all over the place – the walls, the panelling, the doors, everywhere. Rachel's dad had some oil paintings. It was unbelievable what they were doing.'

'And still no one said anything? Tried to stop them?'

'No. It's hard to explain. Most people were off their faces. Friends of ours. The chavs. Matt's mates. People didn't care any more. You could see it in their faces. People you thought you knew, people you thought you could trust, they looked like strangers, they *were* strangers. It was weird. It's really, really hard to explain.'

'What about you? How did you feel?'

'I was frightened.'

'Of what?'

'Of everything. It was just ... totally alien, totally strange. You feel ... I dunno ... helpless. There's nothing you can do.'

'You could have phoned us.'

'I thought about that. But then you'd have busted us all. And Gareth was right. Rach would have got the blame. She got on OK with her dad but I knew he could be really strict.'

'So you did nothing?'

'I tried to calm things down, tried to keep a lid on things.'

'And no sign of Rachel?'

'No.'

'Matt?'

'No.'

'Gareth?'

'Not that I remember.'

By this time, she said, it was way past midnight. That's when the guy next door had appeared. She'd met him a couple of times before when she'd been round at Rachel's place. According to Rachel, he'd been a bit of a bad boy but made loads of money. He had a nice wife who was friends with Rachel's mum.

'And what happened?'

'He tried to sort a couple of the chavs out. He could see exactly what was going on. If you want the truth, I thought he was incredibly brave, doing what he did. He just picked on the biggest ones and set about them.'

'And?'

'It was hopeless really. There were just too many of them. They got him on the floor, started kicking him. One of them had a bottle. I think it smashed. There was blood all down his face. All the girls were screaming. Just totally manic. That's when I next saw Matt.'

Matt, she said, dragged some of the kids off. Then he got the neighbour out of the house. After that, she wasn't sure what happened.

Faraday was trying to establish a timeline. Marie's treble nine had been logged at 12.39. The force control room had put out a priority alert to units in Portsmouth. Marie had sent her wounded husband back home and then waited in the street for the police. The first of the attending units had logged their arrival time at 12.51. Minutes later, alerted by Marie, they were gazing down at the bodies beside Mackenzie's pool.

Faraday was looking at Sam.

'Let's go back to the last time you saw Rachel,' he began. 'I know it's difficult. I know everything was kicking off. We're not holding you down to an exact time. But roughly when do you think that might have been?'

'I don't know.'

'Try, Sam, just try.'

'It's hard. Stuff like that, you just ...' She ducked her head, knotted her hands in her lap.

Suttle reached across, put a hand a hand on her shoulder.

'An hour?' he suggested.

She shook her head, blew her nose.

'Longer?'

'I think so.'

'Much longer?'

'I don't know. I just don't know.' Her head came up. Her eyes were shiny with tears. 'This is really important, isn't it?'

'I'm afraid it is.' Faraday again.

'Then I'm really, really sorry.' Her hand opened and closed around the ball of Kleenex. 'I'm pretty useless really, aren't I?'

Winter had an address and phone number for Matt Berriman within minutes of Mackenzie's departure from Gunwharf. Bazza had named a couple of likely streets in Somerstown and Winter's call to 118118 had done the rest.

Margate Road was a shallow curve of terraced houses close to the heart of the area. One end of the street had become home for aspirant families with a bit of money to spend on window boxes and a shiny brass knocker for the new front door. The rest of the properties had been swamped by students, Asians and troubled loners fleeing the usual army of demons.

Matt Berriman's mum had invested in a nice display of fuschias. Winter stepped out of his Lexus to find her perched on a pair of wooden steps, watering her hanging basket.

'Mrs Berriman?'

'That's me.'

'The name's Paul Winter. Friend of a friend.'

'Which friend?'

'Friend of your boy's.'

'Matt?' She glanced down at him. 'A guy your age?'

She was a tall woman, striking, with a mop of greying curls. She wore a faded kaftan and her feet were bare on the wooden steps. A single silver ring adorned a middle toe.

When Winter asked whether Matt was at home, she shook her head.

'No.'

'You know where?'

'No idea. I haven't seen him since yesterday morning.' She had a flat London accent. 'In trouble is he?'

'Why would that be?'

She looked down at him, amused, not answering. Then she handed Winter the watering can and stepped onto the square of tiled path that led to the open front door.

'Come in. I've got something on the stove.'

Winter followed her into the gloom of the narrow hall. He could smell joss sticks, heavy and sweet. Ahead, stairs led to the top of the house. From above came the sound of a radio, some kind of sports commentary. Cricket, Winter thought. Maybe the husband.

The kitchen-diner lay at the back of the house. The units looked new and the far corner was dominated by a huge fridge-freezer. A jam jar beside the sink was full of artist's brushes and something white was bubbling in a big saucepan on the ceramic hob. She gave it a poke with a wooden spoon and turned the heat down.

'Nappies,' she said briefly.

Nappies? Winter was inspecting the display of photos on the shelves opposite the window. They were mounted in plastic frames, wedged haphazardly between recipe books, assorted crockery and jars of spices. The same young face, the same broad grin.

'This is Matt?' Winter nodded at one of the photos.

'You should know.'

'I said friend of a friend. Me?' Winter offered her an easy smile. 'Never had the pleasure, Mrs Berriman.'

She didn't believe him. He could see it in her eyes. From upstairs, he heard the *thump-thump* of footsteps.

'You're a cop, aren't you?'

'Why do you say that?'

'Because you get a nose for it in the end. No one's as nice as they look. Do you ever find that, in your line of business?'

Winter blinked. No one sussed him this quickly.

'I'm not a cop, Mrs Berriman.'

'Never?'

'I used to be. But not now.'

'Retired?'

'Sort of.'

'Private then? Some kind of special cop?'

Winter grinned this time. Some kind of special cop. He liked that.

Mrs Berriman had folded her arms. 'So who's this friend? Or aren't I supposed to know?'

'His name's Mackenzie.'

'Baz?' The smile was genuine. 'I haven't seen him for years.'

'But you knew him?'

'I did. Of course I did. He could be a very bad boy if you crossed him but he could be a brick if you really needed something.'

'And you?'

'I really needed something.'

Winter looked at her, wanting more, but she shook her head. Winter nodded at the photos. A couple of times over the last year he'd taken his doctor's advice and risked a length or two at the Victoria Baths. He recognised the tall windows at the deep end, the view down from the tiered seating.

'Bit of a swimmer is he, your boy?'

'Used to be. He was good too. In fact he was better than good. What's this about? Do you mind me asking?'

'Not at all. It's about Rachel Ault.'

'Rachel?' She seemed to sense bad news. 'What about her?'

'You haven't heard?'

'No. Tell me.'

Winter was about to explain when the footsteps, heavier now, clumped down the hall behind him. The boy must have been sixteen stone, maybe more. He was wearing a grey shell suit with a pair of blue slippers. Winter found it difficult to guess his age but he'd barely started shaving and there was a tuft of cotton wool beneath his button of a nose. The huge head seemed to wobble on his shoulders and he had his arms wrapped around his chest as if he was trying to parcel himself together.

He grunted something that Winter didn't catch. Through a pair of thick lenses he stared at the pair of them.

'This is Richard. My youngest.'

Winter nodded a greeting. He caught a smell of something sour. More soggy nappies, he thought. Poor bloody woman.

'What are you after, Ricky? Only the man's busy.' She asked the question very slowly, spelling it out.

Another series of grunts.

'I don't know, love.' His mother seemed to understand. 'Back upstairs now. I'll fetch it later.'

'Now.' Much clearer this time.

'Later. Do as you're told.'

The boy was gazing at Winter. He stepped closer, reached out, touched his face. Winter held his ground.

'All right, son?' He extended a hand.

The boy studied it for a long moment. The expression on his face might have been a smile but Winter wasn't sure. Then he felt his mother brush pass, intercepting her son as he lunged at Winter's hand.

'Best if I put him back to bed,' she explained. 'He bites a bit when he gets excited.'

Winter watched her coax the boy towards the stairs. He was shouting now, but nothing made much sense. They began to climb the stairs. Then Winter heard the sound of a door opening and footsteps overhead. Seconds later came the radio again, much louder this time. Winter had been right. The cricket.

She was back within minutes. She didn't volunteer any kind of explanation about her son. Instead, she wanted to know about Rachel Ault.

'I'm afraid she's dead, Mrs Berriman.'

'Rachel?' She couldn't believe it. 'Rachel Ault?'

'Yes. I thought you might have known. It's been all over the telly, the radio.'

She shook her head, shocked, still trying to absorb the news.

'How?' she said at last.

Winter explained about the party in Craneswater. There'd been some violence, some fighting. Things had got out of hand.

'And Rachel? She got caught up in all that?'

'It seems so.'

'And Matt?'

'He was there too.'

'Fighting?'

'Helping.'

'Helping in a good way?'

'We think so.'

'Who's we?'

'Me.' Winter risked a smile. 'And Bazza.'

She nodded, beginning to believe it now. The kettle was on the hob. She filled it, turned on the gas ring, swore when the ignition wouldn't work. Winter watched her trying to find a match.

'Did he come back last night? Matt?'

'No.' She shook her head, preoccupied. 'But that's not unusual.'

'And he hasn't been in touch? Hasn't phoned at all?'

'No. But that's not unusual either.' She gestured at the kitchen. 'I like to think of this as his home but I think that says more about me than him.'

'So where's he living?'

She wouldn't answer. At length Winter asked her about the relationship with Rachel Ault.

'It's over. It's been over for weeks now. That's why I'm surprised about last night. Matt being there.'

'He never mentioned a party at all?'

'Not to me.'

'So why do you think he went?'

She shook her head. She said she hadn't a clue. Breaking up with Rachel had been a big thing in Matt's life. He'd done his best to play the tough guy, pretending everything was cool, but underneath she knew that it had crucified him. That's probably why he'd started to come off the rails.

'Like how?'

'Like drinking too much. Like borrowing a friend's car and driving like a maniac.'

He'd been done for some lunatic speed on the M27, she said. A big fine and a year's disqualification.

'And you think that was down to splitting up with Rachel?'

'Has to be. They'd been going together for years. She earthed him. She gave him a centre. And no one knew that better than Matt.'

Winter pushed for more. She made the tea, found some oatcakes, talked about the swimming, the early years, the relentless training, the dawn starts, the growing suspicion in her own mind that she'd somehow mothered a prodigy.

'He just grew into it,' she said. 'And the more he did it, the harder he tried, the better he got. I just watched him change. Physically, he started to look amazing, my boy, and it changed him inside too. He started to believe in himself. He'd always been quite cocky, quite mouthy, but this was something different. By the time he started winning serious races he really had something to boast about, and you know what? He didn't bother. He just let the cups and the medals and all the stuff in the paper at weekends speak for themselves. It was a kind of arrogance really, but it seemed to suit the person he'd become. Awesome.' She shook her head. 'Sometimes I couldn't believe he was the same child.'

'And Rachel was part of all that?'

'Completely. Like I say, she earthed him. She was a totally different character. Sane. Sensible. Patient. Kind. Matt never knew how lucky he was.'

'Until it ended.'

'Exactly.'

'And was it too late? Was it definitely over?'

'You're asking me?'

'I am.'

'I'm not sure.' She was frowning now, thinking hard. Eventually her head came up. 'You're telling me he was definitely at that party last night?'

'Yeah.'

'Then I imagine the answer's no.'

Winter left the house minutes later. Matt's mum was back upstairs again, attending to her other son. Fumbling for his car keys at the kerbside, Winter's attention was drawn to a white Skoda backing into a tight parking space across the road. The face in the passenger seat was all too familiar, a veteran D/C on Major Crime, and when the driver got out to lock up he too turned out to be CID.

They'd spotted Winter already. As they crossed the road, he greeted them beside his new Lexus.

'Bit late, aren't you?' Winter nodded back towards Berriman's front door. 'Tea's getting cold.'

Chapter six

Mandolin's second management conference was over. As the inquiry's principals filed out of Martin Barrie's office in readiness for the full squad meet, Faraday lingered beside Jerry Proctor at the long table. He had a sequence of crime scene shots pumped back from Sandown Road on his laptop and Faraday wanted a second look. The shots, barely an hour old, covered the downstairs rooms at the party house. Proctor flicked through them, explaining the geography of the house with the aid of a floor plan at his elbow.

'This is the entrance hall. This is what our lads saw when they first walked in.'

Faraday gazed at the laptop. The carpet in the Aults' hall was strewn with debris: smashed china, glass, empty crisp packets, DVD boxes, items of clothing, half a dozen bottles, crushed tinnies, even the remains of a bunch of flowers. In one corner, upended, lay a fire extinguisher, a dribble of foam clearly visible from the nozzle. A couple of paintings on the staircase had been tagged in black and then attacked with a knife, and someone had splintered the wood panelling that ran along the hall. Boot height, he thought, looking at the damage.

'What's that?' Faraday indicated a yellowing puddle on the carpet.

'Vomit. Apparently it's everywhere. And this too.'

Proctor keyed another set of images. This must be the lounge, thought Faraday. He tried to picture what it must have looked like prior to the party: the long crescent of sofa, the low occasional tables, the piles of newspapers and magazines, the modest-sized TV, the carefully placed wall lights, the glint of bottles on the cocktail cabinet, the freshly bought tulips in the fluted vase, the antique-looking dining table in the recess of the big bow window, all of it testament to lives shaped by restraint and good taste. Now, though, the room was laid waste: the furniture upended, the upholstery slashed, the cushions spilling feathers over the wreckage of the carpet. Someone had attacked the

TV with what looked like a wooden mallet and most of the far wall had become a blackboard for the tagger with the aerosol. *Cunt asked for it*. Went one line of graffiti. *Cunt got it*.

'Cunt?' Pondered Faraday.

'Rachel, presumably. Though that's a guess.'

'And what's that?' Faraday pointed to something brown smeared on the door round the handle.

'Shit, I'm afraid. I warned you, Joe. This place is a zoo.'

As Proctor sped through image after image, Faraday sat back, trying to imagine the feel of the property, its smell. Zoo was kind, he thought. No animal would inflict this kind of damage, this kind of insult. Even Gail Parsons, with her talk of train wrecks and bomb incidents, was wide of the mark. There was something evil going on here, something deeply personal he'd never before associated with the city he thought he knew. Not just drugs. Not just coked-up kids with nothing better to do. But the frenzied application of extreme violence, an opening salvo in God knows what kind of war. These people, whoever they were, cared for nothing. The house they'd so casually occupied had spoken of decent lives, decently lived. And they'd trashed it.

He got to his feet, wondering whether that same indifference to consequences, that same terrifying irrationality, extended as far as the bodies beside the pool. Was it rage that had killed Rachel and Gareth? Had they been two more targets of opportunity in some kind of grotesque class war? The have-nots settling a debt or two? Was it simple anarchy, the work of the fuck-you-and-fuck-the-rest-of-the-world lobby? Or could it have been more personal – more intimate – than that?

He glanced across at Proctor, wanting to take this debate further, but Proctor shook his head. Parsons was running a tight ship, he muttered. Best not to keep the lady waiting.

The first *Mandolin* squad meet took place in the Major Incident Room at the far end of the corridor of first-floor offices. Workstations, each one with its own PC, lined the walls and there was a separate area for the D/S in charge of Outside Enquiries. With the MIR at full throttle, the workstations were largely manned by civilian indexers, feeding in more and more data from the flood of interviews, statements and doorstep enquiries. It was this developing jigsaw, correlated and cross-referenced by the HOLMES software, that should offer the *Mandolin* management team their first glimpse of pathways forward through the evidential swamp. In theory, one or more of these pathways would lead to court. In practice, as Faraday knew only too well, it was rarely as simple as that.

He found himself a space beside the door and leaned back against the wall, surveying the faces around the room. The fact that DCI Parsons had managed to lay hands on so many D/Cs was a tribute to the closeness of her relationship with Willard, as well as to the spreading ripples of last night's events in leafy Craneswater.

Normally, the Major Crime Team relied on a core of detectives serving full time on the squad. Reinforcements, if necessary, would come from other MCTs in the west and north of the force area. On this occasion, though, Parsons had pressed for extra pairs of local hands, Pompey D/Cs with an ear to the ground, and Willard had obviously risked the wrath of their bosses on division to try and bring *Mandolin* to an early conclusion. With the nation's gaze riveted by events in leafy Craneswater, now was no time to squabble over manpower.

The duty Detective Superintendent, still acting as Senior Investigating Officer, made a couple of opening comments. *Mandolin,* he said, showed every sign of being a runner. His own commitments prevented him from staying with the investigation and so Mr Willard had taken a policy decision to hand the SIO role to DCI Parsons until Martin Barrie returned from leave. Under the circumstances, he was therefore happy to give her the floor.

Parsons nodded, stepping forward. Without consulting her notes, she quickly summarised progress to date. For the time being, she said, they were treating the riot and the double murder as linked crimes. This would give them a mountain to climb in terms of evidential footwork but the sheer scale of the vandalism and damage at 11 Sandown Road posed a challenge that might one day put *Mandolin* in the investigative textbooks. Every last detail, she insisted, had to be nailed down. She wanted no excuses, no short cuts. With a huge audience watching their every move, this job had to be faultless.

She called on Jerry Proctor for an update on the various scenes of crime. Proctor, Faraday knew, hated these presentations. He was a gruff man, interested only in results, and had no time for showboating or unnecessary drama. The scene by the pool, he confirmed, had yielded blood and other forensic evidence. The stamp mark on Gareth Hughes's cheek was being matched to sole patterns through a private forensic databank and details on make and trainer type should be available by noon tomorrow. The hunt for the knife used on Rachel Ault was ongoing.

'What about CCTV?' It was Willard. He'd slipped into the meeting while attention was fixed on Proctor. 'Has Mackenzie got cameras?'

'No, sir. I understand he's thought about installing a system but decided against it. If anyone's ever silly enough to try anything there'll be cheaper ways to sort it out.'

There was a ripple of laughter around the room.

'Shame.' Willard grunted. 'Go on.'

Proctor turned his attention to Mackenzie's house. He'd had a couple of investigators inside the property all day but so far they'd found nothing to challenge Mackenzie's version of what had happened: no incidental damage, no sign of any kind of struggle. In all probability they'd be releasing the scene at some point tomorrow.

Next door, meanwhile, another forensic team was moving through the party house, room by room. They'd started on the ground floor and so far they'd cleared four rooms. The place, he said, had been comprehensively wrecked, and in terms of potential evidence they were overwhelmed with samples. Blood, semen, shit, vomit, DNA traces from glasses and fag ends, multiple fingerprints, all the chaotic leavings you'd associate with a hundred or so partying youth. Teasing any kind of pattern out of all this was going to require hundreds of man-hours of analysis and discussion but for the time being, in the absence of anything as unlikely as a confession, he had no choice but to work slowly upwards through the house until the job was complete.

'Do you have an estimate on that, Jerry?' It was DCI Parsons this time.

'Hard to say. Thursday at the earliest. Depends, really.'

She nodded and scribbled herself a note. Then she turned to Willard.

'The Aults are booked onto a Qantas flight leaving Sydney on Wednesday afternoon, sir. They arrive at Heathrow at six in the morning next day. I'm arranging a FLO to be on hand. They're going to need a lot of support.'

Willard nodded. Although Judge Ault was no stranger to serious crime the Family Liaison Officer would try and buffer them from the worst of the shocks to come.

Proctor resumed. Mobiles and digital cameras, he said, were going to be key to the investigation. The mobes seized in Sandown Road were now awaiting analysis. He was anticipating hundreds of still images and possibly hours of video footage. A POLSA search in the grounds of the Aults' house, he added, had recovered a further nine mobiles. More grist for the evidential mill.

'What about PCs? Laptops?' Willard again.

'As far as we know, there were two in the house but they were both upstairs so we've yet to get there. Ault's got a PC. The girl, Rachel, had a laptop.'

'And you think they're still there?'

'No idea, sir. The laptop's probably gone. Along with a load of other stuff. It's impossible to say until the Aults get back.'

The meet went on. When Parsons asked Faraday for a summary of progress on the interviews, he did his best to simplify the worst of the complications.

The partygoers, by and large, were extremely reluctant to offer any kind of worthwhile account of exactly what had happened. Some of them, he suspected, had been so bombed that they simply couldn't remember. Others, especially friends of Rachel, were clearly frightened. They'd seen what some of the more violent kids could do and the last thing they intended to offer was themselves as a target for reprisals.

A third category – the majority, to be frank – were saying absolutely nothing. They'd stolen into Craneswater under cover of the gathering darkness, necked or nicked everything they could lay their hands on, and generally had a fine old time. When challenged about invitations they'd simply mumbled about a general invite, a form of words that seemed to have more to do with Facebook than trespass. The whole fucking city knew about the rave in Sandown Road, they seemed to be saying. So we just turned up.

Faraday glanced down at his notes. His suspects' list now numbered seventeen. These youths, mainly male, mainly white, would be subject to further interview this evening. In the absence of forensic evidence or incrimination from another source, they'd be released on police bail by midnight. Tomorrow, he anticipated a start on comparing ninety-four witness statements, no matter how brief. In conjunction with the emerging picture from Scenes of Crime, plus developments on the intelligence front, he'd hope for some kind of solid timeline within a few days.

'One other thing, boss.' He was looking at Gail Parsons. 'We re-interviewed Rachel's best friend this afternoon. If we're looking for motive, the lad Berriman definitely has some questions to answer.'

Briefly, he outlined the relationship that Rachel had so recently broken off. Gareth Hughes had taken Matt Berriman's place. And Berriman had been less than pleased.

A hand went up at the back of the room. It was one of the D/Cs who'd seized Berriman's laptop at Margate Road. He was looking at Faraday.

'One thing I forgot to mention, boss. Guess who we met coming out of Berriman's place?'

'Who?'

'Paul Winter.'

It took a while for Winter to pin down an address for the dead boy-friend. The Pompey phone book had dozens of entries under 'Hughes' so he put a call in to a contact on the *News*. Lizzie Hodson was a mate of Jimmy Suttle's. Winter had met her himself on a couple of occasions and he knew she was intrigued by what had taken an ageing cop to a new career on the Dark Side. In return for the promise of a drink and a chat later in the week, she agreed to make a few enquiries and call him back.

His phone was ringing within minutes. Hughes, it turned out, had lived with his family on Hayling Island. Winter, impressed with this speedy bit of research, asked how she knew.

'Jimmy told me,' she said.

'Did you mention my name at all?'

'Of course not.'

Hayling Island was on the other side of Langstone Harbour, an area of land the size of Portsmouth. Flat, featureless and ribboned with rows of neat little retirement bungalows, it had always struck Winter as an invitation to an early death, but towards the south of the island there were avenues of more substantial properties, expensively alarmed against predators from across the water.

Orchard Lodge, Sinah Lane, lay behind a thick laurel hedge. From the Lexus, with the window down, Winter could hear the *tick-tick* of a water sprinkler. More faintly came a surge of applause from some kind of crowd.

Pushing in through the big double gates, he braced himself against the attentions of a black Labrador. The dog was young, still a puppy, and it danced round Winter's feet as he made his way to the front door. The house looked pre-war, solidly built, with half an acre of so of encircling garden. Most of the garden was lawn, newly mown. Winter knocked again, watching the arching throw of water as the sprinkler ticked round.

'Can I help you?'

The voice came from an upstairs window. Winter shaded his eyes against the last of the sunshine. The woman seemed in no hurry to open the door.

'It's about Gareth ...' he began.

'Who are you?'

'My name's Winter. Paul Winter.'

'Are you a journalist'

'No.'

'Then why are you here?'

It was a good question. Winter was still coming up with the answer when the front door opened. A man this time, overweight, middle-aged, in jeans and a faded pink T-shirt.

'What the hell do you want?' Winter caught the scent of alcohol on his breath. His eyes were filmy. 'Don't think we've had enough for one day?'

'I'm sorry. Bad time.'

'It bloody well is. So what do you want?'

Winter produced an iPod and held it out. The man stared at it a moment. When nothing registered, Winter turned it over. On the back, two smiley cartoon faces carefully drawn in blue pentel.

'That belongs to Gareth. Where on earth did you get it?'

'It came from a good friend of mine. Marie Mackenzie. She gave Gareth and Rachel a lift to the station a couple of days ago. Gareth left it in her car.'

'Mackenzie?' The name had rung a bell. 'Next door to the Aults, you mean? The house with the pool?'

'Yes.'

'And you say he's a friend of yours?'

'Yes.'

'OK then. I suppose you'd better come in.'

Winter stepped into the cool of the house. Beyond the gleaming expanse of parquet flooring in the hall lay the living room. England were batting on the big wall-mounted plasma screen and Winter watched as the batsman stroked the ball towards the distant boundary. More applause.

'You must be Mr Hughes.' Winter glanced across at him.

'That's me.' He was pouring himself another glass of wine. 'Gareth's dad.'

He picked up the iPod, staring at the faces again, then turned round. He had his son's complexion, his son's freckles, though his pale skin was blotched with alcohol.

'This has been a nightmare. I'm sorry to be blunt but we've pretty much had it with the press people. You know something? They never leave you alone. TV are the worst. Think they own the bloody world.'

They'd had crews down from London, he said. They'd camped out in the road, put up the satellite dishes, then phoned through on their mobiles, pleading for an interview. At first he'd told them to bugger off, wanted nothing to do with them, but then his wife had pointed out the nuisance to the neighbours. Give them what they want, she'd said. And then they'll leave us all in peace.

'And did they?'

'Yes. But then more arrived, press people as well. No bloody manners, any of them, and no bloody imagination either. Just the same old question. How did we feel? How do you bloody *think* we feel?' He swallowed a mouthful of wine. 'I kid you not, total nightmare.'

Winter sympathised. He'd had dealings with the media himself, often. Tact wasn't their middle name.

'*Tact?*' The word triggered a fresh outburst. 'These people wouldn't know the meaning of the bloody word. All they want is grief. It's not even news. Just some poor bloody woman sobbing her heart out.'

'That would be me ... ?'

Neither Winter nor Hughes had heard her come down the stairs. She stood barefoot on the carpet. She was wearing a silk dressing gown and her hair was wet from the shower. She looked vague, Winter thought, a stranger in her own house.

'Mrs Hughes?'

'Yes.'

Winter apologised again for the intrusion and said he was sorry about Gareth. He'd come to return the iPod and offer condolences from the Mackenzies. Mr Mackenzie, he said, had been the one grown-up to try and do something about the madness next door. He'd got injured in the process, quite badly injured, but at least he'd had a go.

'I didn't know that.' Her voice was low, emptied of all passion. 'I thought the police ... .'

'They intervened later. By then it was too late.'

'I see.'

She asked Winter to sit down. She wanted to know more. Her husband had turned away, once more refilling his glass and then staring up at the cricket. Grief, thought Winter, walls you off. He'd seen it countless times.

'Tell me about the party.' She settled in the armchair across from the sofa. 'Tell me what you know.'

Winter obliged. A conversation with Bazza had given him a picture of the state of the Aults' place and the rest wasn't hard to make up. An invasion of kids from the other side of the tracks. Too much booze. Too many drugs. Things get out of hand. The script, he said, writes itself.

'Except that two young people died.'

'Exactly.'

'Not died, Helen. They got themselves *killed*. There's a difference.' It was Hughes. He was still watching the Test match. The way he put it sparked anger in his wife's face.

'You make it sound like it was their fault,' she said.

'Well it was, in a way.'

She looked up at him in disbelief. Booze, thought Winter. And anger. And loss. He doesn't mean it. He's just run out of things to say.

Hughes turned round at last, and reached down for the bottle. He was looking at Winter, his face beaded with sweat.

'Tell me I'm wrong,' he said. 'Tell me the world hasn't gone crazy. Tell me it's not a jungle out there. Tell me ...' he frowned, staring down at his glass, fighting to control himself '... that bloody boy of mine will be home tonight.'

He began to sob, his whole body shaking. When his wife got up and stepped across, he tried to shield himself, fending her off. She put her arm around him and led him away. Winter heard their footsteps on the stairs, the soft murmur of her voice, then the sound of a door closing. His glass had dripped red wine across the carpet. Winter was still watching the cricket when she returned.

She sat down, saying nothing, staring at the window. The silence between them thickened. Finally, Winter said he ought to leave her in peace.

'No,' she said. 'Don't.'

At length she got up and fetched a wine glass from the drinks cabinet in the corner. Winter, assuming she needed a drink, reached for the bottle.

'This is for you.' She gave him the glass. 'You knew Gareth?'

'Never had the pleasure, Mrs Hughes.'

'But Rachel? You knew her?' She seemed glad of someone to talk to.

'A bit.' Winter emptied the bottle. 'This relationship of theirs. Quite recent, wasn't it?'

'Very.'

'Had he known her before?'

'Not really. They were in the same year, at the same school, so they weren't *total* strangers, but to be honest I think the whole thing took Gareth a bit by surprise. Not that he didn't ... you know ... fancy her. Anyone would. She was attractive. She was bright. She was a wonderful girl. But I don't think he ever quite worked out why she'd picked him.'

'Picked?'

'Yes.' She reached for the remote and switched off the TV. 'I get the impression she made all the running.'

Rachel, she said, had been in another relationship for years. Friends of Gareth's regarded her as practically married. Then suddenly there she was, turning up with Gareth for Sunday lunch, a neat little pile of roast lamb pushed to the side of her plate.

'A vegetarian?'

'Definitely. And a girl who knew exactly what else she wanted in life. I think Gareth was a bit bewildered to begin with. He didn't know quite what to make of her. His father just told him to enjoy himself.'

'While it lasted?'

'Exactly. His exact words.'

There was a stir of movement overhead, then silence. Winter wondered how long he'd got.

'They were keen on each other then? Rachel and your boy?'

'Very. I know Gareth. He was quite a shy lad. In a way she overwhelmed him. I suppose I should have worried but I didn't. I was probably wrong but I think he needed a bit of that in his life.'

'A bit of what, Mrs Hughes?'

'A bit of oomph. A bit of adventure. A bit of passion. Don't get me wrong. He was a lovely boy. He was kind. He was sensible. He had nice friends. He worked really hard. But looking back I don't think he ever took risks.'

'And Rachel was a risk?'

'Yes. Because Rachel is the kind of girl you'd fall in love with. And Gareth had never risked that in his life.'

The kind of girl you'd fall in love with.

'You mentioned someone else. A previous boyfriend.'

'Of Rachel's, you mean?'

'Yes.'

'Yes.' She nodded. 'His name was Matt.'

'Did Gareth ever talk about him at all?'

'A couple of times.'

'In what context?'

'Just things that Rachel had said. How different Gareth was to her last boyfriend. How simple life could be.'

'Did they ever meet? Gareth and Matt?'

'Not to my knowledge. The last week or so, to be honest, we barely saw anything of Gareth.'

'How come?'

'He'd moved in with Rachel.'

'At the Aults' house?'

'Yes. They made no secret of it. In fact Terry and I were glad he was able to keep an eye on her. I imagine it would have suited the Aults too, Gareth and Rachel keeping the house in one piece.' She offered Winter a bleak smile. 'Bit of a joke really, isn't it? Under the circumstances ...'

Winter, for the second time, said he was sorry. Incidents like this were kicking off all over the country. It was like a germ, spreading from city to city. Today Pompey. Tomorrow the world.

'And you think that makes us feel better?'

'I'm sure it doesn't.'

'You think anything will make us feel better?'

Winter studied her for a moment or two. His own wife's death had left him emptier than he'd ever imagined possible.

'No,' he said. 'Not for a long time.'

'But in the end?'

'Yes.' He nodded. 'In the end, yes. Something happens. Something comes along.'

'Always?'

'Always.'

'Is that you being kind? Or do you know?'

'I know nothing, Mrs Hughes. Except you have to wait a while.'

She picked up the iPod, weighed it in her hand.

'What do you do for a living, Mr Winter?'

'I work for Mackenzie.'

'And before that?'

'I was a copper.'

'A detective?'

'Yes.'

'A good one?'

'The best.'

'I'm not surprised.' The smile didn't reach her eyes. 'It's the way you ask the questions, isn't it? And what you make of the replies?'

Chapter seven

The second round of interviews with *Mandolin*'s list of suspects began shortly after seven o'clock. Faraday had organised interview teams at custody suites in Fareham, Havant, Waterlooville and Portsmouth, and briefed the TIAs to press for as much detail as possible. In particular, he told the Tactical Interview Advisers, he wanted a full account of bloodstains found on the suspects' clothing, plus the names of the individuals with whom they'd spent most of the evening. In this way, matching one statement against another, he was looking for the kind of discrepancies that might offer leverage once he had a fuller picture of what had happened.

Of the seventeen suspects, six had been shipped down to the Bridewell. Ahead of the interviews, each of them conferred with the duty solicitor. Faraday, dead on his feet, had put Matt Berriman at the head of the list, determined to take his first good look at how the lad shaped up under pressure. It was still too early to talk about prime suspects but in terms of motivation Berriman faced some obvious questions.

D/C Bev Yates would again be partnering D/C Dawn Ellis in the interview suite. Faraday had talked them through the earlier exchange with Samantha Muirhead, and together with the Tactical Interview Adviser they'd agreed a shape for the next couple of hours. Yates and Ellis were veterans at this kind of work: good listeners, highly experienced, expert at preparing the kind of traps that might lead a cocky adolescent into a reckless boast or two. Ellis in particular, with her baby face and affection for off-the-wall T-shirts, was all too easy to underestimate.

Faraday settled himself in the monitoring room. Only this morning it had been Bazza Mackenzie's face on the video screen. Now he found himself looking at a tall well-built youth with a savage grade one and a pair of startling blue eyes. He was still wearing the grey shell suit Thames Valley had found in their custody suite and the top, several sizes too small, emphasised the breadth of his chest and shoulders. He had a scorpion tattoo on the side of his neck and a tiny silver Yang buttoned one earlobe.

Even on the video feed it was impossible to ignore Berriman's sheer physical presence. This was a lad who'd compel attention wherever he went, Faraday thought. His smile for Dawn Ellis seemed to fill the screen.

Yates had talked earlier to the interviewing D/C at Newbury and had a sheaf of notes on the table in front of him.

'You didn't tell us much about Rachel this morning,' he began.

'That's because no one asked me.'

'Wrong, Mr Berriman. We asked everyone whether they knew her or not. It was a standard question.'

'And I said yes. It was her party. She'd invited me. Is that a problem for you guys?'

'Not at all. But you didn't say you'd been going out with her for five years, did you?'

'No, you're right, but like I said ...' he shrugged '... it never came up.'

'But you *did* go out with her?'

'Yeah.'

'All that time?'

'Ycah.'

'Until recently?'

'Yeah.'

'And it didn't occur to you that's something we might have been interested in?'

'I'm not sure I thought about it. No one told me she was dead until later.'

Berriman held Yates's gaze. There was a hint of accusation in his voice. My girl, Faraday thought. My Rachel.

Ellis took over. She wanted to know everything about the relationship: how it started, how much it had mattered, why it had crashed and burned. The latter phrase made Berriman flinch, and Faraday began to sense that Sam Muirhead had been right. Behind the mask of seeming indifference, he'd missed her. Badly. And he'd wanted her back.

Yates had seen it too.

'So who ended it, Mr Berriman?'

'She did.'

'How?'

'*How?* We had a fucking great row, that's how.'

'Go on.'

'Go on what? You want to know what we said?'

'I want to know how it was between you – why Rachel suddenly decided to call it a day, what actually happened.'

'Who said it was sudden?'

'You're telling me it wasn't?'

'I'm telling you it's none of your business.' He was leaning back in the chair, smiling again, untroubled, back in control, determined to stay out of reach.

Yates held his eyes, then glanced sideways at Dawn Ellis. Her voice was soft. She was trying to help.

'She's dead, Matt. Someone killed her. You don't need me to tell you that's serious. She deserves the best we can do for her. Don't you think that's reasonable?'

'Of course I do.'

'So why don't you tell us as much as you can?'

'About what?'

'About you and Rachel.'

He thought about the proposition for a moment or two, his long fingers drumming on the table. Then he seemed to make some kind of decision.

'OK.' He leaned forward. 'If you're asking me whether she mattered, the answer's yes. She mattered a lot. Now, like you say, she's dead. So how does that work?'

'We don't know, Matt. That's why we're here.'

'But you think I can help?'

'Yes.'

'Because I was at the party?'

'Yes.'

'And you're telling me someone killed her?'

'Yes.'

'How?'

'How what?'

'How did they kill her?'

There was a long silence. Matt Berriman had the steadiest eyes. They belonged to someone much older, Faraday thought.

'Let's talk about the party,' Ellis said at last. 'Tell us exactly what happened. Pretend we know nothing.'

Berriman pursed his lips. Then his head came up and he began to describe the way it had been. He'd come across the party, he said, through an invite posted on Rachel's Facebook page. He'd passed the word on to a mate or two and thought it might be a laugh to go along.

Yates interrupted. 'But Gareth Hughes was going to be there. The new guy in her life. And you'd have known that.'

'I would?'

'Yeah. It was part of the invite. *My new squeeze.* You're telling me you didn't spot that?'

'OK ...' He shrugged. 'So I knew.'

'Yet you still went.'

'Yeah.'

'Why?'

'Because ...' He tipped his head back, stared up at the ceiling. 'Because I was nosy, I suppose. I wanted to know what this bloke looked like. I wanted to know what she saw in him. Like I said ... nosy.'

'And hopeful?'

'Always hopeful.' The smile again. 'Always.'

Yates nodded, scribbled himself a note. Ellis wanted to know if he'd arrived alone.

'No. I had some mates with me.'

'Who were they?'

'I can't remember.'

'You can't remember or you're not going to tell us?'

'I can't remember. I've got mates everywhere. It could have been a thousand blokes.'

'And were they invited?'

'Probably not.'

'Did that bother you?'

'Probably not.'

There was a silence. Ellis looked down at her notes. Yates stirred.

'Don't piss about, Matt. Just give us an answer.'

'No, they weren't invited.'

'So why take them along?'

'I didn't take them along. They just came. There's a difference.'

'You mean you couldn't stop them?'

'It wasn't a question of stopping them. We'd been drinking. We'd had a few. Like I say, it was a laugh. Those blokes don't get to go to Craneswater every night of their lives.'

'You make it sound like an expedition.'

'It was. Sort of.'

'Not for you though, surely?'

'How come?'

'Because you'd have known the house. Because you'd been there before. Quite a lot, I expect.'

'When I was with Rach, you mean?' He shook his head. 'Not really. She came round my place most of the time.'

'But you knew the house? Knew your way round it?'

'I'd been there, yeah.'

'So that made you a bit special, didn't it? As far as your mates were concerned? Big pad like that? Ex-girlfriend's place? Giving them the full tour?'

'That's bollocks.'

'Why?'

'Because you make it sound like my mates are going to be impressed by shit like that.'

'You're telling me they're not?'

'Of course they're not. That's why it's bollocks.'

'OK.' Yates accepted the rebuff. 'So what was the point then? You're not showing off. You're going mob-handed. You know her new bloke's going to be there. You know it's going to be awkward. So why bother?'

'I told you. I thought it would be a laugh.'

'I don't believe you, Mr Berriman. I think it was more than that. I think you were closer last time when you said you wanted to scope him out. Maybe make him just a little bit nervous. And having mates around would make that easier, wouldn't it?'

'Suit yourself.'

'But wouldn't it?'

Berriman shook his head, refused to answer. Then came a whispered conversation with the duty solicitor before she turned back to Yates.

'Mr Berriman's happy to talk about what happened at the party,' she said. 'But he's not prepared to help you speculate. As far as I'm aware, he's a witness not a suspect.'

Ellis nodded at once. Yates seemed less certain.

'When did you become aware that things were getting out of hand?' It was Ellis.

'After about an hour. There were loads of blokes in there by then. Loads.'

'And did you know these people?'

'Some of them, yeah.'

'Had you mentioned the party to them?'

'No. One or two maybe, but no, not that many.'

'So how come they were there?'

'Because word goes round. Blokes were on their mobes all over the house. Party time. Come on round. Help yourself.'

'To what?'

'To whatever's going.'

'Were you aware of drugs on the premises?'

'Yeah.' He nodded. 'There was a load of white. Don't ask me where it came from because I don't know.'

'You don't think it was Rachel's friends?'

'Rachel didn't do drugs. Not if she could avoid it. There was her old man too. He could be a nightmare, believe me.'

'So it wasn't Rachel's mates?'

'I doubt it.'

'All these people …' It was Yates this time. 'When did it all start getting out of hand?'

'You're asking me for a time? I haven't a clue. The first thing I knew, some guy said there was a bunch of them trashing the old man's study. I went up there. They were right.'

He described the kids dancing on the desk, stamping on the pictures, pissing all over them.

'Who were they?'

'I've no idea. But they were young, really young. Total idiots.'

'Anyone else with them?'

The question seemed to catch him by surprise. 'There was a girl,' he said at last. 'A bit older.'

'Name?'

'Haven't a clue.'

'You'd never seen her before?'

'Never.'

'Description?'

'Tats. Piercings. And she shaved her head.'

Yates made a note, studied it a moment. Then he was looking at Berriman again.

'You mentioned Rachel …'

'Yeah. She was in a right state. I'd never seen her so wrecked. She was trying to stop the kids, like you would, but there was no way.'

'So what happened?'

'I sorted them out.'

'Stopped them?'

'Absolutely. They were out of order. Toerags. All of them.'

'And Rachel?'

'I tried to sort her out too.'

'How?'

Another pause. He looked uncertainly at Ellis, then at the solicitor beside him. She told him it was OK to answer the question.

'I took her to the bathroom. She needed cold water, a bit of a wash. She needed to sober up.'

'Was she pleased to see you?'

'Yeah.' He nodded. 'She was.'

'Grateful?'

'Yeah. Of course.'

'So how long were you in there? In the bathroom?'

'A while.' He shrugged. 'I can't remember exactly how long. Like I say, she was in a bit of a state.'

'And the pair of you were talking?'

'Of course.'

'What about?'

'Stuff. I can't remember.'

'Did you talk about Gareth? Did you ask her about Gareth?'

'Yeah, I might have done.'

'And what did she say?'

'That's none of your business.'

'But you remember? You remember what she said about Gareth?'

'Yeah.' He failed to mask a smile. 'Of course I do.'

'And did you have sex with her?'

'That's none of your business either.'

'But you're not denying it?'

There was a long silence, broken – in the end – by Dawn Ellis. She wanted to know what had happened after Berriman and Rachel left the bathroom.

'I've no idea. I think I went downstairs. It was kicking off big time by now. Total chaos.'

'And Rachel?'

'I don't know where she went.'

'So when did you next see her?'

'I didn't.'

'Not at all?'

'No. Like I said, it was fucking bedlam, blokes out of their head, madness.'

The next thing that happened, he said, was a visit from the neighbour next door. It was obvious they were looking at big trouble because the music was just getting louder and louder. You could probably hear it on the Isle of Wight.

'And did you know this guy?'

'Yeah. His name's Mackenzie. He used to know my mum. He can be a bit heavy himself sometimes, and he set about some of the blokes the minute he came in. They weren't having any of that so pretty quickly he's got himself a serious ruck. I remember someone bottling him. That's out of order too, so ...' he shrugged '... I lent him a hand.'

'By wading in?'

'Yeah.'

'Again?'

'Yeah.'

He described bundling Mackenzie out of the door. His wife was waiting in the street. He knew she'd have called the Old Bill and he was right. The next thing everyone knew there was a army of cops outside – vans, blokes in full ninja gear, the lot. This, if anything, just made things worse.

'How come?' Yates sounded genuinely interested.

'Because it's attention, isn't it? It's celebrity? It's what we all want? Blokes were taking loads of pictures on their mobes, sending them to their mates, sending them out to the whole fucking world. We all knew we'd made the news. We knew we were going to be famous. The Craneswater ruck. And we were there.' He shook his head. 'Weird when you think about it.'

The interview came to an end minutes later after Berriman had described getting in a van for dispatch to Newbury. Faraday scribbled himself a note to make the forensic on Berriman's seized clothing and footwear a priority. Then he became aware of voices. Berriman had stepped into the corridor and was asking Dawn Ellis for a lift home. Faraday heard Ellis laughing.

'You think I'm some kind of taxi service?'

'Of course not.' Berriman had paused outside the door. 'Never hurts to ask though, does it?'

It was nearly dark by the time Faraday left the Bridewell. Berriman had been released on police bail, walking out into the gathering dusk with barely a backward glance. Reports from the other interview teams spoke of a mixed bag of results. A couple of the suspects had been remarkably gobby. Most had added little to their previous statements. A couple had gone no comment. Come the morning, Faraday and Suttle would begin their first review, piecing together all the accounts, trying to coax them into some kind of narrative. In the meantime he needed to get away.

He threaded the Mondeo through a maze of Southsea streets, avoiding the remains of the Sunday night traffic, and hit the seafront just west of the pier. The last of a spectacular sunset had spilled across the Solent and he could see lights pricking the soft grey shadow of the Isle of Wight. This time yesterday, he thought, he and Gabrielle had been halfway through a perfect weekend. Now, twenty-four hours later, he was almost too tired to find a parking space.

He switched off the engine and wondered whether he had the energy to risk a walk. He needed to clear his head, to fill his lungs with the sweet chill of the night wind, to build a dyke against the images that kept crowding in: the wreckage of the life the Aults had built, their daughter's sightless eyes staring into oblivion, the turmoil in Major

Crime as he and countless others fought to bring this monster to heel. It wasn't simply a question of spilled blood, of lives needlessly taken. There was something else going on here, something that belonged in a nightmare, and the more he thought about it, the more depressed he became. Berriman had described the experience as weird. Weird was right. But weird was just the start of it.

Nearly an hour later, back home in the Bargemaster's House, he tried to share this thought with Gabrielle. She'd picked up bits and pieces of news from the radio during the day, enough to anticipate a late supper, and now she was stirring a pot of cassoulet. Another bottle of Côtes-du-Rhône stood open on the kitchen table. The house smelled of garlic and goose fat.

'*Combien?*' She couldn't believe it.

'Well over a hundred kids. We laid hands on ninety-four. The rest would have gone before we arrived.'

'Including *les coupables*?' The guilty ones.

'Almost certainly. What would you do if you'd just killed someone? Hang around? Tell the world? Wait to get yourself arrested? No –' he reached for the wine, filled two glasses '– the way I see it we've got ninety-four witnesses and absolutely no clue where to go next. We'll crack it in the end, we'll get some kind of result, but life just shouldn't be like this. We are what we are because we still have some shred of respect for each other. That's what makes us civilised. That's what brought us out of the swamp. Last night tells me that might be coming to an end. Christ knows what happens next.'

Faraday rarely made speeches. He mistrusted emotions as raw as these. He was about to blame the outburst on exhaustion when Gabrielle turned from the stove. She'd been tactful enough to hide her surprise.

'*Merci.*' She tipped the wine glass in salute. '*À justice.*'

Faraday took a deep swallow of the wine, feeling better at once. Over the past few months, no matter what the pressures, he'd tried to shield this new life of his with Gabrielle. He seldom discussed particular inquiries, or the people he worked with, or the way that one job seemed to fold seamlessly into the next. In the distant past, nearly three decades ago, he seemed to remember volunteering for this treadmill, little realising exactly where the journey might take him. Were things really getting worse? Were people any nastier now than they'd always been? In truth he hadn't a clue but suspected that Gabrielle's guileless toast would do no harm.

'To justice,' he replied, 'whatever that might be.'

Later, fighting sleep, Faraday led her to the sofa. Mahler's Fifth was playing on the hi-fi. Outside, through the open French doors, the softer passages were underscored with the gravely whisper of the rising tide. It had started to rain, a thin drizzle that blurred their view of the harbour.

They lay together for a while, her head on his chest. For months now, funded by a grant from a French university, Gabrielle had been exploring gang culture on Portmouth's inner-city estates. An anthropologist by trade, she'd been more used to researching Third World hill tribes on the very edges of civilisation but she'd been struck from the start by the parallels she'd discovered in Portsea and Buckland. The same reliance on friends and extended family. The same instinctive reactions in times of feast or famine.

Faraday had always kept the small print of her work at arm's length, a mark of respect as well as an acknowledgement of her independence, but at times like these he couldn't resist asking her how it was going.

'It's fine,' she said. 'I was in Somerstown today. Just for a couple of hours. There were two kids I had to see.'

'And?'

'Only one turned up.'

'So where was the other one?'

'You'd arrested him.' She got up on one elbow, touched him lightly on the cheek. 'I should be angry, *n'est-ce pas*? My precious schedule ruined by some grumpy policeman?'

'You're telling me he was at the party? In Craneswater?'

'Of course. Like most of his friends.'

'You've talked to some of these kids?'

'Of course not. You'd locked them up.'

'But you will talk to them? In due course?'

'*Bien sûr*. That's my job. That's what I do.'

Faraday looked down at her, feeling the first tiny tickle of apprehension. Potentially there were issues here. Turf. Procedure. To whom did these kids belong? Were they raw material for a French anthropological treatise on UK gang culture? Or were they fodder for the courts?

'Maybe we should have regular conferences?' he suggested. 'Maybe we should compare notes?'

'Sure.' She smiled back. 'And maybe we shouldn't.'

Chapter eight

Willard again. He can't keep away, Faraday thought.

'Joe?' The Head of CID beckoned him into Martin Barrie's office. 'This won't take long.'

Gail Parsons was still in residence, her paperwork spread across the Det-Supt's desk. She seemed to treat Willard on level terms, two grown-ups with a mutual interest in squeezing the last trickle of juice from the *Mandolin* lemon, and when Faraday stepped in through the open office door it was Parsons who waved him into the empty seat. Squatter's rights, Faraday thought. Leave it too late, and Martin Barrie will return to find himself banished to the corridor.

'This is bigger than we thought, Joe.' It was Parsons.

'How come?'

'The city council have been banging on the Police Authority's door. They're not happy. And neither is the Chief.'

'And that's our problem?'

'It could be if we don't pull our fingers out. You know the way the bureaucracy works. Next thing we know, they'll start calling for an official inquiry. As if we don't have enough on our plates.'

Faraday looked blank. His job description suggested he was a detective. The luckless occupants of Sandown Road had doubtless been having a moan about the breakdown of law and order, and after Saturday night he didn't blame them.

'But what's all this got to do with us? Keeping the peace isn't down to CID. Not last time I looked.'

'Don't be obtuse, Joe.' It was Willard. 'Gail's right. Like it or not, we're all in the spotlight. In a perfect world we'd all keep our heads down, but on this job that's not an option.'

Faraday nodded, said nothing. Willard's comments on Sky News had made headlines in the national press. Quoted in a longish article in this morning's *Guardian*, Hampshire's Head of CID had refused to retract a word of his earlier interview. Indeed, he'd gone further. The

78

UK, he said, was facing the very real possibility of anarchy. Keeping the peace was a numbers game. There weren't enough policemen, there wasn't enough resource. As soon as the kids sussed the odds, the game was up. Not just in leafy Craneswater but everywhere else. If you thought you were safe, if you thought this kind of behaviour would pass you by, you'd better think again.

Gabrielle had spotted the article first, sliding it across the breakfast table for Faraday's attention.

'Game?' she'd queried.

Now, sitting in Martin Barrie's office, Faraday was still wondering where this debate was supposed to lead. Willard would never have opened his mouth in the first place without sanction from above, and that meant that his comments carried the authority of the Chief Constable. In one sense, it was an obvious tactic, a bid to stifle howls of protest from the likes of the Craneswater Residents' Association. In another, it was remarkably high risk. Under a government addicted to spin, nothing carried greater danger than the truth.

'We're doing our best,' he said at last.

'Of course you are, Joe. I'd expect nothing else.'

'So what else …?' He gestured round at the three of them.

Willard glanced at Parsons. Whatever was coming next, Faraday sensed it had been her idea.

'Witness statements, Joe.' She was looking at a list of names he'd sent through yesterday morning. 'What's the strength?'

'It's mixed, as you'd expect. Most of these kids weren't interested in helping us out. They knew they were looking at trespass or criminal damage and the last thing they wanted to do was land themselves in it.'

'And the others?'

'They're mainly friends of Rachel's.'

'And there's detail?'

'Lots.'

'Pretty graphic?'

'In places, yes.'

'What about pictures?'

'The mobes are at Netley. We're having a session this morning. I'm told there's yards of the stuff.'

'And ownership?'

'The material belongs to whoever shot it. The mobes too, of course.'

'But you've got Regulation of Investigatory Powers Acts on this lot?' The question came from Willard.

'Of course, sir.'

Under the Regulation of Investigating Powers Act, *Mandolin* had been obliged to get formal authority to access messages and images from the seized phones. The RIPA forms were a pain to complete. More grit in the investigative machine.

Willard was looking at Parsons again. She bent forward, intense, businesslike, eyeballing Faraday.

'A lot of these images would have been sent to friends before we seized the mobes, am I right?'

'I imagine so, yes.'

'And we could access those numbers from the mobes?'

'Yes.'

'Well then ...' She was looking at Willard now, one eyebrow raised.

At last Faraday began to understand where the conversation was heading. This wasn't about *Mandolin* at all. This was about politics.

'You want to get some of this stuff out there,' he said flatly. 'You want faces, stories, details, pictures. You want it in the papers. You want it on the telly. You want to scare people stiff. Am I right?'

'You are, Joe.' Parsons nodded. 'We can't release statements, of course, and we won't.'

'Names and addresses? Phone numbers?'

'No way. Not coming from us. Not directly.' She paused. 'You're working with young Suttle on the witness statements. Mr Willard tells me he's close to a reporter on the *News*. Would that be right?'

Faraday nodded. A year ago, with Major Crime stalled in the hunt for the killer of a property developer, Lizzie Hodson had been more than helpful.

'So what are you saying?' He was looking at Willard.

'Nothing, Joe.' He smiled. 'This conversation never happened.'

Winter was at Victoria Baths by mid-morning. He paid for a spectator ticket and took the stairs to the rows of tiered seating that looked down on the big pool. Already he could hear the yelp of young voices. Kids, he thought, attending by the busload from some school or other.

He was right. He found a seat and settled in. A movable barrier separated the shallow end from the rest of the pool. The shallow end was black with kids while a handful of others were swimming laps up and down the pool itself. Among them, occupying a roped-off lane of his own, was Matt Berriman. His mum, half an hour earlier, had told Winter he'd find him here. He'd popped by Margate Road first thing and made a call to someone at the pool, she explained. She didn't know the details but gathered he needed space to do some serious training.

Winter watched him as he prepared to turn at the deep end. His long body seemed to carve a rippleless furrow through the water, moving without visible effort, and when the time came he somersaulted underwater, pushing off again with a single thrust of his legs. The manoeuvre was accomplished in a blink of the eye, his powerful arms already reaching ahead, his head turning for the first breath, water sluicing past his open mouth, and Winter found himself mesmerised by the way he'd made the pool his own.

A couple of the older girls in a nearby lane had stopped to watch him. They giggled as he swept past, then one of them tried a few strokes herself, splashy, uncoordinated, useless. Her feet found the bottom again and she squeezed the water out of her eyes in time to see him turn at the other end, alone in his bubble, totally beyond reach.

A woman appeared from a door at the end of the pool. Ignoring the bedlam at the shallow end, she strode towards the lane occupied by Berriman. She was tall, with cropped black hair. Her tracksuit was badged *PN* on the back, and she paused halfway down the pool, then squatted on her haunches, waiting for Berriman to stop. Two lengths later, he pulled up beside her, folding his arms on the edge of the pool. A conversation followed. The woman demonstrated an arm movement. Her limbs were as long as Berriman's. Then she reached out and squeezed his shoulder before getting to her feet.

Berriman began to swim again, faster this time, the water churning behind him. She watched for a moment or two, a smile on her face, then she looked up. Winter raised a hand. He hadn't a clue who she was but he sensed she was worth a conversation. When she disappeared the way she'd come in, he left his seat and took the stairs back to the front lobby.

He found her beside the drinks machine, trying to steady a plastic cup beneath a thin stream of black coffee.

'And you are?' She hadn't turned round.

'My name's Winter. Paul Winter. You got a moment?'

For the third time in two days Winter found himself missing the warrant card. In the Job an encounter like this would be child's play. He'd sit her down, explain his interest, have a chat. Out on your own, meetings with total strangers were an entirely different proposition

Keep it simple, he decided. Stick to the truth.

'I work for a guy called Mackenzie' he said. 'Two kids died by his swimming pool last night.'

'I know. One of them was Rachel Ault. I used to coach her.' She juggled the hot cup. 'You want one of these?'

She took him into an office at the back of the building. A wallboard had been gridded in blue, a list of names down one side. Morning sessions started at 05.30. You were expected back in the pool at 16.30. The corkboard behind the door was covered in newspaper cuttings and snatched photos. In one of them he recognised a younger Rachel Ault looking up the camera as she climbed from the pool. The Speedo costume flattened the contours of her body but she had a smile that would turn heads in any pub. Lucky guy, thought Winter, thinking of the torpedo in the fast lane.

He took a sip of coffee. It was scalding.

'You coach him too? Matt Berriman?'

'Coached. Past tense. He chucked it in a couple of months ago.'

'Would that be after he split up with the girl? Rachel?'

'Before. I think she'd seen it coming. I certainly had.' She eyed Winter a moment. 'So where are you going with all this? Do you mind me asking?'

'Not all. And if I had an answer, I'd tell you. Like I say, I work for a guy called Mackenzie. He—'

'I know Mackenzie.'

'You do?'

'Yes. Matt's mum used to talk about him. You should get in touch with her if you want to find out about Matt.'

'I just did.'

'And?'

'She was very helpful. Can't have been easy, with that other boy of hers.'

'You're right.'

Winter was waiting for more detail. When nothing happened he asked about Matt's mother and Mackenzie. How come they'd once been friends?

'She didn't tell you?'

'No.'

She studied Winter for a long moment, then shrugged.

'When the kids were really young she had all kinds of trouble with the father. He used to beat her up. Regularly. She thinks now it had to do with Ricky. He was pretty odd even then. But at the time this guy was making her life a misery.'

'And Mackenzie?'

'He sorted him out. Alice Berriman had been a school mate of Marie's. They all used to party together, drop the tabs Bazza was flogging, go to the same gigs. Bazza knew Alice well.'

Winter nodded, beginning to understand. *He could be a brick when you really needed something*, Alice had told Winter earlier.

'So Bazza came to the rescue? Is that what you're saying?'

'Yes. She phoned him up one day in a bit of a state and he went straight round and put the guy in hospital. After that, according to Alice, there wasn't a problem. She was grateful, as you might imagine.'

'And does Matt know about all this?'

'I've no idea. He may do. Mackenzie used to come to some of the swim meets in the early days, when Matt was starting out, but I haven't seen him for years.'

Winter remembered Bazza's intervention on Saturday night. It had been Matt who'd saved him from a serious slapping. A blood debt settled, Winter thought, half a generation later. Very Pompey.

'How much do you know about the party on Saturday night?'

'Only what Matt told me.'

'Did he stay on after Mackenzie left?'

'Yes.'

'And he was still there when the Old Bill arrived?'

'Yes. And he ended up in a cell in God knows where.'

Winter nodded. A party on that scale would stretch his ex-colleagues to breaking point.

'They nicked him?'

'They asked him to come along as a witness. I gather it was virtually the same thing, though. If you said no, then you'd be arrested.'

Winter, in his head, was back on Major Crime. He understood the mindset; he could picture the likes of Faraday trying to boil down busloads of pissed youth to a list of prime suspects. You started with the obvious. You started with opportunity. And then you looked for a motive.

'How did the interview go?'

'I've no idea, but he had two of them. One yesterday morning up in Newbury. Then another in the evening, back down here.'

'I'm not surprised. He's got a problem, hasn't he? Ex-boyfriend of one victim? Jealous as fuck of the other one? And this is a lad who knows a thing or two about violence?'

'That's a bit strong, don't you think?'

'Not if you're a copper. And not if he has a criminal record.'

'You know about that?'

'His mum told me. Flat out on the M27 in some friend's BMW.'

'I expect he was upset.'

'Sure. I expect he was. Doesn't work in court, though, does it?'

She accepted the point with a nod, then drained her coffee. Winter could still hear the echoing shriek of kids splashing about in the pool.

'I didn't catch your name,' he said.

'Nikki. Nikki Dunlop.'

'You work here?'

'I work for the club. Northsea. I keep an eye out for prospects – kids from school – and take them to the next level.'

'Kids like Matt and Rachel?'

'Absolutely. Though they were both exceptional.'

'You'd know Matt well then?'

'I'd like to think so.'

'So how's he doing?' Winter hunted for the right phrase. 'Under this kind of pressure?'

'What kind of pressure?'

'Coppers sitting him down, asking him the hard questions, getting in his face. This is a murder inquiry. They don't fuck about.'

She thought about the question for a moment, gazing down at the empty cup in her lap. Her hands, Winter noticed, were huge. Finally, she looked up at him again.

'You think Matt would be thrown by something like that?'

'It's possible. I used to be CID. Most kids are all mouth, even these days.'

'And you think Matt's like that?'

'I've no idea. That's why I'm asking the question.'

'Sure.' Her eyes had strayed to a sports bag tucked untidily beneath the desk. 'There's two things you ought to understand about Matt. The first is he wouldn't have put a finger on Rachel, not a single finger. He'd never have touched her, let alone killed her.'

'You know that?'

'For sure.'

She held Winter's gaze. Something in her eyes spoke of defiance.

'And the other?'

'Matt was a sprint specialist. He wanted to be the best, the fastest. Blokes like him swim fifty metres. That's nothing, that's a blink. I took him to the national squad. Last year, before he packed it in, he got that close to the British record.' Two fingers, a millimetre apart. 'It took him five years to swim that single race, five years of sessions you wouldn't believe, five years of total dedication, five years for 22.3 seconds. This is a man who's asked himself some serious questions. Handling a couple of interviews would never have been a problem. Not if he knew it wasn't down to him.'

Winter fought the urge to applaud. It wasn't defiance he'd seen in her eyes. It was pride. All the same, one word snagged.

'Man?' he queried.

'Sure.' She smiled at last, getting up. 'That's the whole point.'

She said she had a couple of conversations to finish in the pool. Maybe he ought to talk to Matt himself.

'Here?'

'Of course. Be my guest. I'll tell him to get changed.'

In a break between meetings, Faraday asked Jimmy Suttle to come to his office. The young acting D/S appeared minutes later, taking the proffered seat and spreading the interview statements across the desk.

'This is half of them, boss. In fact less than half. I'm sparing you the rubbish.'

Faraday gazed at the pile of forms. Gail Parsons had been right. This was a monster.

'You've been through the lot?'

'Every page. Ninety-four statements. If you're asking me if we're looking at any kind of real breakthrough, the answer has to be no.' His hand rested lightly on top of the pile. 'Our guys went for open account, just the way we asked them. They obviously wanted to know pretty much what happened, in pretty much what order. When Rachel or the lad Gareth come into the frame they've obviously pressed for more detail but it's all pretty chaotic. No one wants to commit themselves. Either they were too pissed or they've got something to hide or they just don't like us.'

'And that applies to Rachel's friends?'

'Most of them, yes. I haven't had time to look at the interview vids or listen to the audio, but reading this stuff, as far as her friends are concerned, you just get the impression that they just want to forget it all. I think there's probably a bit of guilt there too. Maybe they could have done more. Maybe they *should* have done more.'

'To save her life?'

'To chuck the chavs out.'

'So why didn't they?'

'Good question. We know some of the bigger lads, the rugby crowd, were squaring up to have a go, but the girl we interviewed, Samantha, obviously talked them out of it, just the way she told us. In retrospect, that might have been a mistake.'

'Why?'

'Because at that point the numbers weren't too horrific. It's hard to get a real handle on this stuff time-wise but I'd guess around half ten for the face-off. After that, they were doomed. Look ...'

Some of the pages on the desk were tagged with Post-its. Suttle quickly leafed through until he found what he was after. He indicated a couple of lines flagged in green Pentel. Faraday glanced at the name of the top of the page. Jeremy Manningham. Unusually, this was a direct quote.

'It was unbelievable,' he'd told the interviewing officers. 'They just kept coming and coming. One minute we'd been looking at maybe a dozen of them, tops, then the gawkers were everywhere. You couldn't move for bloody Stone Island and Lacoste. Horrible ...'

'Stone Island?'

'It's chav gear. You buy it cheap at Gunwharf.'

'Gawkers?'

'Chavs. But that's not the point, boss. This guy happens to have got it bang on the nose, but a lot of these kids, mates of Rachel, are basically saying the same thing. After half ten or around there, the place was just swamped. It's kids with mobiles. It's the invading army. It's reinforcements. Some of the estates must have been bloody *empty* by midnight.'

'So the kids we nicked? The ones we carted away for interview...?'

'Tip of the iceberg. A lot of the chavs had gone by then.'

'Empty-handed?'

'Hardly.' He nodded at the statements. 'No one's naming names but obviously a lot of the Aults' stuff walked. Literally.'

Faraday sat back, gazing at the rooftops beyond the car park. Until the judge and his wife returned there'd be no prospect of a proper audit, but Suttle was surely right. Saturday night would have turned into a free-for-all, the Christmas of your dreams. Help-yourself time. A real gift.

'So we're saying it's all down to the chavs, are we?'

'For it all kicking off? Definitely. For a spot of pillaging, a spot of social revenge – no question. The rest – Rachel, the boy Hughes – I've no idea.'

'What about Rachel herself? Any glimpses?'

'Plenty. Everyone's agreed that she was pissed, in fact extremely pissed, but no one's suggesting she was slutting it up. Apparently she started drinking early, just the way we heard it from her mate, and my guess is she probably never stopped. As things got tricky, she seemed to lose her grip completely. A couple of the girls talk about her being in tears, really emotional, mainly because of what might happen to the house. One of them said she was terrified of her father, especially of what would happen if we got involved. That might be a bit strong but once things really kicked off she's in a place no one wants to be. All these kids kicking the shit out of the family heirlooms and fuck all she can do about it. Not nice.'

'What about the incident in the old man's study? The kids on the desk?'

'Most of them didn't see it, not for real. Word got round, of course, like it would, but it was mainly in connection with the lad Berriman. One of the PGS girls said he put the rugby lads to shame.'

'Did they see Berriman as a chav?'

'Oddly enough, no. But I think that's because a lot of them knew him. He'd been with Rachel for years, of course. That made him human, gave him visiting rights.'

The phrase made Faraday laugh. On another double murder, barely a year ago, Suttle had played a blinder, again in the intelligence role. This time he showed every sign of repeating the trick.

Faraday had been thinking hard about Rachel. At some point in the evening she must have left the party and gone next door to Mackenzie's place. Which meant, in turn, that somebody must have seen her.

'They did, boss. At least I think they did. And the timeline makes sense.'

Around half eleven, he explained, the wreckers had moved into the Aults' kitchen. A bunch of Rachel's mates had been in there, mainly girls, watching in disbelief as a food fight started. Eggs from the fridge. Bags of flour. Bottles of tomato sauce. Jars of pickle. Anything they could lay their hands on.

'Apparently the stuff was everywhere – mayonnaise, balsamic vinegar, pesto, the lot.'

Faraday nodded. He'd seen the Scenes of Crime shots on Proctor's laptop. One of the kitchen walls looked like an early Jackson Pollock.

'And Rachel?'

'Two of these girls say she came into the kitchen. They remember because she was so upset, as she would be, but there was something else about her. She was holding her hand to her face as if someone had smacked her. One of the girlies tried to talk to her but she didn't want to know. At one point her hand came down and there was blood around her mouth.'

'Did she say anything?'

'Nothing they mentioned.'

'Then what?'

'She left.'

'*Left?*'

'Went out through the back door. I got a plan of the property from Jerry. Here ...'

He unfolded a sheet of paper from his jacket pocket. Number 11 Sandown Road was surrounded by a largish garden. The kitchen door, said Suttle, opened onto the side of the garden that adjoined number 13. Getting into Mackenzie's place via the street wasn't an option because his electronic gates were locked.

So access had to be over the shared wall.

'And that's possible?' Faraday was gazing at the plan.

'Jerry says yes. There's a pile of wood stacked against the wall next to a little gazebo thing. Just here.' Someone had marked the position with a pencilled cross. 'He says it would be easy just to climb on the wood pile and hop over the wall. Especially if you knew the garden well.'

'Which she did.'

'Of course.'

Faraday nodded.

'And Hughes? The boyfriend?'

'Apparently, around this time he was looking for her. One of the rugby guys said he had a conversation with him. He said Hughes was pretty much out of it too.'

'And what happened?'

'The witness didn't know.'

'What about the girls in the kitchen?'

'They'd moved on.'

'So no one saw Hughes leave?'

'Apparently not.' Suttle was looking at the pile of transcripts.

Faraday pushed his chair back from the desk, easing the cramp in his legs. Hughes and Rachel had had the run of the house for the best part of a fortnight. Hughes would have got to know the place, got to find out about the short cut to next door. Given the chaos at the party house, unable to find Rachel, he might well have concluded that she'd legged it over the garden wall. In a full-scale riot attention would have been turned elsewhere. It was more than possible, therefore, that Hughes had followed her.

'Did anyone else leave?'

'Not that anyone's saying.'

'Not Berriman?'

'Hard to be certain.'

'What does that mean?'

'One witness talked of a tall bloke going out through the front door. She remembered because a neighbour or someone had been on the doorstep having a moan about the noise and some of the chavs were trying to barricade themselves in. The tall bloke wasn't having it.'

'Did she know Berriman, this witness?'

'That's not clear.'

'Was she a friend of Rachel's?'

'She says she was, but one of the interviewers left a note on the transcript. He thinks she was lying. To cover her arse.'

'So it might have not been Berriman? Is that what we're saying?'

'Yes, boss.'

'And time-wise?'

'That's not clear either.'

Faraday frowned. Another thought. 'How come the girls in the kitchen were so sure of the time?'

'Easy. There was a clock on the wall. It came down during the food fight.' Suttle was grinning. 'And it stopped at twenty-five to midnight.'

Faraday reached for a pad and began to construct a timeline. At around nine the first party guests arrive. An hour or so later Berriman turns up with a bunch of his mates. After that comes a small army of intruders. Soon afterwards the first real sign of trouble.

By around eleven, kids are trashing the old man's study. Matt Berriman intervenes. Afterwards he takes Rachel along to the upstairs bathroom, locks the door. They may – or may not – have had sex together. Either way, she's last seen half an hour later, stepping out into the darkness of the garden. Her boyfriend, Gareth Hughes, appears to be looking for her. Matt Berriman may – or may not – have left by the front door.

An hour later the Mackenzies arrive back from a dinner party. It's obvious that events next door are out of control. Bazza intervenes, sparking yet more violence, while his wife makes a treble nine. The call is logged at Netley at 12.39. In the party house Matt Berriman comes to Bazza's rescue and bundles him out into the street. His wife packs him off home, then waits for the cavalry to arrive.

At 12.51 the first response units turn up. By one o'clock Marie's relaxed enough to go home and check on her husband. Minutes later she's back on the street, looking for a policeman. Two bodies beside her swimming pool. Both of them dead.

Faraday went through the sequence afresh, testing every link with Suttle. Then he eyed the transcripts again.

'What else?'

'Not a lot, boss.'

'How about all the charlie? Where did that come from?'

'No one's saying for sure, but a couple of Rachel's lot mentioned the name Danny. None of them are brave enough to take a look at a face or two but the name's still in the frame. I put a call into Drugs Intel, still waiting on a reply. The coke market's up for grabs just now, the way I hear it.'

Faraday got to his feet and stepped across to the window. Until Suttle appeared with his bursting files of witness statements, he'd felt remarkably rested after the nightmare of the weekend. Now, confronted yet again with the sheer scale of this investigation, he barely knew where to turn.

At the centre of everything, burned deep into his brain, were the pale dead faces of the two victims. The statements, later, might prove crucial. But at this stage they were simply a kaleidoscope of impressions, a prism through which you caught fleeting glimpses of the last hours of Rachel Ault's young life. She was pissed. She was distraught. She hadn't got a clue what was going on. Was that any kind of way to end it all? In a fog of vodka? Weaving from room to room in a house you thought you knew? Driven to seek some kind of solace, some kind of peace and quiet, next door? Wrecked beyond description?

For the umpteenth time he tried to imagine a chain of events that could have taken her to Mackenzie's place, could have led to a confrontation, could have somehow accounted for a knife plunged deep into her belly. In truth there was a multitude of explanations. Jealousy. Revenge. Blind rage. Alcohol. Payback. Whatever. But where to start?

Faraday shut his eyes a moment. Lately, he knew, the job had started to get the better of him. Now, a vague feeling of inadequacy had sharpened into something much closer to despair. Her face again, her eyes, the way that death had opened her lips. The unvoiced question: why is this happening to me?

'There's just one other thing, boss . . .'

'What's that?'

'One of the chavs, a girl. She's there in a couple of the statements – more than that, maybe half a dozen. No one's giving her a name, and no one appears to have known her, but basically they're all saying the same thing.'

'Which is?'

'That she was scary. Really scary. Shaved head. Face furniture. Tats. The lot. Even her mates seemed to be frightened of her.'

'Are we talking girlfriends?'

'Blokes too. No one ever went near her.'

Faraday nodded. Matt Berriman had mentioned someone similar in Ault's study. Shaved head. Tattoos. Getting the lads to piss on the family photos.

'Do we have a name?'

'No. It seems she was with a younger kid, a boy. He was the one who tagged all the pictures.'

'With the black aerosol?'

'Yeah. They used a knife too.'

'A *knife*?'

'Exactly. The lad did the tagging. She did the rest.'

'With the knife?'

'Yeah.'

'What kind of knife?'

'No one's saying.'

'Shame.'

Faraday remembered the Scenes of Crime shots on Jerry Proctor's laptop, the shreds of canvas hanging from the artwork on the Aults' wall. Most of the stuff had been portraits. Faces slashed, he thought. Lives disfigured.

'We need the mobe footage.' He was thinking aloud. 'You want to give Netley a ring?'

Chapter nine

Winter had waited nearly half an hour by the time Matt Berriman stepped into the office at the swimming pool. He looked up from a month-old copy of the *News*, his patience wearing thin.

'What sort of time do you call this? Channel swimming, is it?'

Berriman ignored him. He bent low, then stuffed his towel and deodorant into the holdall beneath the desk. Winter had been through the bag already. The weekend's coverage of the party in the *Sun* and the *Daily Mail*. A packet of Rizlas, a wallet of Virginia Gold and a small cube of blow wrapped in silver foil. A pint of milk. A paperback copy of *King Lear*. And, tucked inside the book, a scrap of paper with a multi-digit number. Out of habit more than hope Winter had made a note of the number. It looked like a phone number but he didn't recognise the prefix. Later, he might give it a ring.

Berriman was standing by the door now. Watching him swim, Winter hadn't realised he was so tall.

'Nikki tell you I was here?' Winter asked.

'Yeah. She said you wanted a word.'

'She's right.' Winter wrinkled his nose. 'Where do you fancy? Only the smell of chlorine makes my eyes go funny.'

They went to a nearby café, La Parisenne, tucked into a triangle of pavement beside the torrent of city-centre traffic. It was Berriman's choice. He took a table in the sunshine while Winter fetched cappuccinos and a couple of pastries from the counter inside. For mid-morning, the place was packed.

Back outside, Winter eased the collar of his shirt. It was hotter than he'd expected. He was beginning to sweat.

'Full of bloody students, isn't it?' He gazed round at the other tables. 'Beats me where they get the money.'

'Most of them are foreign.'

'This lot?'

'Yeah. Nik says you're a cop.' Berriman had wolfed the first chocolate croissant and was reaching for the other one. 'D'you mind?'

'Not at all, son. All that exercise.' He sat back. 'Nik's wrong. I *was* a cop. It makes a difference.'

'Yeah? How does that work?'

'It means I know what to look for. It also means someone else pays my wages.'

'Nik says it's Mackenzie.'

'Nik is right.'

'He's a bit of legend, that man. Doesn't put up with any shit. You mind if I give him a ring? Only he tried to phone when I was in the pool.'

Without waiting for an answer, he produced a mobile and keyed in a number. Seconds later he was talking to Mackenzie. Winter could hear the rasp of Bazza's voice above the kerbside growl of a nearby delivery truck.

Berriman listened while Mackenzie offered his sympathies. It had been a shit weekend for one and all. Rachel was a nice girl. Must hurt like fuck to lose her like that.

'You're right. I appreciate it.'

'Your mum says you've been with the Old Bill. Don't let those bastards grind you down. Talk to my mate Paul. He knows most of them better than their mums do.'

'Would that be Paul Winter?'

'Yeah. Fat bastard. Needs to lose a few pounds. Not that he ever fucking listens.'

'I'm looking at him now.'

'You are?' The news made Mackenzie cackle with laughter. 'Make sure the old cunt picks up the tab then. Not that he's paying.'

The line went dead. There was a smile on Berriman's face.

'Respect.' He nodded at Winter then looked at his empty plate. 'How about another couple of those croissants?'

Faraday was on the phone to Gail Parsons when Suttle dropped by his office in Major Crime. The DCI was up in London with Willard, attending an emergency get-together at the Home Office. Media coverage of the weekend's events in Sandown Road had alarmed Downing Street and one of Brown's special advisers wanted a full report on the new Prime Minister's desk by close of play. There was talk of a new task force to explore something Parsons called the urban interface. Faraday hadn't got a clue what she was talking about but assumed it wouldn't do her career prospects any harm. Just now she needed to know whether there was anything tasty she could put in the Home Office pot.

'Not much, I'm afraid.' Faraday summarised the new intelligence about Rachel leaving the party. The assumption was that Hughes had also found his way next door.

'And that's all? Ninety-four interviews and that's it?' She sounded disappointed, and Faraday found himself wondering what kinds of promises she'd been making. All those extra bodies she'd won from Willard came at a price.

'It's early days, boss. If anything happens, you'll be the first to know.'

'You don't sound hopeful.'

'I hope I sound realistic.'

'Realistic's fine, Joe. Realistic has its place. Up here they deal in fairy dust. As you well know.'

Faraday, waving Suttle into the spare chair, started to laugh. So far he'd never associated Parsons with a sense of humour. She must have the door closed, he thought. And she must be more than desperate.

'I'll bell you,' he said. 'If anything turns up.'

She began to protest again, telling him to look harder, make a few calls, talk to Jerry Proctor, unearth *anything* for God's sake that might keep these people off her back. Then, without warning, he was looking at a photograph that Suttle had slipped onto his desk. The resolution wasn't perfect and one corner of the shot had gone inexplicably black but there was absolutely no doubt about the face. The last time he'd seen her, she'd been dead beside a swimming pool. Now this.

He peered hard at the digital readout across the bottom. 23.08, it read. 4/8/07.

Parsons was still telling him to get his act together. Glancing up at Suttle, he told her to hang on a moment.

'Where did this come from?'

'Scenes of Crime recovered it from Rachel's bedroom first thing. Jerry had it shipped it across to Netley and asked for priority. It turns out to be Gareth Hughes's phone.'

Faraday was still staring at the photograph. Someone's penis filled Rachel's mouth. She had her eyes closed and she seemed to be smiling, though it was hard to tell. The shot had been taken from above, presumably by whoever she was pleasuring. Light gleamed from wall tiles at the back.

'So that's Gareth Hughes?'

'I'd say not, boss. Hughes was ginger.'

Faraday looked harder. Suttle was right. The pubic hair was clearly black.

'Who then?'

'We're still working on it but a copy of this has gone to the blokes doing the Aults' house. They've matched the background against the upstairs bathroom. It's a perfect fit.'

Faraday nodded. The old man's study, he thought. The kids pissing all over the family's precious photos. Matt Berriman hauling them off. Then taking Rachel along to the bathroom for a quiet chat.

'So how did this get on to Hughes's phone?'

'It was mailed from another mobe.'

'Did we seize a mobe from Berriman?'

'No. I checked. But we've got the sender's number and Netley's checking with the headquarters Phone Unit. They should come up with caller ID.'

'So Berriman could have given his phone to someone else? Someone who left early? Just in case?'

'Could be. Or he hid it after we turned up mob-handed. He knows the house, remember. Either way, this is a guy who thinks things through. Which, in my book, makes him sus.'

'It does, son. It does.'

At last he returned to Parsons. She was still on the phone. By now he was beaming.

'Bit of a turn-up, boss. Are you sitting down?'

Winter was interested in Berriman's choice of reading. Berriman had rolled himself a spliff from the contents of the holdall and the bag still lay open on the pavement beside the table.

'Shakespeare?'

'Sure.'

'Just for pleasure?'

'No.' He produced a lighter, expelled a plume of smoke. Heads turned downwind.

Winter wanted to know more. A Somerstown boy tucked up with *King Lear*? The combination was hard to believe.

'You should get a life then, Mr W. I know blokes who read this stuff every day of the week.'

'You're kidding me.'

'Not at all. Why me? Why now? Because it was Rach's idea.'

'She put you up to it?'

'She said I ought to go back into education. She suggested sports management. I don't think she meant to patronise me but that's the way it felt.'

'So you went for the Bard?' Winter nodded down at the book. 'Just to make it hard for yourself?'

'Sure.' Berriman ignored the dig. 'It's a degree course. Comparative Drama. Shakespeare. Ibsen. Arthur Miller. All the greats.'

'Here? At the uni?'

'Yeah. I talked to the admissions people and they said I had a year to get my shit together. A couple of half-decent A levels and I'd be in. It's cheaper here, for one thing. Plus Oxford's not that far away.'

'When was this?'

'A couple of weeks ago.'

'So you hadn't given up? On Rachel?'

'Never.'

'Because you knew you could get her back?'

'Yes.' He didn't take the answer any further.

Winter glanced down at the paperback again, trying to measure the journey Berriman would have to make from a handful of GCSEs to full-time study. Was it a fantasy? Some half-arsed bid to get back inside Rachel Ault's knickers? Or did he mean to stay the course? He looked up, watching Berriman making another call. 22.3 seconds, he thought. After five years thrashing up and down that fucking pool.

At length Winter took the conversation back to the party. His guvnor, Bazza Mackenzie, was less than pleased at what had happened. It was Winter's job to come up with some answers. Preferably before Thursday.

'Why Thursday?'

'Because that's when Rachel's mum and dad arrive back. Baz phoned them last night. The father's in a terrible state.'

'I know. I phoned them myself. I'm not sure answers are what he's after. What he's after is his daughter back. How do you get round that?'

'You don't. You leave it.' Winter frowned, trying to imagine this conversation. 'So what did you say?'

'I said I was really, really sorry. I meant it. I said she was a lovely girl.' He nodded. 'Yeah ... truly fucking outstanding.'

For the first time Winter detected a catch in his voice. He remembered the number he'd found in the paperback. Berriman must have got it from Bazza.

'Bazza wants names,' Winter said at length. 'And, given where Rachel ended up, I'd say he's got a bit of an interest.'

'Sure. I hope he's a patient man.'

'So why don't you tell me?'

'Tell you what?'

'Tell me the way you see it.' He beckoned him closer. When Berriman didn't move, Winter leaned forward across the table. 'You're still in love with the girl. She means everything to you. You spend half the night reading *King Lear*, the rest of the time wondering how else you can get her back. Then, bang, she's gone. She hasn't run off. She isn't in Australia. Someone's killed her. Now that's a situation a bloke like you isn't going to walk away from. Not when you were there.'

'There?'

'At the party. Feeling the way you do about her.'

'I see.' Berriman hadn't taken his eyes off Winter's face. 'Go on.'

'So tell me what's gone through that brain of yours. Tell me what you'd do in my situation. Given that Mr Mackenzie has absolutely no fucking time for patience.'

'I'd jack it in.'

'You mean that? Seriously?'

'Yeah. I'd jack it in because you want names and there's no way I can help you.'

'Why not?'

'Because it's not what we do. Not where I come from.'

'Because I'm asking the heavy questions? Because I was a copper? You think that's grassing?'

'Yeah. Once a copper ...' He shrugged then glanced at his watch.

'What about Mackenzie?'

'Mackenzie's different. But the principle's the same. This is between me and a bunch of other guys. It's got fuck all to do with you, and fuck all to do with Mackenzie. We sort it out the way we sort it out. Mackenzie would know about that. Back in his time it would have been exactly the same for him.' He offered Winter a lazy smile. 'Or have I got that wrong?'

'Not at all, son, but no one died. Least of all in your own back garden.'

'So what?' He got to his feet then stretched. 'Shit happens.'

He bent for the bag, hoisted it to his shoulder, then nodded a thanks for the coffee and croissants. Winter scribbled his mobile number on the back of the bill and handed it across.

'You'll need this,' he said. 'Once you've had a think about it.'

Berriman glanced at the number, folded it into his jeans pocket and then sauntered away. Two girls at a nearby table watched him until he rounded the corner and disappeared. Then came the *beep-beep* of a car horn and Winter turned back to see a driver waiting for the lights to change. She raised a hand, looking directly at Winter, and it was a moment before he made the connection. Nikki Dunlop, he thought. Driving a BMW.

Chapter ten

It was Jimmy Suttle who brought news of the new Facebook page to the hastily convened management meeting. His late arrival drew a tight-lipped reprimand from Gail Parsons but Suttle barely spared her a glance.

He handed round a set of photocopies. Even Parsons couldn't hide her curiosity.

'This went up this morning.' He'd checked with Facebook. 'Around half ten.'

Faraday found himself looking at a photo of Rachel Ault. She was leaning against a ship's rail, her head framed by the wide blue spread of Portsmouth Harbour. The sun was in her eyes and someone must have cracked a joke because the grin had a spontaneity that seemed to Faraday totally unposed. Her friend Sam had been right, he thought. She was a lovely girl.

The page was titled 'Rachelsbash' and it took Suttle to point out the obvious.

'Think RIP,' he said. 'Think memorial. It's the kids' way of saying goodbye.'

He was right. The page was full of tributes from her friends. Some were awkward. Others were over-sincere. A couple simply buckled under the weight of grief. But every single one was garlanded with lines of kisses. 'You were chocolate,' one girl called Maddie had written. 'Ever in our memories, always in our dreams,' someone else had managed. 'LVU4EVR' went a third, 'SLPWLL'.

Once, Faraday thought, you said all this with flowers. Now you got together with your buddies, found a little corner of the Internet, and built the victim a shrine.

Another tribute caught his eye at the foot of the page.
Thou art a soul in bliss; but I am bound
Upon a wheel of fire that mine own tears
Do scold like moulten lead ...

Faraday mouthed the lines, tasting the blank verse.

'*King Lear*.' Suttle had seen it too. 'Act Four, Scene Seven.'

Heads turned round the table.

'Shit, Jimmy ...' It was Proctor. 'How come you know that?'

'I googled it.'

'Impressive. I thought kids these days never picked up a book in anger?'

'Wrong. These are posh kids, remember? Grammar School kids. They've got a bit of class, a bit of style. This is turning into a national wake. It'll be the chavs' turn next. We hold our breath.'

'What are you expecting?'

'T-shirts. My money's on *The Craneswater Ruck Survivors' Club*. Up on eBay by the weekend. Serious bidding starts on Sunday.'

Another look from Parsons failed to silence the laughter. She called for a minute of silence in memory of Rachel Ault and Gareth Hughes. Heads bowed round the table and even Proctor closed his eyes.

The meeting resumed. Parsons asked Faraday to summarise the results of Jimmy Suttle's trawl through the interview transcripts. Faraday did so then flagged the obvious lines of enquiry.

'Number one, we've got ourselves a timeline. It's not perfect, in fact in places it's bloody wobbly, but it's a start. We know when it all kicked off, and once we get a look at the mobe images this afternoon we might be able to tie some of the damage to particular individuals. They'll become the subject of a separate criminal damage inquiry which I'm guessing we'll offload. As far as Rachel is concerned, we can put her in the party until about eleven. That's when the kids trashed her dad's office. After that she was locked in the upstairs bathroom with Matt Berriman. The next time we see her is in the kitchen, thirty minutes or so later, en route into the garden. She's very upset and she appears to be bleeding from some kind of facial injury. So the assumption has to be that she's off next door. She's had enough. The lad Hughes must have joined her at some point because Mackenzie's wife found them both by the pool. But we don't know when he turned up or how he got there. What we *do* have is this. Jimmy?'

It was Suttle's turn to hand round half a dozen photocopies. The sight of Rachel on her knees in the upstairs bathroom brought conversation to a halt.

'Fuck.' It was Glen Thatcher, the D/S in charge of Outside Enquiries. Another slap on the wrist from Parsons. Language this time. And a bit of respect.

Thatcher mumbled an apology. But where did an image like this come from?

Suttle explained about the discovery of Hughes's mobile. A series of images had been sent to his number at 23.08. This happened to be the most explicit. The sender, after negative billing checks, had turned out to be someone with a pay-as-you-go phone, but Scenes of Crime had a positive ID on the background tiles in the mobe shots. The only person with whom Rachel Ault had shared a bathroom appeared to be Matt Berriman. Berriman, of course, was also an ex-boyfriend.

'We definitely know that?' Still Thatcher.

'About Berriman?'

'About him being the only person she had in the bathroom?'

'No, not for sure, of course we don't. But unless she's gobbing every one she can lay her hands on, it's a reasonable assumption. Berriman had just done her a big favour, remember, in her dad's office. Maybe she was saying thank you.'

'So Berriman videos her and then sends the pictures to Hughes?'

'Of course.'

'To wind him up?'

'To tell him the way it is. Think dog. Think lamp post.'

Faraday shuddered. Suttle's metaphor was brutally accurate.

'Revenge then?'

'Ownership. The way I see it, he's telling Hughes his time is up. Rachel's back where she belongs. And if you're after proof, then take a look at this.'

'So we need to be thinking about Hughes's reaction. Is that what you're saying?'

'Exactly.'

Heads nodded around the table. Then Jerry Proctor extracted a note from his file. One of his investigators had phoned him with more information about Rachel's bedroom. Now might be the moment to table it.

'OK, boss?' He paused for long enough for Parsons to give him the go-ahead. 'We've got traces of blood on Rachel's duvet. Not a lot, and there's no indication of how long it's been there, but enough to make us ask a question or two. Especially now. With this.' His massive hand settled briefly on Suttle's photo.

Parsons understood at once the implications.

'You're suggesting Hughes was in the bedroom with Rachel? After he got a look at what she'd been up to?'

'I'm suggesting it's possible.' He glanced down the table towards Suttle. 'Unless we're thinking she was somewhere else in that last half-hour before she left?'

Suttle shook his head. 'No one seems to have seen her. It's certainly not in the witness statements.'

'Then it would make sense, wouldn't it, boss? She does the business on Berriman then goes up to her bedroom. Hughes is the new boy-friend. He might be downstairs somewhere. He might be up there waiting for her. He might be anywhere. Then his mobile goes off. He cops a look at the bathroom shots then goes ape. They're both pissed. There's a row. He slaps her around. She does a bunk, runs off into the night, hops over the wall, ends up next door. She's had enough. She wants a bit of peace and quiet. She wants to think about things. In due course Hughes follows.' Proctor paused, looking from face to face. 'Is it just me or does this story tell itself?'

Heads turned towards Parsons. For a moment Faraday thought she was going to ask for a round of applause. Instead, another voice. Jimmy Suttle.

'That's terrific, Jerry. Except they both ended up dead. So where does that fucking leave us?'

The Mackenzies had been back in residence for barely an hour by the time Winter turned into Sandown Road. He parked the Lexus outside and sat behind the wheel for a moment. A carpet of flowers covered the pavement outside Bazza's house, and there were more bouquets outside the Aults. He got out and bent to read some of the cards. *Rachel, we loved you*, went one. *Gone but never forgotten*, someone else had written. *Our Candle in the Wind*, a third.

Winter stepped over a beautifully wrapped bunch of roses and pushed through the open gates. Finding the front door locked, he made his way round the back of the property, skirting the pool. Apart from a footprint or two in the flower beds, there was no sign that Scenes of Crime had ever paid a visit.

The kitchen opened on to the rear patio. Winter found Mackenzie inside, monstering some flunkey or other on his mobile. Next door, in the lounge, he could see Marie fussing around, giving an armchair a nudge, plumping cushions, picking up scraps of paper, putting her own scent back on the place. In the kitchen, even with the windows open, you could smell the chemicals the Scenes of Crime guys had used. Latent prints, he thought. Blood. Whatever.

At length Mackenzie brought his conversation to an end. The bruising on his face, yellows and a livid purple, had the makings of a decent sunset.

'Nice flowers, Baz.' Winter nodded towards the road. 'You should fetch some in here.'

Mackenzie was more interested in the Scenes of Crime team. 'Those bastards have been through my office,' he said. 'They've done the filing cabinets, the drawers in the desk, the lot. I know they have.'

'So what? It's a waste of time, isn't it? Now you're Mr Respectable?'

'Too fucking right. And Mr Angry too. You know what we're up to tonight? Me and Marie? We're having the neighbours round, the whole fucking street. There comes a time when you want a bit of action for all the fucking council tax you pay and that time is now. So guess who else is coming?'

'Tell me, Baz.'

He named the local MP, a long-serving Lib Dem with a reputation as a table thumper. In Mackenzie's view, he too would shortly be earning his keep.

'I want questions in Parliament.' He seized a copy of the *Daily Telegraph*. 'Have you seen this?'

Winter settled into a seat at the kitchen table. The surface still felt sticky. Chemicals again, he thought.

Mackenzie had opened the paper at one of the feature pages. The article was titled 'The Morning After The Night Before'. Winter skipped from paragraph to paragraph, aware of Mackenzie hovering above him. He'd yet to put the kettle on. Shame.

'Well?'

'He's got a point, Baz.'

'She, mate. She's got a point. In fact she *is* the fucking point. She's a mother; she's got kids of her own; she lives in a nice fancy part of Surrey; her old man toodles off to the city every morning, scores tons of moolah. Everything's sweet, everything's cushty. The kids are in private school. They've just bought half a chateau in France. They've got it well fucking sorted. Then what? She turns on the telly on Sunday morning and – bang – she's looking at a pad just like hers, same wood panelling, same high ceilings, same fucking taste in wallpaper for all I know. Except it looks like something out of the Blitz. It looks like some fucker's dropped a bomb on it. Why? Because we've lost it with the kids. Totally fucking surrendered. White flag. Doors wide open. Help-yourself time. This isn't some shithole in Salford or Birmingham. This is *Craneswater*. This is the bit of England where you pay getting on for a million quid and expect something in return. Like peace of fucking mind, for starters. Or am I wrong?'

Winter looked up to find Marie standing by the Aga, miming applause. In the last twenty-four hours, he thought, she must have heard this a thousand times. At full throttle Bazza could fill an entire newspaper single-handed, the more right wing the better. Any day now he'd consider running for Parliament himself.

'Write them a letter, Baz.' Winter tapped the article. 'Get it off your chest.'

'No, but look mush, here …' He frowned, trying to find a particular quote. 'Here it is. "Violence is like a rash. Unreasoning violence. Inane violence. A violence bred of boredom, of envy, of simple greed. It spreads and spreads. Unchecked it will infect us all. The time for decent people to take a stand is now. Otherwise we may be facing the slow death of a thousand Craneswaters. And by that time, believe me, it will be too late."' He looked up, beaming. 'There, mush. Spot on. Couldn't have put it better myself.'

'She's a politician, Baz.' Winter had spotted the woman's byline at the foot of the article. 'She's a Tory. She's got an agenda. She's beating the drum.'

'Of course she is, mush. But does that make her *wrong*? No fucking way. This country's going down the khazi, mate, and someone needs to get a handle on it.' He half turned in the chair, looking for his wife. 'Ain't that right, love?'

'Definitely.' She glanced at her watch. 'Were you serious about young Danny or shall we have coffee?'

Minutes later, with Mackenzie at the wheel, Winter was setting off to find a young drug dealer called Danny Cooper. A couple of Bazza's older lieutenants, still on modest retainers, had called in to say that the local Drugs Squad were calling house-to-house at certain addresses, eager to have a chat with the lad.

Word on the street suggested that he'd turned up at Saturday's ruck with a decent stash of high-quality cocaine. He'd been flogging it for silly money, throwing yet more petrol on the firestorm that had engulfed 11 Sandown Road. There were stories of thirteen-year-olds from Portsea coked out of their heads, of one girl who'd put so much up her nose she'd ended up in a cubicle at the A & E. Some of these stories had featured in the local *News*, part of their ongoing coverage of a story that had ballooned to national proportions.

'Peter's gonna be reading all this shit.' Mackenzie frowned, gunning the engine. 'And that man's no fool.'

Winter nodded. As a Crown Court judge, Peter Ault would doubtless know exactly how Baz had made his money, but like so many other establishment figures he obviously got some weird buzz from finding himself sharing a fence with an ex-drug baron. Unless, of course, his precious daughter ended up dead beside next door's pool.

'Lots at stake then, Baz.'

'Too fucking right.'

'And this Danny Cooper? I thought he was supposed to be some kind of protégé of yours? The young apprentice? The new kid on the block?'

'That's bollocks.'

'No, it's not, Baz. You told me yourself.'

'Did I?' He shot Winter a look. The Range Rover was misfiring badly.

'Yeah. You said he was a good lad – sound, solid. You said he read the market well, didn't take silly risks.'

'I was talking about the property game.'

'No, you weren't; you were talking charlie.'

'Wrong, mush. Since when do I talk about charlie these days? No need, is there?'

Winter knew it was a question that required no reply. In tight corners like these Bazza had a habit of talking to himself. When the facts weren't to his liking, he invented a set of new ones. That way he'd still be ahead of the game.

The Range Rover was slowing to a halt, trailing a thin plume of blue smoke. Winter looked up at a block of newly converted flats on the seafront.

'This is where Westie lives.' Winter started to laugh. 'It must be fucking serious.'

Westie was the most inventive of Bazza's heavies. After a decade of relying on home-grown muscle from one or other of Pompey's travelling families, seasoned men of violence, Mackenzie had finally settled on an ex-pro footballer from the West Midlands to keep the scrotes in order.

Westie was tall and black. He had a flat Birmingham accent and a reputation for being something of a psycho. He'd developed an impressive line in persuasion and appeared to take a genuine pleasure from hurting people. He rarely left a victim without taking a photo or two and was rumoured to keep a scrapbook of the choicer snaps, though Winter had never seen it. Nowadays, thankfully, Bazza only wheeled him out on special occasions.

He appeared at the kerbside moments after Bazza's blast on the horn. Can't wait, Winter thought.

Mackenzie, gazing at the steam curling from the Range Rover's bonnet, told him they needed to swap motors. There was something buggered in the radiator and he'd get the AA down later to take a look. Westie's treasured Alfa Romeo was parked across the road. It was black, polished daily. They drove north, sticking to the maze of terraced streets, bypassing the traffic. After the badlands of Somerstown, Westie pointed the Alfa east, towards Fratton and Copnor. Danny Cooper, it turned out, was camping with his Auntie Maddie in a house near the top of the city, trying to keep his head down. The Filth, said Bazza, were knocking at all the wrong doors.

Westie was plugged into his iPod. These days he favoured a long white raincoat with epaulettes. Underneath he wore black jeans and a black collarless shirt. He'd grown a neatly trimmed goatee beard and flashed a heavy gold Rolex at anyone who might be impressed. Westie had never had much time for irony, Winter thought, but now it was beginning to show.

Number 98 Tennyson Road was a terraced house with a brimming wheelie bin wedged in the tiny rectangle of garden. A poster for the Spiritualist Church hung in the front window. Westie eased the Alfa to a halt.

Auntie Maddie had evidently been expecting the visit. She answered the door within seconds, gave Mackenzie a smile and said she hadn't seen young Danny since before lunch. She thought he might have gone shopping. Probably back later.

Bazza returned the smile and pushed past. A nod sent Westie into the lounge on the ground floor. After the lounge he checked the kitchen. Then he was back. He shook his head. No Cooper.

Bazza and Winter followed Westie upstairs. Cooper was in the tiny bedroom at the rear of the property, sprawled under a purple duvet, feigning sleep. When Westie gave him a shake, he slowly rolled over, rubbing his eyes. Winter was looking hard at the duvet.

'Mr M,' Cooper mumbled. 'Nice to see you.'

Bazza nodded. 'Sick, are you? Only it's the middle of the afternoon.'

'Knackered.'

'Too knackered to give me a ring this morning? Like I asked you? Too knackered to remember your fucking manners?'

He stepped back, giving Westie the room he needed. No gestures, no instructions, just a couple of feet of floor space between the wall and the bed. Westie reached down, dragging Cooper out of bed. Underneath the duvet he was naked. Beside him, curled in a tight foetal ball, was a girl in her early teens. She was so thin, so small, that only Winter had realised there'd been two people in the bed. She too was naked.

Westie hesitated. Bazza told him to throw her out. He scooped her up and dumped her on the landing outside, smothering her screams with the duvet.

'Shut it,' he yelled. 'Just fucking shut it.'

The screaming stopped. Cooper was terrified. Winter could see it in his eyes. He was crouched on the bed, his back against the wall, his knees tucked under his chin. He was a well-built lad barely out of adolescence. He had a Chinese tattoo on one bicep and badly needed a shave.

'Listen,' he kept saying. 'Just please fucking listen.'

'Sure.' Bazza settled on the bed beside him. 'How long will it take Westie to boil a kettle? Only that's how long you've got.'

'To do what, Mr M?'

'To tell me what kicked off at that fucking ratshit party on Saturday night. You were there, Danny. I know you were. So don't even bother to tell me different. We understand each other? *Comprende?*'

'Yeah, sure, yeah, whatever.'

'So tell me, son. What happened?'

'I dunno.'

'Yes, you do, son.'

'I don't. I swear. I got texted. A bloke I trust. I gave him a bell back. He said there was open house in Craneswater. *Craneswater?* You have to be fucking joking. He said it wasn't no joke. Then he gave me the address. It was right next to your place, Mr M. Number 13.'

'So you went? Because of that? Because of *me*?'

'Yeah. The way I figured it, you'd know about the party. So I thought I'd make a bit of a contribution.'

'With half-price bags of toot?'

'Yeah.' He swallowed hard, staring up at Mackenzie's battered face. 'Kind of two-for-one offer. Bit of a thank you, like. All the favours you've done me.'

Bazza stared down at him a moment, then he bent low, his mouth to Cooper's left ear. His voice was low, barely a whisper.

'Listen, shitface. Are you hearing me?'

'Yes, Mr M.'

'There never were any favours. Never. They never happened. We never met, never talked, not even on the mobe. I never lifted a finger to help you, not in any way, not once, and you know why? Because you're a twat.' He straightened up. Winter heard footsteps clumping up the stairs. Westie, he thought.

Bazza hadn't finished. He wanted to know more about the party. In particular he wanted a name or two.

'Like who?'

'I dunno, do I? Otherwise I wouldn't be asking. Twat.'

'But what kind of name?'

'The kind of name that might give my friend here a chance.' Bazza nodded in Winter's direction.

'Chance?'

'To find out which evil cunt put two bodies in my back garden. Is this news to you? Or don't you read the papers?'

Cooper nodded. Of course he read the papers. It had been all over the telly too. It was the talk of the city. He'd heard you couldn't see Sandown Road for flowers. He'd heard people were wearing memorial fucking T-shirts. Unbelievable.

Westie had appeared at the door. Steam from the kettle curled in on the draught along the top landing. Winter was starting to feel uncomfortable. Bazza sometimes let these situations get out of control.

'Well? You gonna tell me or what?'

'I've got nothing to tell, Mr M.'

'You're a fucking liar, mush. You've got your ear to the ground. You *know*.'

'Know what?'

Bazza was losing patience. Winter could sense it.

'Tell me, son,' he said. 'Save yourself a lot of grief.'

'Listen ...' There were tears in Cooper's eyes. He'd been around long enough to understand what came next. He bunched his knees together, then began to hug himself, his knuckles white, his whole body swaying backwards and forwards. He nodded towards Westie.

'Just tell that fucking ape to get back in his tree. Then I'll tell you.'

'You will, son. You will.'

Bazza glanced at Westie. No one called him an ape, least of all this quivering lowlife. He stepped forward, held the kettle high, then slowly tipped it. The scalding water splashed on Cooper's knees. He screamed, reached for a nearby towel, exposing himself. More water. Lots of it. The entire kettle. Higher up.

'Just tell me, son. Just give me some names. Westie likes doing everything in threes.'

Cooper's eyes had widened. Steam curled from his groin. The scream became a whimper. This was a pain he'd never even contemplated. He tried to get the words out. Failed completely. Westie stepped forward again. This time he had a Stanley knife in his hand. Bazza stopped him.

'Talk to me, son. Take your time.'

Cooper's breathing slowed. He gulped. Tears were pouring down his face. He looked like a kid, Winter thought. He felt soiled by even being in the same room as these animals.

Mackenzie was still waiting for an answer. At length, to Winter's surprise, he got what he wanted.

'She calls herself Jax.' His eyes were closed now.

'Jax who?'

'Jax Bonner.'

'And she was at the party?'

'Yeah. But you want to be fucking careful, Mr M. She carries a blade. She's off her head. She doesn't care who she hurts.' His eyes opened, pleading for this nightmare to stop.

'Where do we find her?'

'I've no idea.'

'Yes, you have.'

'No.' He shook his head. 'You're wrong, Mr M. I haven't got a clue.'

'So how do we find her?'

'Fuck knows. Ask anyone. Ask the social fucking services. They all know her. Jax Bonner.'

Another face had appeared at the door. It was the girl from the landing. She was staring at the patches of damp on the bed, at Danny Cooper's crimson thighs.

Bazza, Winter sensed, was on the point of leaving. Then he bent low again, gave Cooper a pat on the shoulder.

'Remember what I said about you and me?' He grinned. 'Never happened, right?'

'Yes, Mr M.'

'Else we'll come calling again. And next time Westie might stay the night.'

Chapter eleven

Jimmy Suttle, on Faraday's orders, left the Major Crime suite early for once. The inquiry wasn't going well and everyone knew it. The so-called golden hours, the first precious day of any investigation, had come and gone and *Mandolin* was no closer to linking names to the bodies beside the pool. Worse still, the squad's every move was under intense scrutiny. The press and telly were still queuing at *Mandolin*'s door. The bosses in Winchester – even the normally unflappable Willard – were constantly on the phone demanding updates. There were rumours of a serious ruck with the Craneswater Residents' Association. Only the new DCI seemed to be holding her nerve.

Suttle turned out of the car park and inched into the rush-hour traffic, heading for Gunwharf. He'd spent the last hour or so with Faraday and a DVD from the Comms Intelligence Unit containing the best of the images from the seized mobiles at the party house.

For Suttle, the experience had been odd. His previous twelve hours had been devoted to going through hundreds of pages of witness statements. The stiff prose that most interviewing detectives reserved for these forms rarely did justice to real life. You listened to someone describing six hours of drunken madness, you did your best to get the right facts in the right order, you added a verbatim quote or two, and you asked for their signature at the end. What you rarely pinned down was the raw experience of being there.

The Netley images, downloaded from umpteen mobiles and a couple of digital cameras, changed all that. This was the movie of the book and one look at the swirl of faces, the crazy camera angles, the sheer press of bodies surging from room to room was as good as being there. Watching this stuff, hearing the soundtrack, Suttle could smell the weed, could feel the thump of techno deep in his bones, could sense how quickly you'd abandon every shred of restraint.

He tried to imagine himself as a friend of Rachel's, tried to figure how he'd feel about this army of strangers crashing in from the dark.

First off, you'd be spooked. There might even be a hint of menace. But then the booze would kick in, and whatever else, and pretty soon you'd tell yourself you were all here for a good time. Some of the girlies you might fancy. Some of the blokes might be a laugh. Pretty soon everyone would be your mate.

He'd watched a mad circle of guys dancing together, tinnies in hand. He'd admired the chest of a dark girl in a red top, exposed by her leering boyfriend. He'd grinned when another youth had hosed her down with foam from a shaken tinny. And when Faraday had replayed footage of kids wrecking the judge's study, he'd begun to understand how even this might somehow be part of a quality night out. The party, in the end, had been about abandon. No rules. No grown-up bollocks about behaving yourself. Let's just rinse the fucker.

Faraday of course hadn't seen it this way. He wanted – needed – to squeeze the footage for evidence, for clues, for faces, for names. He wanted to tally one sequence against another, to confirm a timeline from the flickering digital readouts, to somehow tease order from this night-long helping of chaos.

Tomorrow Suttle was to make arrangements for Samantha Muirhead to see the footage. She'd been there. She knew many of these people. She could put names to some of the faces. But for the time being, this afternoon, he and Faraday had treated themselves to a preview.

Spotting Rachel had been a priority. A couple of the mobes had belonged to friends of hers. There were plenty of images from early in the evening: Rachel sucking booze through a straw from a shallow glass dish, Rachel dancing with a girlfriend, Rachel showing her arse to the camera as she fed a DVD into the player beneath the Aults' telly. A bit later someone else discovered her in the kitchen, necking with Gareth. Suttle recognised the boy's ginger hair and the pale blue shirt later photographed by the CSI at the poolside. He was thin and a bit clueless and watching him back Rachel against the kitchen fridge Suttle began to wonder quite what the attraction had been. She was too quick for him, too natural, too lively. In the kitchen she'd licked the side of his face and then stuck her tongue in his ear, winking at the camera as he tried to wriggle free. In short, to Suttle the new boyfriend seemed a bit of a prat.

Faraday had noticed it too, but the D/I's real attention had been caught by later shots of Rachel. By now she was obviously pissed. She carried a different glass in every shot and the glass was never empty. Often she was with the same bunch of friends, Gareth among them. In company she seemed to mother him.

Twice Suttle caught glimpses of Matt Berriman, tall and commanding, body-checking his way through the scrum in the background, and on both occasions it was obvious that Rachel had clocked him too. Faraday had paused the footage at this point, leaning forward to peer at the screen. There'd been a wistfulness, he said, in the way she looked at him. She was there and she wasn't there. She'd become a ghost at her own party.

This phrase of Faraday's had stayed with Suttle. Ghost was right but ghost was a word he'd never have dreamed of using. He'd got to know the D/I well over the past year or so and he'd come to recognise just how different this man was from the other detectives on the squad. Working with Paul Winter on division, Suttle had let the city get in his face. That was the way Winter liked it, down at street level, touching hands, bending arms, calling in favours, baiting evil little traps. He talked the language of the toerags he so artfully screwed and took enormous pleasure in putting them away. But Faraday wasn't like that at all, not remotely. Faraday was a watcher. He stood back. He analysed. He thought hard about stuff. And above all he tried to understand what it was like to *be* someone else. Suttle had seen it time and time again, this bid to get inside other people's heads, other people's lives, and it had been the same this afternoon, with Rachel. Ghost was spot on, he thought. And in a way it applied to Faraday as well.

Suttle drummed his fingers on the steering wheel. The lights by the dockyard gates took an age to change.

He checked his watch. Five to six. Shit.

Lizzie Hodson was on the point of leaving when Suttle finally made it to Gunwharf. He'd phoned earlier, catching her between stories at the *News* offices, and she'd agreed to meet him at the Customs House, a pub beside the canal that ran the length of the new development.

He saw her the moment he rounded the corner from the main square, a small, slight figure in jeans and a linen jacket. She was sitting at a table in the sunshine, folding a copy of the *Guardian* into her canvas satchel. Still out of breath, he mumbled an apology and nodded at her empty glass.

'Another?'

He'd known Lizzie for a while now and he'd liked her from the moment they'd first met. She'd been one of a handful of journos invited to a presentation on the work of the Major Crime Team, an exercise in transparency that the Media Department had quickly come to regret. With her degree in political science and her stubborn determination to separate the bullshit from the truth, she'd concluded that the Major Crime set-up represented an awful lot of money targeted on offences that affected a tiny fraction of the city's population.

Most of us, she'd written in a subsequent *News* feature, never came across homicide, or kidnap, or serial rape. Nobody would dream of querying the phrase 'Major Crime' to describe offences like these but ask most people in the street what really bothered them and the answer would be vandalism, and the yob culture, and the kind of unthinking selfishness that badged more and more areas of daily life. This conclusion had won Lizzie few friends at force HQ but she'd said yes when Suttle phoned to suggest a drink, and it was barely weeks before a brief affair had settled into friendship. With her usual frankness Lizzie had always insisted she was a lesbian at heart, but even now Suttle didn't believe her.

He returned to the table with the drinks. Lizzie checked her watch.

'I've got half an hour,' she said. 'It's yoga tonight.'

Suttle took the hint. He hadn't thought this thing through and realised he didn't know where to start. Willard wants to get his own take on the party across, Faraday had told him. He thinks Saturday night is the tip of the iceberg. We're all on the *Titanic* and we're all doomed. Find out whether she's interested. Then let's see how we can help.

'It's Sandown Road ...' Suttle began.

'Surprise me.'

'The bosses think the real story deserves an airing.'

'Bosses?'

'Willard.'

'I bet.' She nodded. She knew Willard.

Suttle shot her a look. She wasn't making this any easier.

'Are you bloody interested or what?'

'Of course I'm bloody interested. It's my job to be interested. But since when did they employ you as a PR man? Stick to the day job, Jimmy. PR sucks.'

'Is it that obvious?'

'Yes.'

'Then I'm sorry.'

'Fine.'

He looked up at her, risked a smile. 'How about I give you a couple of phone numbers? Kids who'd be happy to talk about what happened? Kids who might have sent footage to their friends before we seized their mobes? You could access that stuff. You could use it.'

'It's sorted, Jimmy. We've got more pictures than we can ever use. Kids are sending stuff in by the bucketload, and what we haven't seen is there for the taking anyway.'

'Where?'

'The Facebook memorial page?' She started to laugh. 'Don't tell me you haven't seen it.'

'Of course I've seen it.' He looked at his glass. So much for Willard's clever schemes. 'So there's nothing we can help you with?'

'I didn't say that.' She reached across the table and touched his cheek. It meant she was sorry. She asked him how the job was going. He told her about passing his sergeant's exams. All he had to do now was wait for a vacancy.

'And when will that happen?'

'Christ knows. Skippers' jobs are thin on the ground just now. It could be months. Longer even. Staying on Major Crime would be favourite but I'd have to be bloody lucky.'

'Or bloody good.'

'Quite.' He nodded. He wanted to get back to the party. If he couldn't interest her in mobile footage or witness details, how else might he help?

She studied him a moment. The party itself, she said, was already old news. They'd caned the arse off the story in all of today's editions and there were a couple of major feature pieces lined up for tomorrow. By Wednesday something else would have kicked off and the world would be moving on.

Suttle wasn't having it. 'You're wrong,' he said. 'Willard thinks there's more to it than that. He thinks we're stretched to breaking point, and from where I'm sitting I have to tell you he's right. You know one of the really big problems we had on Saturday night? Finding enough Crime Scene blokes to make a decent start on Sunday morning. And you know why? Because of the European Working Time Directive. They were running out of hours. It's the same for the uniforms, the same for us lot. Two of these parties on the same night and we'd be calling the army in. Three, and you'd start thinking NATO. People don't realise, Lizzie. They take peace and quiet for granted. They shouldn't.'

'Sure. Of course Willard's got a point. But there's a problem here because he's said it already. Yesterday on telly and this morning in any paper you choose to name. They've all been quoting him. The end of civilisation's a great story but not if it's yesterday's news.'

'OK.' Suttle shrugged. 'So what else can I offer you?'

'Is that a serious question?'

'Try me.'

'How about Paul Winter?'

'Winter?' He was staring at her. 'Why Winter?'

'Because he works for Mackenzie. Because Mackenzie's bloody upset by what happened on Saturday night. And because Mackenzie doesn't let things like this go unresolved.' She smiled. 'Or so we hear.'

'Did Winter say that?'

'No, and even if he had I wouldn't tell you. But think about it, Jimmy. An ex-cop working for a Pompey face. An ex-cop like Winter working for *the* Pompey face. That's a nightmare, isn't it? From your point of view?'

Suttle said nothing. He gazed across the canal towards the apartment blocks that lined the waterfront. Winter lived in one of those pads. Before he'd joined Mackenzie, Suttle had been round there a great deal. Stunning views. Great crack. A limitless supply of cold Stellas from the fridge. In those days, Winter had been recovering from major brain surgery in America and it had been Suttle's pleasure to keep an eye on him. More recently, of course, that friendship had ended but, deep down, Suttle realised he missed the man. Winter had taught him everything he knew. Winter had taught him the difference between paperwork and nailing the bad guys. As time slipped by the Job was becoming unrecognisable, and now, sad to say, there were no Winters left.

He looked up. Lizzie Hodson was right. Our loss, he thought, Mackenzie's gain.

'You think there might be two investigations going on here?'

'Yes.'

'And you think I'm going to be silly enough to confirm that?'

'Yes.'

Suttle held her eyes for a moment, then smiled and got to his feet. His glass was still untouched.

'Good luck with the yoga.' He bent to kiss her. 'And phone me next time he gets in touch.'

'Who?'

'Winter.'

Carol Legge was a small cheerful Geordie in her early fifties with a passion for fairy cakes. She worked for the city's Child Protection Team, and the last time Winter had seen her she'd marked his card about a scrote drug dealer and part-time father called Karl Ewart, triggering a chain of events that put Jimmy Suttle in hospital with a serious stab wound. Two years later Legge was still carrying a hefty caseload for Child Protection, and the news that Winter was no longer working for the Men in Black appeared not to matter.

'So what is it, pet? How can I help you?'

'There's a girl called Jax Bonner. Ring any bells?'

They were sitting in a café in the heart of Fratton. Winter had bought teas at the counter and a packet of fairy cakes from the Easy Shopper round the corner. She sent Winter back to the counter for a knife and a plate, then sliced through the wrapping.

'Tallish? Keeps shaving her hair off? Lots of previous?'

'That might be right.'

'She's a headcase, pet. Totally psychotic. Leave well alone.'

The thought put a smile on Winter's face. He helped himself to one of the cakes, brushed crumbs from his mouth.

'You've dealt with her yourself?'

'Never had reason to. She was on the radar as a nipper but that was before my time. Since then she's become a bit of a legend. Colleagues of mine from the Youth Offending Team take bets on when she'll do something *really* silly.'

'Like?'

'I don't know.' She frowned. 'Burn a house down? Nick a car and drive it into a bunch of mums outside a school? Kill someone? This is a headline waiting to happen. That's them talking, pet, not me.'

'Where does she live?'

'I haven't a clue. Like I say, we don't hold the file.'

'So who do I talk to?'

'I'm not sure, pet. That might be difficult. If she's still school age she'd be at one of the Pupil Referral Units. They call them Harbour Schools now. There's no way she'd be in mainstream education.'

Winter wetted a finger for the crumbs on his plate. Pupil Referral Units were last-chance dump bins for excluded kids. He'd had dealings with them before, when he was still in the Job. Staff at these schools did their best to get their charges back in line but most of the harder cases never bothered to turn up.

'Has she got family?'

'Everyone's got family, pet. It's a question of whether it works or not. In her case I'd say no but I'd be guessing. Like I say, you'd need a look at the file.'

Winter nodded, leaving the next question unvoiced. At length, Legge wanted to know why Jax Bonner had suddenly become so important.

'Saturday night? Sandown Road?'

'You're kidding. She was there? At the party?'

'She may have been. Hand on heart, love, I can't say for sure.'

'*Craneswater?* I'd say that was way out of her comfort zone.' She paused, frowning. 'So how come all this matters to you?'

'I have a friend. Let's call him a client. He pays me to find out stuff. Saturday night he came home to find two bodies beside his swimming pool.'

'Next door, you mean?'

'Yes.'

'That's Mackenzie's place.'

'Yes.'

'You're working for him? Mackenzie?'

'Yes.'

'Goodness me.' She looked startled. 'Bit of a culture shock, isn't it? Kipping with the enemy?'

'Not the enemy, love. Not any more. He's calmed down. He runs a business. He spreads money around. He employs people. He does good deeds. Ask him nicely, and I'm sure he'd sponsor any little scheme your lot might care to dream up.'

'You're serious?'

'Totally. And you're looking at the man that can make that happen.' He found a pen, then scribbled a number on the corner of her newspaper. 'My new mobile.' He helped himself to the last of the fairy cakes. 'Ask for Robin Hood.'

There were evenings when Faraday knew with a troubling certainty that he was going to get drunk, and this was one of them. *Mandolin* had become a media event, making waves across the nation, sending ripples as far as the other side of the planet. Minutes before he'd left Major Crime, Jimmy Suttle had appeared with a cutting from the *Sydney Morning Herald*. TWO SLAIN AT WEEKEND PARTY went the headline. PM WARNS OF ANARCHY.

There were more stories like these, he said. From papers in Europe, in North America, in the Far East. The coverage, while factual, carried an undertone of nemesis, of social debts long overdue for settlement. A commentator in *Le Monde*, in a wounding aside, wondered whether incidents like these wouldn't become the norm in a society that had lost touch with itself. After two decades of Thatcherism, even under New Labour the English battery chicken was coming home to roost.

Lost touch with itself. Faraday, driving home, knew it was true. For more years than he cared to remember family and faith had been dissolving in the teeth of a bitter wind. Lately that wind had become a howling gale. Whichever way you measured it – the divorce figures, *Big Brother*, domestic violence, the weekend army of teenage drunks swamping the nation's A & E departments – society was falling apart. Respect had gone. Not just for each other but for any kind of effort to make a decent fist of life. Failure, by some savage twist of logic, had become a badge of achievement. For countless thousands of kids, cloned by shit television and trashy high-street brands, it was cool to rubbish anything that smacked of genuine effort. You made your mark by hanging out. You found comfort in numbers. You grabbed your pleasures wherever you could. And there wasn't any argument that couldn't be settled with a boot or a knife. Welcome to Cool Britannia.

Back at the Bargemaster's House he uncorked a bottle of Merlot and tried to share some of his anger with Gabrielle. She was on her laptop at the kitchen table, transcribing a pile of notes. She listened for a while, still typing, then stopped when Faraday repeated the phrase that had triggered the war drums in his aching head.

'Lost touch? *Qu'est-ce que ça veut dire?*'

'It means disrupted. It's a question of rhythm. If we were soldiers, we'd be out of step. If we were on the dance floor, we'd be all over the place. The guy used the phrase in *Le Monde* this morning. *La société anglaise ne se reconnait plus.* And he's right. We don't know ourselves any more. We can't hear the music any more. We've lost it. It's gone. We're a mess.'

She pondered the image for a moment. This is her trade, Faraday thought. Trying to figure out ways that groups of individuals become a tribe.

'Music's good.' She nodded in approval. '*Ça accroche.*'

'You think so?'

'Definitely. It works because music ties us together, because music is glue. When the music stops ...' She shrugged.

'We fall apart.'

'*Exactement.* You see it all over the world. You have to *belong*. In Cambodia you see this, in Vietnam, with the mountain people. Beliefs, faith, conduct, *moeurs,* it's all the same. It's glue, it's music. You belong. You sign up. You obey. Here too. Especially here.'

'Where?'

'Here.' She gestured at the pile of transcripts beside the laptop. 'Somerstown. Portsea. Buckland. All these places. Maybe you're hearing a different music but deep down it's the same. You're part of the tribe, of the gang. Like I say, you *belong*.'

'Which matters.'

'*Oui, absolument.* The kids I talk to, most of them have nothing. Family doesn't work for them, school doesn't work for them; they have no exams, no bits of paper, nothing. All they have is time. Time and hunger.'

'For what?'

'For belonging. The biggest club, the biggest gang, is your *société anglaise*. But to join that club you need the right clothes, the right trainers, *n'est-ce pas?* And for that you need money. But these kids have no money. All they have is each other. And so – *voilà* – they make a little gang, a little tribe of their own. It becomes everything to them. It's their family, their Church, their everything. So they link their arms together. And they march in step.'

Faraday was beginning to wonder where this conversation might lead. 'You're describing the symptoms,' he said carefully. 'I'm talking about the disease.'

'But the disease is all about us. You're right, *chéri*. The kids are getting *difficiles* because that's the way your society has gone. You see it everywhere. There's more space between people, more emotional space. That's where the kids get lost. Right there in that space. You know what I never see in these flats? In these little houses? A dinner table. A place where people can eat together. Eating is living. Here, people often do neither. That's why the kids belong to gangs. That's why they're outside the corner stores all night. And you know the important word? *Belong*. They belong there, on the street, with each other.'

'And you're telling me they have rules?'

'*Bien sûr*. Of course they have rules. Break the rules and the gang punish you. Break the rules too often, and the gang throw you out. The worst. *Absolument le pire*.'

She abandoned her chair and perched herself on the edge of the table, facing Faraday. She was on fire now – intense, hunched, a pose he recognised from a handful of previous occasions. Few things touched her as deeply as her work. Like Faraday she committed far too much of herself.

She was talking about a particularly difficult fourteen-year-old from a family in Portsea. His mother, she said, had a new baby and a succession of dysfunctional partners. Some of them spent her child benefit on crack-cocaine. Others beat her up. She was so damaged and so preoccupied with the baby that all verbal communication with her adolescent son had ceased. If the boy wanted anything, he left her a note. On good days it worked. Most of the time he went without.

'So what happened?'

'He decided to go fishing. He'd been down to the little pier in Old Portsmouth. He'd seen the men with their rods. He made a line with some string. These men, they all know each other, a little group, a little family, a little gang, *n'est-ce pas*? They tell the boy they need *maquereaux* to cut up for bait to catch the bigger fish, the sea bass. You fish for *maquereaux* with a hook and a little feather. They show him how. He starts to catch *les maquereaux* and – *voilà* – they give him 50p for each fish. This boy, he saves enough money for an old rod, to catch sea bass. For sea bass the Chinese in the restaurants pay two pounds, maybe three. But he needs a bag, a waterproof bag, to keep the sea bass. In Portsea boys deliver papers from yellow bags. The bag protects the papers from the rain. And so he gets a job. As a paper boy. After two days he quits the job but he keeps the bag. And so now he has three things. He has a nice waterproof bag. He has money from the sea bass. And he has a new gang, a new family. *Courage, chéri.* Life could be worse.'

Maquereaux meant mackerel. As he knew only too well, this little parable of hers was a tiny touch on Faraday's tiller, a reminder that black was an impossible colour to live with, and after a moment's thought he responded with a tilt of his glass.

'*Salut.*' He was looking at her laptop, at the lines of text carefully transcribed from her interview tapes. 'You met more kids today?'

'*Oui. J'en ai rencontré cinq.*'

'Five? Really? And what did you ask them?'

'Today is different. Today I never asked. Today they talked.'

'About what?'

'*Quoi?*' She began to laugh. '*Quelle question.* They talk about your party. And you know why? Because most of them were there. They saw everything. They're famous now, *célèbres.* They had a fine time.'

'Everything?' Faraday couldn't help himself.

'*Bien sûr.* These kids aren't stupid. They watch. They listen. And most of all they remember.'

'Remember what?'

'How easy it was.' She grinned. '*Quelle rigolade.*'

What a laugh? Faraday shook his head and turned away. Then he reached for the bottle and filled his empty glass.

Chapter twelve

Esme, Bazza Mackenzie's daughter, lived inland, on a lush green flank of the Meon Valley. On Tuesdays it had become a habit to drive the children down to Southsea to spend the day with their granny.

Marie had come to look forward to these visits. If the weather behaved itself, the kids liked nothing better than spending the day beside the pool. Bazza, in the spirit of these excursions, had brought them a pair of inflatable armbands each, a little dinghy to splash around in, and an inflatable crocodile for when things got boring. Marie kept the fridge well stocked with chocolate ice cream and party-sized bottles of Coke, and had acquired a bottle of factor 30 for the sunnier days. When Bazza suggested she might give this particular Tuesday a miss, she wouldn't hear of it. The quicker life in 13 Sandown Road returned to normal, she said, the better she'd feel.

Esme arrived earlier than usual. Girlfriends were raving about some 1920s cocktail dresses in a fashion outlet in Gunwharf. A purple sequined number at a 70 per cent discount was a steal and she needed to be down there before the size 12s got snapped up.

Guy, the oldest of the three kids, was a born explorer. At home he thought nothing of patrolling the acres of fenced-in meadow on his own, chasing one or other of Esme's horses. In Sandown Road, once the novelty of the pool had worn off, he'd take a wander round the garden.

At the back of the garden a hedge separated Bazza's property from number 15. The house had been empty for some months and the hedge had seen better days. Since the spring Guy had made himself a tunnel through the tangle of dead briar and discovered a sandpit on the other side. One of his prized possessions was a collection of toy soldiers that had once belonged to Bazza, and every Tuesday he liked nothing better than to crawl through the tunnel with handfuls of his granddad's Nazi storm troopers, and stage elaborate mock battles in the privacy of the hijacked standpit.

Bazza's model soldiers had come with a couple of ancient toy field guns. The guns took broken-off matchsticks as ammo. The matchsticks sometimes got buried way under the sand. Which is how young Guy found the mobile.

The first Marie knew of the boy's find was a fit of giggles from the direction of the pool. Guy had brought back his trophy find from next door's sandpit and was showing it off to his sisters. Thanks to Esme all three kids knew their way round mobile phones. What especially fascinated them were the pictures you could watch.

From the kitchen window Marie could see them crowding round Guy. He'd shaded the mobe from the sun and he was doubled over with laughter. Marie loaded a tray with doughnuts and stepped outside onto the patio. It was Guy who volunteered the phone.

'What's that?' he said.

Marie took the mobile. Without her reading glasses she couldn't be sure but a second look beneath the shade of the nearby tree confirmed her worst suspicions.

'Where did you find this, Guy darling?'

'There.' He was pointing at the briar hedge, proud of himself. 'It was really deep. I really had to dig.'

'You mean next door?'

'Yes.'

'In the sandpit?'

'Yes.

'Fine. I expect you're hungry.'

Ignoring their questions, she handed out the doughnuts and then retreated to the kitchen. Bazza was in his office at the hotel. He picked up on the first ring. Marie still had the mobile. She blew sand off the tiny screen.

'I'm looking at Rachel Ault,' she said briefly. 'With a mouthful of someone's dick.'

Bazza's call caught Winter at home in Gunwharf. He'd spent half the morning trying to figure out ways of finding Jax Bonner. Within minutes he was pointing the Lexus towards Craneswater.

By now Bazza was back at Sandown Road. Guy had returned next door to the sandpit while his sisters watched cartoons on a portable TV Marie had rigged up beside the pool. Bazza sat at the kitchen table. He'd accessed the stored numbers on the phone and noted them down. When Winter stepped in from the patio, he glanced up.

'Bonz? Fearless? Jersey K?'

'Never heard of them.'

'Pete? Dudie? Sprocket?'

'Pass.'

'Rakka? Mum? Nikki?'

'Phone Mum.'

'I just did. No answer.'

Winter nodded. He asked for the phone and checked one of the numbers before keying it in. He waited a second or two, then a grin spread from ear to ear.

He returned the phone to Bazza. He hadn't said a word.

'Well?'

'Her name's Nikki Dunlop. She's a coach down at the pool. Ten quid says she's shacked up with Matt Berriman.'

'His mobe then?'

'I'd say so.'

'And his dick?

'Send her the pictures. She might know.'

Even Marie laughed. When the kids had demanded an explanation she'd said that the girl on the screen had been playing a kind of party game. When they'd asked whether it was a treat or not, she'd said yes.

Bazza wasn't interested in party games.

'Marie says this came out of next door's sandpit. I thought your lot would have done a proper search?'

'Only your garden and the Aults', Baz. They'd need a separate warrant for number 15.'

'You're sure about that? You don't think they planted the fucker?'

'I doubt it. They're not that bright.'

'Bright, my arse. So where does that leave Mr Berriman? I've been telling myself I owe this guy. Now I find his knob halfway down young Rachel's throat and the evidence in my other neighbour's garden. To get to that sandpit you'd probably go through the hedge. That puts him on my property, doesn't it? Or am I missing a trick here?'

Winter didn't reply. The spare doughnut looked too good to ignore. After a couple of mouthfuls, he licked the sugar from his fingers.

'I talked to him yesterday,' he said at last. 'He's got some quaint ideas, that lad.'

'Like what?'

'Like not wanting to grass his mates up.'

'Grassing? To us? How does that work?'

'It doesn't, Baz. And that's what I told him. I got the impression he wants to freelance this thing, handle it himself.'

'That's stupid.'

'I agree.'

'Shall I give Westie a call?'

'The boy may have saved your life, Baz.' Winter was looking pained. 'He certainly spared you a good slapping.'

'That's not an answer, mush. It's Tuesday. The Aults are back the day after tomorrow. Like I told you yesterday, we need a result, a name, maybe a couple of names, something that says I haven't totally screwed up. We had a great meeting last night. The MP bloke's gonna give the Filth a kicking. But Aultie's going to want more than that. He'll want to know who did his daughter. I can't shake the bloke's hand with fuck all to tell him, can I?'

'No, Baz.'

'I'm serious.'

'I know you are.'

'What about the girl Danny mentioned? Jix?'

'It's Jax, Baz. And she's a bit of a problem too.'

'Well fucking solve it, mush. That's what I pay you for. *Comprende?*'

It was late morning before Faraday began to surface from the hangover. A couple of Ibuprofen first thing had failed to still his thumping head and two more when he arrived at the office had been equally useless. Three cups of tea plus a bacon sandwich fetched from a nearby café by one of the management assistants had put something solid in his stomach, and by the time Suttle knocked at his office door the worst of the nausea had passed.

'You look shit, boss.'

'Thanks. Never try to outdrink the French. They've got livers of iron.'

It was true. By the time he'd stumbled off to bed, Gabrielle must have sunk at least a bottle of her own. Then she'd gone back to her laptop.

'What have we got?' The thickness of Suttle's file looked promising.

'Just an update, boss, really. Jerry Proctor rang me from Netley. His lads at the Aults' place are going through the rooms at the top of the house. According to the girl Samantha, Rachel had a laptop. They can't find it.'

'Nicked, you think?'

'That's Jerry's view. They've done the full monty on her bedroom, taken a look at all the other rooms. Sam says she kept everything on it. Emails. Stuff for her Facebook page. Poems. Photos. A bit of a diary. The lot.'

'Shit.'

'Exactly.'

'What about the other computer?'

'That's the PC in Ault's study. The screen got trashed but the computer itself was OK. My guess is it was too old to get nicked. It's at Netley now. They're going to bump it up the queue for hard-disk analysis just in case she'd been using it.'

'What else have they got?'

'Multiple specimens. Jerry says we're talking lots of spillage. I think he means semen.'

'Where?'

'The upstairs bathroom, which we knew about already. The upstairs landing. The Aults' bedroom – that's the bed, bits and pieces on the carpet, stuff on a little armchair. There's shit up there too. Smeared across one pillow.'

'Nice.' Faraday was beginning to regret the bacon sandwich. Suttle hadn't finished.

'So he's asking for a steer, really. Whether or not you want to send the lot away or wait.'

'That's down to DCI Parsons. They're all bagged up?'

'Of course. They're in the fridge at Netley. Ready and waiting.'

Faraday nodded. He'd seen the big samples fridge at Netley. Jerry kept the milk in there as well. He looked up at Suttle, trying to get his thoughts in order.

'We've got semen in Rachel's throat from the PM. Am I right?'

'Yes, boss. Jenny took smears from her body at the scene too. They tested positive for semen from her throat and her vagina.'

'Results?'

'Friday. Tops.' He paused. 'So what about the other samples?'

'Ask the DCI.'

'I just did. She's after your advice.'

Faraday winced. The last thing he needed just now was a face-to-face with Gail Parsons. Seconds later he heard her footsteps hurrying along the corridor. She didn't bother knocking.

'Joe? You've got a moment?'

He followed her into Martin Barrie's office. To his surprise he found himself looking at a bunch of flowers on the window sill behind the desk. They were neatly arranged in a tall glass vase and for a moment he wondered whether they'd come from Willard.

'A woman's touch, Joe.' She'd been watching him. 'Something to brighten our days.'

She settled behind the desk and scrolled briefly through a list of waiting emails. One in particular caught her attention. She reached for the screen, turning it towards Faraday. The message had come from Jimmy Suttle. Parsons must have tasked him to take a look at

Saturday night's CCTV footage and Suttle had responded with a barbed query about exactly where she wanted him to start.

'Hardly helpful, Joe, wouldn't you say?'

Faraday, oddly cheered by the defiant good sense in the message, found himself defending Suttle.

'He's got a point, boss. There are no cameras in Craneswater. The city network doesn't extend that far. A party on one of the estates and we'd have footage coming out of our ears. Nice people don't riot.'

'I was anticipating he might be looking elsewhere.'

'What for?'

'Gangs of youths. Kids who might have left the party early. Faces we wouldn't have seen so far.'

Faraday was trying to grapple with the implications of this search. Pompey on a Saturday night was awash with youths. There were hundreds of kids, thousands of kids. Where, exactly, would you look first?

'You sound like Suttle, Joe.'

'Only because he's right.'

She gave him a look, tight-lipped, disapproving, then enquired about the mobile phone footage retrieved by Netley. She understood they were waiting on a visit from Rachel Ault's best friend. When did she propose to turn up?

'She's coming in at half eleven. Her name's Samantha Muirhead.'

'And what do we think she might be able to tell us?'

'We're after putting names to faces.'

'You're telling me that hasn't happened yet?'

'We've got ID shots from the custody suites but they're just the kids we could lay hands on. We need to start thinking about who we *haven't* met yet. The girl Sam might be able to help.'

Parsons looked Faraday in the eye. He sensed she relished confrontation.

'We aren't doing well, are we, Joe? No one thought this thing would ever be easy, least of all me, but we're losing momentum.' She nodded at the telephone. 'I had Mr Alcott on first thing. He'd just had a call from Mike Hancock. As you can imagine, he's eager for good news, *any* news. The word he's using is underperformance.'

Mike Hancock was MP for Portsmouth South. Terry Alcott was the Assistant Chief Constable in charge of CID and Special Operations. *Mandolin*'s buck stopped at his desk.

'Under*performance*?' Faraday felt the blood flooding into his aching head. Twenty-four hours without sleep over the weekend. The constant drumbeat of phone calls and meetings thereafter. The raised hopes, the false leads, the sheer mountain of evidence, most of it worthless.

And now this: a Senior Investigating Officer who seemed to be paying far too much attention to the noises off. Maybe performance was right. Maybe the press, and TV, and Facebook, and all the rest of the chatter, had taken them into new territory. Maybe this wasn't an investigation at all. Maybe *Mandolin* had become a piece of theatre.

Parsons was still looking at him, still waiting for some kind of explanation. Faraday, irked beyond measure, didn't bother to rise to the challenge. In his view the squad was working flat out. Parsons, like everyone else in the world, wanted instant results but already it was clear that this would never be a three-day event. There'd be no short cuts here, no magic wand, no sudden arrests at dawn with the snappers in attendance and a morning press conference to follow. In the end he sensed they were looking at a tight little knot of circumstance, of motivation, of payback. Untying that knot would take time. If Parsons couldn't see that, if her finger had slipped on the steadying pulse of the investigation, then too bad.

'We need to be patient,' he murmured. 'I'm afraid that's the best I can do.'

Parsons nodded. It wasn't the response she wanted. She returned her PC screen to its previous position and bent to the keyboard. She was never less than direct.

'Martin Barrie comes back on Monday, Joe. My guess is he'll be taking over as SIO. I'd like something substantial in the bank before then.'

Jerry Proctor was waiting in Faraday's office when he returned, minutes later. Two glasses of cold water had made him feel a little better.

'We've got a result on the stamp mark.' Proctor surrendered the chair at the desk. 'I thought I'd run you through it.'

Photos of the pattern on Gareth Hughes's cheek had been sent through to Napier Associates, a private database in York. They carried details of hundreds of sole patterns. Later, if required, they could match a specific pair of trainers against the Hughes imprint.

'And?'

'We're looking for a pair of Reebok Classics.'

'You make it sound like bad news.'

'It is, Joe. This is the Ford Mondeo of trainers, no offence. Everyone's got a pair.'

'Size?'

'Nine to eleven.'

Faraday nodded. Sole lifts only came in three basic sizes. It was the uppers that changed from box size to box size.

'How many did we seize at the house? Have you checked?'

'A couple of dozen. More than half of those were within the size range.'

'Including Berriman's?'

'No. He was wearing Nike Air Max 95s.'

'Shit.' Faraday turned away and gazed out the window.

'You're sure they were Nikes?'

'Positive. I double-checked.'

Proctor wanted a decision on the seized Reeboks. Should he send them all away for full forensic examination? At £600 a shot for the thirty-day turnaround, they'd be looking at a sizeable bill. The premium service, with a speedier result, would cost another £1400 per item.

'Ask Parsons.' Faraday was still thinking about Berriman. 'It's her pay grade not mine.'

A knock on the door revealed Suttle in the corridor. Samantha Muirhead had arrived. He wanted to know whether Faraday wanted to sit in on the viewing session. Faraday said yes.

Suttle fetched Muirhead from downstairs. She'd been waiting a while in the front reception area and was fretting about an impending job interview at a café-bar in Southsea. Suttle promised to run her down there as soon as they'd finished.

Faraday joined them in the Intelligence Cell. Suttle had readied the DVD at the start of the Rachel footage. Sam bent towards the screen, watching intently, and Faraday realised she may never have seen any images from the party. Her own phone hadn't featured on the DVD playlist. Maybe hers didn't have a camera.

Rachel was at the foot of the stairs, fighting off the attentions of a youth in what looked like a striped rugby shirt. The pictures cut to the living room, Rachel sprawled on the sofa with her head in another boy's lap. Then she was in the kitchen with Gareth, winking at the camera over his shoulder as he steered her towards the fridge. Faces came and went in the background.

'That's me.'

Sam was right. She was leaning against the kitchen table, eating a slice of pizza. Suttle hit the pause button.

'Those first two guys with Rachel. You know who they are?'

'Of course. One's called Slaphead. He's in the first fifteen. The other one's really sweet, talented too. He wants to be an actor.'

'Should we be interested in either of them?'

'How do you mean?'

'Was Rachel interested in either of them? Or vice versa?'

'No. They're mates, that's all. And Slaphead's always pissed.'

Suttle nodded, crossing the sequences off a list at his elbow. He played more footage, all of it featuring Rachel with various groups of friends. More names, more dead ends. Then followed an edited sequence showing kids busy destroying everything they could get their hands on. In a court of law this would be prima facie evidence for a criminal damage charge but in every case Samantha was unable to help with names.

After a while she glanced at her watch. Time was moving on.

'There's one other thing ...' It was Faraday. 'People have been telling us about a girl at the party. The way we hear it, she was hard to miss.'

He described the shaved head, the nose rings, the tongue stud, the gallery of tattoos down her arms. Oddly enough she hadn't appeared on any of the images they'd seen so far.

Sam nodded. She knew exactly who they meant.

'Scary woman,' she said. 'You can see for yourself.'

'We can?'

'Sure.' She looked surprised. 'It's on the Facebook page. "Rachels-bash".'

'Since when?'

'Since this morning. You guys ought to check it out.'

Suttle and Faraday exchanged glances. Suttle turned back to the desk. A couple of keystrokes took him into Facebook. Entry to Rachel's memorial page was by open invitation. No password.

Sam was watching over Suttle's shoulder. He followed her prompts. The screen cleared to reveal yet more mobile footage. Faraday felt himself stiffen. These were new pictures, the camera at the foot of the stairs, angled upwards. At the top of the shot a couple of youths were necking cans of Foster's. One wore his baseball cap sideways, the other was squatting down with his back to the wall, scratching himself. Between them and the camera, halfway up the stairs, the girl with the shaven head was slashing at a painting, big diagonal crosses, top to bottom. The angle of the camera hid the painting itself but Faraday couldn't take his eyes off the knife in her hand. Right size, he thought. With a black handle.

'Shit, boss.' Suttle had seen it too.

Faraday wanted to know what it took to upload material like this onto Facebook. Sam didn't understand the question.

'Do you have to be registered? Do you have to be a member?'

'Of course.'

'And how easy is that?'

'You need an email address, a user name and a password. It's really simple.'

'And the email address can be Web-based, boss.' It was Suttle. 'Something like Hotmail or Yahoo. If you're thinking sender details, trying to get a handle on whoever posted all this stuff, it's a nightmare. It might take months. And that's if you're lucky.'

'And tracing the computer it came from?'

'Total no-no. I'll check it out with Comms at Netley but Facebook must handle millions of hits every day. Capturing every single IP address? My guess is you wouldn't even try.'

'So the sender's invisible?' Faraday nodded at the screen. 'Is that what you're saying.'

'Pretty much. We might get lucky but I doubt it.'

Faraday bent forward. The sequence had cut to a close-up of the girl with the knife. Her bony face was pale. There was no shadow of hair on her shaven skull. She was striking, even beautiful. She lunged at the mobile then stuck out her tongue. The tiny silver stud glittered under the nearby wall light. A smile widened into a leer, then she began to lick the lens with the tip of her tongue, blurring the whiteness of her face, before the shot changed again.

Now the ruined portrait filled the screen. Someone had already attacked the picture with a spray can but behind the loops of black paint a man's face hung from the gilded frame, the reflective smile reduced to shreds of canvas. Faraday recognised the picture from Jerry Proctor's laptop. The Scenes of Crime photographer had been there twenty-four hours later.

'That's Rachel's dad.' Sam sounded shocked. 'Horrible, isn't it?'

Chapter thirteen

Five minutes with the phone book had given Winter an address for Nikki Dunlop. She lived in a tiny flat-fronted house near the seafront in Eastney, barely half a mile from Craneswater. Twice he'd called round in the early afternoon but both times there'd been no answer. Now he'd decided to park down the road and wait for her return.

Nearly an hour later the BMW rounded the corner at the end of the road and came to a halt at the kerbside. Nikki Dunlop was behind the wheel. The tall figure beside her was talking on a phone. She was at the front door, looking for her keys, by the time he ended the call and got out. Winter watched, beaming. Patience, he thought. Never fails.

He gave them time to put the kettle on, then locked the car and sauntered across the road. It was Berriman who opened the door. He had a puppy in his arms and his face was pinked with exercise. The pool again, thought Winter.

Nikki appeared behind him. The front door opened straight into the sitting room.

'Invite the gentleman in, Matt. He won't bite you.'

Berriman stepped to one side. He shut the door and let the puppy run free. He dug in his pocket and unwrapped a wafer of chewing gum. Nikki was watching the puppy as it pounced on a cushion and began to drag it across the room. Then she glanced up at Winter.

'Tea?' Her smile was icy.

The minuscule kitchen was at the back. One wall was dominated by a poster for an international swimming meet in Düsseldorf. Shelves on another were home to an assortment of photos, postcards and souvenirs. Some of the photos featured Berriman. Winter was reminded of the kitchen at the boy's home in Somerstown. Wherever he went, wherever he lived, he seemed to leave a calling card.

Winter helped himself to the kitchen stool. He could see Berriman through the open door to the sitting room. He was draped across the imitation-leather sofa, watching *Countdown*. The puppy kept trying to clamber onto his lap. Sometimes he cuddled it but mostly he pushed it away.

'You never called me,' Winter said to Berriman. 'Which is a pity.'

'Why's that?'

'I could have saved you the price of a new mobe.'

'Yeah?' Berriman's finger found the mute button on the remote. 'How's that?'

'This. You want to take a look?'

Winter produced the phone that Guy had recovered from the sand-pit. He fired it up and found the camera icon. Berriman hadn't moved but Winter was aware of Nikki Dunlop standing behind him. The sequence from the bathroom began to play. He dropped a shoulder to give her a better view then glanced round. She didn't look the least amused.

'It's a question of ownership, love.' Winter nodded at the tiny screen. 'We have to be sure who it belongs to. And we're not talking about the phone.'

'Is that how you got my number?' It was Nikki.

'Yeah.'

'So that was you who phoned this morning?'

'Afraid so.'

Berriman was on his feet at last. When he saw the phone, Winter sensed a flicker of alarm in his eyes.

'It's mine,' he said simply. 'Where did you get it?'

'You know where I got it. I got it from where you left it. Just be grateful it was me and not some arsehole detective.'

Nikki was looking hard at Berriman and the expression on her face told him everything he needed to know about their relationship. She'd looked after his best interests for years. On the way to the national squad she must have dug him out of endless scrapes; 132 mph on the M27 was probably the most recent. Now this.

'Where did you leave it, Matt?'

Berriman ignored her question. He had his hand out. He wanted the phone back.

'Sorry, son.' Winter shook his head. 'Finders keepers.'

'That's the last time I saw her. The pictures are mine. They belong to me.'

'Fine. I'll squirt them over. The phone stays with me.'

Winter slipped the phone back in his pocket then spread his hands wide. He wanted no fuss, no aggro. He gave Berriman a smile. The last time they'd talked Berriman had made it plain that he was going to get to the bottom of who'd killed Rachel. He'd made it equally plain that this task was down to him, and him alone. By now, the way

Winter saw it, he'd have made some progress. He'd have been asking around, touching base with old mates, getting a steer or two, maybe even a name.

'Am I wrong, son?'

'Go on.'

'There's a girl called Jax Bonner.'

'Is that right?'

'Yeah. And by now, unless you're stupid, you'll probably know all about her. Why? Because she was at that party. She carries a blade. And the way I hear it, she's a psycho, off her head most of the time. Am I getting warmer?'

Berriman looked away a moment, a smile on his lips. Nikki was watching him carefully.

'Matt?' she prompted.

'I'm not getting into this.'

'Why not? This guy's not a cop. You can help, Matt. You can tell him.'

'No way.'

'Why not?'

'Because that's not what you do. I told him before. No one grasses. Not where I come from.'

'Grasses? You're crazy, Matt. Rachel's dead. This isn't some game. She's dead. Gone. That's why we've got the dog, for fuck's sake. Don't you think you owe her this?' She shook her head, turned away.

Winter was looking at the puppy when he felt his mobile vibrate. 'That was Rachel's dog?'

'Yeah.' Berriman nodded. 'It was.'

Winter nodded, squatted beside the puppy, tickled it behind the ears. Then he fetched out his mobile and checked caller ID. Marie. Pocketing the mobile, he glanced up at Berriman.

'I know some powerful people, Matt. People who make things happen. In this city we can get to anyone, any fucking person you care to name.'

'I don't need that kind of help.'

'You're crazy.' It was Nikki. 'You think you can do it all yourself? Everything?' She shook her head again, exasperated.

Winter got to his feet again while the puppy barked for more attention.

'Listen, son. When I say I can help you, I mean it. You've had time to look for this girl, this woman, this Jax. You'll have turned up something, I know you will. So ... your call.'

There was a long silence. Winter cocked an ear. From next door, through the thin walls, the sound of a child crying.

He turned back to Berriman.

'You gonna help us then? Do the right thing? Only the guy I work for might have a view on some of this. And he's nowhere near as nice as me.'

'You mean Mackenzie?'

'Yeah.'

'After what I did for him on Saturday night? You're serious?'

'I am, son. I know you go back a while. I know you did him a favour. But he's got a crap memory sometimes and just now he wants to know about Jax Bonner. Me? I think you've got that knowledge, and that includes where to find her. Do we understand each other?'

'Yeah.'

'You gonna tell me then?'

'No.'

'Suit yourself.'

Winter stepped towards the door, made to squeeze his way past Berriman into the sitting room.

He didn't move. 'My phone?' Berriman held out his hand. His face was very close.

Winter could smell spearmint on his breath. He looked at him for a moment longer then patted him on the shoulder. 'No way, son,' he said. 'That's not the way it works.'

Outside, in the car, Winter returned Marie's call. She was at home.

'We need to talk, Paul,' she said at once. 'Can you come round?'

'Is Baz with you?'

'No.'

Sandown Road was two minutes away. Winter found Marie in the kitchen, topping and tailing a big pile of runner beans. Esme had called by half an hour ago and picked up the kids. Winter said no to coffee when Marie offered. He wanted to know what was on her mind.

'It's about Saturday night,' she said at once. 'There are a couple of things I should have mentioned but never did.'

'Like what?'

'Like when I first got back from next door. I'd been out on the street, waiting for the police to arrive. Baz had got himself hurt and I'd sent him home, and once the police turned up I went back to check him out. He'd bolted the front door, which was why I went round the side. That's when I found the two bodies.'

'Yeah?' Winter was wondering exactly where this might lead. 'And what else?'

'The kitchen door ...' She nodded at it. 'It was wide open. The light was on inside.'

'How come?'

'I've no idea. Except that Rachel knew where we hid the spare key. I assumed she'd let herself in for some reason. God knows why.'

'Did you tell the police this? At Fareham?'

'No.'

'Why not?'

'*Why not?*' She was staring at him. 'Since when did your lot ever do us any favours? There's Baz upstairs, black and blue, two bodies on our patio, and on top of that the kitchen door's wide open. You've been trying to nail us for years. Something tells me you'd start thinking it was Christmas.'

'Not me, love. *They.*'

'Sorry. You know what I mean.'

'Of course. So what did you do with the kitchen?'

'I turned the light off and shut the door.'

'Locked it?'

'Yes.'

'What was it like inside?'

'Perfectly normal, as far as I could see.'

'No signs of a fight? Any kind of struggle?'

'No.'

'OK.' Winter nodded. 'And Baz? Once you were both released?'

'I told him. Of course I told him.'

'And what did he say?'

'He said to keep it to myself. Just the way I'd done.'

'So why tell me? Now?'

'Because I've just realised what's missing.'

'Missing?'

'From the kitchen. I should have looked earlier. I should have done a proper check. But somehow I never did.'

'And?'

'I've got a favourite kitchen knife.' She nodded at the beans. 'I use it on the veggies. It's gone missing, Paul.'

'Have you told Baz about this?'

'No, but I will. And I'll say I've talked to you as well. This is serious, Paul. If that knife turns out to be the one that killed Rachel, then God knows what kind of shit we're in.'

Jimmy Suttle's first call had gone to the manager of a project targeting young offenders in the city. He'd been to a presentation recently and had been impressed. The manager's name was Bruce Marr. Suttle said he was interested in a girl his support workers might have come across. She was currently featured in a mobe clip uploaded onto a Facebook page. He gave Marr a Web address and suggested he take a look. Five minutes later Marr was back on the phone. It was nearly five o'clock.

'We ought to talk,' Marr said. 'I'd drive down but it's tricky just now. You want to come up here?'

The Preventing Youth Offending Project occupied an office in an Edwardian red-brick villa on the lower slopes of Portsdown Hill. Among Marr's front-line support workers was a soft-voiced Brummie with shoulder-length hair and mischievous eyes.

'This is Paul. He's been dealing with Jax Bonner on and off for years. Frankly, all this is no big surprise.'

Suttle wrote the name down. He'd need to check Bonner's record when he got back.

'Jax?' he queried. 'How does that work?'

'Jane Alexandra.' It was Paul. 'And she's a one-off, believe me.'

Bonner, he said, was her mother's maiden name. She'd married young, to a naval First Lieutenant called Andy Giles. She'd had two babies. The first was a boy, Scott. Four years later Jane arrived. The marriage seemed rock solid. Then Andy had fallen in love with someone else's wife and bailed out. The mother, Stephanie, had done her best to cope but in the end the situation was too much for her. Clinically depressed, she'd swallowed every tablet she could lay her hands on. Released from hospital, she'd set fire to the family home. Only prompt action from a neighbour had saved the kids' lives. 'And the mother?'

'She'd drunk half a bottle of gin and locked herself in the bedroom. There must be worse ways to die.'

The kids, he said, had been transferred to the care of a relative. Jane was seven, Scott eleven. When that didn't work, approaches were made to their natural father. He was happy in his second marriage. The last thing he wanted was two more kids.

'So what happened?'

'They were fostered out. Sometimes that works, sometimes it doesn't. In this case it didn't.'

The regime, he said, was tough but at least both kids were under the same roof. As they got older the bond between them tightened. They became inseparable. At school. During the holidays. At weekends. By the time they came to the attention of the project's team the core situation was extremely clear: Scotty and Jane against the world.

By now Suttle had begun to question the thrust of this story. Briefings like these were rarely so detailed.

'What were they up to?'

'Pretty much everything. These are intelligent kids, middle-class kids, but they're both hugely damaged. The boy, Scott, was probably the more devious. He was into all sorts but he kept his head down. The girl, Jax, was just angry. And she took it out on any one who happened to be in range.'

'Like how?'

'Violence, mainly. She just lashed out. In these situations it's often a question of boundaries. In her case there weren't any. By the time she left primary school, she was close to putting other kids in hospital.'

Moneyfields was a big comprehensive in Copner. They recognised Jax's potential and did their best but finally realised they couldn't cope. Exclusion followed exclusion. By her fourteenth birthday Jax was causing havoc at the Pupil Referral Unit.

'Offences?' Suttle was making notes.

'Shoplifting. Assault. A spot of arson. Check out the records. She did an ISSP and then a spell at a Youth Offending Institute but I can't remember exactly when.'

'ISSP?'

'Intensive Supervision and Surveillance Programme. She'd have been watched, tagged, the works.'

'And her brother? Scott?'

'He was still at mainstream school. In fact he was doing very well. Like I say, bright kids. But his big thing was money. He wanted to dig himself a little hole; he wanted to keep the world at arm's length, and he decided the best way of doing that was to get rich. In his situation I'm not sure I blame him. He'd had a pretty shit time of it so far.'

'So what did he do? To make money?'

'Drugs of course.' He shot Suttle a look. 'What else would you do?'

Suttle nodded, made another note. Paul was right. After a bummer of a life the drugs biz might have been a bright new start.

'And did it work?'

'It did. And he was bloody good at it. We watched from a distance, like you do, but he was obviously cutting the right deals. He was out of school by now, big handful of GCSEs, and he was flogging quality gear. He wasn't silly either. He didn't blow it all on flash motors and trips to Dubai; he invested.'

'In what?'

'Lock-ups. Garages. You know this city. It's impossible to park anywhere. He saw what people needed and he set about supplying it. Last time anyone counted he had dozens of the things. You want to buy a garage, you go to Scott Giles.'

'He didn't call himself Bonner?'

'No. He'd had a big kiss and make up with his natural dad by now. He went back to being Giles. He wanted to bin the past.'

'And flogging gear? He'd knocked that on the head too?'

'No.' Paul shook his head. 'The gear gave him the means to buy more lock-ups. I think they call it capitalism.'

The thought drew a smile from Suttle. He liked this man. He'd got life in perspective, unlike some social workers he'd known.

'So where is he now? This Scott Giles?'

'In Winchester nick. He got five years on a supply charge. This is recent history. I'm surprised you guys don't know.'

A sizeable stash of cocaine, he said, had been found in one of his empty lock-ups. Throughout the trial Scott had insisted on his innocence. He'd never bought the stuff, never left it there, disputed every item of evidence in the prosecution case. Many present at the trial – lawyers, journalists – had agreed with him. But then came the judge's summing-up and after that the jury's verdict was a formality.

'And the judge was ... ?' Suttle sat back, realising at last where this story had been heading.

'Peter fucking Ault.' Paul nodded. 'You guessed right.'

Suttle was returning to Major Crime when he took the call from Lizzie Hodson. Rush-hour traffic on the M27 had come to a halt.

'You said to call you if Winter got in touch.'

'And?'

'He phoned this afternoon.'

'About what?'

'This and that.' She broke off a moment then came back to the phone. 'He left his number too, in case you'd forgotten. You two guys ought to get together, compare notes.'

'Why would I do that?'

'In the interests of justice, Jimmy.' She was laughing now. 'And that new job you told me about.'

'And you? Why are you being so bloody helpful?'

'Because I'm a nosy soul, Jimmy. I'm afraid it goes with the territory.'

Back at the Major Crime suite Suttle found Faraday at his desk. He was on the phone. He was laughing. He waved Suttle into the spare chair.

'Tell him any time. Tell him the house is his.' He listened for a second or two, the smile even wider. 'Absolutely no problem, the sooner the better. *Et toi aussi.*'

He put the phone down. His son, J-J, was coming down from London. He fancied a weekend by the sea. He had one or two friends he might catch up with. He'd bring his camera and a big telephoto for a day out on the marshes.

'But I thought he was deaf?' Suttle nodded at the phone.

'He is but he talks to Gabrielle by email. They've got a big thing going. They chatter away most weeks and she keeps me *au fait*. Like now.' Faraday was inspecting the calendar on his desk. 'She's talking about the coming weekend. We need to get this thing sorted by then. Think you can manage that?' He looked up at Suttle.

'No problem, boss.' Faraday in this mood was becoming a rarity. 'You want some more good news?'

He told Faraday about Jax Bonner and her brother. Slashing the pictures, in the view of the support worker he'd talked to, was absolutely her MO: dramatic, vicious and very, very public.

'This girl's in your face,' he said. 'Show her a book of rules and she'll break the lot. Do her a favour and she'll screw you over. Be around her for any length of time and she'll drive you mad. Why? Because she hates the world. That's him talking, not me.'

'Do we know where to find her?'

'He thinks she's been living with her brother for a while. That's before he went inside. He's got a flat in North End somewhere. She might still be there.'

Faraday nodded.

'You've checked on PNC?'

'Haven't had a chance, boss.'

'You want to do that now?'

'Sure.'

A handful of computers on Major Crime were security-cleared for checks on the Police National Computer. Suttle's was one of them. He was back within a couple of minutes. He had an address for Scott Giles: 91 Merrivale Road.

'When did he go down?'

'June fifteenth.'

'That's this year?'

'Yes.'

'Do we know whether the place was rented? Or did he own it?'

'I think he owned it. According to the guy I talked to, he was good with money. Made a stack of investments.'

'And you're telling me the girl's been living there?'

'That's what the guy from the project thinks. He says she went to a kids' home after the foster parents gave up. Then she got a spell in a Young Offenders' Institute. Then she went to live at her brother's place. They were still very close. Apparently he used to go and see her in the YOI and his was the address she put down on the release form. This would have been last year.'

'So she could be still there? In her brother's flat?'

'Easily. The other thing he told me was about the business the brother ran. Apparently she helped with the lock-ups and the garages.'

'Keeping it in the family?'

'Exactly. And it might still be giving her a living too.' He paused. 'You want to bosh the place? Only we'll need a warrant.'

'That's got to be Parsons' decision.' Faraday was looking for Merrivale Road on the big wall map. 'First off we need to find this bloody girl.'

Suttle disappeared to the Incident Room to organise a couple of D/Cs. No way would Jax Bonner volunteer as a witness but the Face-book footage gave ample grounds for an arrest for criminal damage. When D/S Glen Thatcher mentioned risk assessment, Suttle found himself pausing for thought.

'She's a headcase,' he said at last. 'And she may have done Rachel Ault.'

'Stabproofs, then? Is that what we're saying?'

'Yeah.' Suttle nodded. 'For sure.'

Faraday's call found DCI Parsons on the M27, heading for Winchester. Yet another conference with Willard, he thought.

'Good news, boss. We're looking at our first arrest.'

He told her about Jax Bonner. When Parsons came back to him, he detected a quickening in her voice. As far as Willard was concerned, he sensed she played the terrier in his life. If so, she at last had something to lay at his feet.

Faraday wanted to know about 91 Merrivale Road. If the girl wasn't there, what did Parsons want to do?

'Get a warrant sworn,' she said at once. 'Get Scenes of Crime in there. We're looking for stuff from Saturday night, clothing especially. I'll be back later.'

The line went dead. Suttle was at Faraday's open door.

'You want me on this thing as well, boss? Only I could use a couple of hours.'

'No.' Faraday shook his head. 'If we nick her, I'll want you in the interview suite but that won't happen for a while.' He glanced up. 'Anyone special?'

'No, boss.' He shook his head. 'Just a mate from way back.'

Chapter fourteen

Winter took the call en route to the pub. He'd just stepped out of Blake House and paused on the Gunwharf harbour front while he dealt with his employer. He'd been counting the minutes since he'd left Marie at Sandown Road. The only surprise was that it had taken Baz so long to pick up the phone.

'She told you about that knife that's gone walkabout?'

'Yeah, Baz, she did.'

'What do you think?'

'I think she's right.'

'Right to tell you?'

'Right that you might have a problem.'

'You? What's this *you*?'

'We, Baz. I meant we.'

'Fine. So what do *we* do about it?'

It was an excellent question, to which Winter had been devoting a great deal of thought.

'A year ago it would have been simple,' he said at last. 'Someone was in your kitchen. Maybe more than one. We need to know who and we need to know why. Marie seems to think Rachel was in there and she might well be right, but we need to be sure. A year ago I could have pulled all kinds of stunts. We're talking forensics, Baz. Databases. All that shit.'

'Great, mush. But you're not Filth any more.'

'You're right, Baz.' Winter grinned, checking his watch. 'But just leave it to me, eh?'

The Cardigan was Winter's choice, and on the phone that afternoon Suttle knew at once that he'd been sending a message. The pub lay in Old Portsmouth, a stone's throw from the cathedral. It served decent beer, ample meals, and among the regulars standing at the bar Suttle anticipated a number of faces who'd be on speaking terms with Bazza

Mackenzie. The Cardigan had always been Winter's turf, Winter's local.

The moment Suttle stepped in through the door, fifteen minutes late, he sensed something had changed. Gone was the fug of cigarette smoke, the tight buzz of conversation, the beery eyes, the stabbing fingers. Two elderly men were watching snooker on television. A third was deep in a crossword puzzle while the girl behind the bar was painting her nails. Tuesday night, he thought.

Winter was at a table at the other end of the bar. He'd got as far as page two of the *Daily Telegraph* and the glass at his elbow was nearly empty.

'Stella, son.' He didn't look up.

Suttle fetched the drinks. Winter folded the paper, drained the last of his pint and made space on the table for the next one.

'They know you're meeting me?'

'You're joking.'

'Unofficial then. Our little secret, eh? Cheers, son. Here's to that new job of yours. It's in the bag. I kid you not.'

Suttle ignored him. In these moods – matey, cheerful, seemingly artless – Winter was at his most dangerous.

'Something tells me I should be warning you about perverting the course of justice.' Suttle reached for his drink. 'Or would I be wasting my time?'

'Me?' Winter looked pained. 'Why would I want to do that?'

'Because you're poking around. Because you're doing what we're paid to do.'

'How do you know?'

'Because two of our blokes met you outside Berriman's place in Margate Road. And because you refuse to mind your own bloody business.'

Winter looked amused. Then hurt.

'My boss has just found two bodies beside his swimming pool. A bunch of arsehole kids have given his neighbourhood a bad name. He thinks that *is* his own bloody business. So that makes it mine, doesn't it?'

'No.' Suttle shook his head. 'It's our business. And a year ago you'd have been saying exactly the same thing. It's what you do, mate. It's called behaving yourself.'

'Are you warning me off? Is that why we're sitting here? Only it was you who made the call, remember. Not me.'

Suttle said nothing. Already the last year seemed to have vanished. Within minutes he'd become a D/C again, sitting at Winter's feet. That was the man's talent, his special gift. He could turn you inside out and you'd still be sitting there, enjoying his company.

He changed the subject. 'How is it, then? This new life of yours?'

'Very agreeable, son. If you want the truth, I was a bit bothered to begin with. Looking after a bunch of pensioners in Spain wasn't what I signed up to. But that's gone now, thank fuck.'

Suttle nodded. He wanted to know more. Winter told him about the Playa Esmeralda, Marie's pet project, and about the canny way she'd dressed the job up. He'd flown out there as Director of Security and ended up running poolside games of bingo.

'What about Mackenzie in all of this?'

'He's forever moving on. The man bores easily. He's got the attention span of a gnat. The minute something's in place, he's thinking about his next little adventure. This is all legit, believe me. It might sound dodgy because everything's got his name all over it but in the end it's just money. He's become a businessman, son. And as long as everything's cushty, he's sweetness and light.'

'So what's your job?'

'To keep him that way.'

'Sweetness and light?'

'Too right.' Winter swallowed a mouthful of lager. 'And so far, once I'd binned all that Spanish nonsense, it's been a doddle. Nice motor. Good money. No one giving me grief about my RIPA forms. Like I say, peachy.'

'Until Saturday night.'

'Spot on. And you know why? Because for once dear old Baz does the right thing. He plays the white man. He does the good neighbour thing. He wades in there and does his best to sort these animals out, and you know what he gets for his troubles? A crack over the head with a bottle of Scotch and a bunch of adolescent tossers trying to put him in hospital. You've come across the boy Berriman? The lad who swims a bit? Bazza owes him. Big time.'

'So I gather.'

'You met him? Berriman?' Suttle nodded. 'So what's the story? What do you make of the boy?'

This was dangerous territory, and Suttle knew it. He hadn't come here to mark Winter's card. He glanced over his shoulder. The old guys watching television had gone. The pub was virtually empty.

'I'm way out of line even being here ...' he began. 'You'd know that.'

'Unless they've sent you.'

'They haven't. Sure as fuck they haven't. And if they knew, I'd be busted back to D/C. Maybe even uniform.'

Winter winced at the thought. He'd never bothered to hide his contempt for the woollies, one of the reasons no one in uniform had bothered to turn up at his leaving do.

'Then why make the call?' he asked. 'Why stick your neck out?'

'You want the truth?'

'Go on.'

'Because I'd be mad not to. We're calling this operation *Mandolin*. I'm driving the Intel Cell. You know how intel works. The best stuff often comes off the streets. So I should be out there, running down a few contacts, asking the odd favour, applying a bit of pressure. And that should put me alongside people like you.'

'You think I'm some kind of grass?' Winter sounded genuinely shocked. 'You want to stick me on PIMS? Bung me a few quid for my trouble?'

PIMS was a system for registering informants, yet another layer of bureaucracy to make thief-taking harder. Winter, a D/C who'd relied on an army of informants, had always loathed it.

It was Suttle's turn to grin. The thought of running Winter as a paid grass was delicious.

Winter hadn't finished. He beckoned Suttle closer. 'There's something we need to talk about, you and me.'

'What's that?'

'You know what really happened last year? When you lot were running round after that minister got himself shot?'

Suttle shook his head, thrown by this sudden change of direction. The Goldsmith Avenue killing had stretched Major Crime to the limit. At the time he'd been working with Faraday on another murder, the killing of a property developer in Port Solent, and he'd ended up finding the key piece of evidence that had scored a result on both jobs.

'Tell me,' he said.

'I was with Bazza's lot. On appro.'

'I know. That was the last time we had a drink. It was in the Buckingham. Round the corner. Remember?'

'Sure. And you gave me a hard time. "Disappointment" was the word you used. Or maybe it was disgrace.'

'Bloody right. And so you were.'

'Thanks.' Winter held his gaze. 'Fucking thanks.'

'So what are you telling me? That I'd got it wrong? That you hadn't got pissed? That you hadn't been chucked out on a DUI? That Mackenzie hadn't come along and hoovered you up? Along with the rest of the rubbish?'

'Great, son. Really sharp. And to think I had you down as some kind of detective. Brilliant. Just fucking brilliant.' For once Suttle knew Winter wasn't bluffing. He was upset. Seriously upset.

'So tell me,' Suttle said again. 'Tell me where I got it so wrong.'

'You really want to hear?'

'I just asked, didn't I?'

'OK, son. I'll tell you this once, and once only. And I'll tell you because believe it or not you mattered to me. All the stuff out in America? All that medical shit?' He touched his head. 'You pulled me through. I don't know whether you realised at the time but you played a blinder.'

'Sure. Thanks. So tell me about Mackenzie.'

'It was a sting, son. Willard's idea. The DUI was a set-up, not that the woollies knew. Three times over the limit and I was out on my arse. And you were right about Bazza. He couldn't help himself. All I had to do was wait for the phone to ring.'

'So what was the plan?'

'It doesn't matter. All you need to know is that Willard fucked up. Big time. Willard and the twat D/I from Covert Ops who was running me.'

'Who was that?'

'A woman called Parsons. I was inches away from getting myself totally fucking blown. And in the kind of company I was keeping, you'd only do that once.'

'So what happened?'

'I told Willard to stuff it. Sweetest conversation I ever had in my life. Lasted about ten seconds.'

'And after that?'

'I felt a whole lot better. He and Parsons nearly got me killed. They'd deny it but it's true. Working for Bazza, doing it for real, is sanity compared with where I was this time last year.' He nodded, reaching for his drink.

Suttle took a while to absorb this conversation.

'How do I know you're not still U/C?' he said at last.

'You don't, son, but it's a fucking good question. Proves you've still got a brain in that head. As it happens, I'm not. I'm seriously bent and I work for a man who makes me very happy. If you can put up with the company, I'll buy you a curry. Here's to crime.' He raised his glass. 'Cheers.'

Moments later Winter disappeared to the loo. Suttle rang Faraday on his mobile and asked about progress in Merrivale Road. Faraday told him there'd been no response from the ground-floor flat. The people upstairs had confirmed that a girl with a shaven head was living down there but they hadn't seen her since Saturday. Faraday himself was now in the process of getting a search warrant sworn. Parsons thought there was no percentage in staking the place out in case Bonner returned. In her view the girl had probably fled the city.

Seeing Winter returning from the loo, Suttle brought the conversation to an end. A curry, he'd decided, would be good. Preferably a takeout.

'My place then.' Winter was finishing his drink.

They walked the half-mile back to Gunwharf. Stepping into Winter's apartment, Suttle felt a strange sense of déjà vu, of time telescoping backwards. Back in the pub he'd never seen Winter so emotional, so raw. Something had hurt him badly, Suttle realised, and that something had to do with the times they'd spent together.

While Winter busied himself in the kitchen Suttle stood at the big picture window staring out at the gathering dusk on the harbour. He'd always had respect for Winter. More than that, especially after the onset of the brain tumour, he'd felt affection for the man. He'd never met anyone so alone, anyone with less need for other people. He wasn't solitary in the sense that Faraday was solitary. On the contrary, Winter had an immense gift for mateyness, for making people trust him. But a year working together had revealed another side to the man, an empty space inside that was very close to loneliness, and it had been Suttle's pleasure to become a kind of son. He'd kept an eye on the old boy. They'd had a lot of laughs. And in return Winter had taught him a very great deal.

He was on the phone now, shouting orders to some takeaway or other. Joannie, Winter's wife, had been dead for years. He'd sold up the bungalow in Bedhampton and had no kids. Maybe Mackenzie's filled that gap, Suttle thought. Maybe that's why he's ended up on the Dark Side.

Winter stepped back into the lounge.

'Chicken jalfrezi? ' he said. 'Pilau rice with a side order of sag? Have I got that right?'

'Perfect, boss.' He accepted a can of Stella. 'Tell me about Matt Berriman.'

Winter settled himself on the sofa, slipped off his shoes.

'He'd been with the girl forever. You'd know that.'

'You mean Rachel?'

'Yeah. Baz was close to Berriman's mum once. Nothing intimate, just friends. He did her a favour, way back. He knows the boy but not well.'

'And you think ... ?'

'I think the boy was pissed off with losing the Ault girl. I think he wanted her back. Turning up at the party had a lot to do with that.

But did he kill her? Did he find himself a knife and do the business? Make sure no one else ever had a dip? No way.'

'Why not?'

'He was still at the Aults' place, for a start. Baz turns up, gets himself into all kinds of shit … Who digs him out? Our man Matt. By that time Rachel and the boy Gareth are probably next door, time-expired.'

'How do you know that?' Suttle raised an eyebrow.

'I don't. I'm guessing. But the way I see it, Berriman wasn't there. Berriman was next door partying. Until Baz arrived.'

Suttle conceded the point. The image of Berriman in the interview suite had stayed with him. He'd dominated the tiny space. He'd been sure of himself.

Winter had another question: 'What's the forensic on Berriman? You seized his gear?'

'Of course.'

'And?'

'It's too early to say. He's priority but we're still talking five-day turnaround. Nothing changes.' Suttle paused. 'So we rule out Berriman? As far as Rachel Ault's concerned? Is that what you're saying?'

'Definitely.'

'Because?'

'Because he wasn't next door. And because there's no way a guy like him would have done that. Not to her. Not the way he felt.'

'You've talked to him?'

Winter studied him a moment, then raised his glass. It looked like Scotch.

'What do you think, son?'

'I think yes.'

'You're right. And so am I. He's off the plot.'

Suttle took a sip of lager. The temptation was to share the pictures from the upstairs bathroom, to tap Winter on the shoulder and ask him why – barely an hour before – Rachel would have been on her knees saying a private thank you to her former boyfriend, and why that same Matt Berriman would have promptly sent the evidence to Gareth Hughes's mobile. That was the kind of situation that might easily have led to a confrontation. And the consequences would have been incalculable.

Winter sensed his reservations. When Suttle said nothing, he raised another name.

'There's a girl called Jax Bonner.' he said. 'You'll know the name.'

'Would I?'

'Don't piss around, son. You know who she is.'

'I do?'

'Of course you do. If you don't, you should try looking at that Facebook page of theirs. She shaves her head. She's got a knife. She slashes pictures to bits. Nothing too subtle.'

Suttle didn't react. In the end he knew they'd have to trade information but he wanted to stay in the driving seat.

'There's another name we've come across,' Suttle said at length. 'Scott Giles?'

'Go on.'

'You know him?' Winter shook his head. Suttle knew that meant nothing. 'He's Jax Bonner's brother. He went down for five years a couple of months ago. Possession with intent.'

'Five *years*?'

'Half a kilo of the laughing powder in a lock-up. He's always claimed someone fitted him up. I was just wondering ... given the company you keep ...' Suttle was happy to leave the rest of the thought unvoiced. There was a subtext here. He was commissioning Winter to make a few enquiries, to have a poke around. There'd doubtless be another meet and another after that. It wouldn't be easy, and it certainly broke every rule in *Mandolin*'s book, but it might offer another route to Jax Bonner.

There was a buzz from the video entryphone in the hall. Winter got to his feet. Chicken jalfrezi, Suttle thought.

Winter waited in the hall to sort out the guy from the delivery service. Suttle heard a murmur of voices then Winter was back with the curries.

'Your blokes boshed Bazza's kitchen, didn't they? Scenes of Crime? Full service?'

'That's right.'

'Got anything back yet?'

'No. Netley's swamped. The fingerprint guys are talking gridlock.'

'Shame.' Winter grinned down at him. 'Extra chutney?'

Faraday found the note propped against a bag of vegetables in the kitchen. When Gabrielle was in a hurry, she didn't bother with English. '*Cheri. Il me faut sortir. Rentre plus tard. Sais pas quand. Les pommes de terre et les tomates sont parfaits. Sers-toi. Vas-y. XXX*'

Faraday looked in the bag. The new potatoes were fresh from the garden, still dusted with soil. The tomatoes as well were home-grown. He popped one in his mouth, realising how hungry he was. She was right. *Parfait.*

He checked his watch. It was late, nearly ten, and he wondered whether to knock up some kind of salad and wait for her return. She rarely went out by herself in the evening, and when it came to time she was punctilious, which made the note all the more surprising. *Back later? Don't know exactly when?*

He frowned, spotting her laptop, bagged on the kitchen table. Normally he'd never dream of snooping, of opening up her emails, of prowling through her interview files, but something in last night's exchange had planted a small seed of doubt. She was meeting kids on the inner estates. Some of those same kids clearly knew a thing or two about Saturday night in Sandown Road. It would have been in Gabrielle's nature to have pressed them for details, to have cocked her head and smile her French smile, and laugh at the funny bits. She was brilliant with other people, just the way she'd been brilliant with him.

He remembered the first time they'd met. She'd stepped onto a country bus in northern Thailand, up in the mountains near the Burmese border. The bus had been packed but she'd found a space on the seat in front of him. She'd perched on the seat, sideways on, one brown arm looped over the seat back as they lurched from corner to corner, and within an hour Faraday seemed to have told her his life story. She had a voracious appetite for other people, for the journeys they'd made, for the conclusions they'd reached, and she made the act of sharing deeply pleasurable. At the time Faraday had sensed that he could talk to her forever, and the way it had turned out, he was right.

He found a half-empty bottle of wine in the fridge. He poured himself a glass, trying hard not to visualise what she might be up to. He got the impression that some of these kids were young, barely adolescents. Where would you meet them at this time of night? How would you win their confidence? And what kind of sense would all this material make by the time you'd finished?

He knew she was looking for patterns, for the kind of templates she might apply to other social groups on the very edges of the planet. She'd worked with the Inuit in the high Arctic, with Berber tribesmen in the Mahgreb, with Pathans in the wilder parts of Afghanistan, returning from these expeditions with hundreds of pages of notes and a wealth of photos. To date she'd authored half a dozen academic papers and a slim volume that had been published only last year. This extended essay had sought to apply the lessons of her travels to urban societies in the West, winning applause from the review columns of *Liberation* and *Le Nouvel Observateur*. One of the few copies she possessed had found its way onto the shelf that Faraday reserved for especially treasured books and the sight of it nestling beside *Birds of the Western Palearctic* still gave him a little jolt of pleasure.

From a world that increasingly defied analysis she'd somehow fashioned order. In a society that had become atomised she'd knitted together a powerful case for the warm, complex comforts of kinship. To even attempt a challenge like that demanded not just intelligence but an optimism all the rarer for being so natural, so unforced. All you had to do, she'd once confided to Faraday, was to hide the candle from the draught. He nodded to himself, knowing how much she'd changed this life of his. She was the flame, he decided. And he was the candle.

Faraday's gaze returned to the laptop. To even turn it on would be an act of trespass. To settle down and go further, an act of betrayal. And yet. And yet.

He shook his head, emptied the bottle, made a start on the potatoes, forcing himself back to *Mandolin*. The duty magistrate had sworn a search warrant on the address in Merrivale Road. Inside, he and a couple of D/Cs had taken a cursory look at the flat. To his surprise, it had been clean and reasonably tidy. One of the bedrooms had obviously belonged to the brother, while the girl Jax seemed to have occupied the other. She'd stuck a photocopied picture of herself on the wall above the bed and left a couple of unopened letters with her name on the front on the tiny table beneath the window. There was a pile of her clothes at the foot of the double bed and a stack of CDs beside the player in the corner. The younger of the detectives, eyeing a poster for a band called Achtung Everybody, pitied whoever lived upstairs. His own kid sister had similar tastes in Pop-Punk and it was driving his mum bonkers.

Before they'd left the bedroom the same D/C had spotted the end of a Pompey scarf hanging from a drawer. Inside the drawer he'd found an assortment of socks and underwear, none of it female, and checks in the nearby bathroom had revealed a can of shaving cream and a couple of knackered razors in the bin beneath the sink. Faraday had made a mental note to revisit some of the interviewees who'd noticed Jax Bonner at the party house. Maybe she'd come with company, he'd thought. And maybe that someone had taken the footage on the stairs. He remembered the paleness of the girl's face turning to the camera, and the smear of spittle from her flickering tongue. Maybe she'd known this person. Maybe she even lived with him. Maybe they'd planned the evening together – a raid on enemy territory, a chance to settle her brother's debts. And maybe that payback had extended to Rachel Ault.

Now, ducking into the garden in search of mint for the potatoes, Faraday wondered where a full SOC search might take them. He'd left a uniform outside the property overnight and Jerry Proctor's boys would be making a start first thing. They might find ID for Bonner's flatmate. If not, then DNA from the razors or maybe a toothbrush might give them a hit a week or so down the line. Either way, two names would double their chances of pushing *Mandolin* towards an early result.

He smiled, reminded suddenly of the impending weekend. J-J, he thought, and the chance for a day or so of decent birding. There were reports on one of the RSPB sites of a marsh harrier on the Isle of Wight. All three of them could take the ferry across to Ryde and explore the wetlands south of Bembridge Harbour. They could have dinner afterwards at a favourite pub in Seaview. Maybe even stay over, take a couple of rooms for the night, make a proper break of it. Warmed by the thought, he plucked another sprig of mint and headed back towards the kitchen. As he did so, he became aware of approaching headlights in the cul-de-sac that led to the Bargemaster's House. A taxi stopped, and two figures got out. One of them was the driver. The other, slighter, seemed to be limping.

Faraday watched for a second or two then stepped round the side of the house to meet them before they got to the front door. In the spill of the streetlights Gabrielle's upturned face was caked with blood.

'Been in the wars, mate.' The driver had his arm locked beneath hers. 'I offered to take her to A & E but she wouldn't hear of it.'

Faraday thanked him. He'd take over. He'd sort it. Gabrielle was whispering something. Faraday bent down to her.

'Money, *chéri*. He needs money.'

'You mean the fare?'

She nodded, closed her eyes.

'Please ...' she said. 'Just pay him.'

The driver said he'd picked her up in Cosham, on the mainland. He'd spotted her slumped in a bus shelter and had stopped to help. Faraday asked for a name and a phone number and waited while the driver fumbled for a card.

'Thanks, mate.' He was pocketing Faraday's twenty-pound note. 'I'd go to the police if I were you.'

The driver gone, Faraday walked Gabrielle slowly into the house and settled her on the sofa. One eye was swollen and a cut high on her cheek was still oozing blood, but the wounds looked superficial. When he asked whether she hurt anywhere else, she shook her head. He went to the bathroom and laced a bowl of hot water with antiseptic. Then he returned to the sofa and knelt on the carpet, gently swabbing her battered face with a flannel. Only when she asked for something to drink did he put the obvious question.

'What happened?'

She shook her head. Her eyes were still closed.

'It's nothing,' she said. '*Rien du tout.*'

'Please … just tell me.'

'I can't.'

'*Can't?*'

'It's impossible, Joe. Sometimes it's like this. Not so easy.' She winced at the sting of the antiseptic. 'Maybe I asked for it. Maybe it was my fault. *Tant pis.*'

'Asked for what?'

'Please, no.' She shook her head. 'Maybe later, maybe tomorrow, not now.'

He made a pot of tea, checking on her through the open kitchen door. When he asked whether she'd eaten, whether she was hungry, she shook her head. She was exploring her mouth with her fingers. At length she asked for a mirror.

'*Merde.*' She scowled at her image, running her tongue over her teeth.

'Some kind of mugging?'

'*Non.*'

'But you were robbed? And that's why you had no money?'

'I lost my purse.'

'*Lost* it?'

She sipped at the tea, not answering. When Faraday tried again, more questions, she shook her head. She'd had enough. Her face hurt. Her head hurt. She wanted to go to bed. *Tant pis.*

Too bad? Faraday helped her upstairs. When he tried to undress her, she said she'd do it herself. She was shivering now, her skin cold to the touch. Faraday found a dressing gown and put his arms round her. She nestled her head against his chest then pushed him gently away. Leaving the room, he heard the sigh of the mattress as she got into bed.

Downstairs, back in the kitchen, he closed the door. He found the mains lead to her laptop in a pocket of the bag. He opened the laptop and then plugged it in.

Chapter fifteen

Winter found Mackenzie in his private quarters at the Royal Trafalgar Hotel. Until recently he'd occupied a single ground-floor office on a sunny corner of the building, but his growing empire had demanded more space and so he'd moved upstairs to a suite of rooms with a near-perfect view of the Isle of Wight. With a nod to his days in the 6.57, Mackenzie had dubbed the previous office the Fratton End. His new corporate headquarters, infinitely smarter, had become the Steve Claridge Suite.

Winter sat in front of the desk, waiting for Mackenzie to come off the phone. A huge blow-up of the veteran Pompey striker dominated the office. The photographer had caught him in a crowded penalty area, about to pivot on one leg and lash the ball into the net. Winter knew very little about football but recognised at once why Steve Claridge belonged here. The socks hanging down round his ankles. The muddy knees. The wreck of a haircut. Like Bazza himself, Claridge depended on other people not taking him seriously. Underestimate this man, Winter thought vaguely, and like so many Premiership defenders you'd be sitting on your arse listening to the roar of the Pompey crowd.

'Well, mush? Did you find her?' Bazza appeared to have forgotten about Marie's knife.

Winter assumed they were talking about Jax Bonner. He shook his head. After Suttle's departure last night he'd driven up to Merrivale Road.

'She's gone to ground, Baz. She's got a flat up in North End but the Old Bill were sitting on it last night, marked car across the road, so that tells me they're not expecting her back.'

'And why would they be interested?'

Winter told him about the footage on Facebook. The girl acting as administrator on the site had now removed the pictures of Jax slashing the pictures but they'd been up there for most of yesterday, time enough for even his ex-colleagues to log on.

'She's in the frame then?'

'Definitely. I know fuck all about her background but I gather the flat belongs to her brother. Does the name Scott Giles ring any bells?'

Bazza shook his head. Winter knew at once he was lying. The denial was too quick, a reflex action, almost a twitch.

'Young guy? Early twenties? Recently made a name for himself in the cocaine biz?'

'Pass.'

'You're sure about this? Only a couple of ex-informants I've been talking to this morning say the boy Giles had a serious run-in with Danny Cooper. Same market, same clients, same turf. There wasn't ever going to be room for the two of them so young Danny decided it was time to tidy the place up.'

'He did?' Mackenzie was watching Winter carefully. 'And how might he have done that?'

'I've no idea, Baz. All I've got is rumour. Street talk. You know what it's like around drugs. You can't trust any of these lowlife animals.'

'So what did they tell you?'

'They told me Danny laid hands on a decent stash of charlie, bulked it out with all kinds of shit, wrapped it up in cling film, and parked it in one of Giles's lock-ups. There's some other stuff about a sandwich Giles bought from a corner store up in North End. That was wrapped in cling film as well. It seems the sandwich cling film ended up round half a kilo of cocaine with Giles's prints all over it. They even rescued the remains of the sandwich from the bin where Giles had left it. That was in the garage too. Prints from the cling film. DNA from the sandwich. Bingo.'

'Clever.'

'Extremely.'

'And kosher, do you think?'

'Could easily be. Think about it, Baz. What would you need? Some scrote to follow Giles around, clock the way he spends his days, find out where he buys his lunch. This guy's busy. He's on the move. He's buying and selling gear. He's renting out lock-ups. He snacks on the move. He chomps on the sandwich, eats the best bits, dumps the rest. You wait till he's gone, then go to the bin and help yourself. Wear gloves and you're home safe. Writes itself, doesn't it?'

'Yeah?' Mackenzie was looking thoughtful. 'This Giles kid went down, didn't he? I remember the case now. Five years.'

'That's right.'

'And he's definitely this girl's brother?'

'That's what I'm told. And they were tight too. Still are. Giles is in Albany. She's been going across to visit on the ferry every week. Set your clock by it.'

Albany was a Category A prison on the Isle of Wight. Mackenzie wanted to know why brother and sister had different surnames.

'No idea.'

'So what are we saying?'

'We're playing the copper, Baz. We're wondering about motivation. About opportunity. About MO. We're looking hard at Jax Bonner and we find she's half in love with a brother who's been sent down on dodgy evidence. She knows it's dodgy because her brother's told her so and she trusts her brother. She's a bit of a headcase and so now she's looking for someone to blame. She doesn't think the judge played a blinder at the trial and, who knows, she might be right. She has a bit of a think about it and then one day she hears about a party. She knows fuck all about Craneswater but she doesn't need to. All she needs is a name. And guess what...?'

'Ault.'

'Exactly.'

'Shit. You think she did it? You think she did them both? With that knife? From my fucking kitchen?'

'No idea, Baz. But a year ago there's no way I wouldn't have wanted a long conversation.'

'So that's where they're heading? The Filth?'

'Absolutely no question.' He paused. 'You think we might have a problem with that?'

Jimmy Suttle didn't arrive at Major Crime until lunchtime. The Scott Giles bust had come out of the Serious Organised Crime Squad based at Havant, and Suttle had spent half the morning at Havant nick going through the CPS file with a D/C who'd worked on the case.

Operation *Fiddler*, he told Suttle, had been a pain in the arse. For one thing everyone was a bit puzzled why Giles should have earned himself so much investigative resource. It seemed the lad had done OK from the narco-biz but more and more of his profits were coming from the lock-ups, and that appeared to be a totally legit operation. Indeed, in the eyes of many social workers Giles was a textbook ex-ample of a bad apple hauling himself out of the shit. So why bother spoiling that little aspirational fairy tale?

'Good question.' Faraday had invited Suttle into his office. 'So what's the answer?'

'No one seems to know, boss. To be fair, there was a big question mark about exactly how much weight the bloke had been shifting when he was at it full throttle, but there they had a problem too. Largely because everyone was clueless. My guy had a couple of informants who swore blind he was only playing at it. There was another D/C who had different information. He said Giles was bidding for the big time. In the end *Fiddler* ran with him.'

'So what made the difference?'

'Partly it's covering your arse. Someone says Giles is a major player, you can't afford to ignore it. But then they sorted out some surveillance and it turned out he was a busy little fucker. They laid hands on a deals list and it seemed to be kosher. Giles made regular calls. Often in the nicer parts of town.'

'Where did the list come from?'

'Another tyro. Danny Cooper.'

'Danny Cooper's one of Bazza's boys. He's supposed to have his eye on the crown jewels.'

'Exactly.'

'And he'd know about these clients because Giles might have nicked them off him?'

'Sure, boss. Or vice versa. Put Giles away, and Cooper's got a clear run. Takeover time. Those clients become his clients. Isn't that the way it works?'

Faraday wanted to get back to the trial. What was the consensus on the strength of the CPS file?

'Dodgy. In fact weak. Half the squad thought there was no point submitting it in the first place.'

'Why?'

'Giles must have heard a whisper. Either that or he'd genuinely binned the drugs biz. They boshed his flat, his motor, all his lock-ups. Nothing.'

'Apart from half a kilo of cocaine.'

'Exactly. But that was the following week when Giles was out of town. He'd just taken himself off to Spain for a little holiday. Next thing *Fiddler*'s getting word about a stash of charlie in this particular lock-up. It's a stand-alone place up in Copnor, not even on an industrial estate, and of all his properties it's the only one without any kind of CCTV. Naturally the guys arrive to do the lock-up but there's another funny thing ...'

'What?'

'It's wide open already. Someone's been at it. Clumsy too. Crowbar job. The source says they've got to look under a pile of stuff at the back, nothing too difficult, and guess what? Half a kilo of charlie with bits of Scott Giles all over it. Not just that, but half a sandwich nearby. Tuna salad, if you want the detail. They trace the sandwich to a little shop in North End, seize the CCTV, send the sandwich off for profiling, and bingo … Giles's face on the CCTV tapes, Giles's DNA all over the sandwich. Two strikes, and the guy's got a big problem. They arrested him at Gatwick on his way back from his hols. He hasn't been a free man since.'

'Except he didn't do it.'

'Very probably not. His defence brief at the trial drives a cart and horses through the evidence from the lock-up. What kind of drug baron can't afford a new roll of cling film? Why pollute all that charlie with bits of tuna salad? And why go on holiday with your lock-up door wide open? It wasn't just the charlie he had in there. There was a motor, for fuck's sake, plus a bunch of tools and a Harley-Davidson he was going to do up. Some of the blokes on the squad thought the case was so thin that Giles would do them for false arrest. Then came the judge's summing-up. After that he was lucky not to pull a life sentence.'

The D/C, said Suttle, had been present at the trial. Astonished by this sudden bend in the road, he'd made notes. Judge Ault, he said, hadn't dwelt overlong on the evidence. Instead he'd directed the jury's attention to the plague of drug dealers, big and small, preying on the city's youth. As it happened, most of Giles's alleged deals list had been middle-aged and moneyed. Coordinated raids on multiple addresses had certainly turned up recreational amounts of charlie and weed, but no one was talking and it hadn't been possible to tie any of it to Giles. This, though, was mere detail. The accused, said the judge, was educated, clever and undoubtedly interested in making money. To make money you need money. That money may well have come from drug dealing, and but for one tiny slip Mr Giles might still be in the extremely profitable business of supply.

'One tiny slip?' Faraday was smiling.

'Exactly. Over a grand's worth of charlie and he leaves the door wide open. Not to mention the motor and the Harley and everything else.'

'What about the girl? Any idea whether she was at the trial?'

'Every day. I asked. I took the Facebook photo up to Havant and the D/C confirmed it. She's not hard to spot.'

'And after the verdict?'

'She had a go at the judge. And nearly ended up on a contempt charge.'

'What did she say?'

'She called him a fucking disgrace.'

'Threats?'

'No.'

Faraday nodded. He could imagine the scene only too well. Justified or otherwise, there were few families in the city who didn't take a guilty verdict very personally indeed.

'And your feeling, Jimmy?'

'About what, boss?'

'About Scott Giles. You think he was fitted up?'

'I think it's odds on, yes. The lad had definitely been knocking out serious weight in his time but the lads on *Fiddler* never got to prove it. As it is, he'll probably be back in a couple of years with all kinds of new tricks up his sleeve. And he won't be interested in lock-ups any more.'

'But where does it take us? With the girl?'

'Jax Bonner? She's angry already. Her brother going down like that probably confirms all the shit that's pumping around her fevered little brain. I can imagine she enjoyed taking the knife to that picture. Whether she took it to the daughter as well has got to be a possibility.' He offered Faraday a thin smile. 'No?'

Faraday's head turned towards the window. By now Jax Bonner's photo and details would be with every force in the country. Media Relations was talking to the tabloids about tomorrow's editions and he'd heard a whisper that *Newsnight* was fishing for mobile footage from the party. In some strange way Rachel Ault, and the wreckage she'd left behind her, had become the property of the nation. Look what we've done to ourselves. Look where we're heading.

'The Aults are back tomorrow,' Faraday said softly. 'What a bloody homecoming.'

En route back to the Intelligence Cell, Suttle made a detour to the office Jerry Proctor had commandeered down the corridor. He'd noticed his Volvo estate in the car park. Proctor's bulk hung over the desk.

'Jerry ...?'

Suttle stood in the open doorway. He'd talked privately to Proctor first thing this morning and asked him what he could do to press the Fingerprint Department at Netley to fast-track the lifts from Mackenzie's kitchen. Proctor had naturally asked why but had respected Suttle's shake of the head.

Now he said it was sorted. The guy in charge of the print department owed him a favour or two and he'd been happy to quietly reprioritise.

Suttle said he was grateful.

'So what are we looking at?' he asked.

'I checked in about an hour ago. Most of the prints they eliminated against Mackenzie and his wife. There are a bunch of much smaller lifts but they'd fit the grandkids. Apparently they come down every week. Netley are now looking hard at two other lifts.'

One, he said, was a full set from a glass found beside the sink. There'd also been smears of blood around the lip of the same glass.

'And the other?'

'Two palm prints, both on the top exterior surface of the fridge, about a foot and a half apart. Like this ...' He stood up and held out both arms, palms flat.

'As if you were leaning against the fridge, you mean?'

'Looks like it.'

'Have they ID'd them yet?'

'No. They're going to bell me.'

Suttle was thinking hard. Maybe the Mackenzies had someone in to clean during the week. Maybe the fridge had gone on the blink and a call-out engineer had been wrestling it back in after working on it. There were, he knew, a thousand explanations.

Proctor turned to face Suttle. As he did so, his eyes flicked left. Faraday was standing in the corridor. He must have heard every word.

There was a moment of absolute silence. Suttle knew exactly what was coming next.

'Why the interest in Mackenzie's kitchen?' He enquired. 'And what's so important you couldn't tell me first?'

Winter met Lizzie Hodson early in the afternoon. She'd called him from the Mary Rose Museum in the naval dockyard. She'd been doing an interview and had half an hour to spare before she had to be back at the *News*. It was a lovely day. Did he fancy a meet on The Hard?

The Hard was a busy length of harbour front flanked by HMS *Warrior*. Winter hurried down from Gunwharf, intrigued. First Hodson wanted to know about Jimmy Suttle.

'You two got together?'

'We did, my love. We did.'

'Profitable, I hope?'

'Very. I've got a soft spot for the lad. I must be getting old.'

Talking about Suttle like this felt mildly embarrassing. Was there any other reason she'd suddenly been in touch?

'We took a call in the newsroom yesterday,' she said. 'I thought you might be interested.'

'Who was it?'

'A girl called Jax Bonner. She wanted to talk to somebody about Saturday night. One of the subs has been pulling all our coverage together. He was the guy she talked to in the end.'

'And what did she want?'

'Money. She said she'd sell us her story for ten grand. By that time we were aware of the new Facebook posting. You've seen that stuff? With the knife and the picture?' Winter nodded. 'That gave us a problem. On the one hand, she's probably got some kind of a story to sell. On the other, she's obviously down for criminal damage. Plus the police are circulating her photo. There are rules about this kind of thing and our bosses won't put a foot out of line. Even if we ended up with a reasonable figure, we'd be mega-exposed. Plus we never pay more than peanuts.'

'So no deal?'

'None. In these cases you sometimes end up with a freebie because what the person really wants is publicity, but even so I don't think we'd ever have touched it.'

'So it was a waste of time? Is that what you're telling me?'

'Not at all. The sub was bright enough to 1471 the number. He tells me she phoned again this morning. Same number.' She smiled. 'It was local. You want it?'

Faraday told himself the mid-afternoon trip back to the Bargemaster's House was strictly in the line of duty. Gabrielle was no longer just his lover and his muse. By virtue of the kids she was meeting, of the stuff they were telling her, she may well have become a key source for *Mandolin*. A diligent CID officer like himself needed to know that she was safe.

Last night he'd spent the best part of two hours scrolling through Gabrielle's notes, laboriously scanning page after page of her French, trying to get a fix on the chain of events that had finally put her in the back of a taxi, bleeding and bruised.

None of the interviews carried names or contact details. Instead, she'd capitalised each of the people she'd talked to. K, for instance, sounded like a youngish adolescent from Portsea. She'd talked about how much she missed her dad, how much she worried about her mum, how hard it was to get to school in the morning if you'd spent half the night sniffing lighter fluid.

F, on the other hand, was more forthright. He had a jigsaw of ASBOs across the city and shoplifting in Commercial Road had become a bit of a nightmare. The guys working the street cameras from the CCTV control room had your face on file, and if they spotted you in a banned area then you and the gear got nicked in minutes. Getting home in one piece had therefore become a real challenge. Last time he tried it, keeping to streets where he was legal, he must have done near-on ten miles. No doubt about it. ASBOs made you seriously fit.

There'd been more material like this, pages and pages of it, a montage of young lives briefly caught on Gabrielle's audio tape. Collectively, as Gabrielle had already told him, the interviews spoke of an almost tribal sense of belonging. Most kids talked about their mates, about getting by without money, about helping each other out, about partying in the park with a case of stolen Carlsberg after a mass descent on some corner shop or other. Life, they seemed to be saying, was a laugh as long as you didn't take it too seriously.

Other kids were less convinced. They described the dangers of straying onto the wrong street at the wrong time. They drew a map of tribal Pompey, of fault lines between estates you'd be wise not to cross, of hot spots where you could pretty much rely on a good kicking. One in particular, a girl, talked of spirits briefly lifted by booze or drugs, of a relationship with a Buckland boy which had almost worked, of doors inched open then slammed shut again. She wanted to get out, she'd told Gabrielle. But getting out was so fucking hard.

Leaving the Mondeo outside in the sunshine, Faraday let himself into the house. There was no sign of Gabrielle on the ground floor. Upstairs, the bed was empty. He bent low to the pillow, smoothing the creases, pausing to stare at the ochre smears of blood. The clothes she'd been wearing last night were piled by the window. He picked them up one by one, finding more blood on the jeans, on her favourite Georges Brassens T-shirt. He'd never thought of her as a crime scene before and he found the image deeply troubling. Had he, in some unconscious way, been responsible for attracting her to a project like this? Had she watched him leave for work every morning? Had she seen that same face, wearied by another working day, trying to summon the energy to sustain this relationship of theirs? Had she decided to take her own look at the broken chaotic lives that sometimes threatened to swamp their little boat?

In the end he dismissed the thought. He'd rarely met anyone so nerveless, so independent as Gabrielle. She'd survived alone on the very edges of the civilised world and she had dozens of stamps in her passport to prove it. To her the Pompey estates were probably as exotic and alien as anywhere else she'd been and the hours of interview currently on her laptop were simply another path into the jungle.

Back downstairs, he looked unsuccessfully for a note. He was about to return to the car when he thought to check in the garden. He found her in the hammock he'd slung for the warmer days, swaying peacefully in the breeze from the harbour, her face splashed with sunshine, her eyes closed. He looked down at her for a long moment. The purple bruising round her eye was beginning to turn yellow at the edges. He was about to creep away, relieved, when he felt the touch of her hand.

She rarely called him Joe. She sounded sleepy.

'You should be *au travail*.'

'This *is* work.'

'Me? I'm work? You mean that?' She struggled to sit up, holding the sides of the hammock. For the first time Faraday noticed the broken nails on her left hand. She must have put up a struggle, he thought.

He gave the hammock a nudge. She fell back, mustering a grin.

'Out tonight then?' He said. 'Only it might be wise to book an ambulance this time.'

'It wasn't like that.'

'No?'

'*Non*.' She shook her head. 'You have to be careful. Some of these kids are ...' she frowned, hunting for the word '... *instables*?'

'Unstable. Volatile.'

'*C'est ça*.'

'So what happened?'

'I was unlucky.'

'Are we talking lots of kids?'

'Five or six. Maybe more. I wasn't counting.'

'You knew them?'

'Some of them. It was late too. And dark.'

'Where?'

'Cosham.'

Cosham was a suburb on the mainland, an area where the badlands of Paulsgrove seeped into rows of detached villas on the lower slopes of Portsdown Hill. Another fault line, another stretch of no-man's-land.

'So what happened?' he asked again.

'We were walking. I was looking for a bus. One of the kids wanted money. He was young, maybe fourteen. He was crazy too. He kept saying he wanted his money back. And he kept laughing.'

'His money *back*?'

'*Oui. Vraiment*. I think he was trying to be *philosophe*. Like he'd joined a club. Like he'd paid his money at the door. Like he didn't like what he found inside. So ...' she shrugged '... he wanted his money back.'

'Your money?'

'*Oui*.'

'And you gave him some?'

'No. I never give them money. Food, *oui*. Tea, coffee, Coke, *absolument*. Money?' She shook her head. '*Jamais*.'

'So he took it?'

'*Oui.*'

'All of it?'

'*Oui.* I had no cards, just money. Maybe ten pounds. Not much.'

'And you just handed it over?'

'*Non.*' Her hand strayed to her face. '*Une bagarre.*'

They'd fought. Faraday didn't doubt it.

'And the other kids?'

'They ran away. Afterwards I found a place to sit down. Then the taxi stopped. You know the rest.'

Faraday nodded. In a way she'd been lucky. Kids en masse had a habit of piling in. Maybe they'd run away out of shame. Because they knew her.

'The one who robbed you. You knew him too?'

'No.'

'Description?'

'Tall. Thin. And like I say, he was crazy. *Fou.* The other kids were scared of him. You could see that. Maybe ...' she frowned '... *il planait.* I don't know.'

Il planait meant he was high. Faraday paused, struck by another thought.

'Did he take anything else? Apart from the money?'

'*Oui.*' She nodded. 'He took my phone.'

Winter resisted trying the number until he was back in his apartment. Before Lizzie Hodson had left him at The Hard she'd asked again about Jimmy Suttle, inquiring whether they were going to keep this new partnership of theirs going, and Winter had begun to wonder whether she was using him as some kind of back channel. Only slut journos fed information directly to the Old Bill. Maybe Winter was the next best thing.

He took the cordless onto his balcony and made himself comfortable. The new recliner had come from Ikea in Guildford, a surprise present from Marie. He checked the number against the note he'd made then punched it in.

It rang and rang. Way out on the harbour three canoeists were battling against the incoming tide. Winter watched them for a while, wondering about the spreading wake from a nearby ferry, then gave up on the call. With the 02392 prefix, it had to be a landline. But why would Jax Bonner risk leaving a big fat clue like that?

He sat in the sunshine, knowing how much he was enjoying himself. Thanks to Rachel Ault he was back in a job that had made him what he was: getting in people's faces, hunting down leads, backing hunches, nailing down bits of information until a pattern was staring him in the face. He was good at this. He knew he was.

Freelancing, on the other hand, had its drawbacks. A year ago, nailing down a phone number, he'd have been on to the girlie who kept the reverse directory in the big operations room at Netley. He'd have given her the number and she'd have come right back with an address. Single keystroke. All there on the computer. Simple. Nowadays he couldn't do that. Or not quite as quickly.

He smiled, waving peaceably at a middle-aged blonde on the waterfront, then he lifted the phone again.

It had taken no time at all to memorise Jimmy's new mobe number. Winter's call diverted to messaging.

'Me, son.' Winter stifled a yawn. 'Give us a bell, eh?'

Suttle had been summoned to Faraday's office. To his relief the D/I's spirits appeared to have lifted. A couple of hours ago he'd been preoccupied to the point where Suttle had begun to wonder about his health. Now there was a hint of a smile on his face.

'Jerry's been on, boss. We seem to have a result on Mackenzie's kitchen.'

'And?'

'They've tied the lifts on the glass to Rachel. The palm prints on the fridge belong to the boy, Gareth Hughes.'

One of the CSIs, Suttle said, had taken sets of prints from both bodies before Sunday's post-mortem. The match in both cases was beyond dispute.

Faraday was looking up at Suttle. He hadn't offered him a chair.

'So what does that tell us? Since all this was your idea.'

'It tells us they were both in Mackenzie's kitchen.'

'But when? Earlier in the day? Some time previous to that?'

'No.' Suttle shook his head. 'The glass by the sink had blood on it. I saw the CSI's report. If they're Rachel's prints, odds on the blood is hers as well. She had blood around her mouth when she left the kitchen next door. Remember, boss?'

Faraday nodded. A couple of Rachel's friends had been watching a food fight in the kitchen. They'd seen her leaving by the back door. She'd been upset. She was covering her mouth with her hand. They'd noticed blood.

'So she goes next door?'

'Yes.' Suttle nodded. 'Over the wall would be favourite.'

'And she gets into the Mackenzie's kitchen?'

'Yes.'

'How?'

'I've no idea.'

'And Hughes?'

'He follows her. Unless he's there already.' He frowned then shook his head, dismissing the possibility. 'She gets there first. He follows. Maybe the kitchen door was unlocked. Maybe she had access to the place. Maybe they've got a cat she feeds when they're away, and they trust her with the key. Whatever.'

'And?'

'She needs a drink. Probably water. She knows she's pissed out of her head. There's a glass on the draining board, she helps herself. Hence the blood.'

'And Hughes arrives?'

'Yes.'

'Then what?'

'No idea. Have they had a row? Is that why she's upset? Has he seen Berriman's pictures from the bathroom? Has he slapped her around a bit? Is that why she's bleeding? It sounds pretty plausible to me.'

'But what happens, Jimmy? You must have thought about this, otherwise you wouldn't have been talking to Jerry in the first place.'

Suttle nodded. He'd apologised earlier to Faraday for going behind his back. He'd blamed it on the pressure of events. Now he said he'd had a hunch about Mackenzie's kitchen but he hadn't wanted to bother Faraday with yet another investigative decision.

'That's my job,' Faraday grunted 'That's what it says on my tin. So what's the hunch?'

'I've been thinking about the semen samples. They obviously had sex.'

'Rachel and Hughes, you mean? In her bedroom?'

'In Mackenzie's kitchen. Jerry's boys only found blood in her bedroom next door. That suggests a slapping. If they'd had sex then, we'd be talking rape. I think it happened later, like I say, in Mackenzie's kitchen. Hughes wanted her back. He wanted to know that Berriman's pictures didn't matter. He wanted to put his smell on her. Hence his semen in her fanny.'

'We haven't had the DNA yet. We can't be sure.'

'I know. But it stands to reason, doesn't it? If they didn't do it in her bedroom then there's nowhere else next door on offer. The place was a battlefield. So ...' he shrugged '... it has to be Bazza's kitchen. He wants to shag her. She's all over the place. They get it on. Job done.'

'Then what?'

'Good question.' Suttle risked a grin. 'I'll keep you posted this time, boss.'

Chapter sixteen

The message went up on Rachel's Facebook page mid-afternoon. Winter, who happened to be logged on in search of more glimpses of Jax Bonner, was the first to spot it.

He phoned Mackenzie, found him at the Trafalgar.

'Are you ready for this, Baz?'

Mackenzie grunted. He had his mouth full. He was eating his lunch. Winter bent to the screen, reading the message aloud. It was addressed to Jax Bonner.

'"Danny Cooper fitted up your brother. Don't believe me? Ask him."'

'It says that?' Winter had Mackenzie's full attention.

'Plain as you like, Baz. We used to come across this kind of stuff on motorway bridges and old bits of wall. Remember all that?'

'Where does it come from? Who sent it?'

'Haven't a clue.'

'How do we find out?'

'No idea. These things can be a nightmare, Baz. Last time I tried to trace a Hotmail address, back in the Job, the blokes who knew anything about it pissed themselves laughing. There's all kinds of places you can hide now, believe me.'

'But it's a message, right? To the girl Jax, yeah?'

'Spot on, Baz. And with her track record, you wouldn't want to be Danny Cooper, would you?'

It was another thirty-five minutes before the Facebook posting came to the attention of Major Crime. Jimmy Suttle took a call from Samantha Muirhead. As administrator on Rachel's memorial site she was about to take the message down, but before she did so she thought Suttle or one of his colleagues ought to check it out.

Suttle logged on. Sam Muirhead was still on the line.

'You're right,' he said. 'Straight from the shoulder or what?'

He asked her whether she had any details on the sender. She said the user name was Calico. He or she was using a Yahoo email address. Beyond that she couldn't help.

Suttle made a note of the user name. He'd been onto Comms Intel at Netley about Facebook. Given a crime as serious as a double homicide, to his surprise there turned out to be a procedure for tracing specific postings to an IP address.

He bent to the phone again. Sam wanted to remove the message right away but he persuaded her to leave it on the page until he told her otherwise. Moments later he was in Faraday's office, telling him about the latest posting and saying he'd been unduly pessimistic about Facebook.

'Their legal department is in California, boss. There's something called MLAT. Don't ask me what it stands for but it operates on the embassy-to-embassy level. If we register our interest now, the US embassy in London talks to Facebook and Facebook ring-fences all IP data for ninety days. We wouldn't get a result for months, but if we turn up in Palo Alto with the right pieces of Interplod paper, it's doable.'

'They can come up with a name?'

'An IP address. With that we'd be halfway there.'

'So what's the time frame?'

'Three weeks. Absolute minimum. You want to take a look at the Facebook message? It's on my PC screen.'

Faraday followed Suttle down the corridor. DCI Parsons had just been on to him about the Aults. They were arriving at Heathrow tomorrow morning at silly o'clock. Given Faraday's knowledge of the interview statements, she thought it might be a nice gesture for him to drive up there with the Family Liaison Officer. Parsons had last talked to Peter Ault yesterday, when he and his wife were still in Sydney. They'd been happy to accept the offer of a lift back down to the South Coast. For the time being, until they got their house back, they'd be staying with friends in Denmead. Maybe they could be dropped off.

The prospect of a 4 a.m. start from the Bargemaster's House had filled Faraday with gloom. Now he needed to know about any late developments that might sweeten his conversation with the Aults.

They stepped into the Intelligence Cell. Suttle nodded at the PC screen. Faraday read the message about Danny Cooper.

'Someone's hanging that bloke out to dry. Nothing like reading your own death sentence, is there?'

Faraday found himself nodding. Suttle had a point. If Rachel Ault had paid the price for her father's summing-up, then Danny Cooper ought to keep his door locked at night. Assuming he'd planted the cocaine in the first place.

'So how do we find Cooper? Do we have a duty of care here, or what?'

'No idea, boss.'

Suttle keystroked his way into the database that Hantspol maintained on everyone who'd come to its attention. Cooper was logged for a couple of motoring offences and a sus possession charge that had come to nothing.

'They're giving 67a Lovett Road, Copnor.' Suttle had dealt with the same address on another job. 'That's way out of date. A couple of numpties from Waterlooville are dossing there now.' He glanced round at Faraday. 'Cooper is tied to Mackenzie. Bazza used to say the boy was a real prospect. He doesn't use that kind of language any more but I bet he knows where the bloke's living.'

'Mackenzie? And you're really suggesting he'd come through with an address?'

'I doubt it.'

'Should we be talking to someone close to him, then? Someone who works for him? Someone who might have the great man's ear?' Faraday offered Suttle a weary smile. 'Any ideas, Jimmy?'

Winter was back out on his balcony, enjoying the sunshine. In these situations, he reasoned, it was always better to wait. The trill of his phone caught him drifting into a late-afternoon nap.

'Jimmy ...' He was checking caller ID. 'Thanks for getting back, son.'

'Back?'

'I belled you earlier. Don't you check your messages?'

Suttle said he'd been busy. He needed an address.

'Who for?'

'Danny Cooper.'

'Check RMS.' The force Records Management System.

'We just did. It needs updating.'

'But why ask me?'

'Because you work for Mackenzie. And he'd know.'

'Then I'll have to ask him, son.'

'Of course.'

'And get back to you.' He paused. 'I've got a phone number that might interest you.'

'Yeah? Who for?'

'Jax Bonner. She's been belling the *News*. Your mate Lizzie's been ever so helpful.'

'Jax Bonner?' The quickening in Suttle's voice put a smile on Winter's face.

'The very same. I'm looking at it now. One condition, though. We share the address when you find it.'

There was a silence on the line. Winter was still trying to picture the scene in the Intelligence Cell when Suttle came back. 'No problem. Just give me the number.'

'You'll bell me back?'

'Of course.'

This, Winter knew, was a test. It would be child's play for Suttle to screw him on the deal. Minutes later, to Winter's intense pleasure, the boy was as good as his word.

'It's a public box,' he said. 'in Cosham High Street. Do you have a time on the call? Only we can check the box on CCTV. There's a camera just up the precinct.'

'Talk to Lizzie Hodson. They may have the call logged.'

'Yeah? Cheers. What did Mackenzie have to say about Danny Cooper? Does he have an address?

'Dunno yet, son. He's belling me back any minute now.'

The line went dead. Winter stepped back into the lounge and replaced the cordless on its cradle. Jax Bonner hadn't been as dumb as he'd thought. Only the skint or the desperate used public boxes these days, but if you were in Jax Bonner's situation and wanted to avoid falling hostage to the geeks in the Netley Comms unit, it would be a whole lot safer than using a mobile.

Winter went into the kitchen and filled the kettle. There was another implication here and he realised he'd been slow to spot it. You'd only check CCTV if you thought Bonner had company. And you'd only do that if you had grounds for thinking she was shacked up with someone else. Maybe they've got intelligence from the party, he thought. Or maybe they've taken a proper look at the flat in Merrivale Road and found evidence of someone else in the place.

He made himself a pot of tea and padded back outside to the sunshine. Jimmy Suttle answered his call on the second ring.

'Bazza says he's sorry about Danny Cooper.' Winter reached for the sugar bowl. 'He wrote the address down the other day but he's buggered if he knows where.'

Faraday was in conference with DCI Parsons when his mobile began to trill. He'd recently downloaded a ringtone eerily close to the call of a curlew and even Parsons was impressed.

'Lovely,' she said. 'Do you want to take that?'

168

Faraday checked caller ID, recognising the number at once. 07854 6333524. Gabrielle's mobile.

'Do you mind, boss?' Faraday got up and stepped out of the office.

The voice was young, Pompey accent, no messing. 'You a friend of Gabby's?'

'I am, yes.'

'You know where we can find her?'

'I've no idea. You want me to pass on a message?'

The caller went away. Faraday could hear voices raised in the background. Then the conversation resumed.

'We wants to see her tonight, yeah? Bransbury Park, all right? Usual place.'

'What time?'

'Half seven. And tell her we're really sorry, yeah?'

The line went dead. Faraday gazed at the phone a moment then stepped back into the office. A kid's voice, definitely. He must have accessed Faraday's number from Gabrielle's phone. He'd obviously no idea who he'd been talking to.

Parsons was busy on a call of her own. She and Faraday had pretty much finalised a strategy for dealing with the Aults, and she was already locked into another conversation. Shielding the mouthpiece, she said she'd catch up with him later. Then she nodded at the mobile, still in Faraday's hand, and raised an enquiring eyebrow.

Faraday shook his head. 'Personal call, boss. Nothing for us.'

Back in his own office he shut the door and sank into his chair. He knew he had a decision to make and he knew as well that the consequences of getting it wrong could be catastrophic. He brooded for a while, gazing out of the window, watching a pair of seagulls mobbing a crow. He was back in the bedroom last night, his arms around Gabrielle. He could feel the chill of her bloodied face pressed against his shirt. Nothing he'd done had stopped her shivering. Nothing he'd been able to say had brought her real comfort. She'd been badly frightened. And now this.

Finally he reached for the phone. Sometimes, he thought, you simply close your eyes and jump.

'Jimmy? I need a moment of your time. My office. As soon as you like.'

For the second time in less than a week Winter found Esme's face on his video entryphone. He opened his door and waited for her in the hall. She emerged alone from the lift.

'Where are the kids?'

'Parked at Mum's.'

'You should have brought them down.'

'I wanted this to be private.'

Winter led her into the apartment. She'd inherited her mum's leggy Scandinavian good looks plus a helping of Bazza's low cunning. Bazza had put her through university and law school, but though she was qualified as a solicitor she'd never practised. These days, she always told Winter, three kids, seven acres and four horses were more than enough. All that, plus a husband.

'Tea? Something stronger?'

She shook her head. She didn't want this to take long. She eyed the open door to the balcony then settled herself on the sofa. Winter took the hint and closed the balcony door.

'What's the matter?'

'It's nothing ... I hope.'

She frowned, picking at a nail, then said she'd had a call from her dad late last night. She thought he'd been drinking a bit, which was unusual these days.

'What did he want?'

'A favour. He said he'd been talking to a mate of his. About getting stuff on Facebook.'

'*Facebook*? Baz?'

'Exactly. That's what I thought. But then he told me he was really fed up with all the grief next door and he wanted to do something about it. To be frank, he wasn't very coherent. I think deep down it's about the Aults. He's dreading tomorrow. He just doesn't know what to say to them.'

'They're back?'

'Yes. Mum says they land first thing. They're bound to come down to the house at some point. The police haven't finished with the place yet but they'll still want to see what's going on. Plus, of course, they'll want to talk to Dad.'

'So what did he ask you to do?'

'Post a message.'

'On Facebook?'

'Yes. This mate of his seems to be a bit of a geek. Apparently there are ways of posting untraceable messages. That's what he wanted me to help him do.'

He'd told Esme to get herself onto the Facebook website. That had been easy. She'd registered as Calico because that was her favourite bar on Martinique. Next she had to find a wi-fi network that was unprotected. At this point Ezzie had been out of her depth but it turned out to involve driving around with a bit of kit on loan from

Bazza's mate. Bazza himself would handle that end. Ezzie would do the driving and supply the laptop.

'Baz hasn't got a laptop?'

'He spilled tea all over it. Last week.'

'So you did this thing together? Is that the way it worked?'

'Yes. I came down this morning, dumped the kids with Mum, picked up Dad, then off we went. He had this gizmo on his lap. It signals when you're in range of an unprotected wi-fi network. They're everywhere. People don't bother with passwords. You wouldn't believe it.'

In the end, she said, they'd parked outside a house in Essex Road, chiefly because her father fancied the look of a woman who'd just left the place. She was obviously an airhead because she'd left her wi-fi totally unprotected and it had taken less than a minute to squirt off the posting.

'Where did it go?'

'I told you. Facebook.'

'But whereabouts on Facebook?'

'That page they set up for Rachel.'

'Really?' Winter felt his heart sink. 'And what did the message say?'

She looked at him a moment, mutual allies, then nodded. 'It was about someone called Danny Cooper,' she said. 'And I don't think Dad likes him any more.'

Bransbury Park was a couple of acres of playing fields hedged to the north and east by residential streets. Langstone Harbour was a stone's throw away, and from the front seat of Suttle's Impreza Faraday had a fine view of a couple of old ladies tossing bread to a cloud of gulls. The gulls milled around on the edge of the car park, fighting for scraps, and Faraday watched as one of the youngest stole a shred of crust from a bigger bird. Pompey gulls, he thought. Fearless. Cheeky. Painfully thin.

Suttle sat beside him at the wheel. Faraday had brought a pair of his birding binoculars and the young detective was scanning the expanse of grass in front of them. A broad footpath ran from the car park to the distant muddle of houses. To the left of the path a bunch of kids were kicking a ball around. Closer, maybe a hundred metres, was a brick-built pavilion which housed changing rooms for the winter soc-cer leagues. At this time of the evening the pavilion would be locked but Faraday agreed there was no other obvious place to meet.

It was gone seven. Suttle had borrowed a camera and a big tele-photo lens from a friend. Briefing him, Faraday had kept the details to a minimum. His partner had a professional involvement with kids on the city's estates. She'd run into a spot of bother the previous evening. These same kids were now demanding a meet and she'd agreed to turn up. Faraday was naturally keen to keep an eye on her and welcomed the chance to put a face or two on film. Two birds, he'd added wearily. One stone.

Suttle, intrigued, had asked whether or not this was official. The word had brought a mirthless smile to Faraday's face. Had he informed DCI Parsons about this little piece of free enterprise? The answer was no. Might it fit into *Mandolin*'s developing jigsaw? Possibly not. And was Gabrielle aware that her partner was sitting in a car readying himself to spy on her? For the third time, alas, no.

So why didn't Faraday just sort it out himself? Why involve Jimmy Suttle? It was a good question, exactly what he'd have expected from someone of Suttle's calibre, and Faraday had been equally honest in his reply. His own camera was at home, he'd said, and just now he didn't want to meet Gabrielle face to face. She'd also recognise his car, which would destroy the whole point of the exercise.

'So why not just tell her?' Suttle had queried. 'Why all the sneaky-beaky?'

'Because she wouldn't have it. Either I do it this way or she meets the kids by herself.'

'So it's me doing you a favour, have I got that right?'

'I'm afraid so, Jimmy. Is that a problem?'

'Not at all, boss.' He'd smiled. 'My pleasure.'

A couple of kids turned up on bikes minutes later. They circled the pavilion, carving skid marks on the grass, then threw the bikes down and tried to get into the building. When one kid, the smaller of the two, found the door locked he gave it a kick.

Suttle reached for the camera.

'This lot, boss?'

Faraday nodded. He'd retrieved the binoculars and was concentrating on the far end of the footpath where it disappeared into the sprawl of houses on the other side of the park. She'll come through the estate, Faraday told himself. The Bargemaster's House was a five-minute walk away. Any other approach would mean a huge detour.

More kids had gathered around the pavilion. One of them must have been on the beach because he had a pocketful of pebbles. The women with the bread had gone but the gulls were still circling. The kid with the pebbles took a shot or two, then gave up. His mate, much smaller, was rolling a cigarette.

Faraday watched them, wondering which one had made the call

this afternoon. There were seven in all. They looked to be around twelve or thirteen. Most of them were wearing trainers with hoodies over track bottoms. Thin, hollow faces. Baseball caps pulled low.

'Any good?' Faraday nodded at the camera.

'Not bad. It's hard to get a decent shot at this distance. Faces, especially. Here ... help yourself.'

Faraday thumbed through a succession of shots on the tiny screen at the back of the camera. Suttle was right. Nothing definitive. Nothing that would find its way into one of Jerry Proctor's Scenes of Crime albums.

'Keep at it,' Faraday muttered. 'This has to be the place.'

He raised the binos again, wondering what had kept Gabrielle. It was nearly quarter to eight. Normally she wouldn't dream of being late. He began to wonder whether she'd decided not to come, whether the state of her face had kept her indoors, but then dismissed the thought. On the phone a couple of hours ago, when he'd passed on the message, she'd sounded matter-of-fact about this abrupt summons. Maybe they want to give me my mobile back. Maybe they want to say sorry. *Pourquoi pas?*

She appeared minutes later, a small vivid figure emerging from the estate beyond the end of the path. Faraday muttered a warning to Suttle, aware of him swinging the big lens away from the pavilion. She was wearing a denim jacket over a pair of black jeans. The *Médecin Sans Frontières* T-shirt had been hanging on Faraday's washing line only yesterday. My partner, he repeated to himself. My muse.

'What happened to her face?' Suttle sounded alarmed.

'She got jumped. Last night.'

'By these kids?'

'No. At least I don't think so.'

'You don't *think* so?'

'I don't know. Keep snapping.'

Suttle raised the camera again, riding the focus as Gabrielle got closer.

The kids had seen her too. One set off on his bike. The others followed. They all met on the path. Through the binos Faraday watched them mobbing her. The smallest kid, the smoker, seemed to be doing most of the talking. He kept looking up at her, then touching his own face. Then one of the bigger kids dug in his pocket and produced a phone. Gabrielle examined it, gave him a nod of thanks, stowed it away in her daysack.

Seconds later, like pollen, the kids had gone, just blown away on the evening breeze. They weaved back down the path on their bikes, the young smoker standing on his pedals, his thin body twisted as he gave Gabrielle a farewell wave. Faraday could hear them now, yelling to each other. One of them was heading towards the road that led to the seafront. They streamed past the Impreza, weaving in and out among the parked cars. One of them aimed a playful kick at a nearby van. Then they were gone.

Gabrielle was standing on the path, still watching them. At length she retrieved the phone from her daysack and keyed in a number. Moments later Faraday's mobile began to ring.

Suttle had seen it too. He started laughing. Faraday put the mobile to his ear. Gabrielle sounded very far away.

'I got my phone back,' she said. 'Can you hear me?'

'Just.'

'Where are you?'

'Still at work.' It was a lie, Faraday thought, but only just.

He asked her whether it had been OK with the kids.

'Of course, *chéri*. You shouldn't worry. That's all they are ... just kids.' Her voice was getting fainter and fainter.

Faraday told her to check the battery. Maybe it needed charging. No answer. He watched her inspecting the mobile, then lowered the binos as she turned on her heel and began to walk away.

Suttle was still tracking her through the telephoto. As he took one final shot his mouth curled into a grin.

'This is seriously weird, boss.' He glanced across at Faraday. 'You know that?'

It took Winter more time than he'd anticipated to find the house in Copnor, and it was nearly dark before he was sure of the address. Danny Cooper's auntie opened the door to his knock and he knew at once that she'd recognised him from the previous visit. She stepped back, tried to shut the door in Winter's face.

'It's OK,' Winter told her. 'I just need a word with young Danny.'

'That's what you said before. The state of the boy, you should see him. You should be ashamed of yourselves. All of you. I told Danny to go to the police. You should be locked up, people like you.'

Winter admired her spirit. When she told him Danny had moved out, he was inclined to believe her.

'D'you know where he's gone?'

'I've not the first idea. And if I did, I wouldn't tell you.'

'He's at home then, yeah?'

She stared up at him, saying nothing, but Winter knew he'd got it right. Home was a newly acquired house less than half a mile away. Winter had made a mental note of the address a couple of weeks ago when Bazza had asked him to find a plumber to sort out a new bathroom for the lad.

He ducked back into the Lexus. Salcombe Avenue was five minutes away, a row of terraced houses that went nowhere. Beyond the wall at the end of the road was an acre or so of allotments. The houses backed onto a football pitch beside the railway line. Good place to hide yourself away, Winter thought as he looked for a parking place.

Danny Cooper's was the end property. It was getting dark by now. The windows were curtained at the front of the house, and Winter gazed up, looking in vain for a chink of light. He went to the door and rang the bell. When he got no response, he knocked. Again, nothing. He bent to the letter box and peered in through the flap. In the dim light he could make out a narrow hall. There was a smell of new carpets. He put his mouth to the flap, yelled Cooper's name, but nothing broke the silence.

He stepped back from the door. A path led round the side of the house. He squeezed past a bicycle and a water butt and found himself in a tiny back garden. A rusting bath was upended against the rear wall and he recognised the shape of an abandoned khazi under an old sheet. The back door beside the kitchen window was locked. He peered in through the window. An open bottle of milk stood on the draining board and there were a couple of plates in the washing-up bowl in the sink. On the table, against the far wall, he could just make out the headline on the front page of the *News*. He'd clocked the same story on a placard outside a newsagent's earlier in the evening. I was right, Winter thought. He's back.

He retraced his steps to the front of the house. A couple more knocks on the door. Still no response. He was looking for his car keys when he heard a door open across the street. Moments later a figure appeared from behind a builder's van. His jeans were scabbed with plaster and he was wearing a vest. He padded across the road, barefoot. He looked to be in his thirties, maybe older. He hadn't shaved for days.

'Help you, mush? Only it's normally nice and quiet round here.'

Winter said he was looking for a mate. Danny Cooper.

'Young bloke? Walks with a limp?'

'Yeah.'

'What about him?'

'He doesn't seem to be in.'

'Fucking right, he isn't in. Either that or the geezer's deaf.' He was looking at the Lexus. 'Nice motor. That yours?'

Winter nodded. He might be back later, he said. Just in case Danny came home.

175

'Sure. Help yourself, mate. But keep the fucking noise down, yeah?'

He gave Winter a parting scowl and disappeared behind the van again. Seconds later a front door slammed shut. Winter bent to the Lexus then checked his watch. Nearly nine o'clock.

It was dark by the time Faraday made it home. He'd returned to Major Crime from Bransbury Park, waiting in his office while Suttle transferred the photos to his hard disk and printed off the best of them. His mate wanted the camera back that night and he was keen to get the job tidied up before *Mandolin* took over his life again tomorrow morning.

After a delay sorting out a problem with a USB lead, he slipped the prints into an envelope and handed them to Faraday. In Suttle's view it would probably be possible to ID all the kids except one.

With Suttle clattering down the back stairs to the car park, Faraday had the Major Crime suite to himself. The big incident room at the end of the corridor was empty and everyone else had gone home. *Mandolin,* it was widely acknowledged, had at last settled down. On every investigation he'd ever known the squad took a while to find its rhythm. Sometimes it was a question of days before that happened, sometimes it was even longer. Given the chaos of Saturday night and all the media nonsense afterwards, Faraday knew they'd been lucky to stay in the driving seat. There'd been a bigger helping of frustration than usual, and no one was minimising the difficulties of finding Jax Bonner, but their collective nerve had held. There might even be a chance of a couple of days off at the weekend.

The thought of the weekend put a smile on his face. Gabrielle had been vague about the arrangements but he'd gathered that J-J was taking a train down from London on Saturday. If he got in before midday they could still make it over to the island for a crack at some decent birding.

He slipped Suttle's envelope into a drawer, locked his office and took the stairs to the car park. Traffic on the way home was light. He turned the Mondeo round, ready for the morning, then let himself into the house. On special occasions Gabrielle cooked sea bass with Pernod and fennel. Faraday could smell it now.

He stepped into the kitchen, determined to put the evening behind him. Watching Gabrielle in the park had felt deeply wrong. It was almost as if she'd been another woman, a passer-by who'd caught his fancy. There was a feeling of guilt compounded by a sense of helplessness. Why hadn't he done what Suttle suggested? Why had they never talked this thing through?

She met him at the kitchen door, tilted her face up, put her arms round his neck. She'd been in the bath. He could smell the oils she used. She was kissing him now, telling him how much better she felt, how much saner. She'd found the courage to face the kids, to listen to what they had to say, to tell them that last night didn't matter, that one day she'd come across this *racaille* who'd stolen her money and give him a piece of her mind.

Racaille meant scum. Faraday smiled down at her then touched her bruised face with his fingertips.

'Do you have a name for this *racaille*?'

'Yes. His little brother was there tonight. He said he was sorry.'

'The *racaille*?'

'The little brother. And you know something else, *chéri*? I nearly asked you to come tonight.' She paused, her eyes wide. 'Would you have done that? Would you have come to the park with me?'

Faraday thought about the question.

'There might have been a problem,' he said at last. 'There was something else I had to do.'

'Something important?'

'I'm afraid so.' He eyed the stove, wondering whether the sea bass could wait a while.

Winter got back to Gunwharf minutes ahead of Misty Gallagher. He'd stopped for a pint at the Cardigan and was contemplating a second when she'd phoned him.

'Paul? We need to talk. I'm at La Tasca. Baz has just walked out on me. Mind if I come across?'

La Tasca was a Spanish restaurant on the waterfront across from Blake House. It did a decent line in seafood and Winter knew Misty favoured it for special occasions. He told her he'd be back in ten.

The minute he saw her face in the video entry screen, he knew she was pissed. A couple of years back she'd had an apartment of her own in the neighbouring block. Bazza had bought it off-plan and sent her the key the day the contractors left the site. She'd filled it with leather furniture and a zooful of stuffed animals and made Bazza feel very much at home whenever he deigned to drop in. Nowadays, no less obliging, she occupied an impressive waterside property on Hayling Island, another of Bazza's canny investments in a decent sex life.

She stepped out of the lift and made her way uncertainly down the hall. Winter gave her a kiss at the open door and led her into the apartment. Hot pants and a tight-fitting designer T-shirt normally belonged on much younger bodies but at forty-three Misty Gallagher still turned heads wherever she went. She played the slut with real style. Even Bazza couldn't do without her.

After dark she drank Bacardi. Winter kept a bottle in the fridge but hadn't needed it for months.

By the time he returned to the living room, she was draped across the sofa. Her shoulder bag lay open where she'd dropped it on the floor. Winter counted three condoms among the litter of tissues, Marlboro Lights,and chewing gum.

'And Bazza?' He settled on the other end of the sofa.

'Manic, Paul. I haven't seen him like this since Marie kicked off at Christmas.'

Winter grinned. Marie had bumped into her husband in a lingerie shop in the middle of Pompey. He was buying a handful of expensive French bras. No way would 36C ever have fitted her own gym-honed bust.

'What was the problem?'

'He wouldn't say. Not to begin with. Cheers.' She winked at him. 'Old times, eh?'

A year ago, after Winter had finally turned his back on CID, Bazza had celebrated with the loan of his mistress for the night – part golden hallo, part showing-off. Winter and Misty went back years but this had been the first time Winter had understood Bazza's infatuation for the woman. A week or so later, bloodied in a face-off with one of his new employer's Southampton rivals, Winter had been dispatched to Dubai for a spot of R & R, Misty had been there, waiting for him, another mark of Bazza's gratitude.

Misty wanted to know about Bazza's neighbour. Some judge or other?

'His name's Ault. He's got a big house, just like Baz. He used to have a daughter too. You ever read the papers, Mist? Watch the news on telly?'

'Never.'

It was true. Misty's take on the world was shaped almost exclusively by copies of *OK* magazine. Celebrity, she always said, was more fun than car bombs in Baghdad and starving kids in Africa.

'This bloke's important to him? The judge?'

'Yeah.'

'But why, Paul? He never had any time for people like that before.'

'You're right, Mist. But that's because he's never lived next door to them before. They're all pals now. Him, and Aulty, and the heart surgeon who lives down the end of the road. He'll be playing fucking golf next.'

'He calls him Aulty?'

'Not to his face. You see them together and you wouldn't believe how respectful Baz can be.'

'He's taking the piss then. Must be.'

'That's what I thought, Mist, but I'm not sure. Marie loves it. Thinks Craneswater's turned Baz into a human being at last. They even go to fucking dinner parties. Can you believe that?'

'I'm not surprised. She's been trying to change him for years. Cow.'

She nodded, fingering the glass. Winter loved her nails, a deep scarlet.

'So tonight ...' He yawned. 'What happened?'

Baz, she said, had phoned her last week. Around this time of year he always made a special fuss of her, something to do with when her daughter had been a baby. Trude sometimes came along on these occasions but she was in the Canaries at the moment, making her name as a rep, and so it had been just the pair of them at Mist's favourite corner table in La Tasca.

'The tapas, Paul. Those little prawny things on soft roe. To die for.' She reached for him, extended a hand, pulled him close. She wasn't quite as pissed as Winter had thought.

'And Baz?' he enquired.

'Just talked about the judge all the time. This Aulty. He's been abroad somewhere, is that right?'

'The Pacific. On some yacht or other.'

'And Baz owes him?'

'Big time. The judge and his missus are on the plane as we speak. Should be back tomorrow morning.'

He told her about Saturday's party, about the bodies beside the pool.

'Dead?' She struggled up onto one elbow. 'Baz never said anything about that.'

'He wouldn't. I think he's ashamed of it.'

'Baz? Never. He doesn't do shame.'

'That's yesterday's Baz, Mist. Now it's different. Don't tell me you haven't noticed.'

She was still thinking about the bodies. She had a pool of her own, another token of Bazza's undying affection. She spent most of the summer beside it, stretched out on a recliner, surrounded by bottles of tanning lotion and yet more celebrity magazines.

'He'll have to drain it and start again,' she said. 'Marie would freak out if he didn't.'

'Drain what?'

'The pool.'

'But the bodies weren't in the water, Mist.'

'Doesn't matter. Just close is enough. She'll have got the bleach in by now. She'll want to scrub the whole thing down. Baz too, probably.'

Winter grinned at her. This was a new take on Saturday's tragedy. 'Did you tell him that?'

'I couldn't. Like I said, he never went into details. It was just the judge. What he was going to say to this bloke. How Baz was going to make it up to him.'

'And you didn't ask? Didn't enquire further?'

'I couldn't, my love. You know Baz when he gets like this. He cops a serious moody and there's absolutely fuck all you can say. He never listens at the best of times. Tonight I might as well not have been there. You know what I mean?'

She'd loosened the belt of Winter's trousers. Her hand slipped inside. The nails, he thought.

'So what happened in the end?'

'He walked out on me. I thought he'd gone to the loo. After half an hour, a situation like that, you start getting worried. He's not that young any more, Baz. You can tell sometimes. There's a nice young waiter at La Tasca. Enrique. I asked him to pop into the gents, have a look. No Baz. Bastard.'

'Where did he go?'

'I've no idea. He'd been talking about Westie earlier. That was another thing.'

'Westie?' Winter's heart sank.

'Tall guy? Black? Heavy?'

'I know who Westie is, Mist.' He closed his eyes a moment, then lay back as she eased his trousers away from his belly. 'So why would he want to see Westie?'

'I'm not saying he did see him. It's just the last thing he said, that's all.'

'Like what? What did he say?'

'He said there was no point hanging around. And then he said there was no point paying a fortune to someone like Westie and not getting value for money.' She ducked her head for a moment or two. He loved the warmth of her tongue. 'How's that, Paulie?'

'Beautiful, Mist.'

'Faster?'

'No.'

'Slower?'

'Yeah. You remember that huge fucking bed in Dubai? At the Burj?

I've still got the oils I nicked. They're in the bathroom. You want me to get them?'

He opened one eye, waiting for an answer. Misty's head came up. She pulled off the T-shirt then loosened her hair so it tumbled over her naked shoulders. Then she grinned at him.

'We'll get round to the oils later, my love. Never talk to a girl when her mouth's full.'

Chapter seventeen

THURSDAY, 16 AUGUST 2007. 03.55

Faraday had set his mobile on silent alarm. Already half-awake, he felt the tremor through the pillow. He stole along the upstairs landing, washed and shaved, made himself a pot of tea among the wreckage from last night's meal.

By half past four he was on the road.

The Family Liaison Officer, D/C Jessie Williams, lived in Fareham and Faraday had made arrangements to pick her up in the car park of the Marriot Hotel at the top of the city. He found her standing beside her Fiesta, eyeing a spectacular sunrise. After a year on Major Crime she'd won herself a solid reputation among the more experienced detectives. She knew how to get alongside people, to buffer them from news worse than they could possibly imagine yet still preserve a certain distance. And it was from that distance, as Faraday knew, that you so often conjured a result.

They drove north. Even at this time in the morning the traffic was beginning to thicken. By six o'clock they were on the approach road to Heathrow's Terminal Four. Jessie had the travel details. She'd already contacted Qantas for an update on the Aults' flight. QF319 was slightly ahead of schedule. With luck they should be coming through Customs within the next half-hour.

Faraday parked in the multi-storey. Scenes of Crime had recovered photos of Ault from the wreckage of the judge's study. The least-damaged showed a tall figure in his mid-fifties. The shot had been taken on a marina pontoon. He was wearing a strawberry-coloured shirt and a pair of patched jeans. He had a thatch of greying hair swept back from a high forehead. Horn-rimmed glasses gave his face a certain sternness, though nothing could hide the fact that he was enjoying himself. He was carrying a canvas holdall in one hand and a life jacket in the other. He looked fit, tanned and very obviously happy. God help him, thought Faraday, pocketing the photo.

A steady stream of passengers was already emerging into the

Arrivals Hall. These were overnight long-haul travellers, the walking dead, their trolleys piled high with luggage. Faraday found a space behind the rope while Jessie fetched a tray of coffees from a nearby Starbucks. By the time she got back Faraday was deep in conversation with a Qantas official. It seemed there'd been a problem with Mr Ault en route. He'd complained of chest pains and his wife was insisting on a check-up. They were still airside while staff organised an ambulance to take him to nearby Hillingdon Hospital. It might be best to meet them there.

Faraday had no option but to agree. He got directions to the hospital and finished his cappuccino in the car. The hospital was fifteen minutes away. By the time he'd found the A & E department it was nearly half past seven. Late yesterday he'd agreed a meet with Jerry Proctor at Sandown Road in case the Aults wanted to take a preliminary look at their property. The Scenes of Crime team anticipated releasing the house by mid-morning and Jerry was standing by to brief them.

Faraday punched in Proctor's number. The phone was on divert. He explained the delay at Heathrow and asked Jerry to get in touch. Pocketing the phone, he looked up to find Jessie on her feet beside him.

'This is Mrs Ault.' She indicated a slim pretty woman in a rumpled cotton suit. She was younger than Faraday had anticipated and, to no one's surprise, she looked exhausted.

'Call me Belle.' Her hand felt cold. 'I'm afraid Peter may be a while yet.'

The pain, she said, had come on after they'd left Singapore, first in his chest, later in his tummy. Personally she was putting it down to stress though it made absolute sense to make sure.

'He's very fit, Peter. I can't remember a day's illness since goodness knows when. It's just ... all this ...' The gesture took in the pair of them. Then Faraday felt her hand tighten on his arm. 'Please don't think we're not grateful. We are. It's ungodly, getting up at this hour. It's just hard to know what to expect any more. One moment you're floating round the South Pacific, having the time of your life. The next ...' Another sentence unfinished.

Jessie suggested more coffees. There was a machine in the corner. A staff nurse approached. Somebody from the airline must have phoned because she seemed to understand the situation. She said there was another room available, more private. There was a canteen nearby as well, if they needed something to eat.

Faraday was famished. Belle Ault shook her head. Jessie departed for the canteen with an order for bacon sandwiches while Faraday and Belle followed the staff nurse. The room was furnished with families in mind. Two lines of mock-leather armchairs faced each other across a couple of feet of stained carpet tiles, while the corners of the room were piled high with toys. Faraday did his best to spare Rachel's mother the sight of a line of stuffed panda bears.

Uncomfortable with the silence, she began to talk. The voyage, it seemed, had been the experience of a lifetime. The yacht had once belonged to Peter. It was called *La Serenissima*. He'd loved it to bits but it represented a great deal of money and he'd been gallant enough to sell it when they'd needed funds to buy the house in Sandown Road. The buyers had been very good pals of theirs, equally mad on sailing, and the husband – just retired – had decided to spend the best part of a year on a voyage around the world.

'We were thrilled, of course. That was something that Peter himself had always had in mind. Then our pals threw a dinner party one night and they came up with this plan. They'd divided the voyage into a dozen or so stages. Each stage was in a little white envelope and after dinner we all drew lots to join them on the voyage. Peter's face when she opened our envelope … Fiji to Auckland, via Vanuatu. It was a dream come true. We were so, so lucky.'

Mention of Vanuatu drew Faraday's attention. Not so long ago he'd been in a relationship with an Australian video producer called Eadie Sykes. It hadn't worked out between them, but Faraday had been left with a deep curiosity about Eadie's birthplace.

'Did you come across a place called Ambrym? Part of what we used to call the New Hebrides?'

'We did. Beautiful spot. Enchanting. We anchored in the bay there. Peter caught a bucketful of mullet and we barbecued them that night on the beach. The stars. The heat. We were spoiled to death …' She tipped her head back, instantly regretting the phrase, and Faraday found himself wondering how many more of these traps awaited her in the weeks to come. Readjusting after a trip like this would be difficult under any circumstances. To lose your home and your only child in the space of a single phone call was inconceivable.

She picked up the conversation again but her heart wasn't in it. From Vanuatu, she said, they'd headed south on a course that would finally take them to New Zealand. There'd been flying fish and schools of dolphins. They'd been tracked by an albatross for an entire day and caught a faraway glimpse of a spouting whale. The weather had begun to get colder. They'd even discussed using sleeping bags at night. Then the phone had rung and it was suddenly time to go home. Home was another word she clearly found painful.

She fumbled for a tissue. Blew her nose.

'How has your husband taken it?' A woman's question. Jessie's.

'Badly. As you'd expect. Rachel meant everything to him. I don't know whether you're aware of this but she's not his daughter at all. She's mine, from my previous marriage. But it was Peter who was always there for her, Peter who was the real daddy in her life, Peter who pushed her in the swimming days, Peter who dreamed about Oxbridge. All that's gone now, just ...' she was looking blankly at the wall, the tissue balled in her fist '... gone. No wonder the poor man's got pains in his chest. Wouldn't you? Wouldn't anyone?'

The question, unanswerable, hung in the air. At length Jessie suggested they rearrange the furniture, push two armchairs together, face to face, create a makeshift bed. She'd find a blanket, let Belle sleep a bit. She must be exhausted. Belle nodded. It had been a long flight.

Faraday got to his feet and went to look for the staff nurse. She found him a blanket and said that Peter Ault should be through by midday. The tests so far had revealed nothing. Faraday glanced at his watch. 09.56. Heading back to the family room, he became aware of vibrations from his phone. Jerry, he thought.

He was wrong. It was Suttle.

'Boss? Is that you? We've got another body. Division phoned it in ten minutes ago. I'm going out there now.'

'Where? Who?' Faraday was lost.

'A guy called Danny Cooper, boss. As advertised.'

It was Proctor who took Suttle out to Salcombe Avenue. A Scenes of Crime team was already driving down from Cosham and he needed to brief them before they started on the house.

'So what happened?'

'Apparently this guy's got a girlfriend. She doesn't kip there every night but she turned up first thing because they were going to Liverpool for a couple of days.'

The girl, he said, had a key to the house. She'd let herself in and made tea before taking a cup upstairs. When she got to the bedroom, she thought something was wrong because the door was open and she could see a pillow on the floor. The pillow was covered in blood.

'And?'

'She found him half in bed, half out. Multiple stab wounds. Blood up the walls, all over the sheets, everywhere. His throat was cut as well. Very Gothic.'

She'd freaked out, he said, and run over the road to a neighbour. The woman had come back to the house to check for herself then phoned 999. A traffic car got there first, sealed off the road, did the business. The call came to Major Crime just after nine o'clock.

'How do we know it's Danny Cooper?'

'Driver ID in his wallet. Plus there's mail downstairs that suggests the house belongs to him. His cards have gone and there's no money around so we can tick the robbery box. You're asking for a lot of grief, though, just for a couple of quid.'

Suttle agreed. He was already thinking about Jax Bonner.

'Means of entry? Anyone found a knife?'

'Too early to say. The only people to have gone up there are the two women and the P/C. Jenny Cutler's still duty callout so we're expecting her in a couple of hours. My lads will be in there once they're suited up.'

Jenny Cutler was the forensic pathologist who'd attended the scene at Sandown Road. One strike for continuity, thought Suttle.

He wound down the window. The turn into Salcombe Avenue was barred by blue and white *No Entry* tape. A wave of his warrant card took them past the outer cordon.

Proctor found a space for his Volvo. A Scenes of Crime van was parked at the other end of the road. The rear doors were open and a couple of Crime Scene Investigators were stacking walking plates against the wall of the end house. For the next day or so, with the exception of the pathologist, the house would be exclusively theirs.

Proctor set off down the road. Suttle was about to follow when another figure emerged from a nearby Audi. DCI Parsons was dressed for one of her more important meetings and Suttle found himself wondering who'd merit the beautifully cut two-piece business suit

'Boss?' He stepped across.

Parsons was gazing at the activity at the end of the road. She told Suttle she'd been en route to a seminar at Bramshill when she got the call from Willard. He wanted a steer on whether or not this was linked to *Mandolin*.

'You want me to action that, boss?'

Parsons nodded. She'd been looking forward to Bramshill for weeks. She'd been booked in for lunch with a prominent American criminologist and she'd even read the bloody man's newly published autobiography. Now this.

Bramshill was the nation's police college, a honeypot for officers with Parsons' scale of ambition.

'ASAP means by lunchtime,' she told Suttle. 'You're handling intel. Talk to Faraday. Talk to any one you bloody like but get it done. Balance of probability will do. Send me an email.'

She got back in the Audi. Seconds later she was on the phone. Suttle set off to join Proctor and the CSIs beside the van but then realised there was no point. Jerry was right. Until they'd been through the house, no one would be any the wiser.

He stood in the road for a moment or two, debating whether to wait for a lift back to Kingston Crescent or to call for a taxi. Then one of the uniforms strolled across. Suttle had met him a couple of times before. His name was Roly. He played half-decent football, guesting for the CID team.

'There's a woman lives opposite.' He nodded down the road. 'She thinks someone should be talking to her husband.'

'Why?'

'Apparently there was a bloke round last night, trying to knock the lad up.'

'The lad?'

'Cooper. She says he made a hell of a noise, pissed off her husband rotten. He went out, had a word with the guy, got a good look at him.'

'So where is he? The husband?'

'At work. He's a plasterer. Knock on her door. She's got a number for him.'

It was nearly five to eleven by the time Faraday left Hillingdon Hospital. Peter Ault had emerged earlier than expected from the battery of tests. His ECG trace had been normal, his pulse and blood pressure had been only marginally above average, and on the promise that he'd contact his GP for a more thorough check-up, the A & E registrar had been happy to discharge him.

Faraday had introduced himself. Ault was even taller than he'd anticipated. His height gave him a slightly forbidding air of command and it was easy to imagine him in court or at the helm of an ocean-going yacht. Like his wife, he was deeply tanned. He was wearing deck shoes, and the blazer carried a cheerful stripe, but there was a vagueness in his eyes that Faraday had seen in the aftermath of serious traffic accidents. Tragedy, he thought, is all the more cruel for being so unexpected.

They'd taken the motorway south, the Aults in the back of Faraday's Mondeo. So far Ault had spent most of his time staring out of the side window, his head turned away from his wife. Her hand lay in his lap and occasionally she gave him a little pat but he didn't respond. After Guildford she went to sleep, her head tucked against his shoulder.

Ault had indicated at the hospital that he was happy to be briefed on exactly what had happened at Sandown Road but it was a while before the flurry of calls to Major Crime gave Faraday the chance. On the face of it, the killing in Salcombe Avenue appeared to be linked to *Mandolin*. Suttle was busy testing the intel and Parsons was talking to Willard about possible changes in the command structure. A double murder had already stretched the current arrangements. A third might require a new SIO.

'Exactly how did my daughter die, Detective Inspector?'

They were stationary in traffic at the lights in Hindhead. Faraday caught Ault's eyes in the rear view mirror. It was a lawyer's question: precise, emotionless.

'She was stabbed to death, Mr Ault. You're welcome to see the pathologist's report.'

'Thank you. Mackenzie was good enough to put in a couple of phone calls. I understand she was found beside his pool.'

'That's correct.'

'So there was no question of drowning?'

'None. She never went in the water.'

'That's a pity.'

The traffic began to move. Faraday forced his eyes back onto the road.

'Why is it a pity?' he said at last. 'Do you mind me asking?'

'Not at all. Water meant everything to her. Drowning would have been ...' he shrugged '... appropriate, I suppose.'

Faraday nodded. It was a strange thought but he imagined it might offer some shred of comfort. He began to explain about the party, wondering exactly how much detail Ault had picked up from Mackenzie. It might be a kindness to prepare them both for what they'd walk into at Sandown Road. Scenes of Crime would have left the house exactly as they'd found it.

'So I'm afraid the place will be a bit of a mess,' Faraday warned him.

'So I gather.' Ault was staring out of the window again. 'What else did the pathologist find?'

Faraday hesitated. Was this the time to start discussing body fluids?

'Semen,' he said at last.

'Where?'

'In her vagina. And in her throat.'

Ault nodded. His face was quite expressionless.

'And was she drunk?'

'Yes.'

'How drunk?'

'It's difficult to say. We don't get the tox results for a couple of days yet.'

'You'll have witness statements, though. Probably a wealth of witness statements.'

'Of course.'

'So what do they tell you? About her state of inebriation?'

Faraday was conscious of the big head coming round, of Ault's eyes in the mirror again. This was like being cross-questioned in court.

'She'd been drinking heavily.'

'She was incapable?'

'I didn't say that.'

'And Hughes? This new beau of hers? Was he in the same state?'

'He'd been drinking, certainly.'

'And was he stabbed too?'

'No. He had a head injury. The pathology's not complete yet.'

Ault nodded as if this line of questioning had confirmed some previous suspicion. He's looking to blame someone, Faraday thought. And he didn't much like Gareth Hughes.

'Berriman was at the party too,' Faraday said.

'I know. He had the grace to put a call through to the yacht. He told us how sorry he was. About Rachel.'

'You liked him?'

'Very much. We both did.'

'And Rachel?'

'She was head over heels. For years. In a sense I suspect they grew up together. My wife thinks they were like brother and sister but she was wrong: it was much, much more than that. I loved seeing them together. They were so close, so *physically* close. Believe me, Detective Inspector, it was a major disappointment when they went their separate ways.'

'To Rachel?'

'To me.' A brief wistful smile.

They drove on in silence, Ault meditative, his head tipped back, his wife still asleep beside him. Finally Ault asked whether there'd been drugs at the party.

'Yes.' Faraday nodded. 'There were.'

'What kind of drugs?'

'Cannabis and cocaine.'

'In quantity?'

'Yes.'

'How do you know?'

'From witness statements, Mr Ault.'

'And what do they tell you, these witness statements?'

Faraday caught himself frowning. While he had immense sympathy for the Aults, he was beginning to resent this drumbeat of questions.

'It was cheap,' he said at last. 'In fact remarkably cheap.'

'What was?'

'The cocaine.'

'How cheap?'

'We think twenty-five pounds a gram.'

'That's very cheap indeed. As I understand it, that's less than half price. And the source?'

'We're still developing the intelligence.'

'I see.' He removed his glasses for a moment and rubbed his eyes. 'And do we know why this cocaine was so cheap?'

'I'm afraid not.'

'Pity.' Ault's fingers found the rocker switch for the electric window. The roar of road noise filled the car and he put his head back, letting the draught lift the greying thatch of hair.

Minutes later Faraday mentioned Scott Giles.

'I understand you sat at his trial, Mr Ault.'

'That's correct.'

'Was there any ... ah ... reaction afterwards?'

'In what sense?'

Faraday hunted for the right word. Feedback was too limp. Jax Bonner didn't do feedback.

'Did you have any contact with his immediate family? Might there have been threats?'

'To whom?'

'To you.'

'On what grounds?' Ault was engaged now. 'You're suggesting the jury were mistaken? You think they got their verdict wrong?'

'I'm suggesting nothing, Mr Ault. In these situations we look for motive. That's our job. One of the uninvited guests at that party was Giles's sister. She has a record for violence. She appears to be unstable. There might be grounds for thinking she was upset.'

'With me?'

'Yes.'

'Because of some miscarriage of justice?'

'As she may have seen it ...' Faraday slowed for a roundabout '... yes.'

'So she killed my daughter? Some primitive act of revenge? Is that what you're suggesting?'

Faraday nodded. Ault was clearly upset. Next he'd be blaming himself for Rachel's death.

He brooded for a while. Then he shook his head. 'I've had no communication whatsoever from the family. This girl's name, Detective Inspector?'

'Jax Bonner.'

'Jax.' The smile was icy. 'Very colourful. You've talked to her?'

'She's disappeared.'

'I see.'

Faraday was wondering whether now was the moment to describe the state of Ault's portrait. Jax Bonner had slashed it to shreds. The evidence was beyond dispute. Later, he thought. Once he's had a little time to reflect.

'I'm afraid there may be an issue with robbery as well,' he said instead. 'We haven't been able to compile any kind of list as far as your house is concerned but one or two items are clearly missing.'

'Like?'

'Rachel's laptop for one thing. Evidentially it's obviously of interest to us but it seems to have disappeared. In time we may be able to recover it but I'm afraid there's no guarantee.'

'You shouldn't bother.'

'Why not?'

'I've got it. It's in the luggage. She lent it to me for the cruise. And I must say it was immensely useful.'

His wife began to stir beside him. Ault spared her a glance, no more. Then he tipped his head back again and closed his eyes.

'Can you hazard a guess about the last few days? Since we got the news? Can you imagine what people like us *do* in a situation like that?'

'I can't, Mr Ault. It must be awful.' It was Jessie.

'Awful, I'm afraid, doesn't quite do it justice. Unreal is closer. You get a call like that, a voice you've never heard in your life, and you want to pretend it's some kind of nightmare. You want to tell yourself it hasn't happened. But then you log on to one of the news sites, BBC, Sky, and there it is – your house, your front door – and you realise that it must be true. Your daughter really is dead. Not unreal at all. Surreal.'

He hadn't slept at all on the voyage back to Vanuatu, he said. He'd stood two watches back to back, and then gone below when the skipper insisted he try and rest.

'And did you?'

'Of course not. You think. You reflect. You dwell. You dig down through the years. She used that laptop like a diary, like a best friend. I could hear her voice. I could share her thoughts. I could practically *touch* her. So close. Yet gone. Just like that. Gone forever.'

Gone, Faraday thought. His wife had used exactly the same word. So simple. So final. Gone.

They were approaching Petersfield now. Very soon they'd have to make a decision about Sandown Road.

Faraday found Ault's eyes in the mirror. They were moist behind the big horn-rimmed glasses.

'We can carry on down to Southsea if you want to, Mr Ault. I have the Crime Scene Coordinator standing by. He's the one to talk to about your house.'

Ault thought about the proposition for a moment. Then he shook his head. 'Not yet,' he said, 'if you don't mind.'

Chapter eighteen

D/C Jimmy Suttle found Winter in a deckchair on the nudist beach, tucked away in the shadow of a disused MoD facility on the long stretch of shingle that curved towards the mouth of Langstone Harbour. Park up where you see the other motors, Winter had told him. I'm the fat bastard in the red deckchair.

To Suttle's relief Winter was fully clothed. It was a beautiful day, barely a wisp of cloud in the sky, and Suttle could feel the heat rising from the pebbles beneath his feet. An elderly couple nearby were sharing a picnic on a square of plaid blanket. The woman poured tea from a Thermos and then passed a sandwich to her partner. They had skin the colour of old leather.

To his surprise there was another deckchair beside Winter with a pile of clothes spilling out of a green Jaguar sports bag.

'Company?'

'Yeah.' Winter was finishing an ice cream.

'Friend?'

'That's a bit strong, son. More like associates.'

'Plural?'

'Yeah, people I need to talk to. One of them told me she likes getting her kit off before taking a dip. Thought I might pop along and keep her chair warm for when she's had enough.'

'She knows you're here?'

'No, not yet. Neither of them do.' He nodded towards the blue shimmer of the sea. It was low tide and Suttle was still searching for a couple of bathers when Winter pointed towards the distant smudge of the pier. 'There and back. Apparently, it takes them about an hour.'

'*Swimming?* That distance?'

Winter nodded. He wanted to know what was so important it had got Jimmy out of his precious Intelligence Cell.

'You haven't heard?'

'Try me.'

'About Danny Cooper?'

Winter's head came round. The Calvin Klein shades didn't suit him at all and Suttle wondered whether he'd borrowed them.

'What about him?' Winter said.

'He's dead. The girlfriend found him this morning. You didn't know?'

'Why should I?'

'Because you were there last night. Looking for him.'

'I was?'

'Yeah. I don't suppose the bloke across the road introduced himself but his name's Mick.'

'He gave you a description?'

'Yeah. Balding. Overweight. Shiny trousers. Sweating fit to bust. You want me to go on? He clocked you and more to the point he clocked the motor. How many cars like that turn up in Salcombe Avenue?'

'It was hot last night.' Winter sounded defensive. 'Hot enough to make anyone sweat.'

'So you *were* there ... right?'

'Yeah.' He nodded. 'I was.'

'Why?'

'*Why?* Is that a copper's question? Or is this my ex-mucker being nosy? Only there's a difference, son.'

'There is?'

'Of course there fucking is. So tell me. Is this official? Do I bell my brief? Put my sandals back on? Let you drive me to the Bridewell? Or do we have a little chat here? In the sunshine?'

Suttle looked down at him a moment. Then he draped his jacket over the back of the other deckchair, moved the sports bag and made himself comfortable.

'Good decision, son.' Winter was demolishing the last of the ice cream. 'Did I tell you about your mate Lizzie? She asked me to pass a message. She says to tell you she's had enough of the sapphics.' He glanced across at Suttle and raised an eyebrow. 'Sapphics? Me neither. I had to look it up. I think it means she's not a lezzie any more, not this month anyway. Could be you're in with a chance.'

'Pimp now, are you? As well as my scumbag informant?'

'Very funny. Tell me more about Danny.'

Suttle gave him the facts. He held nothing back because he knew so little in the first place. Cooper, he said, had been stabbed. The attack had been violent, even frenzied. A knife had been used. Blood everywhere.

'Was the knife recovered?'

'I've no idea.'

'Witnesses?'

'Pass. You know the way these things work. Isolate the scene first. Then think about house-to-house.'

'But it's a cul-de-sac, son. People come and go. People watch.'

'Sure. And one of them clocked you. Which is why I rang.'

'Very thoughtful. I appreciate it.'

'You're not answering the question, Paul. You were there last night. And you'd help yourself by telling me why.'

'I owed the bloke a conversation. There were one or two things we had to sort out.'

'Like what?'

'I can't tell you. It was confidential, to do with the business. Bazza gets funny about stuff like that. He's a very private guy. You might have noticed.'

'This is murder, Paul. The machine's cranking up. Like it or not, it's going to spit your name out.'

'This bloke across the road's been statemented?'

'Of course he has. It'll be on HOLMES by now. I don't want to labour the point but you're not hard to miss. Balding? Overweight? Flash motor? This guy took the reg number, Paul. Not the whole plate but enough for a match. Seriously, you need to be thinking about things.'

'Thanks.'

'I mean it.' Suttle paused, letting the message sink in.

Winter propped the shades on his peeling forehead and gazed out to sea.

'You'll have to make this official,' he said at last. 'There's no way you can't.'

'That's right. It might not be today, and it probably won't be me, but it'll happen.'

'So why now? Why the call? What do you want to know?'

'I just need a bit of a steer. Does that sound reasonable?'

'Go on.'

'Was last night anything to do with Sandown Road?'

'You mean the girl? Jax Bonner?'

'I mean Sandown Road.'

Winter took his time.

'This is me being nice to you,' he said at last. 'I can't swear by it. And you lot sure as fuck won't get anything out of me if I end up in the Bridewell. But for old times' sake, Jimmy ...' he nodded '... the answer's probably yes.'

Suttle knew this was as far as he'd get. He checked his watch. 12.32.

DCI Parsons had stipulated lunchtime as a deadline for a preliminary report. He struggled out of the deckchair and retrieved his jacket. As he did so he became aware of two figures emerging from the water. They paused in the shallows, stepped out of their costumes and bent to rinse them before walking up the beach. The man was tall, well-built, broad shoulders, flat belly. The woman was older. Their hands touched briefly. They were laughing.

Winter was already reaching for a towel, aware of Suttle's interest.

'You're right, son. Matt Berriman.'

Faraday was at Kingston Crescent by two o'clock. The sight of Willard's Saab convertible in the car park braced him for yet another meeting.

He found the Head of CID in conference with Gail Parsons. The flowers on the window sill were beginning to wilt in the heat and Faraday detected a hint of weariness in the flap of her hand as she directed him into the spare chair. A plate of sandwiches at her elbow had barely been touched.

Willard wanted to know about the Aults.

'We dropped them off in Denmead,' Faraday told him. 'They're going to drive down tomorrow. I'll get Jerry to the house to meet them. Jessie Williams too.'

'How have they taken it?'

'Badly. As you'd probably imagine.'

'Do you think they're disappointed?'

'Disappointed?'

'That we haven't got a result yet?'

'I've no idea, sir. I don't think they've even got that far. They're still trying to cope with what's happened. Nothing we do is going to change any of that, is it?'

'You don't think so? He's a judge, Joe. He's not some punter off the street. He understands the system. He knows how these things work. He's bound to have a view on how we perform.'

'That's not going to happen. Not yet anyway.'

'How do you know?'

'Because the guy's away with the fairies. You can see it in his face, in his eyes. He's lost it.'

'That sounds like jet lag.' It was Parsons. 'I think Mr Willard's right. We need to be extremely careful where we tread.'

'Meaning?'

'Meaning he'll be watching us. Every step of the way. He's pals with Richard Brooke. Or maybe that's passed you by.'

Brooke was Chairman of the Police Authority. Faraday was tired of this conversation. He'd been here before only days ago. Politics again.

'We do our best, boss. As I'm sure you know.'

The silence was far from comfortable and Faraday wondered how long the pair of them had been up here fretting about Judge Ault. At length, Parsons' eyes strayed to her PC. Jimmy Suttle had just sent through a preliminary assessment of the Cooper killing. In his view there was a probable link to *Mandolin*.

'Based on what?'

'On the Facebook message posted yesterday. The one that mentioned Cooper by name. That has to be more than coincidence. Scenes of Crime have recovered some diary material from Scott Giles's flat in North End. Some of this stuff also mentions Danny Cooper and it appears to be in Bonner's handwriting.'

'We're treating her as a suspect?'

'Prime facie, I'd say yes. She has motive. Suttle's come up with a couple of calls she made to the *News* on a local number, so that would suggest she's still in the area. It looks like Suttle's also taken some other soundings.'

'With whom?'

'I'm not sure.' She was peering at the screen. 'It doesn't say.'

Willard broke in. He'd made a detour on his way in to check out the location for himself. If you were looking for a bit of quiet stabbing, he said, you couldn't do better than Cooper's place. The garden backed onto a football pitch. To the north there was a bunch of allotments. In terms of approach, no one would be any the wiser.

'Entry?'

'Through the kitchen door at the rear.' Parsons had just been briefed by Jerry Proctor. 'Scenes of Crime found the lock forced. They're thinking crowbar or tyre lever or something similar.'

'They've recovered a weapon?'

'Not so far. The house isn't big. I get the impression they should be through by this time tomorrow. They'll bosh the garden before they leave and we're doing a full POLSA search on the football pitch and the allotments.'

'Prints?'

'A few. I'm still waiting to hear from Netley.'

Faraday nodded. Lifts from the scene would be sent electronically to the force Fingerprint Department. Once Cooper and his girlfriend had been eliminated, the rest would be matched against a huge database.

'So what are we thinking?'

'We don't know. Not yet.' She glanced at Willard. She seemed to be waiting for some kind of cue. Faraday wondered whether he'd decided on a change in *Mandolin*'s command structure and whether this was the moment he'd find himself looking at new responsibilities. As it turned out, he was right.

'A name's come up already,' he said. 'And it raises certain issues.'

It was mid-afternoon by the time Jimmy Suttle got a reply on the photos he'd emailed earlier. He was looking for names to attach to the faces he'd snapped in Bransbury Park and copies had gone from his hard disk to a number of agencies in the city. Some could be sticky about imparting this kind of information but a call to the uniformed Inspector who sat on the city's Crime and Disorder Partnership appeared to have done the trick.

'The lad's name is Edmonds, boss. His mates apparently call him Jersey. No one knows why.'

Faraday had just stepped in from the corridor. He was standing beside Suttle's desk inspecting the best of last night's shots. Jersey Edmonds was the smallest of the kids, the one who'd waved to Gabrielle as they'd pedalled off towards the beach, the one she'd mentioned last night.

'Does he have an elder brother? This Jersey?'

'No idea. You want me to find out?'

'Please.'

Suttle scribbled himself a note. Faraday shut the door. They had the Intelligence Cell to themselves. Faraday helped himself to a seat beside the window.

'We need to talk about Paul Winter,' he began.

'I know.'

'You've seen the statement from the guy in Salcombe Avenue?'

'I met him this morning. I passed his name on to the Incident Room. Who actioned it?'

Faraday named a D/C on the *Mandolin* squad. He'd interviewed the plasterer on a building site in the city centre, less than half a mile from Kingston Crescent.

'It has to be Winter. Or that's what Parsons is assuming.'

'She's right.'

'You've seen him?'

'This morning. He admits it. He says he was there.'

'What else did he say?'

'Not much. He told me it was a business call but he wouldn't go into details.'

'He's still working for Mackenzie?'

'As far as I can gather.'

'Doing what?'

'I dunno, boss. Chasing blokes like Danny Cooper, I suppose.'

'And he gets a Lexus for that?'

Faraday let the question hang between them. When Suttle declined to take the conversation any further, he outlined Willard's concerns. Winter, in the view of the Head of CID, was openly working for one of the tiny handful of Pompey faces to have made the New Scotland Yard list of nominals. SOCA Nominals, convicted or otherwise, were the top UK underworld figures deemed important or successful enough to warrant serious attention. The party in Sandown Road appeared for once to have put Mackenzie on the side of the angels. Yet here was Paul Winter, an ex-CID officer and now one of Mackenzie's key lieutenants, implicated in a murder scene.

Suttle wondered whether 'implicated' wasn't too strong.

'You think last night's visit was some kind of coincidence?'

'I've no idea, boss. But we can't arrest him for knocking on Cooper's front door.'

'Even when he won't tell us why?'

'We haven't asked yet. Not properly.'

'But I thought you said you'd talked to him this morning?'

'I did.'

'On what basis?'

The question stopped Suttle in his tracks. He'd been crazy to be so casual about the meet with Winter, crazier still to admit it. He nudged his chair towards the desk and reached for the photo of the kids.

'Sometimes you take short cuts.' He lifted the photo. 'Sometimes it's easier that way.'

'I don't doubt it. You think last night in Bransbury Park was a short cut?'

'I was doing you a favour, boss.'

'And this morning? With Winter? Were you doing him a favour too?'

'How do you mean?'

'By warning him about Salcombe Avenue? By marking his card? By giving him a heads-up?'

'He'd have found out anyway.'

'Of course he would. You know that. I know that. But now he has a chance to get a story together.'

'If he needs one.'

'You think he doesn't?'

'I think he's extremely savvy. In fact I think he's one of the savviest blokes I've ever met.'

'And did that make him a good cop?'

'It made him a bloody effective cop.'

'So how do you measure that?'

'By the blokes he potted. I worked with him for more than a year. I lost count in the end.'

'Great. So how come he ends up working for Mackenzie?'

Suttle bit his tongue. A couple of days ago he'd have been asking exactly the same question but after the curry in the Gunwharf flat he realised there was another side to Winter's story, altogether less shameful.

He looked Faraday in the eye, wondering how much he really knew about Paul Winter.

'Appearances can be deceptive, boss,' he said quietly. 'Winter was never an easy guy to read.'

'What does that mean?'

'Here? Now?' Suttle gestured at the files scattered across his desk. 'As far as *Mandolin* is concerned?'

'Yes.'

'OK.' Suttle nodded. 'The way I see it, Winter is a resource we can't afford to ignore, not if we want to progress this thing. He works for Mackenzie. Presumably Mackenzie trusts him. Mackenzie himself also has a very big interest in getting this thing sorted. Those kids died by his swimming pool, remember. It's his reputation on the line. So my guess is that Mackenzie has cut Winter some slack, let him off the leash.'

'To do what?'

'To come up with a name or two.'

'For Rachel and Hughes?'

'Yeah. And maybe Danny Cooper too.'

'You know this?'

Again Suttle fell silent. Faraday was clever. Already Suttle knew he'd said far too much.

'Willard and Parsons want to play it by the book,' Faraday said at last. 'They always regarded Winter as a liability and absolutely nothing's changed. In fact it's much, much worse. He's well and truly on the Dark Side and he doesn't care who knows it. At the same time they're thinking what you're thinking, and because they're only human they want it both ways.'

'So what happens next?'

'They're suggesting we make a formal approach to Winter, offer him informant status.'

'He'd piss himself laughing.'

'And then?'

'He'd tell us to fuck off.'

'That's exactly what I told them.'

'And?'

'They said it has to be done. Done and recorded.'

'In the Policy Book? To cover Parsons' arse after the shit's hit the fan?'

'Of course.'

'So who makes this official approach.'

'You, Jimmy. And that was my idea, not theirs.'

Winter was still on the beach. The prospect of a hot afternoon in the sunshine had attracted a modest turnout of naturists and he was admiring a shapely redhead with a cheeky tattoo on her arse when Berriman mentioned yesterday's posting on Facebook.

He was face down on his towel, his head pillowed on his folded arms. Nikki Dunlop had gone home.

'You think Jax Bonner saw that posting?' said Winter.

'I think she'd sussed it already.'

'What makes you so certain?'

'I'm not. But I've been asking around and people who know her say she never talks about anything else. It's the court case, all the time. The judge. The dodgy evidence. Danny Cooper.' He rolled over, grinning. 'What she's not going to do to that fucking man.'

'What kept her then?'

'I dunno. People say she's flakey, a real headcase. She'd do a total stranger, really hurt them, for no good reason. Then you come up with someone who's really asking for it, someone like Danny Cooper, and she holds off. Or maybe bides her time.'

'And Rachel?'

'Rachel never asked for it. Rachel was different.'

'But you think Bonner did her?'

'I know it.'

'You saw it happen? You saw her do it?'

'No.'

'How do you know then?'

Berriman got up on one elbow and scratched himself. Then he lay back, his eyes closed.

'Because it couldn't have been anyone else. There were lots of ways of getting at Ault but Rachel was by far the best. This woman's off her head, remember. Plus she'd been sticking shitloads of cocaine up her nose.'

'That would be Danny Cooper's cocaine.'

'Yeah.' Berriman nodded. 'Weird, isn't it? He was knocking out gram bags at twenty-five quid that night. *Twenty-five quid*. Bonner bought a couple. I watched her do it.'

'Where did she get the money from?'

'Bonner?' he opened one eye. 'Apparently she's minted. Not minted exactly but definitely OK for dosh. Now her brother's inside, she gets all the rents from the lock-ups. You're talking hundreds of quid a week, easy.'

'Cash?'

'Could be.'

'So how does she collect it? With half the world chasing after her?'

'Good question. If I knew, I'd have been the first to find her.'

'And?'

'Danny Cooper would still be alive.'

The Scenes of Crime team finally released 11 Sandown Road at four o'clock in the afternoon. Five days' intensive work had yielded tray after tray of DNA swabs, umpteen seized items for detailed investigation, plus enough sets of finger and palm prints to keep the Netley specialists busy for months to come. In time, as Proctor pointed out in a testy exchange with DCI Parsons, there'd be enough cross-checked forensic evidence to compile a reasonably lawyer-proof account of exactly who had been where. Add the hundreds of images captured on seized mobiles and you might even end up with a detailed timeline. Quite how this would help progress the search for the killer or killers of Rachel and Gareth remained to be seen but the house itself could now be returned to its rightful owners.

It was Jessie Williams who phoned the Aults' Denmead friends to pass on the message. She spoke to Belle. Her husband, she said, had taken two strong sleeping tablets and gone straight to bed. In the morning she'd be phoning the family doctor to book an appointment for more medical tests. Peter had insisted there was no need but she was going to do it anyway. The next couple of weeks wouldn't be easy. The last thing Peter needed at this point in time was a heart attack.

Jessie Williams reported the conversation to Faraday. In her opinion the Aults might be wanting access to the house as early as tomorrow morning. The locks had been changed on the front door and someone needed to be on hand with a key. In the meantime, as requested, she'd made arrangements for a D/C to drive across from Netley to bag and tag Rachel's laptop. The contents of the hard disk would be cloned and analysed. Given the time scales involved, she added, it might be a gesture to offer to buy Ault a replacement machine.

Faraday turned the suggestion down.

'He doesn't want a replacement,' he pointed out. 'He wants the one we've seized. Just now it's probably the closest he can get to her.'

'He'll have to wait then?'

'I'm afraid so.'

'He won't like that at all.'

She was right. Something about this morning's journey down from Heathrow had begun to trouble Faraday. Peter Ault, he realised, could be a truly forbidding figure. Not just to a jury in court, or to a possibly innocent man in the dock, but maybe to Rachel as well.

Until this morning he hadn't realised that Rachel wasn't his natural daughter but a two-year-old he'd inherited when he'd met and married Belle. In one sense, Faraday told himself, it didn't matter. He'd brought the child up. He'd doubtless lavished upon her every kind of attention. Yet there'd been no kids to follow, no kids he and his wife could truly call their own, and now Faraday was beginning to wonder whether the judge hadn't invested too much of himself in Belle's daughter. He'd been rightly proud of her – of her achievements, of her prowess in the swimming pool, of her success in the Oxbridge exam – yet there was something else in his face that was altogether darker.

Even when the party was totally out of control Rachel had never lifted the phone to the police. Close friends of hers, in interview, had put this down to fear of how her dad would react if drugs were found and proceedings followed. Fear was a strong word but Mr Ault, they said, could be truly scary. At the time Faraday had been disinclined to place much weight on these comments but now, having met Ault in the flesh, he was starting to have second thoughts. There was something in his manner, in the way he'd chosen to cope with her death, that sounded an alarm bell deep in Faraday's head.

He mused a little longer, staring out of the window. Then his hand found the phone. He checked his mobile for Jessie Williams's number. She confirmed she had the new key to 11 Sandown Road.

'Is there a problem, boss?'

'Not at all. My guess is they'll want to see the house at some point tomorrow. Give me a bell before you take them round.'

'Why's that?'

'I'm coming too.'

Chapter nineteen

Winter finally found Mackenzie at a café-bar in the middle of Southsea. He'd been phoning him all day, without success. Marie thought he might have gone to London. Staff at the Royal Trafalgar said they hadn't seen him since early, when he'd helped himself to a plate of food from the breakfast buffet and retired to his office to make some calls. Now, he was sitting by himself at a corner table reading a copy of the *Daily Express*.

'She never did it, mush. Bloody police out there don't know their arse from their elbow.' He tapped a photo of Kate McCann beside a local detective in Praia de Luz. 'What's the Portuguese for Filth?'

Winter stood at the table. The café-bar was filling up.

'You want to go somewhere quieter?'

'Why?'

'Because we've got a couple of things we ought to talk about, Baz.' Winter offered him a thin smile. '*Comprende?*'

They walked the length of Palmerston Road. Mackenzie's Range Rover was parked beside the Common. The AA, he told Winter, had diagnosed piston failure. He'd need a new engine. Another five grand down the khazi.

Mackenzie turned left, towards Craneswater. Winter said he'd prefer a longer walk.

'Where to, mush?'

'The seafront.' Winter nodded towards the low grassy battlements of Southsea Castle. 'Do you good.'

Mackenzie was defensive by now. He wanted to know what was so fucking important it wouldn't wait until tomorrow. Marie was doing a barbie tonight. She'd got loads of tiger prawns from the fish market. He was already on a yellow card for turning up pissed last night. If he was late, she'd be vile to him.

'So where did you go last night, Baz?'

'What's that to you?'

'I need to know.'

'Why?'

'*Why?*' Winter seldom lost his temper. 'I came on board to look after your interests, Baz. That's why you took the risk on me. That's why it's turned out OK. That's why you pay me shitloads of money. So I'll ask you the question again. Where did you get to last night?'

Mackenzie shot him a look. No one talked to him like this.

'I was out.'

'Where?'

'Gunwharf. What is this?'

'Then where?'

'What do you mean, *then* where? If you must fucking know, I was out with Mist. We had a meal. We had a few laughs. I probably drank too much. Then I came home and got an earful from Marie. No big deal. Just another Wednesday night. OK?'

'Sure.' Winter sidestepped a curl of dogshit. 'Someone did Danny Cooper last night. I expect you've heard.'

'Yeah. Little cunt.'

'That someone went to town on him. Blood fucking everywhere.'

'How do you know?'

'I just do, Baz. It's what you pay me for.'

'OK.' Mackenzie nodded, coming to a halt. 'So the boy got himself killed. And from where I'm looking, I know who that someone was.'

'Yeah?'

'You don't see it?'

'See what, Baz?'

'See who must have done it? Must have taken a knife to him? All that shit about the court case? Scott Giles going down for a long one? Because of Danny stitching him up? This is seriously worrying, mush. Do I have to spell it out?'

'You think the girl killed him, Jax Bonner.' Winter said. A statement not a question.

'Of course she fucking did.'

'Broke into his house and cut his throat.'

'Yeah, stands to reason.'

'And you think she put that message on Facebook as well? Just to get the ball rolling?'

'Haven't a clue.'

Winter nodded, staring down at him. Then he began to walk again, towards the seafront. Mackenzie watched him for a moment or two then followed. By the time he caught up, he was out of breath.

Neither man spoke. They climbed the slope beside the castle and found a bench. Winter told Mackenzie to sit down. For once in his life he seemed to be listening.

'Did Ault come back to the house today?' Winter asked.

'No. Tomorrow. Belle phoned Marie.'

'And what are you going to tell him?'

'I'm going to tell him I'm fucking sorry.'

'About Rachel?'

'Yeah. And the house. And everything.'

'You think it's your fault she died?'

'Of course not, mush. But I should have been smarter, shouldn't I? I should have kept a better eye on things. Marked the girl's card.'

'About what?'

'About all the shitbag scum in this khazi of a town. Hold open house like that and you're asking for trouble. I should have seen that coming.'

'You couldn't. Not without checking out the invite on Facebook.'

'Fair play, mush. But Aulty's not going to see it that way, is he? Aulty's going come back to a fucking horror show. Plus his precious daughter's lying in a fridge somewhere waiting for someone to ID her. I need a name, mush. I need something that's going to make him feel better. I need to make him understand I've taken this thing seriously. He's going to expect it. I know he is.'

'And then you can be friends again? Mates?'

'Yeah.' He nodded, biting his lip. 'No reason why not, is there?'

Winter turned his head away. Miles away a huge tanker was nosing up the Solent towards Southampton. He watched it for a moment, wondering how far to take this conversation. Closer, in the shallows beneath the castle, two kids were battling over a lilo.

'I tried to find Westie today,' he said at last. 'Any idea where he might be?'

'None, mush. Why should I?'

'Because you'd know.'

'Would I?'

'Yeah. I also phoned Barbara. She sent a cab to Westie's place last night, at three in the morning. The cab took him to Gatwick. And you know who ordered the cab in the first place?'

Mackenzie said nothing. Barbara was the supervisor at the cab company he'd recently bought. 'You had no fucking right,' he said at last.

'To make the call? You're wrong, Baz. I had every fucking right.'

'You're behaving like a nonce. You're not a cop any more, mush.'

'Yes, I am. And I'll say it again, that's why you pay me.'

'To put me on the spot? To make me look a twat?'

'To protect you from yourself, Baz. There's a difference.'

'Yeah? So how does that work?'

Winter put his head back, turned it towards the sun.

'You went off to find Westie last night,' he said softly 'You told him to sort Danny Cooper out. Why? Because you're shit scared young Danny's going to end up answering a lot of hard questions about all that charlic at Rachel's party. That's going to get back to your mate Aulty. And your mate Aulty's not going to be best pleased. Am I getting warm, Baz? Or is this just a bent old copper barking up the wrong fucking alley?'

Mackenzie was staring at the kids on the lilo. Winter hadn't finished.

'And maybe there's more,' he said. 'Maybe you had some kind of hand in Danny fitting up the girl's brother because you thought Danny deserved encouragement. Good young prospect. Chip off the old block. Don't ask me what kind of hand because I don't know. All I can remember is Westie pouring boiling water all over the boy, and he doesn't do that unless there's a fucking big problem. But jugging the kid didn't sort it. Not in your head. Not with Aulty expected any minute. So you pop along to let Westie off his lead and next thing you've got him on the phone in the middle of the night with another big fucking problem.'

'Yeah? You really think so? Well, mush, let me tell you something about Westie. The bloke's lost it. The man's a liability. He's got a whack of money. He won't be back.'

'So you did see him?'

'Yeah.'

'Told him to go round to Danny's place?'

'Yeah.'

'Told him to kill the boy?'

'I told him to finish it.'

'Same thing isn't it? In Westie's book?'

'Dunno, mush.' Mackenzie shrugged, turning his head away. 'Westie's gone. He's off the plot. Good fucking riddance.'

'Sure. But you think it ends there?'

'Of course it does. He's careful, Westie. Wears gloves. Takes his time. I told him about the house. Go through those allotments; no one would ever see you.'

'Soil? Trainers? Sole patterns?'

'He wears Guccis.'

'What about his car? Afterwards? You're telling me he's not got a drop of blood on him? After what he'd done to the boy?'

'Fuck knows. If you're worried about Barbara, I'll square her. She's good as gold, that woman. The cab driver too. All it takes is money, mush. You should know that.'

There was a long silence. Mackenzie wanted this over. Winter could tell.

'It's still outside Westie's flat,' Winter said at last. 'I checked this afternoon.'

'What is?'

'The car. The Alfa.'

'So what?'

'It's a crime scene, Baz. It'll have Danny Cooper's blood inside it, maybe on the seat off Westie's kaks, maybe on the floor off those nice Guccis. And you know what else they'll find if they have a proper look?'

Mackenzie was still watching the kids. He shook his head.

'Prints, Baz. Yours and mine. From Westie's first little house call the other day. Remember?'

Faraday, over supper, broached the subject of the kids again. After last night he sensed it would be safe to stray onto Gabrielle's turf. She'd been frightened by the mugging, not simply in the obvious way but because it had been an abrupt reminder that no one was immune from these sudden spasms of violence, least of all a nosy French anthropologist with too many questions to ask.

'You told me last night you've got a name for the kid who jumped you.'

'*Oui?*'

'You want to tell me?'

'*Pourquoi?*'

'Because I might be able to do something about it.'

She shook her head, speared an asparagus stalk.

'*Non,*' she said. 'It's nothing. Maybe the boy needs the money. Maybe he's starving. *Ça ne fait rien.* Me? I have everything.' Her hand closed over Faraday's and gave it a squeeze.

'But you'll be careful from now on?'

'*Oui, absolument.*' She smiled at him. She appreciated his concern. 'Tell me something. The party on Saturday. The one where the girl died. There's a photo in the paper. I saw it yesterday. Jax Bonner?'

Faraday smiled. She pronounced it *bonheur*. *Bonheur* meant happiness.

'What about her?'

'You really think she did it? Killed the other girl?'

'I think we need to ask her some questions.'

'But you think she might have done it?'

208

'I think she could be dangerous.'

'*Chéri* ...' She put her fork down. 'You won't answer my questions.'

'That's because I can't.'

'So careful. So *prudent*.'

'Of course. You'd expect nothing else.'

'But you know where this girl lives?'

'We have an idea, yes.'

'So you've seen? You're watching her?'

'No. We've searched her house. She's gone.'

'*Alors* ...' She was frowning, weighing her next question, and looking at her face Faraday was suddenly aware that she knew. She knew about this girl. She might even have met her. Talked to her. She knew everything.

Faraday reached for her hand again, felt it curl round his.

'When I say dangerous, I mean she hurts people. I expect she hurts people for lots of reasons, but I'm a copper, not a psychiatrist, and it's my job to find her before she does it again. Because she will. Unless we stop her.'

'So you think she *did* kill the girl?'

Faraday made a habit of weighing questions like these extremely carefully. In his heart he knew he couldn't be sure but now wasn't the time to say so.

'Yes.' He nodded. 'I think she did.'

It was dark by the time Winter met Bazza Mackenzie on the seafront, directly opposite the block where Westie had a flat. Mackenzie pulled in beside the Alfa. He was driving Marie's Peugeot cabriolet, a present from last Christmas. The window purred down and Bazza waited while Winter crossed the road.

'OK, mush?'

Winter sniffed the night air, wondering whether Marie did prawns with her garlic. Mackenzie's mouth and jaw were still shiny with grease.

'Never better, Baz. Spot of twocking? Bring it on.'

He knew the idea was reckless but just now he couldn't think of an alternative. All it took was a single clue, a single oversight on Westie's part, and for most of his ex-colleagues it would suddenly be party time. A chance sighting of a black guy picking his way across a bunch of allotments? Something Westie might have left in Cooper's house? It didn't matter. Once the Major Crime lot had a name in the frame, they'd start looking for an ageing Alfa Romeo. And what they'd doubtless find inside didn't bear contemplation.

Mackenzie got out of the Peugeot. He had a screwdriver in one hand and a tyre lever in the other. It wasn't elegant but seconds later, with the door frame dented, he was sitting behind the wheel of the Alfa.

'Turn off that fucking light, Baz. I'm sure it'll all come back to you.'

Mackenzie reached up and tried to kill the courtesy light but without success. Then he bent to the dashboard and began to fumble around beneath it. Winter wasn't sure about his boss's hot-wiring skills and he certainly took his time, but in the end the engine coughed into life. The courtesy light had at last gone out.

'There you go, mush.' Mackenzie stepped out, looking pleased with himself.

Winter made himself comfortable, adjusting the seat and the rear-view mirror. Mackenzie was back behind the wheel of the Peugeot. He'd given Winter directions to an industrial estate in Portchester, up on the mainland. He'd be following behind, keeping an eye on things, but if they got separated in traffic they'd meet at the end of the journey.

'Look for Perfect Glazing,' he said again. 'Geezer called Barry.'

Winter backed carefully out, waiting for a couple of lads on scooters to whine past, then set off towards Bradford Junction. It was a while since Winter had a working knowledge of every CCTV camera monitoring the major junctions, and there'd doubtless be extra ones, but the route he'd chosen to get them out of the city still felt pretty safe.

He settled down, checking the mirror. He could see Bazza's face as they passed each street lamp. Mackenzie's fingers were drumming on the steering wheel and Winter wondered what music he was listening to. From time to time the Alfa's courtesy light flickered on.

Beyond Bradford Junction, Winter nosed into Fratton Road, then pulled a hard right, entering a maze of side streets that would spit him out at the city's northern end. Bazza was still tailing him.

Most of these streets were one-way, with cars parked on both sides of the road. Winter took it easy, keeping his speed down. On a Thursday night traffic was light. One of the busier roads he had to cross was Stubbington Avenue. He slowed the Alfa to a halt, waiting for a car from the right. Moments later he realised it was a traffic patrol car. Two uniforms peered out at him as they passed. Then the driver hit the brakes, stopped. Winter was already pulling out. He gunned the Alfa, aware of Bazza behind him. The traffic car was reversing fast into the road they'd just left. The driver had already switched on the blues. Next he'd hit the siren. Shit.

Winter eyed the speedo. Fifty in streets like these was asking for trouble. He tried to relax, tried to tell himself he was making the right decision. With his reputation there was no way he'd risk a stop-check. These guys would like nothing better than the chance to drive him down to the Bridewell and book him in. And what would happen then? Once they had a proper look at Westie's precious fucking Alfa?

He took a chance on the next intersection, never taking his foot off the throttle. Thankfully the road was clear in both directions. Bazza followed, a squat figure hunched behind the wheel, and it occurred to Winter that he was probably enjoying this. Being a grown-up businessman doubtless had its advantages but nothing beat the raw adrenalin buzz of a traffic car halfway up your arse. So how come the woollies had stopped in the first place? Winter shook his head. He knew there were a million explanations. Someone must have clocked them on the seafront and phoned the car in, he thought. Two dodgy guys round an Alfa. Too fucking right.

They were in North End now, and with a cold certainty Winter knew they were running out of options. The next intersection would take them onto one of the main roads funnelling traffic off the island. If they got that far, they were dead.

Winter was still debating whether to risk a high-speed turn into one of the side streets to the left when he heard a squeal of brakes behind him. Then, milliseconds later, came the sound of tearing metal and splintering glass as the police car smashed into Marie's new Peugeot. Already, in the rear-view mirror, the accident was receding. In seconds it would be no more than a dot. Winter, slowing for the turn into the main road, heard the sound of his own laughter. Bazza, he thought. What a fucking star.

The big roundabout at the top of the island took him onto the dual carriageway that ran to the foot of Portsdown Hill. Within minutes, he knew, the woollies would have every traffic car in the city looking for him. He took the Alfa up to seventy, slowing for the new junction beside the Marriott Hotel. Thankfully, the lights were green. He powered across, then slowed for traffic on the other side. Under normal circumstances the Marriot to Portchester was a five-minute drive. Tonight, once he'd passed a couple of dawdlers, he did it in three. He knew the industrial estate well. He'd spent hours here over the past decade, plotted up with half a dozen other guys, waiting to lift some scrote or other. Perfect Glazing was round the back of the estate next to the railway line.

He turned the Alfa onto the forecourt and killed the lights. After a while a figure emerged from the shadows and strolled across to the Alfa. Winter wound the window down. Barry Cassidy. An old face from the 6.57. From far away came the howl of a siren. Then another, much closer. Barry was grinning. He nodded at the gaping mouth of the industrial unit.

'In there, mush. Quick as you like.'

Jimmy Suttle gave up on Winter shortly after eleven. He'd spent the best part of the evening in a fish restaurant in Gunwharf. One of the management assistants on Major Crime had been raving about the Loch Fyne in the old Vulcan Building, and Lizzie Hodson had been happy to join him.

Now, strolling along the waterfront, Suttle paused beside Blake House. He was still curious to know why Berriman had been of such interest to Winter. *Someone I need to talk to*, he'd said. He looked up at Winter's apartment. The lights were off in the windows at the front and when he rounded the corner there was no sign of life in the kitchen or either of the bedrooms. Earlier he'd warned Lizzie that he might have to bring this evening of theirs to a premature end. Now there seemed no point.

He stepped back onto the waterfront, pausing to watch as the big night ferry to Ouistreham rumbled past. He and Lizzie had been talking earlier about a promotional offer in the *News*. Twenty quid all up for two night crossings and a day ashore. Watching the huge white bulk of the ferry, he wondered whether she'd been serious.

'Fancy it?' He nodded towards the harbour mouth.

'France?' She nodded. 'Yeah.'

'You're serious?'

'Definitely.'

'How's your French?'

'Not bad.' She slipped her arm through his. 'Maybe we ought to practise first.'

Chapter twenty

Faraday took the call from D/C Jessie Williams as he was driving to work. The Aults had just phoned. They'd been offered a lift down to Southsea and they'd be in Sandown Road around nine o'clock. Jessie had agreed to meet them outside the house. Was Faraday still interested in joining the party?

Faraday checked his watch. Nearly ten to nine.

'I'll meet you there.' He checked his mirror and began to signal left. 'Hang on till I arrive.'

As it turned out, his was the first car to make it to Sandown Road. He parked opposite the Aults' house and got out. After a week of sunshine the weather was on the turn. The forecast first thing had warned of rain by lunchtime. Already he could feel the first shivers of wind stirring the trees along the road.

The Aults arrived within minutes, dropped by their friend at the kerbside. Faraday half-listened to the two women making arrangements for a lift back to Denmead later. Belle clearly wasn't planning on moving back in, not yet.

The car drove off, leaving Faraday and the Aults on opposite sides of the road. At that moment there came a whirr from the electronic gates next door and another figure stepped onto the pavement. At first Faraday didn't recognise Mackenzie. He was wearing a neck brace and walking with a pronounced limp. His head was crooked, cocked to one side as he limped down towards the Aults. Then came the trademark grin and the pumping handshake.

It was Belle who asked him what had happened.

'Car crash,' Mackenzie explained. 'Got whacked up the backside. You think I'm bad, you should take a look at the Peugeot. Marie's livid. I'm blaming the guy behind.'

Belle began to sympathise but Mackenzie's eyes were on her husband and Faraday remembered the scene in the interview room moments after Dawn Ellis had broken the news about Rachel Ault. Mackenzie must have been rehearsing this moment all week, he thought. What do you say to a man who's just lost everything?

'Peter? You OK?'

'OK?' Ault was looking pained. 'Hardly.'

'I'm sorry. Really sorry. If there's anything ... you know ...'

'Thank you.'

'I mean it. We both do. Marie's got the guest suite ready, in case you fancied kipping round our place ... you know ... while you get things sorted. Be handy, just next door.'

'Thank you.'

'I'm serious.' He glanced towards their house. 'I don't suppose you'll be dossing down here for a while, will you?'

Ault looked down at him, saying nothing. Icy was a word that didn't do justice to the expression on his face. Mackenzie dug his hands in his pockets, doing his best to warm the exchange with a grin, but Ault shook his head and turned away.

Moments later Jessie Williams's Fiesta coasted to a halt beside them. She was sorry she was late. Traffic again.

Faraday joined them on the front door step while Peter Ault wrestled with the new key. Mackenzie had beaten a retreat.

Once the door was open, it was the smell that hit Faraday first, a foul gust of Scenes of Crime chemicals, stale cigarette smoke, spilled alcohol, sodden carpets and a ranker – more human – odour. Ault paused on the threshold and for a moment Faraday thought he might turn on his heel, find himself a bus, take the train to the airport, go back to Australia. Under the circumstances he wouldn't have blamed him. Not for a moment.

'Darling?' He turned to his wife. 'Do you really want to do this?'

She nodded, holding her nose. She looked like she wanted to throw up.

'You're sure?'

'Please, Peter,' she muttered, 'Let's just get it over with.'

Faraday and Jessie Williams followed them into the hall. Scenes of Crime had been as good as their word. They'd touched everything, moved nothing. This was the way Faraday remembered it from early Sunday morning. All it needed, he thought grimly, were the war cries from the Force Support Unit as they cornered the last of the stroppier kids.

Ault was gazing down at the remains of a bottle of wine. He picked up the bottle, sniffed it, examined the label.

'They went through the lot?'

'I'm afraid so, Mr Ault.' It was Jessie.

He nodded, said nothing. A padlocked door beside the staircase led down to the basement room he'd used as a cellar. The door had been kicked in then wrenched from its hinges. Ault bent to retrieve a scrap of yellow paper. It was a Post-it. He showed it to his wife. The warning was handwritten. *Locked*, it went. *Keep Out.*

'That's Gareth's handwriting,' she said. 'At least he tried.'

Ault raised an eyebrow, said nothing. He looked briefly at the wreckage that had once been his lounge and then turned to mount the stairs. Faraday stood back then followed. The study was on the left at the top of the stairs, the door already open. Ault lingered a moment on the landing, staring in. His leather-topped desk was covered in the smashed frames of the photos trashed by the kids. The sour taint of urine hung in the air and there was glass underfoot. You could hear it crunching as Ault crossed to the window. An old engraving of the Victorian Dockyard that hung beside the window had been tagged in black. The message couldn't have been simpler. *Lying cunt.*

Something else had caught Ault's eye. He was staring at the PC on his desk. Someone had put a boot through the screen.

'Where's my computer?' He was looking at Faraday.

'I'm afraid we seized it.'

'For what purpose?'

'We need to download the hard disk. We think there's a chance that Rachel might have used it to send the Facebook invite. We'll need to evidence that.'

Ault nodded.

'So when do I get it back?'

'Just now that's hard to say. I'd give you a firm date if I could but we're snowed under.' Faraday gestured round at the ruined study. 'I expect you'll understand why.'

'Of course, Inspector.' It was his wife. She was playing the diplomat.

Ault was looking at the drawers from the desk, both upside down on the carpet.

'These were locked,' he said stonily. 'I assume they were forced.'

'I'm afraid so. It's the same everywhere. Downstairs in the lounge. In the bedrooms. Everywhere.'

Belle was looking alarmed now. Faraday told her that Jessie Williams would be taking down a list of everything valuable that seemed to be missing. That was partly why they'd both come along.

'Partly?' Ault had sunk into the revolving chair behind the desk. 'So why else would you be here?'

'Moral support, Mr Ault. A time like this we find it often helps.'

'Do you?' He began to inch the chair left and right, getting the feel of it. At length he stood up again. He'd had a collection of antique coins in one of the drawers. In the other, as far as he could remember, was his address book.

'And the coins have value?'

'They do, Mr Faraday. But not as much as the address book. Lose that and you lose part of your life.' He gazed round for a moment then shook his head. 'This, to be frank, is terrifying. We left this place in good faith. It was our home. Maybe Rachel was foolish to do what she did, throw a party like that, but never ... *never* ... would you expect to come back to something like this. I feel ...' he frowned '... defiled. Dirtied. These people must hate us.'

Faraday nodded. There was nothing to say. He was right.

The tour of the house went on. The Aults' bedroom was the next room they checked. The sight of days-old faeces caked on the pillows of the big double bed drew a gasp from Belle. She went to her dressing table. The contents of the drawers were scattered across the carpet. She was about to get down on her hands and knees to search for particular items when Ault pulled her back.

'Don't bother. The good stuff will have gone.'

She looked up at him, mute, compliant, shocked.

'Of course,' she whispered. 'Silly of me.'

Last on the tour was Rachel's bedroom. Jessie went ahead, armed with the Scenes of Crime map of the house. If the Aults were going to need serious support, then it was surely here. She opened the door and then stepped respectfully back. It was Ault, once again, who went in first.

Faraday could see most of the room through the open door. The duvet cover on the bed had gone. Ault wanted to know why.

'It went off for analysis, Mr Ault. We found traces of blood.'

'Whose blood?'

'That's a question we can't yet answer.'

'Rachel's?'

'Possibly. Possibly not.'

'You're suggesting she might have assaulted someone else?'

'I'm suggesting she might not have been here at all. It was open house. As you can see.'

Ault turned back to the room. A poster for a swimming meet in Düsseldorf was hanging on the wall over her bed. The poster was covered in signatures. Ault stepped across and examined them. Finally he found what he was after.

'There.' His long bony finger hovered over a scrawl of crimson Pentel. 'That's Matt's signature. If she'd still been with him, this would never have happened.'

Faraday, aware of the anger in his voice, shook his head.

'But he *was* here, Mr Ault. And it did.'

Winter awoke to the *beep-beep* of the video entry phone. He rolled over, fumbling for his watch. Nearly half nine. He found a dressing gown and padded through to the hall. Whoever had their finger on the buzzer downstairs wasn't giving up. He squinted at the tiny screen then hesitated. It was Jimmy Suttle, trying to shelter from yet another downpour.

'Are you there, boss?'

For once in his life Winter hadn't a clue what to do. Last night he'd got a cab home from Portchester. He hadn't been in touch with Bazza. Had one of the uniforms ID'd him before the chase began? Or was this visit of Suttle's purely social?

'For fuck's sake, mate ...'

Winter shrugged, then buzzed him in. If it happens, it happens, he told himself. Better to be nicked by the likes of Jimmy than by a posse of gloating woollies.

Suttle was at his door moments later, soaking wet. He wanted tea, toast and a natter. To Winter's relief, he didn't mention the word 'arrest'.

They talked in the kitchen while Winter hunted for bread.

'What's this about then?'

'I'll tell you in a minute. We pulled your boss last night. Has he been in touch yet?'

'Baz?' Winter feigned amazement. 'Why would you do that?'

'Dangerous driving. We had a traffic car after a nicked Alfa. Mackenzie was in the way. Said he got panicked by all the fuss and put the anchors on. He totalled the traffic car and put a fucking great dent in his wife's Peugeot. Bit of a result, really.'

'Yeah? So what's the story on the Alfa?'

'Hard to say. Neither of the traffic guys managed to get a good look at the Alfa's reg plate because Mackenzie's Peugeot was always in the way.'

'No ownership checks then?'

'Obviously not.'

'OK was he? Baz?'

'Whiplash, apparently.' Suttle touched his own neck. 'Plus a bit of a leg injury. The woollies had to take him to the QA in the end. Mackenzie was threatening them with all kinds of grief if they didn't.'

'Health and safety?' Winter was laughing now. 'Don't tell me.'

Suttle wanted Marmite on his toast. When Winter couldn't find any, he settled for marmalade. Winter carried the tray in from the kitchen. Suttle eyed the dressing gown from the sofa.

'Where did you get that?'

'Hotel in Dubai.'

'It looks like silk.'

'It *is* silk, son. Pay two grand a night, and no one minds if you nick it.'

'Your money?'

'You're joking. I get my gear from British Home Stores.'

'I meant the room.'

'I know you did, son. Eat this fucking toast, will you?'

Suttle demolished the toast. He said he owed Winter for last night.

'How come?'

'Lizzie Hodson.'

'She came across?'

'She certainly did. I think we're in love.'

'About bloody time.' He reached for Suttle's plate and tidied up the crumbs with a wetted finger. 'You didn't come all this way to tell me that, though, did you?'

Suttle shook his head. 'I've been talking to Faraday ...' he began.

'And?'

'Our bosses are seriously upset at some of the strokes you seem to be pulling.'

'Like what?'

'Like turning up at Berriman's mum's place before we got a look at it. Like obviously having an interest in Berriman himself. Like visiting Salcombe Avenue an hour or so before the lad probably gets the chop. Like hijacking a deckchair on the nudist beach and waiting until Berriman turns up.'

'You told them about that?'

'Not in so many words. Not yet anyway. But there's definitely something happening here. People like Willard call it a pattern.'

'Willard's bothered? About me?'

'He is, mate. Which kind of makes this official.'

'They know you're here?'

'They fucking sent me.'

'Why?'

'Good question.' Suttle was warming up now, Winter could see it. 'To put it bluntly, mate, they don't know what to do with you.'

'With me or about me?'

'Makes no difference. Put it this way. There's one school of thought says it might be better to give you lots of rope and see where you go ...'

'And the other?'

'We lock you up.'

'You'll need a fucking good reason. Last time I checked arrest without grounds was still illegal.'

'Precisely. So the thinking is—'

'You give me lots of rope.'

'Pretty much.' Suttle nodded. 'Yeah.'

'But what the fuck does that mean?'

'It means you become an informant. We register you. We put you on PIMS. We give you money. We might even discuss limited immunity, if it comes to it.'

'If it comes to what?'

'If we find that you're ...' Suttle frowned '... implicated in some way.'

'But in what, son? What the fuck are you talking about?'

Suttle looked at him for a long moment. Then he grinned.

'I take it that's a no.'

'No to what?'

'Putting you on PIMS. Taking advantage of your matchless contacts.' The grin widened. 'Giving you lots of rope.'

Winter stared at him, the penny beginning to drop. Was this some kind of joke? Probably not.

'Too fucking right it's a no. I'm a working man, son. I have a career in front of me. I earn decent money. I've got prospects, somewhere nice to live. I've got an employer who looks after me, sees me right. Have you got all that? Can you remember it? Or do you want me to write it down? For when you report back?'

'I told them already.'

'Word for word?'

'Pretty much. I told them you'd piss yourself laughing. Then tell us to fuck off.'

'And what did they say?'

'They assume everyone else in the world sees it their way. Welcome to fairyland.'

'You're talking about Faraday?'

'No, Willard. And a woman called Gail Parsons.'

'She's lethal.'

'I know. I work for her. So does Faraday.'

'On Major Crime? She made DCI?'

'Yeah. And she's no intention of stopping there, either. Another reason to get you onside.'

'Are you serious? I risk my neck again? To help that fucking woman get even further up Willard's arse?'

'Nicely put. I'll pass it on.'

'Do, son. Do. My pleasure.'

'Mind if I use the loo?'

'Help yourself.'

Suttle got to his feet and left the room, conscious of Winter wagging his head behind him. He'd enjoyed the exchange immensely and was oddly glad that Winter hadn't let himself down.

In the bathroom Suttle used the loo, then soaped his hands in the tiny basin and inspected his face in the mirror. Last night had been a revelation. He didn't know what Lizzie Hodson had been up to since the last time they'd tried each other out but he certainly wasn't complaining.

Drying his hands, he spotted a screwed-up scrap of paper in the waste bin. It was bright orange. Curious, he smoothed it out. It was a Post-it with the same hotel logo as Winter's silk dressing gown. Scribbled on the non-sticky side was a one-line message. *Guess who made up for a shit Wednesday night?* Underneath was a name he recognised. *Mist. XXX*

He glanced in the mirror again, scarcely able to believe his luck. He knew Misty Gallagher. For a couple of months, years back, he'd been silly or brave enough to have an affair with Trudy, her daughter. At the time Bazza Mackenzie had treated Trudy as his own kith and kin and the relationship had, in the end, put Suttle in hospital with severe bruising and a couple of broken ribs. Trudy had almost been worth it, though. As, all too clearly, was her mother.

He slipped the Post-it into his pocket and returned to the lounge. Winter was still on the sofa. The big plasma TV was on and he was glued to a programme about property abroad.

'Why the interest in Berriman?' Suttle asked.

'My boss owes him. Wants to say a proper thank you.'

'Like how many times?'

'As many as it takes, son. Kids these days ...' he finally glanced round '... they never fucking listen.'

Suttle nodded. No way was Winter in the mood to drop even a hint or two about Berriman. Suttle picked up his plate and left it in the kitchen. On his way out of the apartment he paused again beside the sofa.

'One thing I forgot to mention, mate. Wednesday night. When Danny Cooper got the chop.'

'Yeah?'

'You're down as an action. Expect a knock at the door.' He grinned, thinking of the Post-it again. 'An alibi for Wednesday night might be useful.'

Chapter twenty-one

Nearly an hour later Faraday was summoned to Martin Barrie's office. He knew already that Willard had driven down from Winchester and was aware that DCI Parsons had called a management review meeting for midday. As the Danny Cooper murder appeared to be folding neatly into *Mandolin*, he wondered who'd be shuffling the cards in the pack when it came to Martin Barrie's return. The Detective Superintendent in charge of the Major Crime Team was back from a fortnight in Minehead on Monday and it was inconceivable that he wouldn't play a major role in what was now a triple homicide.

Parsons clearly shared this thought. Faraday could feel the tension in the office as he stepped in from the corridor. The big conference table could seat eight with ease. With just three of them there was nowhere to hide.

As a courtesy on these occasions Willard ceded control of the meeting to Parsons. Her turf, her call. She had a modest pile of paperwork at her elbow and on top Faraday recognised a plan of the Salcombe Avenue area that must have been drawn up by Scenes of Crime. Normally these documents would be littered with symbols indicating finds of interest: footmarks, physical damage, foreign objects possibly left by an intruder. The SOC map, alas, looked bare. Not a good sign.

Parsons was brisk. Nearly a week into *Mandolin* the time had come for a review. Going forward, she said, the squad needed to be clear about its bearings. At the full management meeting she'd be flagging the optimum lines of enquiry. As Deputy SIO, before she finalised her thoughts, D/I Faraday should naturally have an input.

'So ...' she spared him a wintry smile '... let's start with the party. Where do you think we are, Joe?'

Faraday took his time. There was a subplot here, as everyone on the squad knew. In all likelihood, unless the next three days produced a breakthrough, Parsons would be replaced by Martin Barrie as SIO. Before that happened, for the sake of her precious CV, she needed to tidy up.

'The way I see it, boss, we need to be absolutely sure of our ground. Was Rachel Ault murdered? Yes. Was Hughes killed as well? Probably.'

'*Probably*, Joe?' It was Willard.

'He'd clearly been in some kind of fight, sir. The forensic suggests he fell backwards and cracked his head. Someone stamped on his face. There are a lot of holes in there, as any defence lawyer will tell you. We could be looking at death by misadventure. We could be looking at manslaughter. It depends on exactly at which point he died.'

Willard nodded, reached for a biscuit from the plate at his elbow. Parsons hadn't taken her eyes off Faraday.

'But Rachel didn't stab herself, did she?'

'Of course not.'

'So what's your gut feeling?'

Gut feeling was an unhappy phrase. Faraday hesitated, remembering the Scenes of Crime shots by the pool: the paleness of Rachel's face against the cold paving slab, her eyes wide open. If only she and her new boyfriend had gone to the pub for the evening. If only.

'Three possibilities,' he began. 'In no particular order. Number one, the girl Jax Bonner tracked them both next door. Motivation? Payback for the judge. Opportunity? Ample. She may have seen Rachel in a bit of a state. That makes her vulnerable, there for the taking. She may have seen her leave the party house. She may have followed her. There may have been some kind of confrontation. Bonner had a knife – we can evidence that from the mobe footage on the stairs. Plus she left the party before we arrived and sealed the place off. On the other hand, there were two of them, Rachel and Hughes. So are we really saying this girl Bonner sorted them both out?'

'Maybe she wasn't alone, Joe.' Willard again.

'Sure. And there's evidence to support that.'

'Really?'

'Yeah. In the first place we know she came with a bunch of other people. One of them filmed Bonner on the stairs. We have witness statements that put her alongside a younger kid. He's the one with the spray can who did the tagging. There's a problem, though.'

'Which is?'

'The stamp mark on Hughes's face. We've sized it at nine to eleven, a Reebok Classic. That's a big shoe. We know it can't be Jax Bonner because shoes recovered from her bedroom are size 6. The kid she was sharing with is size 8.'

'Size 9 might fit him. Especially if they were nicked or borrowed. That's conceivable, Joe. And Reebok Classics are everywhere.'

Faraday conceded the point with a nod.

'This is a review, boss. There's a strong case against the girl, I don't deny it. She's got a lot of questions to answer.'

'Like why she's gone to ground.'

'Exactly. Those bank statements we seized at her brother's house? Someone's been accessing the account through ATMs over the past week, three withdrawals in all. I was talking to the bank this morning.'

'Local ATMs?'

'One in Cosham, one in Drayton, one in the city.' Drayton, like Cosham, was on the mainland.

'So where's she living?'

'Very good question. We've checked all her brother's lock-ups, just in case, and we've been tracing kids who probably know her. None of them have a clue where she is.'

'Big surprise.'

'Quite.'

'But she's hardly low profile, Joe.' Willard was losing patience. 'The publicity? The TV appeal I did? You're telling me *no one*'s seen her?'

'I'm telling you what I know, sir. "Gone to ground" is a good phrase. I assume she's got a roof over her head. All we need is an address.'

'As simple as that.'

'Quite.'

Parsons was looking at her watch. Faraday took the hint. Time to move on.

'The other guy we're obviously looking at is Matt Berriman,' he said. 'He certainly has the motive as far as Hughes is concerned. He's also got the right size feet.'

'We seized his footwear at the party?'

'Yes.' Faraday nodded. 'Nike Air Max 95. Right size but a completely different sole pattern.'

'And the rest of his gear?'

'We're still waiting on forensic. The custody file from Newbury said there was nothing obvious on his jeans or T-shirt but the results should be through today or tomorrow.'

'But he could have done it? He could have gone next door?'

'In theory, yes. We have one witness that thinks she saw him step out of the front door but can't remember exactly when.'

'And what does Berriman say?'

'He told us he'd gone out to get some air. That was before Mackenzie turned up. He said it was madness in the house. We gather he didn't like the music either.'

'He was gone for long?'

'He says a couple of minutes.'

'Anyone see him come back?'

'No. But he was definitely in the house when the kids trashed the study, and afterwards when he took Rachel to the bathroom. And he was back by the time Mackenzie started scrapping.'

'So he could have gone next door, is that what you're saying?'

'It's possible, yes. But then you have to ask yourself another question. He's been with Rachel for years. By all accounts he wants her back. They've just got together in the bathroom. Why on earth would he then stick a knife in her? Gareth Hughes, I can understand. That sounds plausible. They have a confrontation. Hughes falls over.'

'Then Berriman stamps on him? With the wrong trainer?'

'No.' Faraday shook his head. 'You're right, boss. It doesn't work, does it? It doesn't work with Hughes and for my money there's no way he's going to kill Rachel.'

'Great.' It was Parsons. 'So what's the third possibility?' She put the question to Faraday but it was Willard who answered.

'Mackenzie.' He grunted. 'He leaves the house; he's taken a slapping; he's extremely pissed off; he goes home, finds a couple of strangers on his property, gets one or two things off his chest ... No?'

'But they weren't strangers, sir.' Faraday was trying to be gentle. 'In fact they were anything but strangers. Rachel Ault is the girl he'd promised to keep an eye on and Gareth Hughes is the new man in her life. He knows them both. So why on earth ...' Faraday shrugged, leaving the sentence unfinished.

Willard pushed the plate of biscuits towards Parsons. Faraday was watching her face. This was going from bad to worse.

'Let's talk about Danny Cooper, Joe. You definitely think there's linkage?'

'Yes.'

'Why?'

'Number one because he was at the party. Number two because he was *important* at the party. And number three—'

'Why important?'

'Because he was the one supplying all the cut-price cocaine. Think bees. Think honeypot.'

'And that gets him killed? Four days later?'

'I've no idea, boss. But—'

'Number three?' It was Willard.

'Number three, we have the Facebook posting addressed to Jax Bonner. "Danny Cooper fitted up your brother." There's no indication who sent it, not yet, but that puts Cooper right in the middle of this whole mess. The real damage at the party came from the kids around Bonner. She had a grudge against Ault. Cooper was there with his little bags of toot. And word on the street puts Cooper down for the stash that sent Bonner's brother away.'

'So Bonner killed Cooper?'

'Circumstantially, the answer has to be yes.'

'But Scenes of Crime have found nothing. Am I right?'

'They've found blood, which would appear to be Cooper's. They've found damage to the rear door.'

'But no weapon?'

'No, sir.'

'No prints? No sole marks? Nothing in the allotments or the football ground at the back?'

'Nothing. Yet.'

'No witness statements? No sightings?'

'None.'

'And you're telling me a girl did that? You're suggesting she was *that* good?'

Willard had a point. Faraday admitted it.

'I'm talking motivation, sir. Not MO.'

'I can see that. But it's a bit neat, isn't it? This whole Facebook thing? A bit crude too? Think "cui bono?" Joe. Who else stands to gain from Cooper's death? Who maybe didn't want him around any more?'

It was a good question. Willard hadn't got to Head of CID for nothing. There was an exchange of glances. Then Parsons intervened.

'We need to talk about Winter,' she said. 'I understand he's down as one of this morning's actions.'

'That's right, boss. He was looking for Cooper on Wednesday evening.'

'Do we know why?'

'Not yet.'

'And what about Suttle?' Willard this time. 'Has he talked to Winter about what we discussed the other day?'

'Yes. He saw him this morning.'

'And?'

'Unproductive, I'm afraid. Winter told him to fuck off. They're Suttle's words, not mine.'

'No deal? He won't play?'

'No way.'

'How disappointing. I somehow expected better of the man.' Willard glanced towards Parsons. 'So what do we do with him now?'

'We wait, sir.' Parsons sighed, reaching for her files. 'And we see what develops.'

Faraday sensed the meeting was over. In a couple of hours' time they'd doubtless reconvene and he was curious to know how Parsons might conjure some kind of optimism from the frenzy of the last six days. The media, at least, appeared to be losing interest. He hadn't heard mention of a reporter or a TV crew for twenty-four hours now and he for one was glad that the world was moving on.

The DCI was on her feet when there came a knock at the door. It was Jerry Proctor. He'd just taken a call from a contact at the Forensic Science Service.

'And?' Faraday caught the lift in Parson's voice.

'They've got matches on the semen samples from Rachel Ault. I'm not sure where it takes us, boss, but I thought you ought to know.'

'Go on then.'

'The semen in her vagina came from Matt Berriman. The stuff in her throat belonged to Gareth Hughes.'

Parsons digested the news. As did Willard.

'But I thought those pictures from the bathroom showed us—'

'They did, sir. Odds on, that was Berriman.'

'So how come ...?' Willard glanced at Parsons.

'I've no idea.' She was still looking at Proctor. 'They're sure about the science?'

'Totally, boss. They're talking odds of a billion to one. I asked the same question myself.'

'And there's no possibility that the samples got wrongly labelled up? At our end? After the PM?'

'Highly unlikely. Jenny Cutler's the best.'

A silence. Then she looked round at Faraday.

'Joe?'

'No idea, boss. Interesting, though.'

Suttle had also heard the news. Minutes later he was sitting in Faraday's office. It was Faraday who shut the door. His desk was piled high with paperwork.

'You think we ought to talk to Berriman again?'

'Why would we do that?' asked Suttle.

'Because of the forensic.'

'But where would that take us, boss? We sussed they had sex in the bathroom days ago, when we got the pictures off Hughes's mobile.

Now we know he fucked her properly after the hors d'oeuvre. In my book that's good manners.'

'He lied to us in interview.'

'No he didn't, boss. I checked the transcript. We asked him whether he had sex in the bathroom and he blanked us, told us it wasn't any of our business. In any case having sex with an old girlfriend isn't illegal, is it?'

'That's true.' Faraday nodded at the door. 'I just had a meet with Parsons. Willard was there. Nice and cosy. We talked about Winter.'

'And?'

'To be frank, Jimmy, no one knows what to do with him. It's more than awkward.'

'Because he's having a sniff?'

'Of course. Given the relationship with Mackenzie, I'm not blaming the man. Far from it. I just wish we had a better handle on him.'

'But no one ever did, boss. You can't say any of this is a surprise.'

'No, you're right, but you know something else?' He frowned. 'For all our resources, all the blokes we can muster, all the effort we put in, all the strokes we can pull, even then Winter's probably got the drop on us. Why? Because he doesn't have to wade through all this shit every morning.'

He waved a despairing hand at the clutter on his desk. Suttle, for once, wasn't having it.

'You're right, boss,' he said. 'But then he doesn't have to take any of this shit to court, does he?'

Chapter twenty-two

The Aults spent most of the morning at Sandown Road. Belle Ault, with some reluctance, began to clear up the kitchen but her husband told her not to bother. He'd managed to find a recent copy of Yellow Pages and rang a series of industrial cleaners until he found a company who could start at once. They turned up within the hour in a smart new van, two middle-aged women and a Polish adolescent they called Jozef. Jozef was wide-eyed at the state of the place.

'What happen?' he asked one of the women.

'Youth, love,' she replied.

They started work at once under Peter Ault's direction. He'd already piled smashed or unwanted items by the front door and he took them on a tour of the house, room by room, indicating exactly what else needed disposal. Minutes later the growl of a truck announced the arrival of the mini-skip he'd also ordered. The driver dumped the skip in the drive, leaving Belle Ault to worry whether it would be sufficiently big. Already, it was plain that she'd had enough. When Marie rang her mobile with the offer of coffee next door, she willingly accepted. When the offer was extended to her husband, he shook his head.

By noon the kitchen was spotless. The two women departed in the van to pick up a new drum of disinfectant from the company depot while Jozef found his way to Albert Road to buy them all a spot of lunch. Alone in the house, Peter Ault retreated to his study. With a stiff broom he swept the broken glass into a pile beside the door. It was raining by now and when he'd finished with the broom he stood by the window, his hands thrust deep in the pockets of his jeans, staring out. The study was at the side of the house and overlooked the garden. Below, slightly to the left, was the gazebo. Of the list of jobs he'd compiled when they'd moved in last year, it was close to the top. The wood was rotting round the window sills and the roof leaked. It needed some serious TLC and a lick or two of paint.

Something cheerful, he'd thought at the time. Maybe sky blue and yellow. Seaside colours.

'Mind if I come in?'

He spun round. He hadn't heard the footsteps on the stairs. Mackenzie was standing in the open doorway gazing at the pile of glass at his feet. The neck brace gave him a slightly comical look.

'Make yourself at home,' Ault told him. 'You'll excuse the mess.'

Mackenzie wasn't sure whether he was joking or not. He'd come to sympathise, he said. And to say sorry.

'Don't.'

'But I mean it, Peter.'

'Don't,' he repeated. 'It's over. Finished. One moves on.'

'Yeah, but ... the state of the place ... Coming back like this ... That lovely girl of yours ...'

Ault nodded. He'd spread the photos from the smashed frames across the desk. Most of them featured Rachel.

Mackenzie was repeating the offer of a bed for the night. Or several nights. Or for as long as he and Belle needed it. Situations like this, he said, you needed mates around you, support, conversation.

'We have all that already.'

'Of course you do. But I mean close ... handy ... so you can keep an eye on things ...'

It was an unhappy phrase. Ault hadn't been a lawyer for nothing.

'From next door you mean? Over the garden wall?'

'Exactly.'

'The way you promised before we went off on our travels?'

Mackenzie tried to nod then winced with pain.

'I'm sorry,' he muttered. 'Like I said before, I'm really sorry.'

'I'm sure you're sorry. But sorry's not much use, is it? Did you know about this party?'

'No. She never mentioned it, Rach.'

'Were you here when it happened?'

'Only at the end. I did what I could. Took a hiding for my troubles.'

'Oh? I didn't know that.'

'Yeah.' A tiny movement of Mackenzie's head. 'It was Rach's Matt who dragged those animals off.'

'Rach's Matt?' Something else he didn't know.

'Yeah. Matt Berriman. I still owe the boy.'

Ault lapsed into silence, lifting a particular photo then letting it fall to the desk again. At length, he wanted to know about the drugs.

'What drugs?'

'The police seem to think there was cocaine on the premises. Lots of it. Dirt cheap.'

'Yeah?'

'You're telling me you didn't know about that either?'

'Of course not. If I didn't know about the party, how the fuck could I know about any cocaine?' Mackenzie fought to control himself. 'You think they were down to me? All those giveaways?'

'Giveaways?' Ault's eyes gleamed behind the heavy glasses. 'When you say you know nothing?'

It was a trap, artfully laid. As Mackenzie well knew.

'The police told me,' he said defensively.

'Did they?'

'Yeah. Listen, I'm through with all this shit. The fact is I came over here to say sorry. Think what you fucking like but I meant it when I said you could stay. Where I come from, we can recognise a mate. Is that a bit strong? Or are you getting the drift?'

The two men stared at each other for a long moment. Then Ault eased the chair back from the desk and stood up. He gazed out at the rain then turned back.

'I'm afraid you'll have to excuse me, Mr Mackenzie.' The smile was icy. 'Lots to do.'

Early afternoon, Suttle caught Winter as he was about to leave Gunwharf for the Royal Trafalgar Hotel. Winter buzzed him in on the entryphone, waiting for his footsteps down the corridor.

'You've got a moment?'

'Again?' Winter stepped back into the apartment. 'I'm gonna start charging you lot for my time.'

'You've been interviewed already?'

'This morning. My pleasure.'

'And?'

'You want to find yourselves some decent detectives. Preferably blokes old enough to shave.'

It turned out the Major Incident Room had sent a couple of the younger D/Cs to take a formal statement from Winter about Wednesday night. Someone had evidently done a risk assessment, given Winter's track record with the squad, and the upshot was the dispatch of two detectives who'd never met him. That way, according to the lippier of the two D/Cs, there'd never be any suspicion of bias.

'So what happened?' Suttle settled himself on Winter's sofa.

'Read the statement. It's not long.'

'Surprise me. So what did you say?'

'I told them what I told you. I had business with Cooper. He wasn't in. I went round the back, just in case, but he still wasn't in. That gives you the start of a timeline, doesn't it? The kitchen door's intact. Therefore it must have happened after I left. A breakthrough, son. And like I told your guys, you get that for absolutely free.' He grinned. 'Not going so well, is it?'

Winter was right, though Suttle didn't give him the satisfaction of an answer. The noon management meeting had wound up after less than half an hour. Parsons had declared herself extremely happy with progress but no one was fooled for a moment. She's feathering her nest, Proctor growled afterwards. She's putting the best gloss on a pretty shit week and hoping to God Martin Barrie treats himself to an extra month in Minehead.

'So what are you after, son? Only some of us have a living to make.'

'It's about that kitchen of Mackenzie's. You dropped a hint, remember? About fast-tracking the forensic?'

'Did I?'

'Yes. As it happens, I listened for once. Fuck knows why.'

'And?'

'It turned out to be worth it. They matched two sets of prints to Rachel and Hughes. Hers were on a glass on the draining board. His were on the fridge. Watch me ...'

Suttle got up and stepped into the kitchen. He leaned against Winter's fridge, his outspread palms taking the weight of his body. Winter watched from the open doorway.

'They got the prints from the PM?' he queried.

'Yeah.'

'So the happy couple were in Bazza's kitchen? Yeah?'

'Yeah.'

'Where's the proof it was that same night?'

Suttle pushed himself off the fridge. Déjà vu, he thought. Virtually the same question Faraday had asked.

'She left blood on the glass as well as prints. Someone must have smacked her. Those results came through too. It had to be that night. Had to be.'

'Young Rachel knew where Marie hid the key.' Winter was frowning now. 'She'd keep an eye on the place sometimes when they were away. I've heard Marie mention it. So she's in the kitchen. She's pissed. And he's in there too. It's babes in the wood. They've done a runner from next door and they're all by themselves. So what happens next?'

Suttle said he hadn't a clue. He knew Winter liked to pump up the pressure, hopscotch from one supposition to another, squeeze the known facts as hard as he could. It had been part of his MO as a serving detective. Some of his ex-colleagues used to ridicule the more ambitious jumps but Suttle had seen where some of these expeditions had led.

'There's something else ...' he began.

'Like what?'

'We sent off semen samples. They swabbed Rachel's fanny and her throat, got a result from both.'

'And they got matches too?'

'Matt Berriman in her fanny. Hughes down her throat.'

'Is that right?'

'Yeah.'

'Busy girl then.'

'You'd think so.'

'Does Berriman know this?'

'I expect he'd remember.'

'Don't fuck around, son. I'm asking whether you've put it to him.'

'No.' Suttle glanced up at the clock on the wall. 'But then we probably don't see him as often as you.'

Gabrielle very rarely phoned Faraday during office hours. Faraday had never worked out whether this was deliberate, instinctive respect for his territory, or whether she simply had nothing to say that couldn't wait.

He bent to the phone.

'Where are you?'

'It doesn't matter. You have a pen, *chéri*?' She gave him a mobile number.

'Where does that take me?'

'A boy called Connor. He knows about the party.'

'He was there?'

'For a little while, yes. But you're right about the girl. She frightens him. She frightens a lot of the kids I talk to. You should talk to him, *chéri*.'

'He knows I'm a copper?'

'He knows nothing. Except that I trust you.'

'And that's enough?'

'That's for you to say. *À bientôt*.' The line went dead.

Faraday stared at the number for a moment or two. His instinct was to hand it on to Jimmy Suttle. He was in charge of the Intelligence Cell. Leads like this were part of his job description. More to the point, he was much younger than Faraday and if the last week had taught him anything then it was the sheer depth of the gap that had opened up behind his own generation. Even recently he'd fooled himself he understood kids. Now he wasn't at all sure.

At the same time, though, Gabrielle had entrusted this number to him and not to anyone else. Trust was important to her. She'd just said so. Which meant that Faraday, in turn, should stick to the rules.

He reached for the phone on his desk then changed his mind. Using his mobile would be better.

The number rang and rang.

'Yeah?' It was barely a whisper. Faintly, in the background, Faraday could hear an adult's voice, a woman, plenty of echo. He must be at school, Faraday thought.

'Who are you, Mister?'

'The name's Joe.'

'Who?'

'Joe.'

'Shit.' Ever fainter. 'Gabby's bloke?'

Winter was in his office at the Royal Trafalgar when Mackenzie limped in. Winter, who'd tried him several times on his mobile during the course of the day, thought at first that Bazza was pissed. He looked up, seeing this squat, stiff figure with something white supporting his chin.

'You OK, Baz?'

'Very funny.' Mackenzie sank into the chair Winter kept for occasional visitors. 'Believe me, mush. If I thought there was room for another painkiller ...'

Winter got up. One of the cleaning women was chasing a Hoover along the thin strip of carpet outside. Winter gave her a wave and shut the door, turning back to Mackenzie.

'So what happened?'

'You know what happened.'

'I saw the crash. You think I should have hung around?'

'Don't be daft, mush. It was the best I could do at the time. I thought it was a laugh. Especially when I told them it was their fault.'

The Filth, he said, had been crap. No sense of humour. Not even an apology.

'There's bits of Marie's new motor all over the road, and their radiator's leaking stuff everywhere, and I'm hopping around hanging on to the back of my neck, and all they can do is bang on about speed limits and getting in their way. I gave them an earful, mush. Scaring me like that. Blue lights. Sirens. And me twice their fucking age.'

They'd wanted to take him down the Bridewell, he said, on a dangerous driving charge plus sus obstructing the course of justice, but he wasn't having it. In the end they'd agreed he might have an injury. When he asked for a lift to A & E they wouldn't hear of it. Health and safety meant they had to call an ambulance. The people in the road thought it was something off the telly. One old girl had taken a shine to him.

'Two cups of tea and a slice of Madeira and a bit of a sit-down when I said I felt faint. The ambulance blokes said I got off lightly. Necks break easier than you might think.'

'So how do you feel now?'

'Shit. And my leg hurts like a bastard. Even Marie feels sorry for me.'

When Mackenzie wanted to look round he had to move his entire body. Winter realised he was checking the door.

'It's closed, Baz. What's the problem?'

'This whole thing.'

'What whole thing?'

'The party. What happened. Rachel and her mate by the pool. Ault ...'

'And?'

'Let's just forget it. Tell you the truth, mush, I got the bloke wrong. Turns out he's a cunt.'

'Who?' Winter was lost.

'Ault. He comes back today with his missus. I nip next door, like you would. I tell him how sorry we are, what a shitheap the house is, how he can stay as long as he likes round our place. I couldn't have been sweeter with the guy. And you know what? He just blanks me.'

'He's just lost his daughter, Baz. And he only had one of them to begin with. He's probably a bit upset.'

'Upset? Of course he's fucking upset. Anyone would be upset. But this guy's giving it to me like I was in court. He thinks I did it, mush – he thinks it was my fault. I could see it. It was all over his face. *Mister* Mackenzie? Who the fuck does he think he is?'

Winter sat back. The implications were clear. No more investigations. No more running round playing the detective.

'It might not be as simple as that, Baz. Not the way I see it. You're right to want to get to the bottom of this and you know why? Because they ended up in your back garden.'

'It's history, mush. It's gone.'

'No, it hasn't.'

'No?'

'I'm afraid not. You remember the Scenes of Crime blokes? Crawling round your place for a couple of days?'

'Yeah?' Mackenzie had forgotten for a moment about the pain.

'They found a couple of sets of prints in your kitchen. One of them was Rachel's. The other belonged to the lad Hughes.'

'He's never been in my kitchen.'

'He has, Baz. The night he died.'

'But how do you know?'

'I just told you. They got lifts.'

'But how do you know that?'

'The same way I found out about Danny Cooper and all that blood all over his bedroom walls. I talk to people, Baz. People I trust.'

'The Filth?'

'Of course. You think I'm the only one who ever bent the rules? It's blokes like me, Baz, that keep good citizens like you safe at night. Leave it to the other muppets and you wouldn't get a wink.'

'So who is this bloke?'

'A friend of mine, Baz. He's got a name but there's no way I'm giving it to you. Just trust me, that's all. Think you can cope with that?'

Mackenzie wanted to say no but Winter managed to head him off. The Old Bill might well be back, he said. They were light years from a result and they'd barely survived the weekend's media storm. Add some serious aggravation from the Craneswater Residents' Association plus a forthcoming extraordinary meeting of the Police Authority, and they'd suddenly be in the business of reinvestigating old lines of enquiry.

'That means you, Baz. Or putting it bluntly, us. That motor last night, the Alfa. What happens to it now?'

'I've got a guy's gonna take it round a place I know for a steam clean. Inside and out. Clean like you've never seen clean.'

Winter was shaking his head. Give me patience, he thought.

'No, Baz. No way that motor leaves the double glazing place. You need a guy round there to strip off the plates, the engine number, anything that can tie it to Westie. Then you either need a complete refurb inside – new carpets, new seats, the lot – plus a respray on the outside before you find the money to ship it abroad and find a buyer. Or you invest in a can of petrol and burn the fucker. I'd go for the petrol option personally, but that's down to you.'

'You're serious?'

'Yeah, and so would you be if you'd done my job. Forensics these days, we're talking single-cell DNA. Westie would have left gallons of the stuff. I'm telling you, Baz, it's a no-brainer.'

Mackenzie had the grace to look impressed.

'So what are you saying then, mush? Only I've had enough of going on my knees to fucking Ault.'

Winter sat back, enjoying this rare moment of authority.

'I'm saying – suggesting – that I do what you wanted in the first place.'

'Remind me.'

'Put a name alongside those bodies of yours.' He smiled. 'For everyone's sake.'

Chapter twenty-three

Connor said he was fourteen but Faraday didn't believe him. He was Pompey-thin, with gelled hair, bitten nails and a look of permanent anxiety in his wide blue eyes. A blue Henri Lloyd top hung on his bony frame. On the cusp between childhood and adolescence, he talked in a low mumble with an occasional cackle of laughter when something struck him as funny.

He'd agreed to meet on condition Faraday bought him a Big Bucket at the Kentucky Fried. It had to be the KFC in the Pompey Centre, next to Fratton Park, because Connor was on multiple ASBOs, and most of the rest of the city was out of bounds to him.

Strictly speaking, Faraday was taking a risk on a meet like this. Best practice demanded specialist officers who worked with juveniles all the time and maybe an appropriate adult to sit in. The paperwork alone would have taken hours.

'How come the ASBOs?' Faraday helped himself to a chip.

Connor looked round, disappointed at the lack of audience. Rain pebbled on the big glass windows. The place was empty.

'Assault and battery, bit of happy-slapping, bit of twocking. Yeah, and I nicked a speedboat.'

'How come?'

'Dunno. It was just there.'

The boat, he muttered, had been tied to a mooring buoy on Langstone Harbour. Connor and a couple of mates had been eyeing it for a while. They'd waded out at high tide and helped themselves, just for the laugh, but then the tide had turned and they'd found themselves drifting out through the harbour mouth. Only an alert coastguard had saved them from a night in the English Channel.

Faraday vaguely remembered the story from a piece in the *News*. THREE LADS IN A BOAT.

'So what happened?'

'The Old Bill was waiting when we got towed back. Five of them. Well funny that was.'

As well as the ASBOs, Connor was now on curfew. He pushed the chair back from the table, rolled up one leg of his Adidas track bottoms and insisted Faraday take a look at the electronic tag. The curfew, he said, had originally been for ten in the evening. Now it was seven.

'So how come you were at that party on Saturday?'

'Never said I was, did I?'

'But you know about it?'

'Course. Everyone knows about it. Fucking laugh, mush.'

One of his brothers, he said, had gone. First thing he knew he'd been sitting at home watching the football on the telly with the old tit.

'The old tit?'

'Me mum. My brother, see, him and another geezer had found all this wine, bottles of the stuff. He don't know nothing about wine, Clancy, so he phones the old tit to find out whether it's any good.'

'He hadn't tried it?'

'No, mush. It was a bottle, like I say, not opened or anything, and there's loads more where that came from. Clancy, right, he don't drink wine. But he wants a little earn, yeah?'

'And your mum?'

'She don't know nothing about wine neither, so Clancy says what he'll do, like, is bring a load home anyway because all the good gear had gone already.'

'Like what?'

'Dunno.' He sat on his hands, shrugging. 'iPods? Phones? Cameras? Jewellery? Any moolah lying around? Any bugle going spare?'

'Bugle?'

'Toot. White. Cocaine.'

'And was there?'

'Dunno, mush. Like I say, I weren't there.'

'And the wine?'

'Clancy had a load away.'

'How did he carry it?'

'Pillow cases. Off the bed. He had a bit of flange up there, anything to get his dick wet, Clancy. Nicked the pillow cases after, like.'

'And the wine? He sold it in the end?'

'Dunno. Might have done. The old tit tried a bottle. Said it was all right.'

Faraday nodded, wondering what Peter Ault would make of this conversation. Precious wines laid down for years. Necked by the old tit.

Connor had barely touched the food. Faraday told him it was getting cold. The boy looked at it a moment then pushed it away.

'Ain't hungry, mush. So what's this about?'

Faraday explained a little more about the party, knowing full well that none of this would be news to the likes of Connor. There'd been loads of damage. Two people had died.

'And you wanna know about a sort called Bonner, yeah?'

The directness of the question startled Faraday.

'Yes,' he agreed, 'I do.'

'Why's that, then?'

'I need to talk to her.'

'About them bodies?'

'Yeah. And one or two other issues.'

'Yeah, but it's the bodies really, innit? Cos me and my mates know she's off her head. I had a ruck with her once. She gobbed at me, just for nothing, like. And you know what? I had a fag on and I put it out in her face ... bang ...' One thin arm shot out. 'Just like that. She went mental. Silly old moose.'

'That was recently?'

'Yeah.'

'And you've seen her since?'

'Fucking joking, mush. She carries a blade.'

'All the time?'

'Yeah. She's fucking psycho too. Don't get me wrong, mush. I'd fight her if I had to. No way no bird's ever gonna slap me around. But you don't go looking for it, do you? Not in this fucking city. Not the way it is. There are people want to hurt you out there, really hurt you. And she's one of them. She's fucking dangerous, mush. Like I say, off her head.'

'You know where to find her?'

The question put a new light in Connor's eyes.

'Why's that then? You wanna talk to her?'

'Yes. I just told you.'

'But you're serious? You really wanna do it? Arrest her? Get her sent away?'

'We'd see.'

'See, fuck. She's well evil. I'm telling you.'

'So where do I find her?'

The frown put years on Connor's face. He reached for a plastic spoon and gave the congealing beans a poke. Watching, Faraday wondered whether he might be older, not younger, than fourteen.

'You want an address, like. Yeah?'

'Yeah.'

'That might be hard.'

Faraday nodded. He knew exactly where this conversation was going.

'How hard?'

'Fucking well hard. And fucking dodgy too, a sort like her.' He stared at Faraday.

'So what's stopping you?'

'Nothing, mush.' He was sitting on his hands again. 'But yer gotta have a little earn, ain't yer?'

On the mobile Matt Berriman had told Winter he was busy. When Winter persisted, he finally agreed to meet. He was working in the university library. Around half five, if Winter was offering, he could do with a lift back to Eastney.

He emerged fifteen minutes late in the company of a striking-looking girl with long brown legs and a fall of jet-black hair. He said goodbye to her on the pavement beside Winter's car. She had a throaty laugh and reached up to kiss Berriman on the lips before she strode away.

'Italian.' Berriman folded his long frame into the passenger seat. 'Here for the summer.'

He wanted to know what was so important it had kept Winter at the kerbside. There was no hint of apology.

'We need a little chat. It's about the party. The Old Bill are getting warm. Better now, with me ... eh?'

Winter drove down to the seafront. The incessant rain had stopped at last but the chill in the wind had kept the beach virtually empty. He found a parking space beyond the pier and killed the engine. Two middle-aged women were trying to master rollerblading on the promenade. Skating skirts at forty was a bad idea.

'Well?' Berriman was watching them too.

'It's about Rachel, son.'

Winter had never called him son before. Berriman didn't much like it.

'Matt'll be fine,' he said. 'If it's OK with you.'

'Sure, son.' Winter shrugged. 'No offence. Listen, we need to make one or two things clear. I'm not a copper, whatever you think. That's number one. Number two, Mackenzie pays my wages. You might think that's got nothing to do with you but you'd be wrong. Why? Because Mackenzie likes you. And because he also owes you. He doesn't want to see you in trouble. And that goes for me too.'

'What kind of trouble?'

'The worst. *Serious* shit.'

'To do with Rachel?'

'Yeah. And the boy Hughes.' Winter glanced across at him. 'Are you with me now?'

Berriman nodded, then reclined the seat a couple of degrees and closed his eyes.

'Go on,' he said.

'You shagged Rachel in the bathroom that night at the party. She did you a favour or two first but then you got it on properly, the way you used to, the way she preferred it. Afterwards, you sent the pictures you'd done earlier to Hughes. Am I right?'

'Go on,' he said again. 'I'm listening.'

'Rachel went off with Hughes a bit later. She must have got into a ruck of some kind because she was bleeding around her mouth. Maybe Hughes saw those pictures. And maybe he took offence. Why? Because Rachel didn't much like oral sex, not the full deal. So a bit later they're next door in Bazza's kitchen, just the two of them. Rachel's pissed. Hughes is fucking angry. Rachel wants to make it up to him. And he knows just what she can do to say sorry. Am I getting warm?'

This time Berriman didn't react. His face was a mask. His head was tipped back in the plushness of the passenger seat. He might have been asleep.

'You followed them next door, son. I don't know exactly when but my guess is you got there to find them at it in the kitchen. The light would have been on. Hughes was standing in front of the fridge, leaning on it, his hands out straight. From outside that kitchen door you can see in but at first you haven't got a clue what's going on because he's in the way. But then you start wondering why his shorts are round his ankles and why Rachel's on her knees in front of him. And then you get it. Because you can't fucking ignore it. And then it gets a whole lot worse because Hughes goes the whole way and you know that's just totally out of order. Why? Because she hates it. Because she's always hated it. Which means he's kind of taken advantage ... and that wasn't something you could live with, son. Not after you'd just shafted him with those pictures.'

'So what did I do then?' Berriman's eyes were closed. 'If all this isn't total bullshit?'

'I think you probably waited for a bit. I think you didn't know what to do. I think you waited and I think that after a bit he headed for the door. Rachel was at the sink by now, gagging. Afterwards she had a glass or two of water. Hughes knew he hadn't played a blinder. He *knew* he'd taken advantage. And so out he came. By that time you've had a good look at Rachel. Someone had given her a slapping. It's obvious. And it has to be Hughes. He left the kitchen. To get back

241

to the party, he had to pass the pool. That's where you stopped him. I haven't a clue what you said. You might have said nothing. Whatever happened, you smacked him. He went backwards, cracked his head, knocked himself unconscious. For good measure you stamped on him, stamped on his head, on his cheek, whack. Because he was trash. Because of what he'd just done back in that kitchen. Yeah?'

No response. Not immediately. Then Berriman opened one eye.

'And what about Rachel?'

'I dunno. Did you stick a knife in her? I doubt it. Did you sort Hughes out the way I just described? Yeah ... definitely. In a court of law you'll need a fucking good brief, son. Otherwise you're looking at a long time in crap company.'

Berriman was frowning. 'This stamping thing.' One eye briefly opened. 'Would that leave a mark?'

'Yeah. Almost certainly.'

'But they took my trainers. In fact they took the whole fucking lot. So why haven't they arrested me? If what you say is true?

'A very good question, son. And one I'm hoping you can help me with.'

'Else?'

'Else we're back to square one. The people I used to work with aren't dumb. They're slow but they're not stupid.'

Berriman nodded. There was a long silence. The women on the rollerblades were dots in the distance. Finally, Berriman struggled upright, adjusted the rear-view mirror to check his hair, and then opened the door.

'You've still got my phone,' he said.

'I know, son. And you should be thinking about that too.'

The news from the Major Incident Room came to Suttle moments before he left the office. D/S Glen Thatcher, in charge of Outside Enquiries, had just been talking to one of the D/Cs working on the Danny Cooper killing. He'd been doing a follow-up on a call from a manager at G.A. Day, a big DIY store on Burrfields Road. The manager had been working through the night on Wednesday, battling to finish a stocktake before the accountant's deadline the following morning. He'd left the building for a stretch of the legs and a fag around three in the morning. Standing beside the main gate, doing nothing in particular, he'd become aware of a car parked nearby. The car had attracted his attention because the interior light kept flickering on and off.

'The manager got in touch this morning. His wife told him about Salcombe Avenue and he remembered the car.'

'What time did he jack it in at work?'

'Around half five. It was daylight. When he drove out onto the Burrfields Road the car had gone.'

'The G.A. Day place is across from the allotments.'

'Exactly.'

'With Salcombe Avenue on the other side.'

'You've got it.'

'Did this bloke get a make at all?'

'Yeah. He's a bit of a car buff. Says it was an Alfa Romeo.'

'Did he get a look at the reg plate?'

'Afraid not ... but here's the good bit. One of the civvy indexers has a boyfriend in Traffic. Apparently a patrol got involved in a collision last night. They rear-ended a Peugeot up towards Hilsea. It seems they were chasing a car reported nicked and the Peugeot kept getting in the way. The boyfriend swore the target was an Alfa.'

Suttle nodded. The coincidence was interesting, little more. Thatcher hadn't finished.

'The traffic guys got details of the Peugeot driver,' he said. 'Take a guess.'

The indexer had left a number for her boyfriend in case anyone wanted to talk to him. Suttle returned to the Intelligence Cell and lifted the phone. The P/C's name was Grant. He was downstairs in Traffic, preparing to go out on patrol. Suttle took the stairs two at a time.

Grant had been in Pompey for less than a year. Wednesday night he and his oppo had taken a heads-up from the force control room about a sus vehicle theft. He said someone had rung in about a couple of guys acting suspiciously on Southsea seafront. The car involved was down as an Alfa.

'How did they know?'

'No idea. You'll have to check.'

'So what happened?'

'We clocked an Alfa in Stubbington Avenue. It was waiting to come out from Randolph Road. We'd taken the call literally minutes beforehand. Time-wise it looked quite promising.'

He described backing into Randolph Road, then setting off in pursuit.

'The problem was the car in between, the Peugeot. Fair play, the guy couldn't let us past because it's too narrow with all the parked cars up there but he had at least a couple of chances to pull over when we came to intersections and he never took them. Then, out of nowhere, bam, he hits the brakes. We had no chance. He must have known that.'

'And this was Mackenzie?'

'Yeah. I didn't know him from Adam but my oppo told me about him later. Bit of a local face? Would that be right?'

Suttle nodded. A bit of a local face. Too right.

'And the Alfa?'

'Gone.'

'So they might have been in convoy? Is that what you're saying?'

'Easily. Though this guy Mackenzie wasn't having it. Kept threatening us with his brief. Talked about doing us for harassment.' He glanced at his watch. 'Are we through? Only my oppo will be waiting.'

Suttle returned to his office. The shift supervisor in the control room at Netley checked the 999 log for last night's activity. The call about the Alfa from Southsea had come in at 22.21. The caller had left a name and number. Dermott Callaghan, 02392 348567. Suttle lifted the phone again. For a long minute nothing happened. Then came an Irish voice, old, uncertain. Suttle introduced himself, explained the circumstances, said he'd like to come round.

'When?'

'Now.'

'Why?

'To say thank you, Mr Callaghan.'

He took an address, grabbed a pad and collected his Impreza from the car park at the back. Southsea seafront was five minutes away. He parked across the road from the parade of converted hotels and boarding houses, and located the block of flats. Callaghan was only too happy to buzz him in.

There was no lift. Suttle took the stairs to the fourth floor. Callaghan was waiting for him on the top landing. He must have been eighty at least, a bent figure in a soup-stained cardigan with smoker's fingers and wisps of snow-white hair. The effort to make it as far as the landing showed on his face. He was holding on to the banisters, fighting for breath.

The flat smelled of roll-ups and a weak bladder. Suttle began to wonder how often this old guy got out. Beside the window was an armchair surrounded by a litter of open newspapers. Across the room a new-looking TV was tuned to the evening news. There was a phone on the floor beside the armchair. A nearby ashtray was brimming with fag ends.

'I do the horses most days.' He'd sunk into the armchair. 'Keeps me out of mischief.'

Suttle glanced down at the newspapers, all of them open at the racing pages, runners ringed in green.

'And you ever get lucky?'

'You're talking to an Irishman, son. Luck doesn't come into it. Me and horses ...' He started to cough. A box of tissues at his elbow. Balls of Kleenex at his feet.

'So how do you lay hands on your winnings?'

'Brett.'

'Brett?'

'Yeah. A lovely man. He collects for me, and does lots else as well. Kind as the day is long, that fella.' He nodded at the view. 'Phoning your lot was the least I could do.'

Suttle stared at him then stepped across to the window. He could see his own car parked across the road, then the wide spaces of the Common, green after all the rain.

'You're talking about the car last night?'

'Sure. It was Brett's. That's why I knew it was an Alfa. Black thing. Light of his life, it is.'

'What's Brett's surname?'

'West. Mr West to you.'

'What colour is he? If you don't mind me asking.'

'Not at all, son. He's black. Just like that car of his.' He paused, looking up at Suttle, his eyes milky with age. 'You're telling me you've found it? Only I'd like to tell him myself.'

Suttle phoned Faraday as he clattered down the stairs towards the street. 'Boss? Where are you?'

'In the car park. Off home.' A pause. 'Why?'

'Something's come up. I'll be back in five.'

He drove fast, one eye on the mirror. He knew Brett West from way back. Brett West was the heavy who'd been waiting for him outside the club in Gunwharf the night he'd been in there with Misty Gallagher's daughter. Brett West was the guy who'd stepped into Suttle's path and pushed him backwards into the arms of two other blokes before breaking his jaw. Brett West worked for Bazza Mackenzie.

Faraday was back in his office by the time Suttle returned to Major Crime. One look at his face told Suttle he'd have preferred to have this conversation on Monday.

'My son's come down early.' He nodded at the phone. 'What's up?'

Suttle explained about the 999 call, the Alfa on the seafront, the traffic guys colliding with Bazza Mackenzie minutes later. Suttle had never believed in coincidence. Neither did Faraday.

'So what are we saying?'

'The guy who phoned it in saw two blokes by the Alfa. He's old.

His eyesight's crap. We've got no detail on these people but he knows the car. He thinks he remembers another car beside it on the seafront, a motor he hadn't seen before. He says it was a lighter colour. The traffic guy says the Peugeot was sky blue. We can put Mackenzie in the Peugeot, no problem.'

'So who was driving the Alfa? Assuming you've got this right?'

'Someone who works for Mackenzie.' Suttle at last sat down. 'Someone who knew there was a good reason to swift the bloody thing away.'

'Winter?'

Suttle nodded, said nothing.

There was a long silence then a brief knock at the door before Gail Parsons appeared. She was wearing a raincoat. She was off home for the weekend.

'Come in, boss.' Faraday said heavily. 'Join the party.'

Chapter twenty-four

The search warrant on Brett West's seafront flat was sworn within the hour. Suttle prepared the paperwork and Faraday drove it to the Old Portsmouth address where the duty magistrate and his wife were hosting a dinner party for friends. He and Faraday conferred in a small study at the front of the house. Faraday explained the circumstances. Attempts to find Brett West had come to nothing. They had his address and his mobile number from the old man at the top of the block. West wasn't answering the door, neither did he respond to calls. There were reasons, therefore, to conclude that he might have fled the city.

'Or simply gone away?'

'Indeed. But we have witness evidence of an Alfa in the vicinity of Salcombe Avenue on Wednesday night.'

'The Danny Cooper murder?'

'Yes.'

'And you're saying West drives an Alfa?'

'Yes.'

'And the target car involved in the incident last night?'

'An Alfa.'

'I see.' His hand reached for the proffered pen.

Faraday, armed with the warrant, drove back to the seafront. Parsons was already there, parked across the road. The duty call-out Scenes of Crime team were due any minute from Cosham and the DCI wanted to brief them before they started on West's flat.

Faraday parked up and walked across to Parsons' Audi. A chill in the air seemed to promise more rain and he paused for a moment to catch a pair of swans flying low towards the black silhouette of Southsea Castle.

Parsons got out of the car. Suttle was with her.

'Joe?' She was looking eager, buoyed by the prospect of a breakthrough.

Faraday was gazing up at the apartment block across the road. West lived on the third floor, number 11. Scenes of Crime would need to scoop up everything obvious, first priority, before they began the search for forensic evidence that might tie West to the Cooper killing. A full intelligence search could come later, once they'd finished.

'Mobes, paperwork, anything related to travel plans, notes by the phone.' He was thinking aloud. 'If we've got this thing right, my guess is he's gone already.'

'Gone?'

'Fled. Gatwick? Heathrow? He could be anywhere by now.'

Suttle agreed. He'd already contacted Immigration and Special Branch to run checks at both airports. As soon as he'd got a Production Order, he could start work on West's credit cards. A transaction on an airline ticket would come up with a flight number and a destination. Assuming he'd left the country.

A flash from a pair of approaching headlights announced the arrival of the Scenes of Crime van. Faraday stepped aside as it swung into the vacant parking bay. Parsons was looking more cheerful by the minute. All we need now, Faraday thought, is Willard. Maybe she's belled him already. Maybe she's thinking she might yet survive as SIO. Maybe tonight's developments might protect her from the implications of Martin Barrie's return.

Suttle was talking to the Crime Scene Investigator as he pulled on his forensic suit. Faraday joined them, detailing what they needed from the flat. Another van was approaching – bigger, badged with the Hantspol logo. The on-call imaging specialist had driven over from Netley.

The CSI, now suited up, began to unload gear from the back of his van. He was about to cross the road with an armful of stepping plates when a black Lexus approached. It swept past the parked vehicles and Faraday caught a glimpse of the face behind the wheel as it registered the kerbside scene

Suttle had clocked it too.

'Winter,' he murmured with a shake of the head.

The invitation to dinner had come from Marie. She'd hoped the Aults might turn up as well but a late phone call from Belle had presented their apologies. Peter, she said, had a foul headache and was anticipating an early night. They were still with their friends in Denmead. Maybe another time.

Winter also had a problem with the invite. He'd fixed to meet a business contact for a pint at eight and wouldn't be free until – say – half nine. On the phone Marie had broken off to confer with her husband, returning to say that would be fine.

'Half nine.' It had the force of an order.

Winter parked the Lexus in the street and walked round the back of the house to find them in the kitchen. Bazza had got rid of the neck brace but still appeared to be in pain. Whether this accounted for his mood, Winter didn't know.

'I've just had fucking Westie on from Spain.' He nodded at his mobile, abandoned on the kitchen table. 'You know how much I bunged him Wednesday night? Before he got in the taxi? Fifteen grand. That's cash, mush, that's moolah. And you know what he wants now? Another hundred.'

'A hundred *grand*?'

'Yeah. And I get the impression that's just for starters. He says he's there for good. He says he needs to buy a place.'

'But he's right, isn't he?'

'Of course he's fucking right. But since when am I his fucking banker?'

'Since Wednesday night, Baz.'

'Yeah? Well fuck Westie. He can go and flog ice creams on the fucking beach for all I care. Get a proper job for once. You know what he said to me just now? When I offered him one of them apartments in Marie's place? He said there's no way he's going to be tucked away with a bunch of fucking geriatrics.'

'I don't blame him. I was there, remember. He'd be knitting cardigans by Christmas.'

'Very funny. You want a drink?'

He left the kitchen without waiting for an answer. Winter glanced across at Marie. She was checking something in the oven. She was obviously in the loop.

'So what happened Wednesday night?' Winter enquired.

'Brett phoned. It was God knows how late – three, maybe later.'

'And?'

'Baz went down to the den to make some calls. Then he disappeared for an hour or so.'

'Any idea where he went?'

'No.'

Winter helped himself to a handful of cashew nuts from a bag on the table, wondering where the fifteen grand had come from. Bazza wouldn't keep that kind of money at home, not with the possibility of another visit from the Old Bill.

'You know why Westie's off on his travels?'

'More or less.'

'Baz hasn't spelled it out?'

'He doesn't need to. I'm not stupid. I knew it would end in tears, him and Danny Cooper.' She sighed, closing the oven door. 'He thought the world of the boy to begin with, gave him far too much rope.'

'Rope?'

'Help. Advice. Support, I suppose.'

'Money?' Winter knew he needed to be sure.

'Not to my knowledge. Baz is normally quite canny that way. Not mean just careful.' She paused, biting her lip, checking a detail in the recipe book. 'What happened to Danny, though, is way over the top.'

Winter could only nod in agreement. He remembered Danny Cooper in his Auntie Doris's spare bedroom. Telling Westie to get back in his tree hadn't been clever.

'I think it was Westie he'd upset, Marie, not Baz. Westie can be a bit literal sometimes. He didn't like the boy at all and if Baz gave him the green light the other night, he'd just go ahead and help himself.'

'And that's what happened? Baz gave him carte blanche?'

'I presume so.'

'With no thought of the consequences?'

'Westie? Consequences? Are you serious? The man's a firework. Just like Baz. I'm lots of things just now, Marie, but surprised isn't one of them.'

'But why? Why would Baz be so upset with the lad?'

'It's complicated. This is me playing the copper. Baz was shitting himself about Peter Ault. He thought Ault was likely to ask some hard questions about all the toot at the party. That cocaine came from Danny Cooper at a silly price and it wouldn't take long to put young Danny alongside Baz. The master and the apprentice.'

'So Baz had him *killed*?'

'Baz set Westie on him. He'd done it before but now he really wanted to frighten the lad. He wanted to make sure he'd never grass him up. But give Westie a serious grudge and if he's in the wrong mood you're looking at a death sentence.'

'That's madness.'

'You're right.'

Mackenzie returned with a bottle of champagne and three glasses. He was about to uncork the champagne when Winter told him to sit down. His head came up. He was scowling.

'You what?'

'We need to talk, Baz. All three of us.'

'Why's that then?'

Winter described the scene outside Westie's flat on the seafront. Scenes of Crime. Senior CID. Faraday. The works.

'Today?'

'Just now, Baz. As we speak. You've been up in that flat of Westie's recently? Wednesday night maybe?'

'No.' He shook his head.

'Where did you meet Westie then?'

'Sloppy Joe's'

'Busy?'

'Empty. Had the place to ourselves.'

'Thank Christ for that.'

Sloppy Joe's was a late-night drinking club. Westie evidently went there when he fancied a night slumming it in the back streets of Portsea. No way would the owner or the bar staff do the Filth any favours.

'So what is this?' Bazza was still holding the bottle of Krug. 'Anyone got the bollocks to tell me?'

Winter nodded at the empty chair. Finally he sat down. Marie too. Winter looked at them both. If ever he was to earn the money Mackenzie was paying him, it was surely now.

'Let's start with the Alfa, Baz.'

'It's been moved to a lock-up round the back of that industrial estate,' he said at once. 'And Barry's the only one with a key.'

'You're planning to torch it?'

'Yeah. In the end.' He frowned. 'So what's with Westie's flat?'

'They'll be boshing it by now, Baz. They'll be going through it with a toothcomb. Anything he's left – a speck of Danny's blood, soil out of his back garden, whatever – they'll find. They'll be after intelligence too. They'll want to know what's happened to Westie, where he's gone, how he got there, who paid for his ticket, the lot. All it takes, Baz, is a single mistake, anything that can link him to you on Wednesday night. That's what they'll be looking for, believe me. And if they find it, then we're all in the shit.'

Mackenzie nodded. The stiffness in his neck seemed to have eased.

'He phoned me Wednesday night,' he said. 'Three in the fucking morning.'

'Where was he?'

'Driving back from Salcombe Avenue.'

'A mobe?'

'Yeah.'

'Is he signed up to a plan, do you happen to know?'

'No. He uses pay-as-you-go. He thinks he's a gangster. He thinks it's cool.'

'Excellent. So what did he say on the phone?'

'He told me he'd done Danny Cooper.'

'Killed him?'

'Definitely. And that the place was in a bit of state. He also said he fancied getting away for a bit. I thought that was a cracking idea.'

'And?'

'He talked about Spain. Like I say, he needed money.'

'Did anyone check flights?'

'Not at that time in the morning. I just told him I'd phone for a cab. Gatwick seemed the best bet. Fucking hundreds of flights to Spain from there.'

'So you bunged him money?'

'Yeah. Fifteen grand buys you a nice ticket to Spain.'

'Where did the money come from?'

'A place I use.'

'Mind telling me where?'

'Yes, I fucking do. It's cushty. Safe as houses, mush. That's all you need to know.'

'OK.' Winter was aware of Marie beside him. 'So Westie goes off to Gatwick? Is that what you're saying?'

'Yeah. Sweet as you like.'

'And you?'

'I told him not to fucking come back. Ever.'

'Not best pleased then?'

'About Danny Cooper? You're right. A wet slap's one thing, even a dry one, but cutting his fucking throat is way out of order. You know what else he'd done? He'd taken a photo. Insisted on showing me. Disgusting. What's wrong with the man?' He shook his head then winced and reached for the bottle. As far as Baz was concerned, it was time for some bubbly. Danny Cooper off the plot. Westie gone. No clues. No mobe billings. No phone calls to airlines. Sorted.

Winter waited until the glasses were full. When Mackenzie proposed a toast, he shook his head.

'We're not through, Baz. Not by any means.'

'We're not?'

'No way. My guess is they'll find something. Don't ask me what but Westie's not perfect. He had an hour to leave his entire life behind. There'll be something in that flat, something that ties him to us. Did you ever pay him by cheque?'

'Cash. Always cash.'

'Were there any photos? Times you were snapped together? Social occasions?'

'Plenty. That's not a crime, though, is it? Getting pissed together?'

'Of course it's not. But they're looking for a pretext, Baz. Anything to take you down the Bridewell again. That'll happen tomorrow. I can practically guarantee it. And by then, my son, you'll need to account for every second of Wednesday night. Pretend I'm a copper. Pretend I know a thing or two about the interview routine. You get my drift?'

Mackenzie shot a look at his wife. She hadn't touched her champagne.

'You're telling me you want a little rehearsal? Here? Now?'

'Why not?'

'Because I don't want to, mush. That's why not.'

There was a long silence between them. Then Marie stirred.

'It was Wednesday night you came home pissed, Baz,' she said.

'I'd been with Westie. I told you.'

'I know. I was there. That was me you were breathing Scotch all over. Remember?'

'So why the third degree?'

'It's not the third degree. Paul's right. We need to be ready.'

'Ready, bollocks. I've got a brief. She'll tear them to pieces. Never fails.'

'And Paul?'

'He can have her too, if it comes to it.' He paused, struck by the thought. 'You think it will, mush? You think they'll come looking for you as well?'

Winter nodded. The issue of alibis was fast becoming a problem. He'd been with Misty too. All night. Time for a change of subject.

'Coppers are bastards, Baz. They'll do it out of spite.' He reached for his glass at last. 'Here's to crime.'

Chapter twenty-five

It was DCI Parsons' idea to celebrate Friday night's breakthrough with a curry. A first trawl through Brett West's flat by the Scenes of Crime team had scooped up a number of items, and the place was now secured for the night, with a uniform at the door, pending a return next morning for a full forensic search. Parsons rallied her modest army of troops on the pavement outside. Both Suttle and Faraday had homes to go to but she wouldn't hear of it. They needed a proper conversation. There were issues to be sorted for the following day and she'd order a takeout curry in lieu of dinner. Her shout, she insisted. And a little surprise once they'd got back to Major Crime.

As Faraday had half suspected, this was Willard. Alerted by a triumphant call from Parsons, he'd driven down from Winchester. He'd laid hands on a case of Stella and sat at the conference table in Martin Barrie's office, a half-empty bottle at his elbow, reading an old copy of the *News*.

While Parsons organised the curry, he turned to Faraday.

'Well, Joe ... ?'

'Most of it's circumstantial, sir. He was still logged onto the Internet. The PC screen was showing easyJet flights to Spain. He's got a little table down by the telephone and one of those books of Pompey maps. It was open at the Salcombe Avenue page. The lads found a pile of snaps in a drawer, some of them with him and Mackenzie. Then there was this ...'

Suttle had been expecting the cue. He'd stowed his bag beside the table. He reached in. The book looked like some kind of album. It was secured in a polythene evidence bag.

'We'll spare you the contents, sir. To be honest, we haven't seen the stuff ourselves yet. The CSI talked us through it. We gather it's not something you'd want to see before a meal.'

'Stuff?' Willard hadn't got much patience for games like these.

Faraday came to the rescue.

'There's always been rumours about Brett West, sir. Mackenzie used him as an enforcer for years and paid him by results. Brett started taking photos for the record and the habit stuck. What we've got here is the full story, unabridged.'

'Names?'

Faraday shook his head. 'Faces and dates, according to the CSI. Good as.'

'And we can link this stuff to Mackenzie?'

'That might be tricky. Not too many of these people will be happy to talk to us. Worth a shot, though.'

'Absolutely.' The thought put a smile on Willard's face.

Parsons returned, sliding into the seat beside Willard, who distributed bottles of Stella. Parsons, it seemed, couldn't get enough of the stuff.

'You've done well, Gail.' Willard emptied the remains of his own bottle and uncapped another. 'You've all done well. So what's the plan?'

'Jimmy will be onto the airlines soonest. EasyJet's an obvious place to start. If we don't get a result, we'll look elsewhere. Once we've got a destination airport, I'll talk to Interplod, sort out a warrant.'

Willard nodded. Parsons makes it sound easy, Faraday thought. Willard wanted to know about Mackenzie. Parsons threw the question to Faraday.

'We need to tie him to Wednesday night, sir. In my book that means finding the Alfa. They had it away last night. I'd say that's one hundred per cent. The question is, what did they do with it?'

'They?' So far Willard had only heard a garbled version of the chase through the city's back streets.

'Mackenzie was driving the Peugeot. It turns out to belong to his wife. The Alfa was in front. And no one's seen it since.'

'So who was at the wheel?'

'We're thinking Winter. For one thing, he's aware. If West used it the night before, which he probably did, then Winter knows how much we'd want a look at it. For another, Mackenzie trusts him.'

'How do you know?'

Faraday glanced at Suttle.

'Winter's got his feet under the table big time, sir. It seems Mackenzie's well pleased with him.'

'But how do you know?'

'Stands to reason.' Suttle risked a grin. 'Mackenzie wouldn't have bought him a Lexus otherwise.'

'And that's it? That's your evidence?'

'Of course not. I talked to him this morning. Had a little chat.'

'You did what?' Willard was staring at him.

'We asked him to, sir.' It was Faraday. 'Suttle was with Winter for a couple of years. If anyone knows what makes him tick, it's got to be Jimmy.'

'I see.' Willard took a swallow or two from his bottle. 'So what *does* make him tick?'

The question was unfair and everyone knew it. At the same time even Faraday was interested in the answer. Suttle refused to be bullied. For once he sensed he had the floor.

'Winter's bloody hard to read,' he said at last. 'But I'd say we let him down.'

Willard and Parsons exchanged glances. Faraday, aware of last year's U/C operation that these two had botched, awarded Suttle a silent round of applause. After all the corporate mumbo-jumbo about transparency and taking ownership now came a tiny glimpse of an important truth. They'd certainly let Winter down. Big time.

'Let down how, exactly?' A tiny vein was pulsing on Willard's temple.

'I don't know the details, sir. But I do know how Winter felt about it. Let down was my way of putting it. I'm not sure you want to hear his version.'

'Tell me.'

'I'd prefer not to, sir.'

'Tell me. That's an order.'

Parsons put a steadying hand on Willard's arm. Willard shook it off.

'Well?'

Suttle hadn't moved. His face had paled a little but his eyes were steady.

'He told me you both fucked up. He said you nearly got him killed. And then he told me that working for Mackenzie was sanity compared to what you'd put him through.' He paused. 'Maybe that's why Mackenzie treats him so well. Maybe that's why Winter loves his Lexus.'

Willard's face was a mask. Eventually he asked to see the book again.

'Book, sir?'

'The album thing, with the photos.'

'You mean West's souvenir shots?'

'Yeah.'

Suttle retrieved the album from his bag. Willard fingered it through the polythene bag. Then he looked up.

'I can imagine what's in here,' he said softly. 'Damaged people.

Hurt people. No angels, I'm sure, but people who never dreamed of running into the likes of Brett West. Just think about that for a moment, son. Just think what it takes to be the kind of nasty bastard who earns his living hurting people. Then ask yourself another question: ask yourself what kind of nasty bastard *pays* guys like West to hurt people. Then, if you're still with me, comes the third question, the last question. If Mackenzie's that kind of nasty bastard, what does it take to go and work for him? To bank his money? To break bread with the man? To get pissed with him? And to end up helping the likes of Brett fucking West cut some sad bastard's throat?'

'Helping sounds strong to me, sir. At this stage it's conjecture.'

'Sure, son. And when Winter goes down, as he will, what will you say then? That Mackenzie pulled the wool? That Winter didn't know what he was getting himself into? Winter wore the badge for twenty years. All kinds of people dug him out of the shit. And then he does this to us. The man's a disgrace. He was then and he is now. Thanks to you, thanks to all of you, we're close to putting Mackenzie where that evil little scrote belongs. Winter, fingers crossed, will go down too. Nothing will give me greater pleasure. And I hope that goes for you too.'

He got up, drained his bottle and left the room. In the silence Faraday listened to his footsteps receding down the corridor. Then came the crash of the swing doors at the end as Willard headed for the car park. Moments later Parsons was on her feet. Faraday couldn't be sure but he sensed that she was running down the corridor after him.

'Fuck ...' Suttle was shaking his head. 'Anyone care to tell me what all that was about?'

Faraday extended a hand, gave him a squeeze on the arm.

'You had no choice, Jimmy. In my book he asked for it. Literally, as it happens.'

'Yeah, boss? You think so?'

'Yes. And either you handle it or you don't. He didn't, more's the pity.'

'Great.' Suttle was staring at the album on the table. 'So what do I tell the sergeant's board? Assuming I'm still in the Job?'

Winter was back at Gunwharf shortly after eleven. He'd cut supper short, pleading a headache. Marie's moussaka had been as delicious as ever, but he knew she understood. Westie's recklessness, coupled with his determination to get even, had taken them into new territory. And time was short.

He had to assume they'd be knocking on his door within days, maybe even hours. They'd have a Section 8 warrant, and they'd doubtless do a Westie on his flat. With luck they'd draw a blank on the Alfa, at least for the time being, and what they threw at him in interview would depend on what they'd found in Westie's place. What that something might be didn't bear contemplation but Winter knew it was pointless worrying about it. First things first, he thought.

There were cameras in the undercroft car parking space. He locked the Lexus and sauntered across to the lift, whistling his tuneless whistle. Upstairs he let himself into his flat. Already he'd made a mental list of the stuff he needed to stow away. It wasn't a long list. In fact, putting himself in their shoes, it boiled down to a single item.

He'd already taken the precaution of wrapping it in a Waitrose carrier bag and slipping it into one of the leather slippers he'd liberated from the Burj al-Arab. He retrieved it now, then fetched a screwdriver from his toolkit in the airing cupboard and returned to the corridor. To his certain knowledge there were no cameras here.

At the end of the corridor, on the outside wall, close to the floor, there was a ventilation grille. If anyone came up, he told himself, he'd hear the lift. He bent to the grille, undid both screws very carefully, not marking the paint on the screwheads. The grille came away easily, revealing a cavity big enough for his tiny parcel. He pushed it in then replaced the grille. The paint seal was broken but it was a hairline crack and you'd need to look very hard to spot it.

Satisfied, he returned to his apartment and bolted the door. Through the bedroom window it was impossible to tell but he had to work on the assumption that they'd put surveillance in place. He gazed out at the shadows in the half-darkness, wondering where he'd be if the job had come his way, but there were dozens of possible spots and in the end he pulled the curtains shut and went back to the living room. Beyond the big picture windows the view that had become his life still beckoned him over. He slid the balcony door open, sniffed the saltiness on the night air, watched a couple necking by the railings on the Millennium Promenade. Beyond lay a couple of boats nudging the pontoon. Then came the blackness of the harbour, spiked with the lights of Gunwharf, and the pale looming presence of the Spinnaker Tower. He'd miss all this. He knew he would. He thought about the prospect for a moment longer then turned back into the room

For the first time he became aware of the messages awaiting him on the answerphone. He picked up the receiver, dialled 1571. The first had been left by Misty. She wanted to say hi after Wednesday night. She'd enjoyed it. A lot. The second voice was equally familiar. Jimmy Suttle. He'd rung barely minutes ago. It sounded like he'd had a drink or two. The message was only too clear.

'Take care, mate.'

Faraday finally made it back to the Bargemaster's House close to midnight. In Parsons' absence they'd taken the bags of curry back to Suttle's new flat, where the young detective had done a lot of damage to a bottle of vodka before hauling the chicken jalfrezi out of the microwave and ladling it onto a plate of lukewarm rice.

The exchange with Willard had left him quietly emotional. Suttle was fond of Winter. He thought he'd been a fucking great detective. He understood exactly why he'd binned last year's U/C operation and didn't altogether blame him for putting his eggs in Mackenzie's basket. Aside from anything else, he told Faraday, the old boy appeared to have found himself a family. He thought they cared about him, and when it came to that kind of call he'd trust Winter's judgement.

Faraday had agreed. But the problem, he told Suttle, wasn't Winter at all. As far as he could judge, *Mandolin* was no longer about a Saturday night party that had got out of hand. Neither was it about two bodies beside the swimming pool next door, or even Danny Cooper. It was about Mackenzie. About Operation *Tumbril*, years back, which had totally failed to pot the city's top criminal. About last year's bid to infiltrate Winter into his organisation. About all the other times that Mackenzie had flaunted his wealth and his growing influence, winding up the likes of Willard. The Head of CID didn't like that at all. One day, he said, Mackenzie would find himself in a court of law. And that time, in Willard's view, had probably arrived.

'So that's Winter fucked?'

'Highly likely.'

Suttle nodded, reaching for the remains of the vodka, and minutes later Faraday had left him stretched on the sofa, bottle in hand, eyeing the phone.

Now Faraday swung the Mondeo onto the hard standing at the front of the Bargemaster's House. Already he thought he could hear his son's wild cackle. Earlier he'd talked to Gabrielle on the phone. J-J was upstairs, she said, trying to find some game he used to play as a kid. Bad sign.

The pair of them were sprawled across the carpet in the living room. Between them lay the Monopoly board and J-J was clearly banker. He'd built estates of houses on Leicester Square, Bond Street, and the Old Kent Road, boasted two hotels on Mayfair and Islington, and amassed a tidy fortune in the process. Banknotes fluttered across the carpet as Faraday stepped through the door. Feeling the draught, J-J looked up and Faraday could read the surprise in his face. He thinks I've changed, he thought. He's wondering why I look so much bloody older.

J-J struggled to his feet. The bottle of wine beside the sofa was nearly empty. He must have brought it himself. Faraday never drank Bulgarian red.

Father and son embraced. Faraday caught the familiar scent of roll-ups in the tangle of J-J's hair. He wore it long, much longer than before, and it suited him. Faraday pulled away for a moment or two, taking a proper look, conscious of Gabrielle stepping lightly past towards the kitchen. J-J would be thirty soon, and if you looked hard you could see the onset of early middle age, but in Faraday's eyes he'd always remain the gawky bubbling adolescent who had brightened the years they'd shared at the Bargemaster's House. Deaf since birth, he communicated in a flurry of sign, his hands a blur, and to each of the important relationships in his life he brought a special variation on this intensely personal language. With Faraday he'd always bent into a conversation, closing the physical gap between them, the way you'd share a confidence or a joke, and he was doing it now.

'You look terrible,' he signed. 'What's been going on?'

'The usual,' Faraday signed back. 'Sorry I'm so late.'

'You want to finish the game with me?'

'Why not?'

Faraday got to his knees beside the board. Gabrielle's modest property empire was on the point of disintegration and within three throws of the dice Faraday was virtually bankrupt. Whitehall gone. Two precious railway stations sold for a song. Nothing in the bank but a handful of notes.

'Ask him about his exhibition.' Faraday felt the warmth of Gabrielle's breath in his ear. She'd brought another bottle of wine from the kitchen, something decent this time.

Faraday put the question. J-J was counting his money.

'I got a grant,' he signed. 'From a foundation in London.'

At first the purpose of the grant wasn't clear. There are limits to the amount of nuance that sign can carry, and Faraday had difficulty in pinning J-J down. He been taking photographs of kids in a special school. The kids were handicapped in some way.

'Deaf?' Faraday touched his ear.

J-J shook his head. In his view deaf kids weren't handicapped. He began to sway backwards and forwards, a strange rocking motion. Gabrielle was still beside Faraday. Even she seemed bemused.

J-J tried another gesture, flapping his hands, then a third, hugging himself, determined not to stoop to spelling out a particular word. It was like a game of charades. Finally, his repertoire exhausted, he shot Gabrielle a look and nodded towards the kitchen. She returned with a brochure and gave it to Faraday. Joe Faraday Jr would be hosting a private view of his photographs in a Chiswick gallery in a couple of months' time. The work had already won plaudits in a number of specialist magazines. It recorded a week spent in the company of kids at a residential home in Hammersmith.

Faraday looked up, at last understanding. How would you express autism in sign?

'They were great, these kids.' J-J was back in the world of sign, unpicking the week in Hammersmith with his long bony fingers. 'If you get close to them, *really* close to them, they respond.' He held his finger and thumb a millimetre apart, his eyes ablaze. 'People say you can't reach them.' A violent shake of the head. 'Wrong.'

He plucked the brochure from Faraday's hands and leafed through until he found the shot he was after. A child with an upturned face as bland as the moon was looking into J-J's lens. The fall of light from a nearby window threw deep shadows across the child's features. It wasn't clear whether this was a boy or a girl but there was something profoundly haunting about the eyes. They were the eyes of a cat, mysterious, beautiful, empty, and J-J had somehow judged the shot to perfection.

Janna had had the same talent, the same knack of tuning into a message scrambled by all the other noises off. Faraday had loved her for it, and tried – often unsuccessfully – to express his admiration.

'Your mother could have taken that shot.' He gave his boy a hug, then nodded at the brochure. 'Are we invited?'

Much later, after J-J had finished the second bottle and stumbled off to bed, Faraday led Gabrielle to the sofa. The last couple of days, in a wild burst of optimism, they'd planned their weekend on the Isle of Wight. Now came the moment when he had to tell her he couldn't come. *Mandolin*, like a thousand other operations, had thrown a grenade into the very middle of his private life.

To his surprise, Gabrielle said it didn't matter. The forecast was awful, she said. Rain and wind, and then more rain. More to the point, she'd had a phone call.

'Who from?'

'Connor.'

'The boy I met yesterday? That Connor?'

'*Oui.*'

'And?'

'He's found your girl. He wants money, *chéri.*'

'How much?'

'Fifty pounds. There's something else too. He thinks you're a cop.'

'How come?'

'I don't know. He said it was obvious. But he won't give the address. Not to you.'

'What happens then? For his fifty pounds?'

'He gives the address to me.' She smiled. 'And I go and see her.'

Chapter twenty-six

After a lousy night's sleep Winter was up early. He prowled around the big living room in his silk dressing gown, pausing now and again to peer out at the rain, wondering when to make the call. Eight would probably be too late. Seven, on the other hand, was a big ask, especially at the weekend. Too bad.

The number was slow to answer. She'd definitely been asleep.

'Lizzie? Paul. Listen, I need a favour ...'

He asked her for Jimmy Suttle's new address and only when the silence stretched and stretched did it occur to him that she might be there now, tucked up with the lad, cursing Winter for spoiling the start of a promising lie-in.

'119a Eastfield Road.'

'Milton? I know it. Cheers.'

He put the phone down and headed for the bathroom. Minutes later, showered and shaved, he was riding the lift to the undercroft.

Eastfield Road was one of the streets that latticed the south-east corner of the island. Way back, the endless lines of terraced houses had been built for workers from the naval dockyard. Generation after generation of families had grown up in streets like these but lately they'd been surrendered to a small army of jobbing builders who smelled a profit in subdivision.

A house became a couple of pokey flats. Solitary men of uncertain age shut their front doors on the world while bunches of students upstairs made their lives a misery. When Winter was serving on division the likes of Eastfield Road had featured prominently on the social nuisance index and nowadays he suspected it was probably worse.

Jimmy Suttle had the downstairs slice of the property. A rusting mountain bike was padlocked to a spindly tree in the scrap of garden at the front. Winter buttoned his raincoat and made for the front door. The bottom bell carried no name.

'Jimmy?'

Suttle had taken an age to answer. Naked except for a pair of boxers, he stood in the open doorway, blinking in the thin grey light. His eyes were bloodshot and he turned away wincing when a youth on a big retro Suzuki roared past.

Winter stepped into the house. The door to the ground-floor flat was open. Winter followed Suttle down a narrow hall. The kitchen was at the end. Suttle told him to sort out a pot of tea.

By the time he re-emerged, fully clothed, Winter had found half a loaf of bread and eggs a week past their sell-by date.

'Boiled or fried, son?'

Suttle shook his head. He felt dreadful. He'd necked half a bottle of vodka last night and hadn't touched the pint of water beside his bed. Big mistake.

Winter was inspecting the foil containers heaped on the work surface. Someone had made a half-hearted attempt to seal them up but they were still leaking curry. Winter counted them. There were eleven.

'Good party?'

'Crap. You remember I mentioned passing my sergeant's exams? I shouldn't have fucking bothered.'

'Who've you upset?'

'Don't ask.'

He watched Winter spoon sugar into a mug of strong-looking tea. There were tiny droplets of rain on his coat.

'Drink this, son. Do you the world of good.'

'Thanks.'

'You want me to ask Baz whether he's got anything going at the moment?'

'Like what?'

'Like a job.'

'Great idea.'

'You serious?'

'Of course I'm not.' He blinked again, ran a hand over his face, tried to clear his head. 'So why the social call? This time in the fucking morning?'

'We're in the shit, son. As you lot obviously know ...' Winter nodded at the wreckage of last night's curry. 'I need a steer, that's all.'

'About what?'

'About Westie. You're going to pull us in, I know you are. Probably today. At the latest tomorrow. A quiet word or two about that flat of his would be more than welcome.'

'You want to know what Scenes of Crime found?'

264

'Yeah.'

'I haven't a clue. The blokes start on the forensic this morning.'

'I didn't mean forensic. I meant that first intel scoop, once they'd done the door.'

'You mean last night?'

'Yeah. You're not telling me they found fuck all because I don't believe you.'

Suttle nodded, took another mouthful of tea, then wiped his mouth with the back of his hand. Winter watched his brain beginning to engage.

'We need the Alfa,' he said at last. 'If you're offering.'

'Alfa?' Winter did his best to look puzzled.

'The one you swifted away on Thursday night. You tell me where you've put it, and I'll give you chapter and verse on Westie's flat. I might even get the judge to run to some kind of plea bargain.' Suttle managed the beginnings of a grin. 'We gotta deal here?'

'You're joking.'

'But you know where it is?'

'No way. Last time I saw Westie's Alfa was last week. He got pissed at a party at Bazza's and nearly ran a bloke over in the street afterwards. I had to drive him home, put him to bed.'

'Neat.'

'What do you mean?'

'You're marking my card, aren't you? For when we find your prints?'

'Prints where?'

'In the Alfa ... and maybe in Westie's flat as well. We've got your prints on file, mate. That DUI last year.'

'You think I'm bluffing?'

'Of course you're bluffing. I worked with you, Paul. Remember?'

Winter nodded, helped himself to more tea.

'There *was* something, then ...' he said at last.

'Where?'

'At Westie's.'

'Of course there fucking was. And now it's sitting in the exhibits cupboard, as I'm sure you can well imagine.'

Winter stooped to the fridge, hunting for more milk. The sight of a cube of black resin wrapped in cling film put a smile on his face.

'That could almost pass for Oxo,' he said.

'It is Oxo.'

'Yeah, and I bet it smokes up a treat, doesn't it?' He splashed milk into his cup, reached for the teapot. 'Young Rachel and the boy Hughes—'

'What about them?'

'Something tells me it's not going well. You found Jax Bonner yet? After all that publicity?'

'No. But we will. It's just a question of time.'

'And then what?'

'We'll talk to her.'

'But you really think she did it?'

'It's a possibility, sure.'

'Top lead? Prime suspect?'

'Yeah ...' Suttle was frowning. 'I'd say so.'

'Shame.'

'Why's that?'

'Because you'd be wrong, son. And just now after all this media, all the grief you're gonna get from the Craneswater lot, all those lippy residents, that's going to be a major embarrassment. Not to you, son. Not to you personally. But maybe to others.'

Suttle was staring at him, trying to disentangle the bullshit from something else he sensed might be important.

Winter took a step closer, lowered his voice. He was looking at the remains of the curry again.

'Keep up with me, son. This might be important.'

'You're serious?'

'Yeah.'

'You want me to pass a message?'

'Yeah.' Winter nodded. 'I do.'

'About what? About Rachel? About Hughes?'

'Yeah.'

'And you're telling me you know who did it?'

'Yeah.'

'Evidence? Proof?'

'Both.'

Winter put the mug on the draining board, looked Suttle in the eye, then extended a hand and gave him a squeeze on the shoulder. Seconds later he'd gone.

Faraday had been at his desk in Major Crime since half past eight. He'd rung Gabrielle twice, talked at length to the CSI starting work on Brett West's flat and tried unsuccessfully to get in touch with Jimmy Suttle. Now Suttle had stepped into his office, soaked by the pouring rain, with news Faraday found hard to believe.

'You think he's bluffing?'

'No, boss, I don't think he is.'

'So you think he can deliver?'

'Yeah.' He wiped the rain from his face. 'I imagine he can. Even Winter understands bullshit has its limits.'

'But how? How has he got there?'

'When we haven't? Fuck knows. Maybe he's just better than us.'

'Inconceivable, Jimmy. Out of the question.'

It took a moment for Suttle to realise that Faraday was joking. Last night had clearly had an impact on him as well.

Suttle nodded at the phone on the desk. 'Have you heard from Parsons at all?'

'Nothing.'

'Mr Willard?'

'Zilch.'

'So how do we progress this, boss? As a matter of interest?'

'We don't, Jimmy. You leave it to me.'

He told Suttle to start working the phones. They needed confirmation that West had cabbed it to Gatwick. Calls to the airlines should produce a flight number and a destination. By that time DCI Parsons might be in a position to talk to Interplod and raise an international warrant.

'And Mackenzie? Winter?'

'I just told you, Jimmy. You leave that to me.'

He glanced up and nodded at the door. Suttle, taking the hint, left the office. Faraday lifted the phone and hit the redial button. This time Gabrielle's phone was on divert.

Bazza Mackenzie was having breakfast by the time Winter got to Sandown Road. Marie cleared an extra space at the kitchen table and broke a couple of extra eggs into the frying pan. The smell of the bacon made Winter realise how hungry he was.

He shook the rain off his coat and closed the kitchen door. Bazza was buried in the sports pages of the *Daily Mirror*.

'Haven't been arrested then, mush?'

'Not yet, Baz. Early days.'

'You think they'll get it sorted?

'I think they'll try.'

'Fuck all we can do then, really. Just wait.' At last his head came up. 'Or do we have a cunning plan?'

'No plan, Baz. Except the motor.'

'The Alfa? What about it?'

'My guess is they'll start sieving through the intel on the 6.57. Old names, old faces, anyone they can link to you. Your mate Barry's one of them.'

'Barry's sound, mush. Trust him with my life.'

'But that's the whole point, Baz. That's what you've just done and that's exactly what they'll expect. Which is why they'll be knocking on his door too.'

'You're serious?'

'Absolutely. It's called intelligence, Baz. They've got loads, and times like now, believe me, it comes in fucking handy. So maybe we have a think about the Alfa. Before they get round to paying a visit.'

Mackenzie nodded, then stifled a yawn.

'The Alfa went off first thing this morning,' he said. 'A mate of mine runs a scrapyard up in Swindon. He's got a crusher. Turns any motor into a bunch of teaspoons. Can't do better than that, can we?'

'Went off, Baz? You mean someone's *driving* it up there?'

'Sort of, yeah.'

He shot Winter a wolfish grin. Brian Tallow was another stalwart from the 6.57 days. He ran a removals business specialising in shipping stuff abroad. He had three second-hand furniture lorries, the sides emblazoned with the Union Jack. Winter had used him on a couple of Mackenzie Poolside jobs.

'Brian's running it up there?'

'Yeah. We loaded the Alfa first thing. Cushty, mush. Got anything on today? Only me and a few mates are off on a little outing. Southampton Airport. Half twelve.' Another grin. 'My shout.'

Parsons found it hard to believe. She'd perched herself on the edge of Faraday's desk. Faraday had just told her about Winter.

'He's taking the piss, Joe. He has to be. When someone goes to those lengths it means he's desperate.'

'What if he's not?'

'Desperate?'

'Taking the piss. What if he's been rooting around, asking questions, putting two and two together, maybe talking to some of the kids? What if they tell him stuff they won't tell us? Stuff that's led him to a name or two? He works for Mackenzie, remember. And that gives him access to the kind of pressure we can't possibly apply.'

'I'm not with you, Joe.'

'Have you taken a look at Brett West's souvenir book yet?'

'No.'

'You should. That's pressure, believe me.'

Faraday had donned a pair of gloves and leafed through the album only this morning. Slashed faces. Drilled kneecaps. Wounds no plastic surgeon could ever properly repair. Willard, in a way, had been right. This wasn't simply the work of a psychopath. Mackenzie, in the end, had made it happen.

'And you're telling me any of that assists the course of justice?'

'I'm telling you nothing, boss. Except that it's completely conceivable that Winter has beaten us to it.'

'Then surely it's just a question of time before we catch up.'

'Not necessarily. What if he's laid hands on a key piece of evidence? Something we'd need to make the case? What then?'

'We nick him.'

'But say he's gone to some lengths to hide this thing – whatever it is – away?'

She studied him for a long moment then frowned. 'You're suggesting we do some kind of trade?'

'I'm suggesting we explore the situation. We're in new territory, boss. Winter's sharp. He knows we're up against it. He knows we've got all kinds of people, powerful people, pushing us for a result. Media-wise, the force is still in the frame. We've spent a fortune already and there are lots of bills to come. We're nearly a week on and what have we got to show for it all? Sod all.'

'We've got Mackenzie. And Winter too.'

'That's a supposition.'

'You don't think we can make it stick?'

'Not as far as Rachel and the lad Hughes are concerned, no way. Maybe we can get some kind of result on Danny Cooper. But even then we've got to link Brett West to Mackenzie. You know they've been close. Half the bloody city knows West does jobs for Bazza but that proves nothing, not in a court of law. People won't be in a hurry to testify against Mackenzie. And if you want to know why, you should take a look at that album.'

Parsons shifted her weight on the desk. She hated admitting the force of anyone else's arguments. Finally, with some regret, she nodded at the phone.

'Do you make the call, or do I?'

'What call?'

'To Mr Willard. This is way above my pay grade, Joe. And frankly it's probably above his too.'

Misty Gallagher was ten minutes early for the meet at Gunwharf. She rang Winter from the entrance to the undercroft parking area. She needed the code to raise the barrier. Minutes later she was emerging from the lift and blowing him a kiss the length of the third-floor landing.

'Do I smell coffee?'

'Another day, Mist. I'm late as it is.'

She followed Winter into the flat. A holdall lay on the sofa, half-packed. Winter disappeared onto the landing with a screwdriver.

'DIY time, Paulie?' she called.

'Don't ask.'

A couple of minutes later, Winter was back with something small, wrapped in a Waitrose shopping bag.

'Guard it with your life, Mist. Like I said, no one needs to know.'

'Baz?'

'No one. And keep it somewhere fucking safe. Just in case.'

'Just in case what?'

'Just in case the Bill come looking. We can't rely on them being stupid all the time, can we?' He looked her in the eye. 'You with me, Mist?'

'Of course I am.' She was weighing the little parcel in her hand. 'Best not leave it in the house then, eh?'

'Best where no one's going to find it. It's your call, Mist, but speaking personally I'd dig a hole in that garden of yours and bury it. And I'd do it after dark, yeah?'

'You want it back?'

'Of course I want it back. But not just yet, love.'

He sat beside the holdall and began to pack a modest pile of clothes. Misty watched him, intrigued.

'Going somewhere nice?'

'No idea, Mist, absolutely none. But this is Bazza, isn't it? He's staring a conspiracy charge in the face and we're all off on fucking holiday. Anyone else, I'd say they'd lost it.'

'Conspiracy to what?'

'Murder.'

'You're serious?'

'Too fucking right.' Winter checked his watch then nodded at the package. 'You happy about that? No second thoughts?'

Misty was still digesting the news about Bazza. It turned out he'd appeared first thing this morning, letting himself into the house and banging around downstairs without even bothering to say hello.

'You saw him?'

'I yelled down in the end. He said he was just off out again.'

'What did he want?'

'No idea. It happens sometimes.'

She shrugged and slipped the package in her bag. Then she bent low, kissing Winter on the lips.

'You owe me, you know that?'

'Great.' He managed a smile. 'But some other time, eh?'

Chapter twenty-seven

Gabrielle and J-J took the bus up to Drayton. Connor, as promised, was waiting inside the fish and chip shop across the pavement from the bus stop. The minute he saw J-J, he stepped out into the rain and began to walk away.

Gabrielle caught him further down the parade of shops. Since she'd last seen him, he seemed to have acquired a gold chain. It was looped around his scrawny neck, the bottom disappearing beneath a fold of shirt.

'You never told me about no other geezer.'

'He's OK. A friend, that's all.'

'Why bring him?'

'Because I had to.'

'Who says?'

'My other friend.'

'The bloke I met? He *was* a cop, wasn't he? See ... I was right. And he's your friend too? Fuck that.'

He made to turn on his heel but she pulled him back. Her strength surprised him.

'No bird does that to me.' He brushed his sleeve. 'That's out of order.'

'I'm sorry. I apologise.'

'Yeah?' He was uncertain now, the rain streaming down his face.

'Here.' She nodded at a nearby convenience store. The pavement was dry beneath the plastic awning. Connor was taking a harder look at J-J, who'd sought shelter in the doorway of a nearby estate agency. Something clearly puzzled him.

'What's he like then, this bloke?'

'He's deaf.'

'*Deaf?* You're joking. How does he hear then?'

'He doesn't. That's why he's deaf. Deaf and dumb.'

'Can't talk neither?'

'No.'

'And you think I believe that? You think I'm some kind of cunt? Really stupid, like?'

Gabrielle beckoned J-J over. In a burst of sign she explained that Connor was worried about the fact that she had company.

J-J nodded. Then turned to Connor. He put his head on one side, raised his hands in a despairing gesture then rolled his eyes. Even Connor laughed.

'He's fucking simple, your mate. That's well cool. Do it again.'

'*Quoi?*'

'The hands bit. Like you did just now.'

Gabrielle obliged. This time she signed that Connor needed to get out more. J-J signalled his agreement by winking at Connor and sticking up both thumbs.

'What's that about then?'

'I told him you were going to help us. With the address.'

'Yeah ...?' He frowned. Then his bitten fingers strayed to the tiny gold cross on the chain round his neck. 'You got the dosh?'

'*Oui.*'

'Let me see it.'

Gabrielle took an envelope from her bag. The money was in ten-pound notes. She counted them then returned the notes to the envelope.

Connor turned back to J-J.

'Is he going with you?'

'*Oui.*'

'And you say he's deaf? Really deaf. Can't hear nothing?'

'*Oui.*'

'All right.' His hand came out for the money.

Gabrielle shook her head. She wanted the address first. That was the deal. No address, no money.

Connor was frowning. He took another look at J-J then nodded towards the estate agent's window.

'Over there.'

They left the shelter of the canopy. Jax Bonner had a half-brother, he said. This bloke was the son of the sort her dad had married. He worked as an estate agent, had loads of empty property on the firm's books. Jax was living in one of them. No one had shown any interest in the place for months. He'd given her the key. On the quiet, like.

'So what's the address?'

'There. That one.' They were standing outside the estate agency. Connor's thin finger was pointing at a scruffy bungalow no camera angle could ever beautify. The property was in Wymering. Walton Road.

'What number?'

'Seven.'

'And she's in now?'

'Yeah. She's always in.' Connor pocketed the folded notes, then looked at J-J again. 'She'll like him, Jax. She'll think he's a right laugh.'

Winter took a cab to Southampton Airport, arriving a couple of minutes after half twelve. Bazza was already there, beside the news-stand on the main concourse. With him were three faces Winter recognised at once. Two of them were local mates of Bazza's from way back, both handy scrappers, both football crazy. Winter had used them on the courier service since February and knew they liked a party. The other man was short, thickset, in jeans, new-looking trainers and a Lonsdale T-shirt. His shaven skull was golden under the artificial lights and his mirrored shades made Winter realise he was even fatter than he liked to believe.

Bazza did the introductions.

'Tommy Peters,' he said. 'Face from London. Don't believe you've had the pleasure.'

'Wrong, Baz. We met years ago.'

'Albany,' Peters confirmed. 'I was doing a five for attempted murder. This cunt fronts up one afternoon, tries to turn me into some kind of supergrass.'

'Never worked, though, did it, Tommy?' Winter extended a hand. 'Can't say I blame you.'

Peters refused the proffered handshake. Travelling with Winter was clearly something of a surprise. Bazza took them both to one side.

'Paul works for me now, Tommy. Has done for the best part of a year.'

'And you're telling me you fucking trust him?'

'Tommy, I fucking do. And I'll tell you something else. You will too. Or you're back on the fucking train.'

Peters removed the shades and for a moment Winter wondered whether this little scene was about to turn ugly.

'Give me one reason,' he said, nodding at Winter. 'I'm a reasonable bloke. One'll be enough.'

'OK.' Bazza nodded. 'This morning we had to bin a motor. It happened to be an Alfa. I told Paul here it was going to a scrapyard in Swindon. I chose Swindon because there's only one yard there and I happen to know the bloke who owns it. I won't go into details, Tommy, but that motor can put me inside. Now young Paul, he has half the morning to make a few calls, arrange an interception, get the yard staked out, whatever. That's if I've got him wrong after all this time. And you know what? Not one cunt turned up. I checked with the owner half an hour ago. Clean as a whistle.'

Winter had listened to the story with growing interest. The implications were all too obvious.

'So where did the Alfa really go?' he enquired.

'Basingstoke, you daft cunt.' Bazza shot him a grin. 'You think I'm stupid?'

Mackenzie had hired an executive jet. After cursory passport checks Bazza's party clambered aboard. Seven leather seats on either side of the tiny fuselage left plenty of room for an on-board hostess but to Winter's disappointment Bazza had designated himself master of ceremonies. The flight down to Malaga, he announced, would take three hours. He'd be serving chilled Krug and burgers on the way down, something a bit livelier on the return trip.

'When's that then, Baz?' It was Peters. Evidently he had an important meet with a lawyer back in Slough on Tuesday.

'Tomorrow, Tommy. Or maybe Monday. Depends.'

The plane took off, climbing steeply over Southampton's city centre. As the view was shredded by low cloud, Mackenzie caught a glimpse of St Mary's Stadium, home to the city's football team.

'Fucking Scummers,' he muttered to no one in particular.

Minutes later, with the plane levelling out in bright sunshine, he made his way back to the tiny galley. The pop of a cork announced the first bottle of champagne and Bazza's reappearance with a silver tray and four brimming flutes sparked a round of applause.

Only last year Winter had been on a similar outing – to watch Pompey playing away at Middlesbrough – and the madness of the weekend had left a permanent impression. Not because Bazza allowed himself to become the plaything of the millions he'd stashed away from the cocaine biz, but because he loved to celebrate the reach and the status the money had given him. Twelve months later that instinct to establish himself in life's pecking order was no less strong. Indeed, given the likely consequences of Westie's recklessness, it was probably even stronger. No one, thought Winter, would ever be silly enough to underestimate Bazza Mackenzie. Especially now.

He settled back in the seat, his glass empty, the sun on his face. His eyes closed and he was enjoying the warm anticipation of a little doze when he felt a touch on his arm.

It was Bazza. He had a fresh bottle of Krug and he'd perched himself on the arm of the empty seat across the aisle.

'Splash more, mush?'

'No thanks, Baz.'

'Very wise.'

Winter opened one eye again. He knew Bazza in this mood. He recognised the tone of voice.

'Not just a jolly then?'

'Afraid not.'

Winter twisted in his seat to look back down the plane.

'It's Westie, isn't it?'

'Of course it is.'

'And is that why Tommy's drinking Coke?'

A morning of steady rain had done nothing for 7 Walton Road. Gabrielle pushed in through the gate and picked her way across the broken paving slabs. A steady dribble of water from broken guttering splashed onto the stained single mattress abandoned beneath the front window and a smeared note on the door warned intruders about the resident Alsatian. The note drew a wag of the head from J-J. He'd never liked dogs.

Gabrielle knocked at the door. Moments later a face appeared at the neighbouring window. It was a girl's face. She was wearing a flat cap and heavy make-up. She was beautiful, Gabrielle thought. Full lips, a slash of deep scarlet on a wonderfully pale face.

The face disappeared and moments later the door opened.

'Jax Bonner?'

The girl nodded. She was looking at J-J.

'Your friend, right?'

'*Oui.* Connor? He phoned you?'

'Yeah. Come in.'

The house smelled of damp. J-J padded warily from room to room.

'What's the matter with him?'

'He hates dogs.'

'But why is he deaf? Why can't he hear?'

'*Sais pas.* With some people it's that way forever, from birth.'

'Weird.'

'Sure. But you learn to get by.'

'How old is he?'

'Nearly thirty.'

'He looks younger.' She frowned. 'Weird,' she said again.

J-J had rejoined them, more relaxed now. The dog was outside in the tiny back garden, chained to a drainpipe. J-J found himself a space on the sofa. Apart from the sofa and a single dining chair, the room was bare.

'You've lived here for long?' he signed.

Gabrielle translated. Jax couldn't take her eyes off J-J's hands, always on the move, always shaping fresh thoughts.

'Nearly a week,' she said.

'It's shit,' he signed.

'You're right.' She nodded. 'But better than the Bridewell.'

Gabrielle couldn't translate Bridewell into sign, partly because she hadn't a clue what the word meant. Jax was looking at J-J. She tried to draw a cell with her hands, up and down movements for the bars, then the turn of a key in a lock and an extravagant outward movement as an imaginary door swung open. J-J made her do it again, then gave her thumbs up.

'Prison,' he signed to Gabrielle.

This tiny pantomime broke the ice. For the first time Jax smiled. Her teeth were stained and broken in that perfect face.

'You're the French woman working with the kids, right?'

'Yes.'

'So what's that about?'

Gabrielle moved the dining chair so she could see J-J and then sat down. She explained she was working on a project for a French university. It had to do with gang structures among kids, here and in France. One day it might make a book. In the meantime it was her business to listen.

'And what do the kids tell you?'

'Lots of things.'

'Do they tell you how crap this country is?'

'Sometimes they tell me how crap their lives are.'

'Same thing. Crap country. Crap lives. Except the kids you're seeing are too young to fucking understand it.'

'Connor?'

'He's too stupid. Plus he smokes too much weed. Just like his fucking brother. You know Clancy? I've given him houseroom until we have to move on. He's like Connor when it comes to weed. He tells me he can't sleep without it. Twat.' She paused, staring at Gabrielle. 'So what do you want?' It seemed more than a question. It was a challenge. You've found me here, she seemed to be saying. You've got beyond my door. You've invaded my space. This better be worth it.

'We need to talk about the party.'

'Why? Because your boyfriend asked you?'

'Yes.' She nodded. 'In a way, yes.'

'Connor says he's Old Bill.'

'*Comment?*'

'Filth. Police. A cop.'

'That's right. He is.'

'So why isn't he here?'

'Because he doesn't know where to find you.'

'But you'll tell him, won't you? You're bound to.'

'No. Unless you want me to.'

'*Want* you to? Why the fuck would I want to do that? The Filth are like everyone else. Stitch you up as soon as look at you.'

'You think that?'

'I know it. They stitched my brother up. That's why he's inside. That's why I've been spending a fortune going off to see him every time they bother to give me a fucking visit.'

'And the party? On Saturday?'

'They'll do me for that. I know they will. They'll do me for the two kids by the pool. Prime fucking suspect. They'll do me for every fucking thing. Why? Because they're lazy and because they're evil. You say you live with this bloke? This Filth? Eat with him? Sleep with him? If you think he's a human fucking being, if you think there's an ounce of decency in him, try looking a bit harder. It's under your nose. Shit ...' She shook her head, turned her face away. 'Why do I bother with all this stuff? Why does anyone?'

Watching her, Gabrielle felt the first prickle of fear. The kids were right about Jax Bonner. In moments like this she was out of control, insane, *complètement folle.*

Be careful, they'd told her. She carries a blade. She lashes out. She doesn't care who she hurts.

Gabrielle glanced at J-J. She'd told him a little about the background on the bus coming up: the party, the two bodies, Faraday trying – as ever – to make sense of it all. This girl's the closest they've got to an answer, she'd said. She hates the world and she doesn't care who knows it.

J-J signed a question. Jax wanted to know what it was.

'He's asking whether you killed Rachel Ault.'

'No.' She shook her head. 'I didn't.'

Another question, more complex.

'Would you liked to have done?'

'Dunno.'

'But you might?'

'Maybe.'

'Why?'

'Because she was a spoiled little rich kid. Because life had looked after her. Because she'd got everything. And because she had that arsehole judge as a father. You know something else, though?' She was looking directly at J-J. 'She was lost. You could see it. And it wasn't just us turning up. I watched her. I watched her on and off most of the night. She was pissed as a rat, totally wasted, but her eyes ... Fuck.' She shook her head again. 'You know something? I've probably got a happier life than her. And I mean it.' She broke off, looking to Gabrielle for a translation.

Gabrielle did her best. J-J was looking thoughtful.

'You really mean that?' He wanted to know.

'Yeah. Definitely. I've taken some shit in my life, believe me. I can be a bad person too. I do horrible things. I hurt people. And sometimes I even enjoy it because I think they deserve it, because it gives me a kick to see them in pain, but deep down I know who I am. She didn't. Not that girl. Not that Rachel. She was all over the place. So now I think about it, there'd be no point.'

'In what?' It was Gabrielle this time.

'Hurting her. Killing her. Whatever. No point at all.'

Jax nodded at J-J as if she'd stumbled over a small but important truth. J-J signed that he believed her. The news made her laugh.

'Big fucking deal.' She was looking at Gabrielle. 'So what do you do now? With all this?'

Gabrielle studied her for a long moment, and then got to her feet.

'I go back to my friend,' she said. 'And I translate for him too.'

Chapter twenty-eight

Willard brought the news from headquarters. Force Intelligence, he said, had picked up rumours of a candlelit wake for Rachel Ault and Gareth Hughes, a week on from their deaths. Their friends planned to gather in Sandown Road at dusk. There might be music and readings. There'd doubtless be tears. There might even be more flowers.

Willard had found himself a seat in Faraday's office. Suttle was there too.

Faraday wanted to know where the intelligence had come from.

'Facebook,' Suttle told him. 'It's been up on the Rachel page since yesterday.'

Faraday permitted himself a smile. This was how the madness had begun, he thought. There were no secrets any more. People had forgotten how to be private, how to be discreet. The world of word-of-mouth, of the whispered invitation or the card through the door, had gone. Every life was public property, broadcast, advertised, flaunted. That way you might get to be famous.

'The Public Order boys are doing a risk assessment.' It was Willard. 'The last thing we need is a repeat of last week. The Chief's giving serious thought to having the demo banned.'

'It's not a demo,' Faraday pointed out, 'it's a wake, a farewell.'

'That's not the way he sees it. Neither, I imagine, will our Craneswater friends.'

Faraday shook his head. Madness was too small a word. The prospect of banning a bunch of kids with candles on the grounds of public order was surreal.

'How about Ault? It's his daughter, after all.'

'Ault won't express an opinion either way. We understand he's selling up.'

Faraday nodded. The news came as no surprise. He was a shell of a man, as damaged as the house he'd once called home.

Suttle wanted to know whether the judge had joined forces with

279

the residents' association. If anyone had a case against the forces of law and order, it was surely Ault.

'Not at all. As I say, he seems to have had enough … which is a bit of a bonus, to be frank. The last thing we need is someone of his weight against us. Especially if this wretched thing goes ahead tonight.'

The prospect of another round of press and TV interviews appeared to fill Willard with gloom, a realisation that Faraday found deeply amusing. A week ago the Head of CID had lost no time courting the headlines. Now, with *Mandolin* still empty-handed, he was growling about unnecessary distractions. Live by the media, Faraday thought, die by the bloody media.

'Has DCI Parsons mentioned Winter at all?' Faraday asked.

'Yes.'

'And?'

'And what? You want my personal view? I'd arrest him this morning.'

'On what grounds, sir?'

'Taking the piss. I don't know who had the conversation but it's got Winter's MO all over it. He must think we're simple.'

'It was me, sir.' Suttle had come to brief Faraday on Brett West's whereabouts. 'It was me who had the conversation.'

'Surprise, surprise. You're supposed to be dealing in intelligence, Suttle, not fairy tales. Winter's in a tight corner. He knows the game's up. Personally I'd ignore him but what happens next isn't my decision. Where is he, by the way?' Willard was looking at Suttle again. 'Anyone care to tell me?'

The executive jet touched down at Malaga Airport at 17.23 local time, slowed by headwinds over the Pyrenees. It taxied to a halt some distance away from the line of holiday jets, awaiting a welcome from the charter company's local rep. He arrived in a luxury minibus and shepherded Bazza's party into the cool of the airport's business centre. Arrival formalities were over in minutes. Bazza had prebooked a black Mercedes saloon. Before he sat down with the rep to complete the hire form, he handed Winter a brown leather shoulder bag.

'There's twenty-five grand in there,' he muttered. 'Don't fucking lose it.'

From the airport Bazza followed signs for the city of Malaga. A mile or so down the road he slowed for a rest area beside the motorway. Parked at the far end was a white van. Bazza drew in behind it and killed the engine. Tommy Peters got out. Someone reached across the front of the van and opened the passenger door. Without a backward glance Peters climbed in. Moments later the van was pulling out of the rest area to rejoin the motorway.

Bazza followed, tucked in behind the van. Winter sat beside him, impressed. Bazza had always painted himself as the master of improvisation, thinking on his feet, pulling stroke after stroke, plucking victory from the jaws of defeat, but this was very different. Someone had thought about this, planned it, made proper arrangements. Tommy Peters, Winter thought, with his Lonsdale T-shirt and his Costa del Sol connections. Hence the money.

'We're going to a place along the coast, mush.' Bazza's gravelly voice was barely a whisper. 'Tommy knows a new development there. It's private, empty, cushty. He knows the people who're doing the biz on it. We're gonna drop you outside a bar they're building at the back end of the site. What you do is you go in. You'll have the place to yourself. It's still fitting out but there'll be a table there. There'll be drinks too, and maybe something to eat if the bloke's offering. And then you'll phone Westie.'

Winter took the proffered mobile. With it was a scrap of paper with a number in Bazza's handwriting.

'Where is he?'

'In Malaga somewhere, fuck knows. You tell him where you are. You tell him I've just bought a fucking big stake in the place. You give him the impression I'm gonna be huge around here. The directions are written out for you on a table in the bar. And then you tell Westie you've got a couple of hours, tops, before you have to get back to the airport.'

'What if he wants to meet somewhere else?'

'He won't. Because you also tell him you've got the money.'

'The twenty-five grand?' Winter was looking at the shoulder bag. 'You told me last night he was expecting a hundred.'

'Doesn't matter, mush.. It's all in tens. It looks a lot. Just don't let him count it. Not that he's going to have time.'

'No?'

'No. All you've got to do is sort the cunt a drink, sit him down and have a little chat. Then it's over.'

'Over?'

'Forget it. Leave it to Tommy.'

Winter nodded, paying closer attention to the van. It looked like a builder's van. There were dents in the plastic rear mudguard and the back doors were secured with a twist of rope. With most of Spain a building site, Winter thought, there must be thousands of vans like this all along the coast. In so many ways it was perfect.

They were in the city centre now, heading down a dual carriageway beside the port. The van threaded through the traffic, Bazza behind. A big sign for Almeria took them east, beneath the battlements of a castle. Beyond the traffic intersection Winter glimpsed a circular building half-hidden by smaller blocks.

'That's the bullring,' Bazza told him. 'Me and Marie went once. Fucking animals, the Spanish.'

The van was picking up speed now, helped by a succession of green lights. The city began to thin but views of the sea were screened by an unending ribbon of bars, shops and newish-looking beachside developments. Then, suddenly, the sprawl of suburbs had come to an end and the Mercedes was purring past a huge cement factory. Winter sat back, gazing out at a queue of waiting lorries. Picturesque? He thought not.

Beyond the cement works the road began to dip, and minutes later the journey came to an end. Rincon de la Victoria was a prosperous seaside town wedged between the mountains and the sea. Early evening had softened the brutal heat and the café-bars along the main street were beginning to fill. The van pulled left and there was a puff of blue smoke from the exhaust as the driver changed gear for the climb. The road wound through a residential estate – high whitewashed walls, heavily secured gates, glimpses of an occasional pool – and then they were out on the bare mountainside. On the left yet another development. The van slowed, indicating left. Winter caught sight of a huge roadside placard – *Las Puertas del Paraiso*. The Gates of Paradise.

At this time of the day, as Mackenzie had promised, the place was empty. The Mercedes bumped over the construction road that threaded through the half-built complex. At the end the diggers had levelled a turning space in front of a low two-storey building, more complete than the rest of the development. Beyond, Winter could see nothing but rocky brown scrub.

The van had pulled round in a tight circle. Bazza brought the Mercedes to a halt outside the building.

'Out you get, mush. The bloke's name is Hernandez. Don't forget the fucking phone.'

Winter stepped out of the Mercedes. He could taste the sea on the warmth of the wind. Bazza gunned the engine, leaving him in a cloud of dust. The Wild West, he thought. Without the charm.

The bag looped over his shoulder, he climbed the bare concrete steps that led to a pair of imposing glass doors. Everything was unfinished but the doors opened with a sigh to his first push. Inside, in the gloom, he could smell cement dust and the damp of drying plaster. Ahead, through an opening with no door, lay what he assumed to be some kind of lounge. On the rough concrete floor a table with two chairs at right angles. On the table two bottles of San Miguel. Beyond the table the long curve of a bar covered in blue plastic sheeting.

'*Buenas noches.*'

A thin stooped figure in jeans and a stained white shirt had stepped out of the shadows behind the bar. He looked close to retiring age. When Winter asked if his name was Hernandez, he shrugged as if he didn't know. He gestured for Winter to join him in the lounge and nodded at the beers on the table.

'You want a glass?' Thick English, heavily accented.

'Yeah.'

'Please. You sit there, at the end.'

The table was laid for two, at right angles, just a fork and a plate. Winter studied them a moment, then rearranged the placings face-to-face, aware of Hernandez watching him. Beside his plate was a sheet of paper with directions to *Las Puertas del Paraiso* from nearby Malaga. The directions were in English and Winter looked at them for a while before reaching for one of the bottles. The beer was ice cold. Nice.

Hernandez disappeared, returning with two glasses. Winter drank the first bottle quickly, opened the other. Then he turned his attention to the phone.

Westie answered on the third ring. He was evidently expecting the call.

'You got here OK then?'

'Yeah.' Winter told him how to find the development in Rincon. There was a pause before Westie answered.

'What the fuck are you doing out there?'

'Don't ask, mate. I've got what you're after. Just turn up and it's yours.'

'Let's meet somewhere closer.'

'I can't, son. I'm back to the airport for seven. It's either here or *adiós*. Your call, Westie.'

There was another silence. Winter tried to picture Westie's surroundings. Had he found somewhere to live? Was he in a café? Or walking the beach, eyeing the talent? And how would he get out to this godforsaken place? A virtual stranger to this new life of his?

Finally he was back on the line. *Las Puertas* rang a bell. What was Bazza's interest?

'He owns the fucking place.'

'Yeah?' He began to laugh. He'd be with Winter in half an hour. Be nice to see him again.

Winter put the phone down and emptied his glass. His bartender was nearly invisible in the gloom. Winter gestured at the empty bottles.

'Any chance of another, Mr H?'

Suttle had scored an early result with easyJet. Faraday, working slowly through the pile of paperwork on his cluttered desk, wanted the details.

'Brett West took the Thursday morning flight to Malaga.' Suttle was reading from notes. 'He travelled under his own name. There were no delays on the flight and he'd have been in Malaga by two o'clock in the afternoon. Beyond that I'm afraid we haven't a clue.'

'How did he get to the airport?'

'Speedycab.'

'That's Mackenzie's firm, right?'

'Yep. I've got a name and contact number for the driver. When do you want it actioned?'

'As soon as.'

'Then I'll do it myself. What are we after?'

'A link to Mackenzie. Just using one of his cabs is not enough. We need evidence of payment. If he got a freebie, that could be very interesting. What else?'

Suttle brought Faraday up to date. On the basis of Production Orders, he'd be talking to West's bank on Monday, looking for trans-action details on his two accounts. The same went for his credit card. The force telephone unit was in touch with Orange, and billings on his mobile, with luck, should be available within days.

Faraday nodded. These were routine enquiries, strands in the net that Major Crime threw over life after life. In normal circumstances, with the prospect of a suspect in the custody suite, data like this could trap a man in a lie and occasionally open the door to a confession. But that, Faraday sensed, wasn't going to happen. Not for a while at least.

'You think he's coming back?' he asked.

'No chance, boss.' Suttle shook his head. 'Not until we find him.'

Winter was on his third San Miguel when he heard the clatter of a diesel. Moments later there was the sound of a door slamming, then came the clump of footsteps on the concrete steps outside. He pushed back his chair and looked round. Not one figure silhouetted against the blaze of evening sunshine, but two.

Westie's tall frame stepped into the bar. He was wearing jeans and a white T-shirt. Beside him, smaller but just as lean, was a woman. In the dusty gloom it was hard to be certain but at first glance Winter thought early twenties. Her bare legs were long and tanned. Her hair fell in blond ringlets around a wide pretty face and the smile was unforced.

'Renate,' Westie announced.

Winter stood up and offered the woman the spare seat. Westie, uninvited, took the other. Hernandez ghosted in with a third chair which he placed at the head of the table.

'So how come ...?' Westie gestured round. Bare electric cables hanging from the ceiling. Unglazed window frames. A thin silt of cement dust underfoot.

'I like it. It's like a film set. It's cool.' Renate leaned across the table and put a hand on Westie's arm. She wore a silver bangle on her slim brown wrist. Her English was near-perfect.

'Known Westie long?' Winter enquired.

'Since yesterday. He comes to my gallery. He likes my pictures. He has taste, your friend. He knows what to say, how to say it. We can get a drink here?' She nodded at the empty bottles on the table then began to wind a strand of hair around a single finger.

Winter signalled to Hernandez. Two more San Miguels appeared.

'Sorted then?' Winter was back with Westie, full of admiration. 'No more Pompey slappers?'

'Never, mate. No fucking way.'

'And what about the flat?'

'It's up for sale. Say the word and the mortgage is yours. Good bloody riddance.'

'No regrets? None at all?'

'Are you blind, mate?' He nodded towards Renate. 'Or just fucking old?'

He wanted to know about the money. Winter, increasingly uncomfortable, noticed that Hernandez had disappeared.

'It's down there, Westie. In the bag.'

'You've counted it?'

'No, but Baz has. First thing this morning. Before I got the plane down.'

'What time was that?'

'Early.'

'How early?'

'Bloody early.'

'Which airport?'

Winter sat back. Even the girl could sense the hesitation in his voice.

'Pub quiz is it, Westie? Think of a question? Any question?'

'Not at all, mate. Down here we call it conversation. I'm just asking which poxy airport you flew out of this morning. Gatwick? Big place off the M23? Bournemouth? Heathrow? Only you're starting to make me nervous, mush.' His eyes flicked down to the bag. As they did so

Winter heard the lightest footfall in the shadowed spaces behind the bar.

It was Tommy Peters. He'd appeared from nowhere. He had an automatic in his right hand. The silencer made the gun look enormous. The girl had seen it too. Her hand went to her mouth. Westie had his back to the bar. His big mistake was to look round.

He tried to get to his feet but it was too late. The first bullet took him in the chest, the softest *phutt* from the silencer; the second hit him in the lower jaw, sending a fine spray of blood over Winter. He looked up to see the gun traversing towards the girl. The impact of Westie against the table had sent her sprawling. Now she was crouching on the floor, one arm shielding her upturned face, pleading for her life.

'Easy, Tommy.' Winter tried to get his body between the two of them.

Tommy Peters glanced across, the merest flicker of irritation, before stooping to the girl and putting three more bullets into her head. Two figures materialised from behind the curtain at the back. Winter recognised neither of them. Tommy grunted something about the van then helped them manhandle West's body through the back of the bar. Winter sank back into his seat, hearing their grunts recede into the depths of the building. Then came the sound of a sliding door, metal on metal, from somewhere outside.

Hernandez had appeared with a mop and a bucket. Winter was staring down at the girl. One of the bullets had smashed her cheekbone. An eyeball hung, glistening, in the slant of evening sunlight through the nearby window. Winter had never seen anything as terrible as this. It had happened so quickly, he told himself. There was nothing he could have done to stop it.

Tommy was back with the other two men. They were amused by something Tommy must have said about Westie. They had London accents.

The girl was much lighter. The pair of them carried her out of the bar, Hernandez behind them, mopping up the trail of blood she left behind among the curls of wood shavings in the greyness of the dust.

Tommy Peters picked up the bag and began to count the money. He stopped at twenty thousand, put the blocks of notes carefully to one side, then extracted another seven hundred and fifty.

'Expenses,' he said. 'Tell Mackenzie I'll be in touch.'

Winter nodded, sitting down again, staring at the table, too shocked to pursue any kind of conversation. The bangle on her wrist, he kept thinking. Her smile. The way she wound that strand of hair around her finger. Gone. *Bam*. Wasted.

Tommy produced a plastic bag and departed with the money.

Shortly afterwards Winter heard a cough out the back somewhere as the van fired up. Then he felt someone nudging the table and he looked up, still numbed, to find Bazza Mackenzie counting the rest of the ten-pound notes. The lads were outside in the Mercedes, he said. And they were all going back into Malaga for a drink or two.

He turned round to find Winter getting slowly to his feet.

'You're in a bit of a state, mush.' He nodded at the bloodstains across his shirt. 'Tommy used to be better than this.'

Chapter twenty-nine

Suttle took Lizzie Hodson along to Sandown Road as the last of a cold sunset expired over the low black swell of the Isle of Wight. After a series of hurried meetings the Chief Superintendent in charge of the Portsmouth OCU had recommended that Rachel's wake go ahead, but in case of trouble he'd hedged his bets with an impressive show of pre-emptive muscle. Sandown Road was cordoned off at both ends and the Force Support Unit had turned up in a couple of Transits. Local Public Order units were there as well, parked discreetly around the corner, and Suttle couldn't remember a turnout like this since Pompey and the Saints had clashed at Fratton Park. On that occasion they'd managed to contain a full-scale riot. Tonight they were witnesses to a love-in.

There seemed to be hundreds of kids. Suttle gave up counting the candles. His warrant card and Lizzie's press pass had taken them under the Police *No Entry* tape, and they stood on the pavement across from the Aults' house while the mourners swayed and sang. From time to time voices stilled as someone volunteered a tearful anecdote or a personal memory. References to Rachel's recent performance in a school production of *Cabaret* earned a round of applause. A mysterious aside about the recreational potential of barley sugar soaked in vodka sparked a whoop. Half the world seemed to have been on intimate terms with Rachel Ault, and by the time the gathering began to break up and drift away even Suttle felt he must have known her for most of her young life.

Faraday had asked him to phone before he left. He wanted to know how the evening had gone. Suttle's call found him at home. Evidently he was alone.

'Any sign of the Aults?'

'None, boss. I kept an eye on the house. Everything's locked up, gates included. I couldn't see any lights. I don't think anyone's there.'

'And Mackenzie? Next door?'

'I saw his missus. She came out and had a word with one or two of the kids at one point, but I never saw Bazza.'

'Winter?'

'No.'

'So what happens now?'

'Lizzie and I are going for a drink.'

'Yeah?' Something in Faraday's voice, something almost plaintive, prompted Suttle to ask whether he fancied joining them. They could find a pub round his way, save him getting the motor out.

'Like where?'

Suttle conferred with Lizzie. She knew a place at the end of Locksway Road. The Oyster House. Faraday sounded undecided.

'We'll be there anyway, boss. The walk'll do us good.'

Suttle pocketed the phone. The last of the mourners were wandering towards the seafront. There was a hint of weed in the night air but the uniforms didn't seem unduly bothered. Across the road Suttle recognised the tall figure of Matt Berriman. He hadn't noticed him earlier but assumed he'd probably been there from the start. If anyone held a candle for Rachel Ault, it was surely him.

He pointed him out to Lizzie. She wanted to know who he was with.

'There.' She was pointing at a figure in step beside him, half-hidden by his body, cropped black hair, rangy, older. She had her arm tucked inside Berriman's, and when their steps interlocked, stride for stride, she laid her head on his shoulder.

Suttle admitted he didn't know.

'But you're a detective, Mr Suttle. You know everything.'

'If only.'

'Who do you think she might be?'

'I've no idea.'

'His mum?'

'That's unkind. She looks quite tasty.'

'Older, though. Much older.'

The couple paused at the end of the road. A uniformed sergeant had stopped the traffic to let the kids cross. Berriman and his friend turned left. Suttle and Lizzie were going that way too.

Lizzie quickened her step. With some reluctance Suttle let her close the distance between them. He'd only seen Berriman once, a couple of days ago on the beach. Beyond that, his knowledge was limited to the custody file and the statements he'd signed after both interviews.

He and his companion were talking, naturally enough, about Rachel. Much of the conversation was to do with swimming. At one point the woman wanted to know whether Matt would honestly have gone back to serious training had Rachel still been alive.

'And we were together again, you mean?'

'Yes.'

'You think we'd have got it on again?'

'I know you would. You're telling me different?'

'Maybe. Depends.'

'On what?'

'On what you—'

The rest was lost in the roar of a passing motorbike. The woman began to laugh. Then they ducked suddenly left, towards the warren of streets that led into Eastney. Something in her body language, in the sheer length of her stride, triggered a recent memory. Then Suttle had it. He pulled Lizzie to a halt at the corner of the street. He was still watching her, certain now.

'I last saw her a couple of days ago,' he said. 'On Eastney beach.'

'Yeah?'

'Yeah. She was with Berriman again. And you know what? She hadn't got a stitch on.'

Faraday was already in the pub, nursing the remains of a pint of Guinness, when they stepped in from the street. The landlord was half an hour from last orders and Suttle went straight to the bar, returning with a tray of drinks. Faraday had met Lizzie Hodson on a number of occasions but never in this kind of setting.

Lizzie, with a directness that rather appealed to Faraday, asked him what he normally did on a Saturday night.

'Depends,' he said. 'Normally I've got company. Tonight, as it happens, I'm on my own.'

Suttle remembered the small figure in Bransbury Park. Had she found out about the photos? Had there been some kind of row?

'What about that boy of yours?' he asked instead. 'I thought he was coming down for the weekend?'

'He has. He's here.'

'But not at home?'

'Not this evening.'

'And Gabrielle?'

'She neither. They're out together. Back whenever.'

He reached for his drink and a change of subject. Suttle mentioned seeing Berriman.

'He had company, boss. An older woman. I've seen them together before.'

'Some kind of relationship?'

'For sure.'

Faraday nodded. The last week, thought Suttle, seems to have drained him of everything. 'There's been a development,' he said at last. 'Maybe you can give me a bell later.'

Lizzie took the hint. She was bursting for a pee. Back in a trice.

Suttle watched her pick her way across the crowded pub. Suttle knew that time was short. He leaned forward over the table.

'Jax Bonner?' he queried.

'No.'

'What then?'

'Ault. I got a call from Netley this evening. They've got a couple of guys in the computer department on overtime. One's looking at Rachel's laptop. The other's analysing Ault's hard disk.'

'And?'

'Ault had loads of porn downloaded. It's hidden but it's there. Young girls mainly. Rachel's age.'

When the evening in Malaga started getting out of hand Winter made his excuses and left. They'd started at a bar round the corner from the hotel, Bazza's shout. He'd bought bottle after bottle of chilled cava and enough tapas to cover the tables they'd commandeered. His two mates, Tosh Chatterly and Rob Simpkins, had troughed their way through the marinated squid and cumin-spiked potato balls, determined to add a coat of cheerful gloss to an otherwise shit day. Neither had been present at the killings in *Las Puertas del Paraiso* but they'd seen enough of Winter afterwards to know that something truly vile had happened. Their role now was obvious. They were the court jesters.

Of Tommy Peters, twenty grand the richer, nothing had been seen since. According to Bazza he'd been offered a lift back on tomorrow's charter flight but preferred to make his own way home. Pressed by Winter to justify the risks they were taking, a double killing with a witness, Bazza had insisted everything was cushty. If you pay top dollar, he'd said by way of explanation, you get the best. Tommy was a vicious cunt but had the sweetest connections. By now the bodies would be buried in the foundations of some building site or other down the coast. If he didn't have total trust in the man, he'd have been back on the plane within seconds.

Winter, talking to Bazza in the privacy of his hotel suite, had been obliged to accept it. Westie had made a career out of violence, out of hurting people, and now he'd paid the price. That was the way these deals worked. No one was pretending it was pretty but then Westie himself had been equally brutal, if not worse. Given the prospect of endless demands on Bazza's purse, demands Westie could underline by threatening to turn grass, it made perfect commercial sense to terminate the relationship. The twenty grand to Tommy Peters, he pointed out, was nothing compared to the size of the bill that Westie might one day have decided to present.

Winter had simply nodded. Westie he understood. Westie had it coming. But the girl? After a relationship just one day old? Was that something Bazza could feel proud about? The questions made Bazza uneasy, Winter could sense it, but in the end he'd just shrugged. He'd paid Tommy a great deal of money to sort out a problem. The man had made a split-second judgement about a witness and if you looked at it sensibly he'd probably been right. In any case it was far too late to second-guess the man. Shit happens. *Qué será.*

'And the old guy in the café? Hernandez?'

'Tommy's mates own him. He does what they tell him. No fucking *problema.'*

Now, in the bar, there was talk of going on to a casino that Bazza happened to know. There were quality toms there, Russian girls with a sense of humour and huge tits, and there was no way that life didn't owe them a punt or two followed by some serious frolicking. After the day from hell, a night in heaven. *Qué será.*

Winter, aware that a bottle of cava had made absolutely no difference to the bleakness of his mood, slipped out of the bar and made his way through crowds of people until he found a zigzag path that led up towards the looming battlements of the castle above. He knew he hadn't signed up for this. He knew that his job description had never extended to a triple murder, first Danny Cooper, now Westie and his luckless companion. In one sense it had all been a terrible mistake, a set of events that had simply galloped out of control; but in another he knew that he was kidding himself.

In the Job he'd potted endless blokes who'd run broadly the same defence. It was never meant to happen, Mr W. I never meant to get involved. But look hard at exactly what they'd done and – more importantly – what they *hadn't* done, and you pretty quickly came to a conclusion seldom lost on any half-decent jury. Shit happens because you let it happen. The guilty never bother to say no.

Winter paused for breath, gazing down at the spread of the city beneath him. Beyond the docks lay the blackness of the Mediterranean. Off to the left, behind the hotel where they were staying, the bullring. From here, near the top of the path, you could see down into the ring itself, and he realised with a jolt of surprise that this was where the crowds had been heading. There were tiers of seats bursting with spectators and a flurry of movement on the yellow sand of the arena.

He'd been to a bullfight with Joannie, years ago, and had taken no pleasure from the experience. The ritual killings seemed to him to be savage and unnecessary. These people gloried in blood, in slaughter, in winding up the bulls and then dispatching them for the sake of some macho thrill. There was lots of talk about how dangerous the fighting bulls could be, lots of headlines when one of the top guys got himself gored, but the bottom line was simple. You loaded the odds. You released the poor fucking animal into the ring. And then you killed it.

A blast from a trumpet and a roar from the spectators signalled the parade that started every bullfight. Winter's eyesight wasn't brilliant, and he had trouble making out the details as splashes of colour stalked around the ring, but he sensed the rising excitement from the crowd below. Awaiting the entry of the first bull, it was impossible not to think again about Tommy Peters. He knew the tricks. He commanded a hefty fee. He loaded the odds. And he seldom failed to deliver.

Winter blinked, still trying to focus on the bullring, but it was hopeless. *The girl again. Her innocence. The totally crap card that life had so suddenly dealt her. Her voice, pleading and pleading. Her eyes, staring death in the face. Her beautiful fingers, suddenly lifeless. The wreckage of her lovely face. Could he have done more? Should he have done more?*

Winter didn't know. And that made a surreal evening a whole lot worse.

The lights were on in the Bargemaster's House by the time Faraday got home. He let himself in, recognising the familiar lilt, the voice, the unaccompanied guitar. When she was feeling especially content, Gabrielle would slip her favourite George Brassens CDs into the player and dance. She was doing it now, plaited against J-J, swaying slowly around the living room, her feet bare, her eyes closed, her lips in soundless pursuit of the lyric, and watching them Faraday wondered what his deaf son made of *La Parapluie*.

Very slowly, one shuffling step at a time, J-J revolved. He had Faraday's clumsiness, but as well he had the priceless gift of surrender. He could let go, cast himself off, let the moment take him where it would. Faraday had seen it when he was a child adrift in a world of silence, and he'd always marvelled at the faith the boy must have, and at his courage. The latter, on occasions, had bled into recklessness. J-J sometimes took risks that iced Faraday's blood. But the compensations, the rewards, were obvious. My extraordinary son, Faraday thought, dancing to a music he couldn't hear.

'*Chéri* ...' Gabrielle had seen him at last.

She disentangled herself from J-J and gave him a kiss. Faraday let her lead him into the kitchen, unaccountably relieved. Gabrielle followed, made him sit down at the table, fetched wine, asked whether he'd eaten. He hadn't seen her all day, hadn't been in touch since she'd phoned him from the bus, en route to try and find Jax Bonner.

Faraday cocked his head, raised his glass, the question unvoiced. She grinned back, nodding.

'*Oui.*' she said. 'I found her.'

'Talked to her?'

'*Oui.*'

'All day?'

'No. We went to the island. Walked. Watched the birds.' She broke off.

J-J's scarecrow body was propped in the open doorway. She signed to him about a place they must have found. He nodded, looked at his father, told him about the saltmarsh south of Bembridge, the path that wound through the bulrushes, how quickly they'd left the kids and the trippers, and how, hours later, they'd been lucky enough to find a spoonbill.

Gabrielle, he said, had thought at first that the bird was a big egret. Same colour, same size. They'd seen it first at a distance, flying low over the marshes, but something about the speed of its wingbeats had told J-J that egret was wrong. Later there'd come another sighting, much closer, and the bird's long bill with the flattened bit at the end had confirmed J-J's suspicions. It was only the second time in his life he'd seen a spoonbill and he was glad Gabrielle had been there to share it.

Faraday let this scene wash over him: the music, the warm blush of the wine, his two favourite people within touching distance. J-J understood him. He knew the boy did. He understood his dad's bleaker moods, his isolation, the moments when he was engulfed by a numbing sense of near-total bewilderment. Those moments had always been there since J-J was still in the nest, but now – on his intermittent visits – he brought a different perspective. Deafness, by some strange irony, had conferred wisdom. By making him more curious, by making him look harder, it had given him a unique entrée into other people's lives, other people's heads, other people's hearts. J-J watched. And J-J knew.

'You met the girl too?' Faraday signed.

'Yes.' J-J nodded.

'You talked about Rachel? About her boyfriend?'

'Yes.'

'And what did she say?'

'She hated Rachel,' J-J signed. 'She's full of hate. She hates every-thing.'

'But did she kill her?'

'No.' A brisk dismissive movement with the flat of his bony hand. 'Never.'

Chapter thirty

Jimmy Suttle left Lizzie Hodson in bed. Half past seven on a Sunday morning, he'd agreed with Faraday, was the perfect time to give a Pompey cab driver a shake or two. Apart from anything else, it would signal a certain seriousness.

The cab firm had given the driver's name as Grant Mason. He drove night shifts throughout the week and then retired to an upstairs flat in a street of terraced houses in Milton. It was raining again when Suttle parked up across the road. Mason's cab, badged with Speedy's scarlet logo, was outside his house. Suttle glanced inside as he hurried past. A satnav housing on the dashboard was empty.

Mason, when he finally clattered downstairs to answer the door, had just got out of the shower. Suttle showed him his warrant card and stepped out of the rain. Mason didn't seem the least bit surprised by this sudden visitation. He nodded at the stairs and told Suttle to put the kettle on. Half the night driving pissed kids back from the clubs in Guildhall Walk had left him with a bit of a thirst.

Dressed in a tracksuit, his hair still wet, Mason joined Suttle in the kitchen. He was small and thin, edging fifty. He had a smoker's face, his yellowing parchment skin deeply seamed. He stirred three spoonfuls of sugar into his tea and told Suttle he was welcome to a bit of toast.

Suttle wanted to know whether he'd been driving on Wednesday night.

'Yeah. Course. I drives every night.'

'And can you remember that shift? In detail?'

'Yeah. I looked it up. Barbara on the desk, she mentioned it, said you was interested.'

Suttle had talked to Barbara on the phone. Barbara worked for Mackenzie.

'So talk me through it, Grant.'

'It's Westie, isn't it? Him? That's what you're after?'

The bluntness of the response told Suttle to tread carefully. The going was seldom this easy.

'What makes you say that?'

'Because he's a bad man. Not a rascal, a bad man. Always has been, Westie.'

'You know him well?'

'I've driven him around a bit, as you do. I used to think he was all mouth, Westie, but then you hear things and you get to wonder. Know what I mean?'

'What kind of things?'

'Horrible things. Westie used to have these videos sometimes. It was violence, always violence. He'd tell me the plots, what kind of stuff these guys got up to, what you could do with a hammer drill, stuff like that. I could borrow them off him if I wanted. He was generous that way. Half-decent footballer too, in his time. But a psycho, definitely. Me? I prefer cartoons, preferably *The Simpsons*. Told him too. He thought I was taking the piss.' He peered at Suttle through a haze of roll-up. 'Like *The Simpsons*, do you?'

Suttle began to sense where this conversation was going. He's rehearsed, he thought. He's got all this drivel off pat.

'It wasn't just the videos, though, was it?'

'Fuck, no. Listen to people in this town, and Westie's got a right reputation.'

'For what?'

'For hurting people.'

'For money? Because someone else was paying?'

'Nah, mate. Because he fancies it. Because he's made that way. Sometimes you'll be in the cab with him and he'll be chatty as you like, real gentleman, right laugh. He'll tell you stories from the old days, back when he was on Villa's books, and a couple of times he even comped me a couple of tickets down the Park. Don't ask me where he got them. Probably the players. He drinks in them same bars down Gunwharf, knows a couple of them well. At least that's what he always tells me.'

'So where does the money come from?'

'Fuck knows. Me, I always had him down as a gangster. Maybe he flogs toot. Maybe he pimps birds for a living. I know he's always shagging around because he tells me, every last fucking detail. There's supposed to be good money in them foreign birds, Chinese crumpet especially. Wouldn't surprise me in the least.'

'And Wednesday night?'

'Yeah.' Mason picked a shred of Golden Virginia from his lower lip. 'That was a strange one.'

'Strange how?'

He frowned, taking his time.

'We're still talking Westie, right?'

'Right.'

'OK, so I gets a job at three in the morning. It's Westie's address, the place on the seafront. I get myself down there and give him a tap and he's out of the door like a shot, bang, like he's been waiting half the night. He's got a couple of bags with him, not small bags, and he's sweating fit to bust. That ain't Westie. That ain't the man at all. Westie's Mr Cool. Westie's Mr Iceman.'

'So how come?'

'Dunno, mate. Not then, anyway. Turns out he wants to go to Gatwick. I tell him that ain't a problem on account of I spend half my fucking life going to Gatwick. I could sit in the car and close my eyes and the fucking motor would *take* me to Gatwick. Know what I mean?'

'Tell me about Westie.'

'He's all over the place, doesn't know what fucking day it is.'

'Like how?'

'Like we're sitting in the car, driving out of town, and I ask him where he's off to, like you would. It's an hour and a half to Gatwick. You need a bit of conversation, something to talk about. So one minute he tells me Spain. Then it's Italy. Then it's fucking Greece. Then it's Spain again. So I say Spain's nice. Whereabouts in Spain? And you know something? He hasn't a fucking clue. Lloret? Alicante? Doesn't matter. As long as he gets there, pronto like. So I says to myself, this isn't Westie going off on holiday. This is Westie in deep fucking shit.'

'He told you that?'

'He didn't have to, mate. It was all over his face. You could fucking practically *smell* it on him. Westie's not a bloke who scares easy. He was crapping himself.'

'But why?'

'Dunno. I couldn't work it out. Then he goes all quiet for a bit, won't say a word. We were up round Arundel by then. That time of night, I take the country roads. Anyway, we're cruising along and he suddenly tells me to stop. We're bang in the middle of nowhere, pitch fucking black, and he tells me to pull over. I think he needs to take a piss so naturally I do like he says, pull in. The geezer gets out, Westie, and then disappears.'

'Disappears where?'

'Dunno, do I? He's wearing one of them white raincoats. One

minute I see him by the verge, like, as you'd expect. Then he's found a hole in the hedge or something and he's gone.'

'For long?'

'Dunno. Five minutes?'

'Doing what?'

'Haven't a clue, mush.'

'But you'd ask him, wouldn't you? When he came back?'

'Course.'

'And what did he say?'

'Nothing. He just told me to get a move on. It's getting on towards four by now. It's a funny time to be in a hurry but I'm not paid to give anyone aggro, especially not someone like Westie.'

'You think he left something behind the hedge? Buried it?'

'Dunno. His hands were wet. He kept rubbing them on his trousers.'

'And can you remember where this place was?'

'Give or take, yeah. It's on that road between Slindon and Storrington.'

'But give or take what?'

'A mile or so. Maybe less. Like I say, it was pitch black.'

'But you've got the lights on.'

'Sure.'

'And you go to Gatwick a lot. You just told me.'

'Yeah, but that's normal hours, daylight hours, when normal fucking people want to get to the airport. If there's traffic about, I takes the motorway. Them little country roads can be murder.' He looked up, the ghost of a smile on his face. 'Know what I mean, mush?'

Suttle knew it was nonsense. Clever nonsense, but still nonsense. Someone had marked his card, had a quiet word or two, agreed a script. Westie was an animal. He worked freelance. He made a fortune from pimping foreign toms. He led a colourful life, got himself talked about, hurt people when he was in the mood. Then Wednesday, out of the blue, he does something very silly. Suddenly, he has to get out of the country. But not before an unscheduled stop on a quiet back road miles from anywhere. In real life Grant Mason would never have dared talk about Westie in this kind of detail. Not unless he'd been told to. And not unless he knew Westie would never be back.

'Did he tell you anything else? Westie?'

'Just that he was fucking happy to be off.'

'Nothing about Wednesday night? What he might have been up to?'

'No, mush. And I didn't ask neither.'

'Did you hear about Danny Cooper, by any chance?'

'Yeah.' He nodded. 'It was in the *News*. Bit of a dealer, wasn't he? The way I hear it?' He shook his head, reached for his mug. 'You gotta watch yourself in this town, mush. I always said so.'

Suttle sat back, looking for loose ends, anything he could tuck away for later.

'How did he pay you, Westie?'

'Cash, like always. And a fucking great tip.'

'How much?'

'A score. And he was a mean bastard normally.'

'You give him a receipt?'

'You're joking. Westie didn't do receipts.'

'Did you get the impression he was carrying a lot of money?'

'Haven't a clue, mush. And that's another question you wouldn't ask.' He yawned. 'You gonna make anything out of this? Write anything down? Only I'm off to bed soon.'

Suttle shook his head. Someone might be back to take a formal statement, he said, but it wouldn't happen for a couple of days. Mason got to his feet. He looked, if anything, disappointed.

'How about that place we stopped? You want me to try and find it?'

'Might do. Depends.'

'Yeah? Just say the word, mush.'

Suttle was looking round the tiny living room. He asked whether Mason used a satnav.

'Yeah. We all do. Cabby's best mate.'

'Where is it?'

'In that drawer. Why?'

'I need to take it away. I'm sure the firm will sort a replacement until you get it back. That OK with you?'

For a moment Suttle thought he detected a tiny flicker of alarm. Then Mason shrugged.

'Help yourself,' he said. 'Be my guest.'

Suttle got the satnav from the drawer. It was a TomTom, state of the art. Careful analysis of the built-in memory could retrieve every detail of Mason's recent trips. Suttle slipped it into his pocket and let Mason lead the way down the narrow hallway to the front door. The cabby pulled it open, stood aside.

Suttle stepped into the rain again then shot Mason a look.

'Seen Bazza recently?'

'No, mate.' He returned Suttle's smile. 'A rare pleasure, believe me.'

*

300

Bazza's party was back at Southampton airport by half past ten. An early start from Malaga had been low on conversation. Tosh and Rob were battling industrial-size hangovers while Bazza himself seemed oddly preoccupied. When Winter asked him whether it had been a good night, he rolled his eyes.

'You were better of out of it, mush. I'm getting too old for guys like these. Boys on the piss. Russian fanny. Horrible.'

Winter slept most of the way back, waking up as the little jet bucketed down through low cloud to make a bumpy landing. After a hopeless attempt to get to sleep in his hotel room he'd spent most of the night prowling the streets of Malaga. He'd stopped at every gallery and knick-knack shop, peering in through the window, looking for the name Renate, without the first idea of what he'd do if he found a painting of hers or some other fancy piece of art. Did he owe her memory the asking price? Would parting with money do anything to ease the ache in his heart?

At the airport Bazza settled the balance of the fee for the jet and then walked Winter to the car park. Tosh and Rob, revived by champagne on the way home, were off to The Rose Bowl for the cricket.

'Don't even think about it, Paul.'

They were on the motorway in Bazza's new Mercedes, heading back towards Pompey. Bazza rarely called Winter by his Christian name.

'Think about what?'

'Yesterday. That poxy bar place. Tommy's little party piece. It's business, mate. You win some, you lose some.'

'And she lost.'

'Yeah. She did. It doesn't cover us with glory but I tell you what, it's a whole lot better than the alternative.'

'Which is?'

'The woman still alive, still with a tongue in her head.'

'She said she'd keep her mouth shut. In fact that was the last thing she said. Ever.'

'Yeah, mush, but they all say that. She might have been fond of Westie. She'd only known him a couple of days so she might not have sussed what a clown the man is.'

'Was, Baz. Past tense.'

'Sure. But that's my point. Tommy lets her get away with it. She finds her way home. She lies awake all night, thinking about Westie, what a great shag he was, what a great find, what a great future they might have had, all that bollocks, then – bam – she's down the nick next morning singing her heart out. Fat guy with no hair. Bought me a beer. Supposed to have a whack of money in a bag. English, definitely.

Came in on a flight yesterday. Probably gone already. Seemed to know Westie. You can write every line of it, mush. And it ends with a knock on *your* fucking door. You were protecting yourself, mate. Think of it that way. And you need never see Tommy again in your whole life.' He glanced across. 'Cushty or what?'

Winter said nothing. Bazza was right. Of course he was right.

'What do we do about Westie's album?' he said at last.

'Leave that to me, mush.'

'That's not an answer, Baz. I need to know. We're in the shit as it is.'

'Like how?'

'Like they're not going to give up on Danny Cooper. Like they've still got to put someone alongside Rachel and her fucking boyfriend.'

'Cooper?' Bazza seemed to be having trouble remembering the name. 'What's all that got to do with us? The Alfa's history. I checked last night. Crushed down nicely and already off to a smelting yard. There's nothing in that khazi of a flat that links to us. I only ever paid Westie in cash. There's no cheques, no bank transfers, nothing.'

'So what about the album?'

'Fuck the album. I know every one of those faces. Every single one. They also know me. Westies are two a penny. I can pick another up by lunchtime. They know that, those people. There's no way they'd let themselves down.'

'Simple as that?'

'Simpler, mush. Look for problems, and you'll have a sad old life.' He gave a dawdler a blast on the horn and then swept by on the inside lane. 'You've got a point about Rachel, though. I'd like that tidied up, mush, pronto.'

Parsons called a meeting of the *Mandolin* principals for Sunday lunchtime. Unlike Friday night, there was nothing to eat.

There were five faces around the conference table in Martin Barrie's office. According to Parsons, the Detective Superintendent was due back from leave tomorrow morning, and she was already gathering up the tiny items she'd scattered to make the place feel like home. The flowers, Faraday sensed, would be the last to go. She might even be brave and leave them.

She asked Proctor for an update on the forensic. As far as the killings at the party were concerned, he was able to confirm that the blood beside the pool belonged to Gareth Hughes and Rachel Ault. As far as Matt Berriman was concerned, the forensic checks had revealed no bloodstains.

'None at all?'

'Nothing, boss. Zilch.'

'And you think that wouldn't have been the case if he'd done Hughes and Rachel Ault?'

'Sure. Rachel had stab wounds. We're not talking lots of blood but we'd expect to find *something*.'

'What about Mackenzie? When he sorted out the fight back in the house?' Parsons was looking at Faraday.

'Mackenzie had blood on his head from the scalp wound, and maybe down his face.' Faraday shrugged. 'It needn't have got onto Berriman's gear.'

'So you think his story checks out?'

'I do.' Faraday nodded. There was no evidence, he said, to put Berriman on Mackenzie's property. He'd intervened in the judge's study and hauled the kids off the desk. He'd afterwards had sex with Rachel in the bathroom, left by the front door for a breath of fresh air and returned in minutes to save Mackenzie from a serious beating. He'd surrendered his clothing, as required, and been moderately helpful in both interviews.

'Does anyone have any issues with any of that?' Parsons scanned the faces around the table.

'We don't have a mobile for him.' It was Suttle.

'That's true.'

'Yet he used a mobile in the bathroom. He had to. Otherwise there wouldn't have been any pictures.'

'Good point.' She was frowning at the mountain of statements at Suttle's elbow. 'We must have challenged him on that.'

'We did, boss.'

'Remind me what he said.'

'He said he borrowed a mobile off a kid at the party. Specifically to use the camera in the bathroom.'

'And gave it back?'

'Yes.'

'Do we have a name for this kid?'

'No. Berriman told us the kid was a total stranger. Said he wouldn't recognise him again.'

'So do we believe him?'

'Obviously not.'

'So where is it?'

'I've no idea, boss. If he'd left it in the garden at the Aults, we'd have found it.'

'But you think he definitely hid it for later?'

'Yes.'

'Why would he do that?'

'Because he could see trouble coming. The party had kicked off and there was no way we wouldn't turn up in the end. He'd suss we'd seize all the mobiles because of the damage in the house and he didn't want to risk losing it. Those pictures were important to him. So he left the phone somewhere safe to collect later.'

'It was pay-as-you-go. Right?'

'Yeah.'

'But in that case, if the pictures and the phone were so important, why did he stay at the party?'

'Because of Rachel, boss. He'd put his smell on her. He'd got her back. No way he was going to lose her again.'

Parsons nodded, thinking it over, then looked across at Faraday.

'Joe? You buy that?'

'Yes.' He nodded. 'I do.'

'So where does that take us? To the girl? To Jax Bonner?'

Faraday had been anticipating this question for the last twenty-four hours. To date, despite nationwide publicity, there'd been no sightings of Bonner. Yet here he was, living with a woman who knew exactly where to find the girl. Not only that; Gabrielle had been to see her, talked to her, formed an opinion, along with his son. Was now the time to table these new facts? Faraday thought not.

'Bonner remains a prime suspect,' he said carefully. 'We're obviously moving heaven and earth to find her. She'll surface in the end. These people always do.'

Something in his voice, an unusual caution, touched a nerve in Parsons. Faraday could see it in her face, the tiny raise of her eyebrow, the way she stiffened herself in the chair. *Shit*, he thought.

'What are you saying, Joe?'

'I'm saying we have to wait, boss.'

'And we've no idea where she might be? Which part of the country even?'

'The ATM withdrawals on her brother's business account are all local. You could draw a reasonable inference from that.'

'But who takes out the money?'

'It could be anyone. All you need is the card and the PIN number. If she's aware, then she'll know that most ATMs are cameraed. We'll be talking to the banks again tomorrow.'

'So she *could* be in hiding locally?'

'Yes, that's what I just said.'

'But we still don't know where?'

'Obviously not, boss.'

She looked at him a moment longer then scribbled a note to herself. It was Suttle's turn.

'Given we've yet to lay hands on the girl, Jimmy, what's the strength?'

'I'm with D/I Faraday,' he said at once. 'She's definitely a prime suspect. She hated the Aults. She goes off like a firework. She's got previous for violence. She was carrying a knife. That tells me she needs to answer a question or two.'

'Quite.' Parsons was animated now, looking for a way out of this impasse. The last thing she needed was a Monday morning session with Martin Barrie, incredulous at her lack of progress. The girl's local. She stands out a mile in any crowd. Why on earth haven't you banged her up already?

'Glen? Outside Enquiries? No trace at all of her?'

'None, boss. She's gone to ground.'

'And the kids, Jimmy?' This to Suttle. 'You've been talking to them too?'

'Of course.'

'And?'

'No one's saying a word. They're terrified of her.'

'But you think some of them might know?'

'It's possible.'

'Can't we action that?'

'How, boss? Talk nicely to their parents? Take them round the back and beat the shit out of them? If these were Rachel's friends, we might be in with a chance. Bonner's side of the tracks, we're on enemy territory. They hate us, boss. It's a sad thing to say but it's true.'

The vehemence of Suttle's little speech seemed to shock her. She opened the file at her elbow.

'This is some of the media coverage from last night,' she said. 'Mr Willard emailed me the more important bits.'

She passed photocopies down the table. Despite the lateness of the wake, coverage had appeared in most of the Sunday papers. There were photos too, candlelit young faces looming out of the darkness. If you were looking for a symbol of the times we live in, as the leader writer in the *Observer* pointed out, then here it was. Darkness and light, a candle's width apart.

Faraday's attention was caught by a paragraph in the *Sunday Telegraph*. The reporter had roughly tallied *Mandolin*'s costs to date. These costs included the forensic bills, overtime, invoices submitted by neighbouring forces under the mutual aid arrangements and various sundries. The reporter must have had an inside source because the sums looked right. So far, in his estimate, the Craneswater party had run up a bill of nearly half a million pounds with no arrests in sight.

There were now rumours that a third murder was linked to the party deaths but once again there'd been no arrest.

Parsons hadn't bothered with her own set of cuttings. She'd probably memorised them by now.

'This is not our golden hour, gentlemen.' She closed her file. 'To be frank, I'm disappointed.'

Faraday glanced at Suttle. Like everyone else in the room, he'd got used to Parsons in this mood.

'One other thing, boss.' He raised a hand. 'The stuff on Ault's hard disk. Does that raise any new issues?'

Parsons shook her head. 'There's no offence involved. I've seen the images. This isn't kiddie porn. There's no abuse involved, no violence. It appears to be consensual sex.'

'But aren't they young? Rachel's age?'

'It's hard to tell. In Mr Willard's view it's something of a blessing. He's been wondering why Ault hasn't been more vocal about our performance last weekend.' She offered Suttle a bleak smile. 'Now we know the answer.'

Chapter thirty-one

Winter had never been so glad to get home. He dumped his bag in the hall, circled the big living room, threw open the French windows, stepped onto the balcony. The weather had cheered up at last and the sunshine was hot on his face. Malaga without the aggravation, he thought, beaming fondly down on a young mum trying to teach her toddler to stay upright. No Westie. No London hit men on ten grand a body. Just an hour or two trying to restore some sanity to this life of his.

He made a pot of tea. The Pompey phone directory was under a pile of *Telegraph* magazines beside the sofa. Nikki Dunlop's number was listed. He rang her on the cordless, ready to hang up if she answered. After a while her recorded voice invited him to leave a message. Glancing at his watch, he swallowed the rest of the tea, found his car keys, and headed for the door.

Parking was hopeless in Adair Road. He found a space on the nearby seafront and walked back. He knew it was possible that Nikki was in but hadn't answered the phone. Equally, she might have come back. Either way, he was prepared to take the risk. He wanted this thing sorted.

He tried to visualise her tiny kitchen. The baby he'd heard crying through the party wall had been on the seaward side of the property. He crossed the road and knocked at the house next door. After a while a curtain twitched. He knocked again, then a third time. At last the door opened. A young woman stood blinking in the afternoon sunlight. She was wearing a grubby T-shirt and a pair of shorts. She had curly dark hair and a lousy complexion. She looked as if she'd just woken up.

'Please?' Foreign, Winter thought.

'I'm from the council.' He flashed his plastic driving licence. 'Do you mind if I come in?'

He stepped past her without waiting for an answer. By the time the door closed behind him, he'd squeezed past the buggy in the front room and found himself some standing room beside a pile of laundry. A fan heater was whirring beneath the drying rack and there was a single mattress lying behind it, upended against the wall. The room felt like an oven.

'The council?' He knew she didn't believe him.

'That's right. I'm sorry to call on a Sunday. You are ... ?'

She shook her head. The last thing she owed Winter was a name.

'What do you want?' she said.

'I work for the Noise Abatement Section,' he said. 'We've had a complaint from next door.' He nodded at the wall that adjoined Nikki Dunlop's house.

'Complaint?'

'About the noise. The lady next door ... she says you're very noisy.'

'Me?' She was outraged.

'Yes.'

'She says that? About me? That I make too much noise? *She* says that.'

'I'm afraid so.' Winter softened his tone. He wished he'd brought a clipboard now, really got into it. 'I know it can be hard with a new baby.' He nodded at the buggy. 'I'm not blaming you, love. I'm just here to establish the facts.'

'Nadja's one year old. Maybe she cries a little but only when she's hurt. Or maybe when she can't sleep. You know where we sleep now? Both of us? Here. In this room. And you know why? Because she's so noisy. Not me. The lady next door. So why don't you ask her?'

Winter was eyeing the single armchair. The frame and fabric looked knackered but she'd done her best to brighten it with a couple of cushions.

'Do you mind?' He settled himself in the chair. He was right. It had lumps in all the wrong places. He gave her a smile. 'So tell me more.'

The woman needed no encouragement. First there was the little dog, always barking. Then, because the walls were thin, she could hear every detail of her neighbour's life.

'Everything?' Winter had found a gas bill in his jacket pocket. He began to make notes on the back of the envelope. 'Like how?'

'Like what she does all the time, what she says. There's a man in there with her, a younger man. Sometimes they shout. At night too.'

'Rows, you mean? They're shouting at each other?'

'*Da.*'

'What do they say?'

'Say?'

'I have to have details. For the report.'

'You make a report?'

'Of course.'

'But I can't help you. My English ... not so good.' She raised her hands, angry at herself. 'All I know is they shout. And then my baby, Nadja, she cries.'

Winter nodded, looked concerned, scribbled himself another note, then looked up.

'What else?'

'Everything. The television. The music. So loud. Even the washing machine.'

'Washing machine?'

'*Da*. She has the washing machine upstairs, maybe in the bathroom. It makes a big noise, a very big noise. The other night she does the washing at half past one in the morning time. You think I'm crazy? I tell you no. I look at the clock. Half past one. Dark outside. When the washing machine ...' She frowned, making a circle with her finger.

'Spins?'

'*Da*, it spins, for the drying, then the house ... it shakes.' She nodded. 'Half past one. Dark outside. And you come knocking on *my* door?'

'When was this? Can you remember?'

'With the washing machine?'

'Yes.'

'It's important?'

'Very.'

'For the report?' She was looking at the envelope.

'Of course.'

She nodded, frowned, had a think. Then she nodded again.

'Last night,' she said. 'Last week.'

'Last Saturday?'

'*Da*. Saturday. I tell you true. Half past one. When it comes dark.' The finger again, spinning. 'Everything shaking, like in a storm, everything mad.'

Everything mad. Winter grinned to himself. The woman's name, he'd finally discovered, was Jenica. She was Romanian. Her immigration status was uncertain but she said she had an English boyfriend, the father of her daughter. He worked in the oil business. She'd met him in Romania, in Ploesti. Now he was working on a rig off the south coast of Ireland. They were saving up for somewhere nicer. One day she hoped they'd have a house back in Romania.

Before he left she'd offered him a glass of juice from the carton she kept in the fridge for the baby. She was worried about the report, what the woman next door might say, but when Winter explained that the council had special procedures in cases like this she appeared to believe him. As he left the house, Winter glanced back to see her crossing herself and genuflecting before a creased picture pinned to the living-room wall. He'd seen the picture earlier and hadn't realised it was the Virgin Mary.

Now he debated what to do. It was nearly half past three. He stood on the seafront, wondering whether Nikki Dunlop had decamped to the beach again. Under a near-cloudless sky the sea looked inviting enough and he lingered a moment or two longer, watching a bunch of students daring each other to be the first in. Then he turned on his heel and dug in his pocket for the car keys, shaking his head. Hayling Island, he thought.

Misty Gallagher was on a lounger by the pool when he arrived. He'd parked the Lexus out front and followed the footpath round the side of the house. He heard the radio before he rounded the conservatory at the back, Celine Dion at full throttle, and marvelled that she could doze through a noise like that. Apart from gold bikini briefs, she was naked. There were drips of coconut oil beside the lounger and her body gleamed in the afternoon sun. He looked down at her for a long moment.

'Mist?'

His voice startled her. She struggled upright on the lounger, covering her breasts, then reached for the towelling robe she'd abandoned earlier.

'Don't do that,' she said. 'You're supposed to phone first.'

She wasn't pleased to see him. He shuffled sideways until his shadow fell over her eyes. When she asked what he wanted, he reached down and lowered the volume on the radio.

'The thing I gave you the other day?' he said.

'You want it *now*?'

'Yeah.'

She stared at him a moment longer, then got up and left the patio. Barefoot, she stalked across the lawn. At the bottom of the garden, tucked behind a trellis at the water's edge, was a garden shed. She disappeared inside and re-emerged seconds later. She had a garden fork in one hand and a pair of wellington boots in the other. She dumped them both on the lawn and beckoned him down with an impatient wave.

'These belong to Baz.' She nudged one of the boots with a bare toe.

'The soil's still soaking after all that rain. I'm buggered if I'm going to dig it up.'

She led the way to a patch of garden closer to the house, looked at one spot, then another, then a third. Winter, still wondering why she was being so hostile, began to suspect she'd forgotten the hiding place.

'You could always ring the fucking thing,' she said at last.

'You looked in the bag then?'

'Of course I did. I think it's here.' She indicated an area of recently turned soil beside a rose bush. Winter took his shoes off and struggled into the boots. They were very tight.

'Baz phoned a couple of hours ago,' she said.

'And?' Winter was poking at the soil.

'He was round on Wednesday night. You remember Wednesday night?'

'Of course I do.'

'Apparently he turned up late, really late, half past three in the morning.'

'Did he say why?' Winter had stopped digging.

'No. But that's not the point, is it? I wasn't here. I wasn't in bed. I wasn't where I was supposed to be. The last thing Baz saw of me Wednesday evening was in the restaurant, pissed. He's not stupid, Baz. He might be a headcase sometimes, but the man reads me like a book.'

'So what did he say? On the phone?'

'He wanted to know where I'd been.'

'And what did you tell him?'

'I told him I'd gone to Trude's.'

'Trude's in the fucking Canaries.'

'I know. I forgot.'

'Blinder, Mist. Just what I need.' Winter gazed down at the soil, aware of Misty watching him. Finally he shrugged and set to again, digging very carefully, trying to feel for something solid.

'How far down? Give me a clue.' He looked round, expecting an answer, but she was already halfway across the lawn, heading back towards the pool. Seconds later came the click of her lighter as she settled back on the lounger. This time the robe stayed on.

With *Mandolin* at a standstill and J-J's return to London all too imminent, Faraday got back to the Bargemaster's House in time to catch Gabrielle and J-J debating a change of plan. Last night J-J had been intending to catch a late-afternoon train back to Waterloo but Gabrielle had just made a call to check departure times and discovered that chunks of the journey would be served by a bus service. Now, given the weather, J-J had decided to stay on until Monday. An early train, he signed to his dad, would be perfect.

Gladdened by the prospect of another evening together, Faraday suggested an expedition into the country. There was a stand of trees on Thorney Island that became a daily roost for hundreds of egrets. J-J, like Gabrielle, had always been mad about these stately little birds. High tide was at seven o'clock. They could take the car over to Thorney, park up, then follow the sea wall deep into Chichester Harbour. By seven the trees would be white with the egrets. Gabrielle hadn't seen them since last year. After yesterday's confusion over the spoonbill, she'd be back with the real thing. How did that sound?

J-J was grinning.

'Perfect,' he signed for the second time.

Bazza Mackenzie was cleaning his swimming pool when Winter turned up. According to Marie, Baz had been in a strop for most of the afternoon.

Winter watched him through the kitchen window. When Bazza was angry he had a habit of doing everything very fast. Just now he was moving at the speed of light, pacing up and down the pool, scooping up the odd leaf with his special net, pausing to examine tiny stains in the plastic liner. He was wearing shorts and a pair of flip-flops. Winter noticed that he'd begun to put on weight.

Marie wanted to know about Spain. Bazza had spun her a line about giving some old mates a good time but she knew that Westie had fled on Wednesday night and was far too bright not to have drawn the obvious conclusion.

'Successful, Paul?'

'Yeah, I suppose so.'

'Business trip?'

'Yeah.'

'So will Westie behave himself?'

'Definitely.' Winter nodded, turning away, wary of where this conversation might lead.

'You want to tell me more? Only talking to Baz is hopeless just now.'

Winter shook his head. Then he opened the kitchen door and stepped out into the sunshine.

Bazza was on his knees, scrubbing away at the side of the pool. Hearing Winter's footsteps, he barely spared him a glance.

'I was on to Mist a couple of hours ago,' he said at last.

'I know.'

'Then you're a cunt. And don't tell me different, because you are. Helping yourself ain't on, mush. Not now, not ever. When I say it's OK, then that's cushty. Otherwise you leave the fucking woman alone. I don't care how pissed she was. You're a fucking disgrace.' He was scrubbing harder now, his face reddening with the effort. 'Don't bother fucking denying it either. Only scumbags pull strokes like that. I should sort this here and now, shouldn't I? I should fucking offer you out.'

Winter ignored the threat. He had something else on his mind. He wanted to know about Wednesday night.

'I bet you fucking do. What's the matter, mush? Were you pissed as well? So pissed you can't remember?'

'What were you doing there, Baz?'

'Where?'

'Mist's. On Wednesday night. At three in the morning.'

'None of your fucking business.'

'Is that where you keep the money? Is that where the fifteen grand came from? For Westie?'

'What of it?' The scrubbing began to slow.

'This is important, Baz. Just answer the fucking question.'

Mackenzie at last looked up. He was still livid but there was something else in his face.

'Yeah.' He leaned back. 'Fifteen grand. Cash.'

'And Westie?'

'He picked it up.'

'At Mist's?'

'Of course.'

'He came by cab?'

'Yeah.'

'Brilliant.' Winter dug his hands in his pockets, began to pace up and down.

Bazza watched him for a moment or two. 'What's the big deal, mush? The cabby works for me. I know him. I pay him. No way he's gonna grass me up.'

'Have you got a name?'

'Yeah.'

'What is it?'

'Why do you wanna know?'

'Because we have to talk to him.'

'Done it already, mush. Talked to him a couple of days ago, Thursday it was. Told him the Old Bill would be round. Told him what to say.'

'Great. You want to ring him again? Ask him whether he has satnav?'

'Of course he has satnav. All my blokes have satnav. What the fuck do you think we are, some khazi fucking outfit?'

Winter gazed down at him then shook his head. He heard the kitchen door open. Marie stepped out onto the patio. She was carrying a tray.

'Tea, anyone?'

It was gone six by the time Winter made it back to Gunwharf. Jimmy Suttle answered on his first ring.

'Me, son. We need a meet.'

'When?'

'Now. Quick as you like.'

Suttle began to protest. He had a spaghetti Bolognese on the go. Afterwards, he and Lizzie were off to the movies. Vue were showing *Casino Royale*. She couldn't get enough of Daniel Craig.

'My place,' Winter said. 'OK?'

Suttle arrived half an hour later, furious. He'd binned the spag bol and parked Lizzie in a Gunwharf bar. The movie started at eight. No way was he going to miss it.

'Sit down, son.' Winter nodded at the sofa. 'You want a beer?'

'No.' Suttle didn't move. 'So what is this?'

'Your *Mandolin*.'

'That's got nothing to do with you.'

'Wrong, son. It's got everything to do with me.' He was looking at the sofa again. 'Are you going to listen or what?'

With some reluctance Suttle finally took a seat. Then he checked his watch.

'This better be kosher,' he said.

'Trust me?'

'Never.'

'It's a serious question, son.'

'Yeah?' He stared up at Winter then shrugged. 'Go on then.'

Winter took him back to the party at the Aults. At some time around midnight, he said, young Rachel had had a barney with her new boyfriend. He'd watched the pictures from the bathroom and probably slapped her about a bit. She'd gone next door. She knew where to find a key because she used to keep an eye on Bazza's place when they were away. She'd let herself into the kitchen and had a glass of water. Hughes had followed. She'd made it up to him. Full service. On her knees.

'We know all this.' Suttle was getting impatient again.

'Listen, son. Do yourself a favour. Just fucking listen. Yeah?'

Suttle nodded, said nothing.

'So this is all cushty. She's done what he wants and a tenner says she's back at the sink washing her mouth out. What she doesn't know, what *he* doesn't know, is that Matt Berriman's outside, watching it all. This is the guy she's been shagging for years. This is the guy who knows *exactly* what she likes and doesn't like. This is the guy who's enjoyed a little oral in the bathroom and then shagged her properly afterwards. Now he's watched what she's up to with Hughes. Why? Because Hughes wants it, demands it. Like it's the price she's got to pay. Like it's a kind of punishment. Put yourself in Berriman's place, son. It probably looks like rape. Plus young Rachel's been in the wars. Last time Berriman saw her, back in the bathroom, she was in one piece. Now she's got blood on her face. That has to be down to Hughes, too. Has to be.'

'And?'

'Berriman waits outside. He's a big lad. He's fucking angry. In fact he's insanely angry. And he's waiting. You with me?'

'Go on.'

'So lover boy comes out. There's not a lot to say in that kitchen, not after what he's done. He probably regrets the oral. He knows he won't be flavour of the month. And he's probably sorry about the slapping. But that's not the point because the next thing he bumps into, just there by the pool, is Matt fucking Berriman. This isn't a bloke who's gonna bother with conversation. He's seen what happened. He's seen the state of the girl. He's got a lot to get off his chest. He whacks Hughes. He whacks him fucking hard. Hughes falls backwards, cracks his head, end of story.'

'He's dead?'

'Yeah.'

'Killed by Berriman?'

'Yeah. A good brief, he'd probably get away with manslaughter. But either way Hughes is dead.'

'Killed by Berriman.'

'Exactly. Like I just said.'

Suttle stared at Winter for a long moment then shook his head. 'Doesn't work, mate.' He explained about the stamp mark on Hughes's cheek. The sole pattern had been matched to a Reebok Classic. Berriman had been wearing Nike Air Max 95s.

Winter was beginning to get annoyed.

'Are you here to listen to me or not?'

'I'm just telling you it doesn't work. We're talking hard evidence, *facts*. Anyone can make this kind of stuff up but what the fuck do we say in court? It's a fantasy, mate.' He glanced at his watch and started to laugh. 'You'll be telling me he takes a knife to Rachel next. Stabs the girl he loves.'

The laugh was a mistake. Winter's finger was an inch from Suttle's nose.

'Listen, son. You lot have had a week on this job and from where I'm sitting you've done fuck all. One day you might learn a thing or two about asking the right fucking questions. And one day you might learn to say thank you.'

'This is crap.' Suttle got to his feet. 'If I want fairy tales, I'll stick to *Casino* fucking *Royale*.'

'Help yourself, son. There's the door.'

Suttle made to go. Then he felt Winter's hand on his arm.

'Does Sergeant Suttle sound OK? Or have you given up on all that promotion shit?'

Suttle shook his arm free.

'I don't know what this is about,' he said. 'I don't know where any of this is going.'

'Then just hear me out. And trust me.'

Against his better judgement Suttle sat down again.

'Hughes is dead, OK? Or dying. It now turns out that Berriman's just planted a bloody great clue on his face. The boy's not stupid. He knows he's in the shit. Who does he phone?'

'I've no idea. A mate? His mum? Why doesn't he just fuck off out of it?'

'Because he can't. Because Rachel's there. Because she's in a right state. And the last thing Berriman does is turn his back on her. So I'll ask you again: who does he phone?'

'Pass.'

'I'll give you a clue, son. It's someone he's known for years. Someone who's helped him become the guy he is. Someone who's forced him through years of misery in that bloody pool. Someone he trusts completely.'

Suttle stared up at him. The woman with Berriman last night, he thought. The older woman. The woman with her head on his shoulder. The woman he'd seen on the nudist beach earlier. This was beginning to make sense.

'Something to do with swimming?'

'Spot on, son. Her name's Nikki Dunlop. He phoned her at gone twelve. She lives five minutes away. She hears what he has to say about Hughes, about the stamp mark, about his trainers. He's probably got blood on his jeans, Hughes's blood. This is someone who badly needs a change of clothing.'

'How's she going to manage that?'

'Easy, son. Berriman's living with her. Has been, off and on, for a while. It was her Beemer he borrowed the night he got done on the M27. He keeps some of his gear at her place. Talk to his mum. Nikki's place is home from home.'

'So she turns up with new trainers? New kit? New jeans?'

'Yeah.'

'And then what?'

'Something else happens. My money's on Rachel. She knows all about Nikki Dunlop. Why? Because Nikki's been coaching her too. For years. She knows the woman inside out. And she knows that she's always fancied Matt. That's called jealousy, son. And if you were in the right mood, with access to a knife, you might take it a bit further.'

'You're telling me she tried to stab this woman Dunlop?'

'More than possible. But Nikki's a big woman, a strong woman, and she's not pissed either. Plus ...' the finger again '... she's got her own interest in getting Rachel off the plot.'

'By *killing* her?'

'By stabbing her in self-defence. By sticking her by accident. Whichever way you cut it, Nikki Dunlop is back home by one o'clock, and you know what she's doing? She's putting the washing machine on.'

'How do you know?'

'Because I'm a detective, son. And because I never fucking give up.'

Suttle nodded. He wasn't interested in his watch any more. He looked up. 'You can evidence this?'

'I can evidence the phone. I can evidence a knife. Plus I've found a witness who'll tell you Dunlop's washing machine was going berserk in the middle of the fucking night.'

'Have you got the knife?'

'No. Talk to Marie, Bazza's wife. One's gone missing.'

'What about Berriman's phone?'

'I know where it is.'

'You can lay hands on it?'

'Yes.'

'And the last call?'

'To Nikki Dunlop. At gone midnight. Just like I told you.' He stepped back, shook out a handkerchief, mopped his face. 'I'd take this further but I can't. You need to secure her house. I doubt she's changed the filter on the washing machine. The place might be stiffie time for Scenes of Crime. Then you need to talk to her.'

'Obviously.'

317

'Yeah.' Winter pocketed the handkerchief. 'So where do we go next, son?'

'We?'

'Yeah ... you and me?'

The question hung in the air. At length Suttle glanced at Winter's bag, still lying by the door. It was tagged with a baggage label from Executive Air.

'So where have you been?'

'Spain. Bit of a jolly. Couple of days, there and back.'

'By yourself?'

'Hardly.'

'Successful?'

'Some might think so.'

'Productive? Job done?'

'That's closer, son.' Winter stooped to the bag and ripped the tag off. 'I talked to a guy called Grant Mason just now. I gather you've had the pleasure.'

'That's right. First thing this morning.'

'And you seized his satnav?'

'Yeah.'

'Booked it in yet?'

Suttle didn't answer. At length he stood up. 'We'll need Berriman's phone.'

'Of course you will, son.'

'And I'll also need to talk to someone else.'

'Obviously.' Winter smiled. 'Give him my best.'

Faraday had his mobile on silent when the call came through. The three of them were standing in the long shadow of the sea wall. The stand of trees was fifty metres away, maybe less, clothed in white. The egrets shuffled and muttered in the still warmth of the evening air. J-J was transfixed.

Faraday turned his back on the scene, hunched over the phone, his voice barely a whisper.

'Yeah?'

He listened for a minute or two, nodding a couple of times, aware of Gabrielle watching him. Finally he checked his watch.

'Give me forty minutes,' he said, then snapped the phone shut.

The egrets stirred. A couple hopped into the air. J-J wondered why.

Suttle was back in Winter's apartment moments before Faraday appeared. Lizzie had gone off to see *Casino Royale* on her own.

Suttle said he'd phone her later but didn't hold out much hope of a post-cinema drink. When she'd icily inquired why, he'd pleaded work.

He let Faraday into the flat. Winter was next door standing at the window, nursing a Scotch. On the phone Suttle had given Faraday the barest details. Now, in the hall, he told him the rest.

'And this woman's name again?'

'Nikki Dunlop.'

'Is she on the radar?'

'No, boss.'

'Never been actioned?'

'No, boss.'

'And Winter?' Faraday nodded towards the open door into the living room. 'You think he can stand all this up?'

'Yeah.' He nodded. 'I think he probably can.'

'Right.' Faraday paused for a moment's thought then checked his watch. 'I'll need to talk to Jerry Proctor. Parsons too, if I can raise her.'

'Be my guest.' Winter had appeared. He was offering his cordless.

Faraday thanked him for the offer. He was already calling up Proctor's number on his own mobile.

'Somewhere quiet?'

'Use the balcony.'

Faraday took up Winter's offer. Suttle watched him slide the big plate-glass door shut behind him. He started talking almost at once, his back half-turned, his right hand making sharp downward chopping movements. Suttle hadn't seen him so animated in days.

Winter was watching too. He'd been here before, hundreds of times, raising the bugle, sounding the alarm, calling for Scenes of Crime, arranging for uniforms to seal off a street or a block of flats. He missed it. He knew he did.

At length, Faraday finished the call. When he tried Parsons, her phone was on divert. He left a message asking her to get in touch urgently, then wondered about phoning Willard. First, though, he needed to be absolutely clear about Nikki Dunlop.

He slid the door open and stepped back into the room. Winter was waiting, his glass empty.

'She'll have absolutely no reason to expect us? Am I right?'

'Who?'

'Dunlop.'

'None, boss. I've talked to her a couple of times. She knows I work for Mackenzie. She knows we have an interest in what happened. But I kept it nice and social, the way you do.'

The word 'boss' sparked a smile. Nothing changes, Faraday thought.

'What about Berriman? Might he be there too?'

'I've no idea. What's the plan?'

'We'll arrest them both. Suspicion of murder. Apart from anything else, we have to get them out of the house.'

'Very wise.'

Faraday was already thinking about an interview strategy. He'd been overseeing interviews on *Mandolin* from the start. In the absence of Parsons, he was happy to sort them out.

'You're free tonight?' He was looking at Suttle.

'Of course, boss. You want to team me up with Dawn Ellis? Only she dealt with Berriman on his last interview.'

Faraday nodded, said nothing. He was looking at Winter. 'So what do I tell Parsons? And Willard?'

'I'm not with you.'

'Should they be expecting an invoice? Services rendered? Or what?'

Winter glanced at Suttle, who was studying his shoes. It was Faraday, in the end, who broke the silence.

'They'll start talking about obstructing the course of justice. You know that, don't you?'

'Of course.' Winter went to refill his glass. 'It's the least I expect.'

'They'll also want to ask you about Berriman's phone.'

'Surprise me.'

'Where is it, as a matter of interest?'

'It's around.'

'Have you had it long?'

'You wouldn't want to know.'

'Better me asking these questions than someone else.' Faraday watched the Scotch splash into the glass. 'Don't you think?'

Winter nodded, then smiled at him and raised the glass in a toast.

'So where's the phone?'

'Handy.'

'You'll make sure it gets to Jimmy?'

'Sure.'

He held Faraday's gaze for a long moment. Then, with a nod to Suttle, Faraday was heading for the door. There'd be a briefing at Major Crime in half an hour's time.

Suttle waited for the muffled rumble of the lift. Then he turned to Winter. The object in his hand was a satnav.

'What he didn't say was thank you.' He tossed the satnav onto the sofa. 'Deal?'

'My pleasure, son.' Winter dug in his pocket and produced a mobile phone. Suttle inspected it. He looked up, about to ask about the tiny black specks of earth, but Winter had a question of his own. 'Does Faraday know anything about this?' He was looking at the satnav.

'No.'

'Will he? Ever?'

'No.'

Chapter thirty-two

It seemed to Faraday that the operation went with a smoothness long overdue in the brief history of *Mandolin*.

The Scenes of Crime van parked up on the seafront as the first of the evening's barbecues flared on the beach. A uniformed car swung in beside it. Faraday and Suttle, already in Adair Road, radioed that the target had just returned to number 81. The go signal, at Faraday's suggestion, was *Egret*.

They waited until the uniforms were in sight, then crossed the road and knocked at the door. Inside a dog began to bark. Moments later a tall figure shadowed the pebbled glass.

'Nikki Dunlop?' Faraday offered his warrant card.

'That's me.'

'I'm arresting you on suspicion of murder.' He read the caution, aware of her eyes following the uniforms up the street. If she was surprised, she certainly wasn't showing it.

Faraday had finished. In the slightly comic pause that followed, Nikki asked them whether they wanted to come in.

'Is there anyone else here?'

'No. You want to check?' She stood aside, letting Suttle through. He was back within a minute.

'Nothing, boss.'

Faraday nodded. If there was anything Nikki needed for the next couple of days, then now was the time to fetch it.

'Couple of days?' For the first time she appeared to understand that this was for real. 'Are you serious?'

The uniforms took Nikki Dunlop to the Bridewell. She completed the booking-in procedure and made a call to her solicitor. By now Faraday had DCI Parsons on the phone. He explained the situation and said that he proposed to start the first interview as soon as he'd discussed disclosure with Dunlop's solicitor. Suttle and Ellis would be in the interview suite. So far there was no sign of Berriman though the uniform guarding the house had been warned to expect his return.

'And then what?'

'We arrest him, boss. And bring him down here.'

Parsons was sounding more cheerful by the minute. She was in London, having a meal with a friend. Faraday wondered briefly whether it might be Willard. She wanted to know more about Nikki Dunlop.

'She used to be Rachel's coach at the Northsea Club. Berriman's too. She's known them both for years.'

'And you think she may be implicated?'

'We think she may have killed Rachel Ault. In exactly what circumstances we have yet to establish. I'll keep you in touch, boss.'

'Do, Joe. And well done.'

The interview started at ten to ten. Nikki's solicitor was a veteran of the Magistrates Court, a man she'd known for years. Faraday gathered that he'd seen her through a divorce and several property moves and she certainly treated him like a close friend. Watching on the video monitor from the adjoining room, Faraday could only marvel at her composure.

Dawn Ellis led the first phase of the interview. She wanted Nikki to explain the relationship she'd established with both Rachel and Matt. Could she do that?

'Of course. How far back do you want me to go?'

'The beginning, if you don't mind. Assume we know nothing.'

'Sure.' She nodded. 'Two young people, kids really, different schools, different backgrounds, both highly recommended, both hugely talented. That's where it started. That's where it always starts. You try them out. You explain how hard it's going to be, not just physically but mentally; you start to set them little tests, see how they cope, see how they measure up. In both cases they were excellent. Great attitude. Bags of talent. And fun too.'

'You're all buddies?'

'Of course.'

'How does that work?'

A tiny frown clouded her face. 'Work, how?'

'Being buddies? Being friends? Isn't it sometimes a question of discipline?'

'Of course. But I'm a mum to them, as well as a coach. I'm there to care about them, as well as make them suffer. They were both young, remember. We're talking eleven. Like I say, kids.'

She took the story on. How she'd watched them physically flower.

323

How their confidence had grown. How they'd come to depend on each other a little.

'Is that unusual?'

'Not at all. Swimming's immensely physical, especially competition swimming. For six hours a day you're practically naked around each other. You're super-fit. You're mega-hungry most of the time. If you see a pattern in all of that, an outcome, you'd be right.'

'Outcome?'

'They got it on. Girl and boy. Rachel and Matt. Am I telling you anything surprising?'

'Not at all. What kind of age are we talking?'

'By this time?' She frowned. 'Fourteen, fifteen. Swimmers peak early, especially girls, but Matt was on the edge of the national squad by now and Rachel wasn't far behind. We used to take them away for training weekends – Ponds Forge, up in Sheffield … Crystal Palace sometimes. Give most kids an inch and they'll take a mile, Matt especially.'

'What does that mean?' It was Suttle.

'It means he was hungry. It means he was growing up at breakneck speed. Matt was always a risk-taker. He was the kind of guy who makes things happen. That's why he swam sprints. He had loads of energy, loads of ambition. It was coiled up inside him. It was my job to make sure he released all that power, all that energy, at exactly the right time.'

'On race day, you mean?'

'Of course.'

Dawn Ellis wanted to know about Rachel. Was she similar in temperament?

'Not at all. She had the talent, and she certainly had the drive, but she was much more balanced. Do you believe in astrology at all?'

'Sometimes.' Ellis nodded. 'When it suits me.'

'Then Rachel was Libra to Matt's Scorpio. That's partly why they were such a natural couple. They complemented each other. They were the perfect fit. There was a bit of an issue over Matt's brother too. The lad's severely handicapped. Matt was never too easy around any of that.'

The perfect fit. Watching, Faraday found himself increasingly fascinated by this woman. She was measured. She was intelligent. She'd clearly cared about both her young charges. And, more to the point, she was bringing a rare sense of coherence to the anarchy of that night in Sandown Road.

Suttle wanted to know about the last couple of months as far as Rachel and Matt were concerned. What was Nikki's take on the break-up?

'I wasn't the least bit surprised.'

'You weren't? After everything you've just said?'

'No. Kids change. *People* change. The training began to fall away. You notice it in small ways at first – an excuse here, a headache there, too much homework, whatever. Then the weight starts to go on, Rachel especially. Matt was having substance problems too. Another challenge he could resist.'

'Substance problems?'

'Booze, mainly. The kind of fitness level you need, you've got to be a bit careful. He was using weed too. And being the guy he is, I expect he took a run at one or two other things. Don't get me wrong. This is a guy with huge strength of character, enormous presence. You don't get to swim the way he did without it. But he was always pushing and pushing. That's the way he was built. He couldn't help it.'

'Is that why they split up?'

'Partly. The rest was down to ... I dunno ... life. They grew apart. Different goals. Different values. It happens, as I'm sure you're aware.'

Ellis shot Suttle a look. This was developing into a seminar. Ellis took up the running.

'How did you feel about Matt yourself?'

'I was proud of him. Immensely proud. But I was worried too.'

'Why?'

'The split was Rachel's decision, as far as I can gather. Matt didn't cope well.'

'You were still seeing him? Outside pool hours?'

'Sure. We're talking just a couple of months ago. He wasn't training at all by then.'

She'd seen him in the street a couple of times, she said, and once in a café-bar. They'd chatted, just like the old days, then came the morning when he'd turned up on her doorstep wanting to borrow her car.

'And?'

'I said yes. He had a licence. He said he was insured. He needed to go to a little place in Dorset and apparently the trains were a nightmare. So ... yes, why not?'

'But he got done.'

'As it turned out ...' she nodded '... yes.'

'Doing 132 mph.'

'Yeah.' She smiled. 'My old banger, who'd have thought?'

'And afterwards?'

'We had a chat. Like you do. If you want the truth, I was bloody angry. Not because of the car but because he'd lied. It was a stupid thing to do. And it showed zero respect. That wasn't the Matt I knew and loved.'

'Loved?'

'Yes, loved. Loved as in protégé. Loved as in son. Matt was a very lovable bloke. Still is.'

Ellis made a note. Suttle asked where Matt was now living.

'With his mum, some of the time, when he can cope with Ricky. With me the rest.'

'And do you have a relationship?'

'Yes.' She nodded. 'Just the way we always did. I keep an eye out for him. I make sure he does the little things. I try and make sure he understands the big things. I try and stop him hurting himself.'

'That wasn't really my question.'

'I know it wasn't.'

'Do you sleep with him?'

'I'm not prepared to answer that question.' She broke off to confer with her solicitor. She nodded a couple of times, then she was back with Suttle. 'No comment.'

'Are you fond of him?'

'Of course I'm fond of him.'

'Do you know where he is at the moment?'

'I've absolutely no idea.'

'When did you last see him?'

'This afternoon. He left around lunchtime.'

'But you've no idea where he's gone?'

'None. And that's typical too. He has a life to lead. He's not my property and, before you ask me the question, he never will be. Living full time with Matt would be a nightmare. I love him to bits because he is who he is. But that pretty much rules out anything sensible.'

Dawn Ellis wanted to take the interview forward to the night of the party. Had Berriman been around that day?

'Yes. It was great weather. We go swimming a lot, as you might expect.'

'In the sea?'

'Yes.'

'And in the evening?'

'I was meeting a friend for a drink. I hadn't a clue what Matt was up to. Like I say, I'm not his keeper.'

'He hadn't mentioned anything about Facebook? About Rachel?'

'Nothing. But that would be typical Matt. He loved doing stuff on the spur of the moment. He just followed his nose, really.'

'So what happened?'

'I had a drink with a friend. I just told you.'

'And afterwards?'

'I came home and went to bed. Like you do.'

'You didn't hear anything from him?'

'When?'

'That night? Last Saturday night?'

For the first time she faltered, and Faraday sensed that this was the moment on which *Mandolin* might turn. So far Nikki Dunlop had been a textbook witness. The next second or two, she had to make a very big decision.

'Yes.' She was looking Ellis in the eye. 'He phoned late. Very late. I expect you can check the exact time, can't you?'

Ellis answered the question with one of her own.

'What did he say?'

'He was upset. That wasn't Matt. He said something terrible had happened. That tone of voice, I believed him.'

'So what did you do?'

'He gave me an address. It was in Craneswater. That's half a mile away. He asked me to bring a pair of jeans and a T-shirt and some trainers.'

'And did you?'

'Yes.'

'Did you ask him why?'

'No. I just did it.'

'How long did it take you to get there?'

'I just threw something on and ran. Five minutes? God knows.'

Matt had given her an address in Sandown Road. She was to go into the garden of number 11 and climb over the wall to number 13.

'I knew number 11. I'd been there to meet Rachel's parents a couple of times. They were keen to start her swimming again.'

'And?'

'She wasn't interested.'

'I meant on Saturday night.'

'I did what Matt asked. There was this huge party going on. It was incredibly noisy, all kinds of stuff kicking off. I got over the wall. Matt was waiting on the other side. He said he'd got blood on his trainers and T-shirt and all over his jeans. He took them off there and then and gave them to me. Then he put on the gear I'd brought over.'

'Did you ask him what had happened?'

'Of course I did.'

'And what did he say?'

'He didn't say anything. He just asked me to trust him. He said it would all be for the best.'

'What would be for the best?'

327

'Good question. I just didn't know.'

'Are you sure? This is important, Nikki.'

'I'm sure I'm sure. All I knew was the state he was in. I'd never seen him like that before. He was trembling. He just couldn't control himself. He kept shaking his head. The best, he kept saying. It's all for the best. It was like a mantra, like a prayer.'

'Did you see Rachel at all?'

'No. But then I didn't expect to.'

'You didn't? You didn't associate her with the blood?'

'No way. He loved that girl.'

'So where did the blood come from? In your view?'

'I'd no idea. I know it sounds unreal but that's because it *was* unreal. One minute I'd been asleep in bed. The next I've got a handful of Matt's gear with blood all over it. I just assumed he'd been in some kind of fight.'

She left the house with the clothing and trainers. The party, if anything, was even louder. Back home she put the lot in the washing machine.

'At one in the morning?'

'Something like that. If Matt was upset, then so was I. I just couldn't get my head around it. I waited up that night, waited for him to come home. I must have gone to sleep in the end because it was suddenly daylight. A bit later it was all over the news.'

'And what did you think then?'

'I was appalled. I couldn't believe it. The new boyfriend, I could understand. Maybe Matt had slapped him too hard. He could be quite physical when it suited him. But *Rachel*? No ...' She shook her head. 'That didn't work for me.'

'When did you see him next?' It was Suttle.

'Sunday evening. He just stepped into the house like nothing had happened. I was the one who lost it, not him, not Matt.'

'And what did he say?'

'Nothing. He wouldn't talk about it. It was like it had never happened.'

'The call in the middle of the night? The clothing? The blood?'

'I went through it all. He just shrugged. Shit happens.'

'He said that?'

'Word for word.'

'So how did you feel?'

'I thought he'd gone mad. I thought he was in denial. We rowed a lot about it. I'd scream at him, I'd do anything to try and get through. But then the days went by, and you guys seemed happy enough, and he did too, and I suppose I just blanked off. It was easier that way. It's always easier that way.'

'You never brought it up? All the stuff in the papers? On TV? You never talked about it?'

'Of course I talked about it, at first I talked about it lots. But he just refused to say anything. You've got to understand something about Matt. He takes everything to the wire. He's very black and white. Trust me or don't trust me. In the end I had no choice.'

'You could have come to us.'

'Yeah …' She nodded, tipping her head back, gazing up at the ceiling. 'You're right, I could.'

'Wouldn't that have been a kindness? To Rachel?'

'Sure. Of course it would. But then you'd have come looking, wouldn't you? And we'd have probably ended up here.'

'We? You mean you and Matt?'

Her face stiffened, a mask now. She pursed her lips, refusing to avoid Suttle's eyes. Then she swallowed hard, fighting for control, shaking her head very slowly, and Faraday had a sudden glimpse of the way it must have been, this woman's investment in flesh and blood, in hours and hours of grinding effort, in getting Matt Berriman to the kind of giant he'd become, only to see her dreams dissolve. His bloodied T-shirt on the rinse cycle, he thought. At one o'clock in the morning.

Ellis wanted to know what had happened to Berriman's clothing and trainers once she'd washed them.

'We threw them out.'

'We?'

'I threw them out.'

'Where?'

'I put them in the rubbish. The collection's on Monday.'

Ellis made a note. Another lengthy fishing expedition at the municipal tip. Her head came up again. 'And you've no idea where Matt might be?'

'None. We normally eat together on Sunday evenings. I'd be expecting him around six. Maybe you scared him off.'

Next door, Faraday nodded to himself. A uniform at the front door. A Scenes of Crime van parked across the road. No way would Matt Berriman have been in a hurry for supper.

Ellis was asking Nikki whether she'd like a break when Faraday's phone began to ring. He fetched it out, put it to his ear. It was Parsons wanting an update. So far, Faraday explained, there'd been no word from the Scenes of Crime guys at Adair Road but it was still early days. Given Nikki's admitted complicity, she'd already be facing a conspiracy charge. Under PACE rules, without an extension, they'd have to formally charge her within twenty-four hours. Either that or let her go free.

'So what do we do, boss?'

Parsons took a while to answer. Faraday could hear the murmur of conversation and an occasional clink of glasses in the background. Some fancy London eatery, he thought. With Parsons about to order the champagne.

Finally, she was back on the line.

'Press her on Berriman, Joe. From what you say, there's obviously a relationship.'

'That's true, boss, but I don't think it's as simple as that.'

'You're telling me they're not at it?'

'I don't know one way or the other. They may be. They may not. On balance, I think probably not. But she's protecting him for sure, exactly the way she's always done.'

'Meaning she knows where he is?'

'Meaning she might do.'

'Then go for her, Joe. Give her a shake. We need to lay hands on Berriman asap, and from what you're saying she's our best chance. OK?'

'Sure.' He brought the conversation to an end.

Suttle stepped into the room. Dawn Ellis had gone to the loo while Nikki's brief sorted some coffees. When Faraday nodded at the screen and offered his congratulations, Suttle shot him a look. 'Not quite what we were promised, boss. Winter seems to think she did the girl.'

'Maybe Winter's wrong.'

'Sure, but do we believe her? She's obviously crazy about the guy.'

'You think so?'

'I know so. He's young. He's hunky. He's got it in spades. But he's also in love with his ex-girlfriend. Are we seriously suggesting he stabs her to death?'

Faraday's gaze returned to the screen. Nikki Dunlop was still alone in the interview room.

'There was a phrase she used,' he murmured. 'It'll be on the tape. I should have written it down. "Matt was the kind of guy who made things happen."' Faraday looked up at Suttle. 'He's in control, Jimmy. All his life he's in control. He's a winner. He's the fastest, the strongest, the bravest. He knows there's nothing he can't do. Then suddenly, bang, his girlfriend's left him, he's not swimming any more, and life's not quite so rosy. Some people cope. Some don't. And for my money he didn't.'

'So he stabbed her? Repeatedly? Five times?'

'It's possible. You know it is.'

'And you really believe that?'

'Yes, I think I do.'

The interview began again. Nikki's solicitor registered his concern about the lateness of the hour but accepted Suttle's assurance that this second session would be brief. When he asked Nikki about the likelihood of Berriman knifing Rachel to death, she shook her head.

'I don't believe he could.'

'Could or would?'

'Either. Both. But *could*'s stronger, isn't it? He loved that girl. He was passionate about her.'

'He'd have killed for her?'

'That's glib. You don't murder someone you love.'

'Then who else might have done it?'

'I've no idea.'

'Did you ever ask him?'

'Of course I did. I've just told you. I live with this man. I've known him half his life. He must have been there. He must have seen it.'

'And?'

'Nothing. *Nada*. If he was here, now, it would be exactly the same. You wouldn't get a word out of him. There are some things too private to share. You might get that far. But beyond that ... *nada*.'

'He said that? He told you there are some things too private to share?'

Nikki stared at Suttle a moment, then ducked her head, refusing to answer. Suttle asked the question again, letting the silence stretch and stretch before offering her the chance to make things a little easier for herself. He told her she was already facing an extremely serious charge. Conspiracy to murder could land her with a substantial prison sentence.

She nodded, sat back, looked Suttle in the eye.

'Conspiracy to *what*?'

'Murder, Ms Dunlop. We have two dead bodies. We have Matt Berriman ringing you at one in the morning wanting a change of clothing. According to you, he's offered no satisfactory explanation of exactly what happened. You say you've tried to get the truth out of him and you say you've failed. For everyone's sake, we need to talk to him, and we think you probably know where he is. Or, at the very least, where he might be. Help us at this stage and we'll bring it to the attention of the judge.'

'Really?'

'Yes.'

Her solicitor touched her on the sleeve and Faraday watched their whispered conversation. Finally, she turned back to Suttle.

'No comment.' She said.

'Meaning you don't know? Or meaning you won't tell us?'

'No comment.'

'Fine.' Suttle glanced at Dawn Ellis. Ellis shook her head. Suttle made one final attempt to coax the information out of her then checked his watch. 'The interview ended at 22.16.' He reached for the cassette machine and pressed the stop button.

Still watching from next door, Faraday saw Nikki Dunlop get to her feet. She looked exhausted. As she manoeuvred round the table, she tripped. Her hand went out instinctively, reaching for support. Suttle caught it, steadying her, asking whether she was OK. She nodded, grateful, and asked what would happen next.

'We'll keep you here overnight, Ms Dunlop. And talk again tomorrow.'

'Here? You mean a cell?'

'I'm afraid so.'

She looked at him a moment and shook her head. 'Shit,' she said softly.

Winter was still up, half-expecting a phone call from the Bridewell, when Suttle's upturned face appeared in his video entryphone. He buzzed him in and had sorted a cold Stella by the time Suttle stepped in through the open door.

Suttle opened the can and took a couple of gulps. Winter wanted to know how the interview had gone.

'She coughed to bringing the change of clothes.'

'Jeans and trainers?'

'Yeah. And a T-shirt. They talked by the wall between the two houses. She's saying she never saw either of the bodies.'

'Surprise, surprise. What happened to the gear?'

'She washed the lot.'

'Then what?'

'She says she binned it. That's probably the truth. We'll action the dump tomorrow. Might take a week or two but we'll get there in the end.'

Suttle told him about the rest of the interview. She couldn't get any kind of story from Berriman. Neither did she have a clue where he'd gone.

'And you believe her?'

'No. Faraday thinks she's protecting him.'

'And you?'

'I think he's right. He also seems to think Berriman probably did them both.'

'And you, son?'

'I think she probably did Rachel. I think she took the knife home and disposed of it. Fuck knows where.'

'So what does that make Faraday? Apart from wrong?'

'Unfair question, Paul. Faraday's OK. You're going to owe him, big time. Most D/Is I know would have you down the Bridewell by now.'

'Sure. But he needs me, doesn't he? Because it turns out I was fucking right.'

'About the girl? Rachel?'

'Yeah. Dunlop'll cough that too, in the end.' He reached for Suttle's can and swallowed a mouthful or two of cold Stella. Then he wiped his mouth with the back of his hand. 'What about Scenes of Crime?'

'Nothing. Not yet.'

'You want another tip?'

'Go on.'

'She's got a little office down Victoria Baths. I'd take a look at that as well, if I were you.'

The second interview with Nikki Dunlop started at ten o'clock next morning. Suttle had been at his desk in Major Crime since seven, trawling through interview statements, looking for any scrap of evidence that might be useful in the coming encounter. A night in the cells might have loosened Nikki's tongue as far as Berriman's whereabouts were concerned but as she stepped into the interview room he rather doubted it.

Given the circumstances, Faraday also thought she looked remarkably composed. He settled himself in the monitoring suite, adjusting the volume on the set. The rumour had spread that *Mandolin* was heading for a result and the Custody Sergeant had been thoughtful enough to provide a plate of custard creams to go with Faraday's coffee.

The interview was well under way by the time Faraday's mobile began to trill. So far, Nikki had stonewalled every question, simply repeating what she'd said last night. She had a friend in trouble. She'd gone to his aid. She'd done her best. Whatever happened next was beyond her control.

Faraday bent to the phone. It was the Crime Scene Investigator whom Proctor had tasked to take a look at the office at Victoria Baths. He'd found a pair of trainers in a box at the back of a cupboard. They were Reebok Classics and they looked to be on the big side.

'Blood?'

'Caked, boss. You can see it in the eyelets, in the seams, everywhere.'

'You're serious?'

'Yeah ... real DNA-fest.'

Faraday thanked him. On the point of hanging up, the CSI said he had another bit of news. Just might be of interest.

'And what's that?'

'A knife, boss. Ten-centimetre blade, give or take. Wrapped up in tissue paper in the same box.'

'Jesus.'

'Exactly.' He was laughing. 'How stupid is that?'

Faraday thanked him a second time and hung up. Moments later he brought the interview to a halt while he conferenced briefly with Suttle and Dawn Ellis, sharing this latest development.

Suttle shook his head. Winter, he knew, would be impossible.

'What now, boss?' Ellis nodded at the video screen. 'She's not going to tell us about Berriman. I'm not sure she even knows where he might be.'

'Keep pressing. But start with the trainers.'

The interview resumed. Confronted with the evidence from her office, Nikki Dunlop simply nodded. She'd seen the guys in the grey forensic suits walking up Adair Road, Faraday thought. She's sensed the reach of the Major Crime machine. One way or another, she must have known that this moment would come.

Ellis wanted to nail the evidence down. No shadow of ambiguity.

'These trainers belong to Matt?'

'Yes.'

'And they're the ones he was wearing on Saturday night?'

'Yes.'

'You told us you washed them.'

'You're right. But I didn't.'

'Why not? And why on earth hang on to them?'

'I don't know. I just don't know. I should have got rid of them. I know I should. But ever since last weekend I've somehow thought we might have a proper conversation about what happened. Shouting wasn't enough. Maybe I'd have to force it out of him. Maybe I'd have to stick those bloody trainers under his nose, *make* him look at them, *make* him remember.'

'And the knife?'

'That too. In fact that especially.'

'So you must have assumed ...?'

'I assumed nothing.'

'You didn't think he'd killed her?'

'I didn't think anything. I wanted to *know*. I needed that knowledge.'

'OK. So if he'd told you what really happened? And if it turned out he'd killed them both?'

'Then we'd have to deal with it.'

'We?'

'Yes, we.'

'And how would you do that?'

'I've no idea. It never happened. But there'd have been a way, I know there would, because that's the way it's always been. If you go through the kind of years we had together, then you kind of sign up to each other. Total dependency. Total trust. The going gets rough, you hack it. What you don't ever do is give up.'

'So where would that have taken you? As a matter of interest?'

'I don't know.' Nikki looked round, a sudden vagueness in her eyes. 'Here, I suppose.'

Afterwards

On DCI Parsons' instructions, Nikki Dunlop was charged with conspiracy to murder. Her solicitor's plea for bail was turned down by the magistrates and she was remanded to Winchester Prison.

Later that morning a bather reported a pile of abandoned clothing on the beach close to the Langstone Harbour narrows. The clothes were still damp from the overnight rain. In the back pocket of the jeans the attending PC found a note on blue paper. It read,

Thou art a soul in bliss; but I am bound
Upon a wheel of fire that mine own tears
Do scold like moulten lead ...

It was Suttle, hours later, who remembered the quote. *King Lear*, he said, Act Four, Scene Seven.

The coastguards commissioned a search for Matt Berriman which lasted until nightfall. On Tuesday, at daybreak, it recommenced. When there was no sign of a body the search was called off.

That evening, in a specially convened *Mandolin* squad meet, Willard commended Acting Sergeant Jimmy Suttle for driving the intelligence cell throughout an extremely difficult investigation. The Sandown Road job, he said, had been neither prolonged nor – in the end – especially complex. But everyone had been under the cosh in terms of the media and, speaking personally, he never wanted to see another TV crew in his life. When the ripple of laughter subsided, he added a final word of praise for DCI Gail Parsons. She'd steered the ship through choppy waters with skill and determination, he said, and she was owed a collective debt of gratitude.

The following week Bazza Mackenzie announced the establishment of a fund in memory of Rachel Ault. He'd seeded the fund with a personal donation of £100,000 and proposed to put Paul Winter, a trusted friend and colleague, in charge. Paul's brief was to explore ways of integrating kids into the wider culture in a city as densely packed and volatile as Portsmouth. The word he used, after a glance at his notes, was 'interface'.

That evening he and Marie hosted a dinner in Gunwharf for a couple of dozen of the city's key figures in the world of juvenile offending. Invitations went to social workers, academics, psychologists, sports officials and a priest. Pathways forward were discussed and there was a collective sense that the evening had been a success.

Afterwards, in the privacy of Winter's apartment, Bazza confessed that he felt guilty over Berriman's disappearance. Winter, by taking his new boss at his word, had triggered the set of events that had led to the clothes on the beach. Not for a moment had Mackenzie believed the lad capable of killing his ex-girlfriend and even now he found it hard to believe. Only mad people do something like that, he told Winter. And he'd never had Berriman down as a loony.

The Aults stripped their house of its remaining possessions. The property – cleaned, repaired and redecorated – went on the market at a price of £899,000, but after nearly a month there'd been little interest. During a phone call to Belle Ault Faraday had enquired about her husband's health. Peter, she said, was undergoing treatment for clinical depression. She understood the outlook was promising but it was still early days. When he was a little better they'd start the process of looking for somewhere else to live. Her own preference, just now, was New Zealand. The peace, for one thing. And the quiet.

Five weeks after the discovery of the clothes on Eastney Beach, a man's body was recovered by fishermen off Selsey Bill. DNA analysis confirmed it to be that of Matt Berriman. At the inquest the Coroner delivered a verdict of death by suicide. The funeral, the following week, attracted an even larger congregation of mourners than the earlier service for Rachel Ault. The press turned up en masse, and among the photos published in the following day's edition of the *News* was a shot taken as kids streamed away from St Stephen's Church.

Faraday brought the paper home that night and Gabrielle's attention was caught by a face at the back of the shot. She was looking directly at the camera. She was wearing a black cloak, buttoned at the neck, and the light fell pale on her shaven skull.

'*C'est Jax*,' Gabrielle murmured. 'That's her.'

As late summer gave way to the first chills of autumn, Paul Winter was still expecting a visit from his ex-colleagues. When nothing happened he gave Jimmy Suttle a ring. Suttle confirmed that the investigation into Danny Cooper's death was ongoing. Intelligence from Spain indicated the disappearance of a young German artist from Malaga in mid-August. She'd last been seen in the company of a tall male of Afro-Caribbean extraction whose description matched that of Brett West. While the couple may simply have moved on together, Spanish police were treating her disappearance as suspicious. Should developments warrant further investigation at the UK end, it might pay Winter to have his ear to the ground.

Winter, still digesting the news, asked about Suttle's promotion.

'It came through last week,' he said. '*Sergeant* Suttle to you, my friend.'

Two days later Bazza Mackenzie took a call from Alice Berriman, Matt's mother. She wanted a private chat. Mackenzie invited her to the Royal Trafalgar for lunch. They talked about the old days, and about Matt, and about what had happened at the party.

Alice had produced a letter. She'd found it in her kitchen the morning Matt disappeared. It described exactly what had happened the night Hughes and Rachel had died. Winter had been right. There'd been a confrontation. Hughes had emerged from the kitchen with a knife. There'd been lots of shouting, and then Matt had hit him just the once, enough to knock him off his feet. Rachel had emerged from the kitchen, gone to her boyfriend's aid, tried to revive him.

The fact that he wasn't breathing had freaked her out. The next thing Matt knew, he was looking at the knife. Killing Gareth, she'd said, was the end of everything. In the letter the phrase was underlined. *The end of everything*. Matt knew she was right. If there was no way forward, no way they'd ever be together, then that was the way it had to be.

When she tried to attack him, Matt had grabbed the knife, stabbing her a number of times. He wanted to put her beyond reach. He'd driven the knife in deep and he'd known exactly what he was doing. Sometimes, he'd written at the end, life is black and white, all or nothing. Now, with Rachel's death on his hands, it boiled down to precisely nothing. Very soon the torment would be over. For both of them.

As a postscript to the letter Matt had scribbled an extra line that had, Alice said, offered a tiny crumb of comfort. Not because it softened the overwhelming sense of waste, but because it was, in its own way, so beautiful. She didn't know whether he'd copied it from somewhere else or dreamed it up himself but either way it didn't matter. *You die for what you cherish,* her son had written. *There is no lovelier death in all the world.*

At the lunch table, embarrassed by the tears rolling down her cheeks, Alice wanted to know what to do with the letter. Mackenzie reached across for it, tore it into tiny pieces, and signalled for a waiter to put it in the bin. That evening Alice phoned and said thank you. It wasn't what she'd expected, she said, but then life had never done her bidding.

In mid-October, with the *Mandolin* file submitted to the CPS, Faraday seized advantage of a lull in the ongoing war that was Major Crime and booked a weekend in a hotel in London. On the Saturday afternoon he and Gabrielle attended the launch of J-J's exhibition in Chiswick. The photos had won a review in the *Guardian* and J-J had a modest pile of photocopies for visitors who might be interested. Faraday folded one into his pocket. A couple of sentences from the review had caught his attention. J-J's work opened a door into the mystery that was autism. This was someone, the critic had written, who understood handicap from the inside.

That night the three of them celebrated J-J's success in a Szechuan restaurant in Parson's Green. Conversation turned to Gabrielle's project on the Pompey estates. Her work, she said, was nearly done. Now came the challenge of building all those interviews into a coherent account. J-J, fascinated, wanted to know what the months of research had taught her. She gave the question some thought then signed her answer. After all the questions, all the listening, all the evenings of transcribing her notes, the one word she was left with was *folie*. Madness.

On Monday, back at work, Faraday glanced up from the weekly overtime sheets to find himself looking at D/S Jimmy Suttle. Suttle was newly returned from a break of his own. A week in Crete with Lizzie Hodson had given him a decent tan.

From a Manila envelope he produced two colour prints. Faraday cleared a space on the desk.

'I got to thinking about *Mandolin* again ...' Suttle began.

'On holiday?'

'Yeah. And I realised what we missed.'

He laid the two photos side by side on the desk. One was a shot of Matt Berriman from the Newbury custody suite. The other came from the best of the mobe footage at the party. Faraday gave it the briefest glance.

'That's Berriman too,' he said.

'Exactly, boss. Spot the difference?'

Faraday's gaze returned to the two shots, then he nodded, shook his head, closed his eyes, sat back in the chair. At the party Berriman had been wearing a pink surfie T-shirt. Hours later, at Newbury nick, the T-shirt was white.

'Shit,' he said softly,

'Exactly. So what does that make us?'

Faraday eased his chair away from the desk, clasped his hands behind his neck, gazed up at the ceiling. In truth, with an investigation as complex as *Mandolin*, he could think of endless excuses, but in his heart he knew that none of them was sufficient.

'It makes us stupid,' he said at last. 'And lazy. And somewhat overwhelmed. You agree?'

'Sure.' Suttle nodded. 'And what does it make Winter?'

Another good question. Faraday took his time. From a number of adjectives he finally chose the least despairing. 'Lucky.'

'You believe that?'

'No ...' he shook his head '... sadly I don't.'